Norah was born in Banbridge in 1935 and was an experienced Nurse Tutor, being responsible for Student Nurses within three major hospitals in Northern Ireland. Her main teaching programme was 'A.I.D.S. and H.I.V.' Education.

This is her second novel and she is currently writing her third.

She is married with two children and six grandchildren.

Dedication

I would like to dedicate this book to each of my five brothers who all individually and uniquely made my childhood memories, in spite of many hardships, very happy ones.

Norah Humphreys

THE HOUSE ON WARING STREET

AUSTIN MACAULEY
PUBLISHERS LTD.

A CIP catalogue record for this title is available from the British Library.

ISBN 978 1 78455 154 4

www.austinmacauley.com

First Published (2014)
Austin Macauley Publishers Ltd.
25 Canada Square
Canary Wharf
London
E14 5LB

Printed and bound in Great Britain

Acknowledgements

I wish to thank my husband Ian and all my family circle for their unending encouragement, support and help they gave me during my time of writing this novel.

CHAPTER 1

1976

Thomas sat in his office looking out critically at the furniture display he had just created that morning in the salesroom. He was quite pleased with the results of his hard work. The pink velvet chairs contrasted well with the plush, pale green woollen carpet covering the floor. He was just contemplating whether a couple of side tables with lamps would make his display more homely when he noticed a tall, dark man make his way towards him and he realised it was his cousin, Colin Finlay. He rose from his chair and went to meet him in the salesroom, delighted to see any member of his family come in to his shop.

'It's good to see you, Colin, we haven't been in touch with one another for some time,' Thomas stretched out his hand in greeting as he spoke.

Colin nodded as he returned the handshake and then looking round the salesroom, remarked, 'You have a wonderful display of beautiful furniture, Thomas. Unfortunately most of it would be beyond my reach at present. Besides I only came to see you, to talk to you. I really didn't know who else to turn to. Then, with you having a business of your own, I thought maybe you could help me.'

Colin looked at Thomas almost in a beseeching way, and suddenly Thomas noticed how pale and anxious his cousin looked. He seemed somewhat nervous and ill at ease as he addressed Thomas.

'Is everything all right with your two boys and Margaret, Colin? Is Aunt Dorrie and John well?'

At the mention of his wife and family Colin nodded emphatically and brightened up considerably. 'Is there somewhere we can go to talk, Thomas? – I need some advice and I need a confidante. So I thought of you, I know you are very discreet and I know you can keep a confidence.'

'Of course, Colin, come into my office. We won't be disturbed there,' and Thomas indicated the door at the back of the salesroom. 'I'll just ask Rita, my office girl, to bring us a couple of coffees,' and Thomas proceeded to the back of the shop where a young girl of perhaps no more than twenty sat at a desk, typing diligently.

Once Colin was seated in Thomas's dilapidated office chair, which Thomas usually used for his much needed coffee break, Colin opened his heart to his cousin.

It transpired Colin's worries were centred round his younger brother, Leo. Leo had decided about eighteen months ago, to follow God and become an evangelist. He had given up his "nine to five" occupation in a local ironmonger's office in order to devote his life to Christ. Initially he had hired a local church hall in order to preach the gospel. Although he always insisted he was very poor, he assured his family he was rich in spirit, thanks to God and the Holy Spirit. About six months ago he had approached Colin, who had himself, a quiet but strong Christian faith and suggested that between them, if they could raise the money, they should build their own church.

Although Colin had some reservations, he finally agreed to give up his job as manager in the tobacco factory in Belfast and devote his life and work, with his brother's help, to the Christian ministry. But in the short term, he needed funds because he was going to have to survive on the little salary they earned from their preaching. He had, after all, a wife and two sons to support. After some deliberation, he decided to remortgage his house, then when Leo and he were better established and able to earn an honest wage from their efforts, he would pay the mortgage off.

Now he paused in his story telling and looked at Thomas in a questioning way.

'You must think I've been quite mad, to even contemplate such a thing, Thomas.'

'I'm in no position to judge anyone about decisions they make, I've made a few daft ones in my time, Colin. But I suspect that isn't the end of your story. Is it? There's more.'

Colin nodded briefly before continuing, 'Leo and I have been sharing an office since I joined forces with him a couple of months ago. He arranged a week's holiday in Dublin with Valerie, his girlfriend, and so I have had sole responsibility in the office for the last few days. Unfortunately or fortunately perhaps, I have discovered, although Leo has maintained he is poverty stricken and on the bread line, that he has, in fact, several personal bank accounts throughout Northern Ireland with substantial sums of money in each of them. In contrast, the total sum of money accumulated in the church building fund is a paltry £100.' As Colin detailed all this to Thomas he became more and more distressed, but kept his eyes riveted on his cousin as he revealed the cause for his concern.

'He has just been telling me a parcel of lies,' Colin's voice held a weary, defeated note. 'I fell for it all, fool that I am. All that money from church collections which people freely gave to help build a new church, the most of it is in my brother's bank accounts.'

'Colin, there may be a very simple explanation for it all.' Thomas was anxious to give some reassurance to his cousin.

Colin shook his head sadly 'I was never meant to see those bank statements. They were under lock and key, and because I was curious as to what might be in the drawer, I found the key, opened the drawer and there they were.'

'If you believe this to be true, you must confront Leo with it when he returns from holiday. He has all that money in his accounts, and you have so little.' Thomas was insistent. The truth was he was shocked to the core, that anyone who professed to be an evangelist could possibly be so devious. Perhaps there was some mistake. But from his own past experiences in Kenya and how he was innocently caught up in a fraud case, people simply became greedy and took advantage of certain situations.

'I know I need to do something, but I feel I would like my father to be there when I show these to Leo, as a sort of witness, I suppose.' Colin seemed to brighten up at the mention of his father's name. 'He's a very fair man, Thomas, what do you think?'

'Yes, I think your father needs to know and perhaps he will sort it out between you, I certainly hope so.'

'Thanks, Thomas, and you have just confirmed what my own instincts are in all this, to confide in Dad.'

Colin rose from his seat, hugged Thomas closely and then added, 'I haven't even asked after your mother, or anyone else, for that matter. I'm so sorry. I do think of Aunt Ellen so much and the awful tragedy of Rob's death. I'm so sorry.'

'Please don't worry about any of us. You have enough to think about at present. As you know, Mum is busy preparing for her marriage to Tom Greenlees and we are all very happy about it. You will be getting an invitation any day now, so I hope Leo and you have all this sorted out before then. I'm sure you will.' Thomas returned his cousin's embrace before they headed out of the office and said their goodbyes, Colin promising to be in touch if there were any developments.

CHAPTER 2

Ellen sat very still, mesmerised by the letter on the table in front of her. It was from Maggie, her sister-in-law. And in it she informed Ellen she was coming home, home with her daughter and granddaughter. They had a longing, Maggie wrote, to be at Tom's and Ellen's wedding. Ellen felt lost as she scanned the contents of the letter once more, but the bare facts were there. Maggie, her darling Rob's erstwhile sister, wished to come home to be at Ellen's marriage, she who had never thought it necessary to come home for Rob's funeral. Nor had she shown any interest in his inquest.

She had written Ellen a long letter after hearing of his murder from Eve. In that letter she had expressed her shock and sorrow at his death and the brutality of it all. She sincerely hoped that the perpetrators of such evil would be brought to justice. But since that letter five years ago Ellen had heard nothing. Now here was this news, out of the blue. What was she to do about it all? Where did Maggie intend to stay when she did come back? Ellen felt she could never feel comfortable with her sister-in-law. She didn't know her and if she was honest with herself she had very little interest in getting to know her. Simply because her behaviour as a young girl seemed to affect Rob so much, He only ever seemed to think of her with a real sense of shame. So Ellen was reluctant to offer any accommodation in her home until she knew more about her. Reading through the letter Ellen felt Eve would probably know more about it. Maggie had said in her letter that Eve had written to tell her of Ellen's forthcoming marriage. Gentle, inoffensive Eve had always tried to maintain some contact, however tenuous, with her sister over the years and probably felt it was right to keep her up to date and what was happening with her extended family in Northern Ireland. So she must go to see Eve as soon as she could, in the hope that she might set her mind at ease regarding Maggie's news. Surely she would know what Maggie's long term intentions might be.

Her decision made, Ellen rose from the table in the kitchen, folded the letter and placed it behind the clock on the mantel above the Aga cooker. Tom would be calling later to see her, as he did every evening and had done since shortly after Rob's death four years before. In a mere six week's time, he would be here permanently with her, sharing her bed, and facing her across the breakfast table each morning. Faithful, loving Tom had loved Rob, his best friend for years, too. He had grieved with her, sharing her thoughts and memories, trying to help her bear the unbearable. In six weeks Tom would share the home Rob had loved so much, but was to be denied years of enjoyment in. Ellen had come to realise that Rob would be happy for her. He had loved them both and would be happy for them in the years they had left together.

'It's a beautiful May evening, Ellen, we couldn't wish for better, especially one to drive to Poyntzpass in. Hopefully Eve and Harry will be at home, but if not we'll just call into the Railway Bar and have a quiet drink.' As he talked, Tom was busy putting their dinner plates into the sink and running hot water onto them as he did so. 'I hope Eve can throw some light on Maggie and her family. I only remember her vaguely, a very attractive girl, if my memory serves me right. But Rob rarely spoke of her, only mentioning on one occasion her rather dubious behaviour. I never forgot how upset he seemed to be when he spoke of her. But,' turning to Ellen he went on, 'that's almost fifty years ago and perhaps my memories have become a bit distorted.' Lifting his jacket from the back of the kitchen chair he went on more cheerfully. 'Let's go and see Eve, no doubt she'll be able to give us some details.'

The drive to Poyntzpass always held bitter sweet memories for both Ellen and Tom. Tom, remembering the happy times he and Rob had spent playing in the fields at his parents' home and then their visits to see Rob's father at the railway station. Not to mention their journeys together in Tom's father's car to seaside resorts or to the local dances. As for Ellen she treasured the memories of Rob and herself setting up their first home here, and then the birth of Matthew. So usually their journey to Poyntzpass was a quiet one, where they sat in companionable silence, knowing words were unnecessary between them.

Tom was glad to see Harry and Eve's car parked outside the front door of their cottage. That probably meant they were both at home and Ellen and himself could enjoy an hour or so of their company.

'It looks as if they are at home.' Ellen said quite unnecessarily, as Tom pulled the car to a halt behind Harry's. Before Ellen had a chance to open the car door Eve appeared in the porch, smiling broadly.

'Let's have some tea, Ellen. Then we'll talk and I'll tell you what I know.'

Ellen had immediately, on entering the cosy sitting room, explained the reason for their surprise visit. While Eve had listened to them she indicated the sofa in the centre of the room, then taken their jackets from them.

'Look, love, I'll make the tea and cut up some of that lovely fruit cake you baked yesterday. That will give Ellen and Tom and yourself a chance to talk.' Harry had risen quietly from a seat beside the window, had taken Tom and Ellen's jackets from Eve and was making his way from the sitting room as he spoke

'Thanks, darling, that's a good idea.' and Eve smiled lovingly at her husband as she pulled a chair over beside the sofa where Ellen and Tom were sitting.

'I'll tell you what I know, Ellen, which isn't really an awful lot. When you first told me about your forthcoming marriage, I thought I would write and let Maggie know. Somehow, over the years, I have tried to keep some level of contact with her, even though she never showed any interest in coming to visit any of us. Until now, that is, and perhaps that's simply because of her age, she may have a desire to see us all.'

'Well, perhaps you're right.' Ellen sounded dubious. 'I do know she lost her husband some years ago, but I would never have known it but for you, Eve. The same goes for her daughter Rachel and granddaughter, I feel I know nothing about them. In the letter she sent me she just says they are coming because of my marriage. So I presume it's only for a holiday.'

'That's not what she says in her letter to me, Ellen. She is anxious to return here to live and even more specifically, very keen to bring her granddaughter Lynn here. She feels Lynn might benefit from the slower, more humble way of life here, rather than the fast moving style which seems to be evolving in some parts of Canada.' Eve paused as Harry entered the room carrying a tray laden with cups, pastries and cake and proceeded to set everything out on a table in the corner of the room.

Tom, who had been silent while Eve and Ellen were talking, merely remarked on how tempting Harry's tray of buns and cakes were. 'This is delicious, Eve;' as he helped himself to a slice of fruit cake at the same time watching Harry handing round the tea and pastries.

'She must be very fond of her granddaughter, Eve.'

'She seems to be, Ellen, and I'm sure you remember that Rachel adopted the little girl when her parents were killed in a car crash. The kid was only three years of age when that happened. I do know Rachel only took the child temporarily at first, but then she and her husband applied to adopt her legally. Unfortunately Rachel and her husband, Lewis Compton, split up and divorced about five years ago. So the three generations of women only have one another in their immediate family circle.'

'Oh, Eve, I totally forgot all about the little girl being adopted. Now I remember Rob telling me all about it, and he was thrilled that Maggie now had a granddaughter. That has to be about fifteen years ago.' Ellen was feeling a bit guilty now; Maggie must be seventy years of age, just an elderly relative anxious to return to her homeland and to do the best for her family.

'It is fourteen years ago, Ellen, according to Maggie. Lynn is seventeen now.'

'Where do they hope to stay when they come?'

'Well, she has made it clear she doesn't want to stay with Dorrie and John. She says Dorrie has taken to writing to her and quoting scriptures. And she tells her she prays earnestly for her all the time. So she reckons her sister must be a real 'Bible Thumper' and she would rather not listen to much of that. So in the meantime I have offered her accommodation here, to see how it goes. Having spent a few years in Canada I probably know her better than anyone.'

'At least that's a solution until we get the wedding over, Eve. Then Tom will be moving out of the annexe at Lucie and Paul's house, and I'm sure Paul would let them have it. That is, if they want to move to Belfast.' Ellen was anxious to try to forget the past and make some effort to welcome her sister-in-law into the family circle.

'I never thought of that, Ellen, it sounds a good solution. We will be rather cramped here, this cottage is so small.' Eve sounded so relieved Ellen was glad she had thought of it.

Maggie's homecoming arrangements having been decided, the talk came round to Dorrie and her new found passion for religion and of her two sons' devoutness and their ambition to build their own church. Harry and Tom both expressed their concerns that their nephews were taking on a huge financial commitment at such a young age. And they were totally against them having left steady, regular employment, but Ellen and Eve were confident they both knew what they were doing. They were young, enthusiastic and driven by their beliefs and they would be all right. Besides what they were involved in was wonderful, honest, Christian work and if that were so, nothing could go wrong.

CHAPTER 3

Ellen's wedding day was on June 8th and she was a very happy woman in spite of all that had happened to her, at the prospect of marrying Tom. He had helped her cope with so much; Rob's murder, his inquest and all the trauma and family issues which had inevitably resulted from the horror of it all. There was nothing she wanted more now than to marry Tom Greenlees. Their relationship was a happy, contented one, and as she prepared herself for the drive to the church with Matthew, her eldest son, who would give her away, she was so looking forward to being Tom's wife and demonstrating to him how much she respected and loved him for his unswerving support of her. Ellen knew what Tom and she had for one another was quite unique. It was no mad, impatient passion but rather a quiet dignified love, based on mutual compassion and respect, and she knew such feelings would remain steadfast.

Both the bride and groom had tried their best to have a small, quiet affair, but the numbers just seemed to swell as they organised their guest list, simply because they had so many relatives and friends they wanted to be there to share their day. The church they had chosen was the Methodist one close to the university in Belfast. Ellen's local one held too many sad memories of Rob's funeral and she knew Rob would not want her to be sad today. The venue for the reception was a mere half hour drive from Belfast, a beautiful hotel set in its own secluded grounds and lying close to Helen's Bay. Now though, both Tom and herself were worrying about the wisdom of going anywhere near Belfast for the ceremony. Only three days before, nine civilians had been killed in and around Belfast. The attacks had been committed by both the Provisional I.R.A. and the Ulster Volunteer Force. The truth was people were beginning to realise that no one was really safe anywhere or indeed from either extremist group.

All three of Rob's sisters attended her wedding, which indicated to Ellen their endorsement and their best wishes for her future after the tragedy of Rob's death. Their approval of her marriage was very important to her. She noted Maggie's and her family's presence and how comfortable and at ease they seemed to be with everyone at the reception. It was as if she knew everyone very well and had never been abroad for all those years. Indeed the most remarkable aspect of Maggie's and her family's presence here was their unconcern about any of the troubles which were going on day and daily in Northern Ireland. Ellen could only put it down to the fact that she must really be so delighted to be home that very little else mattered.

Eve and Harry were seated at the same table as Maggie, but their daughter was in England, having found employment there, and was unable to be present. Dorrie and John were also seated alongside Maggie and Eve and their daughter Rhoda, a rather, quiet girl of about eighteen years of age, sat with them.

After a delightful meal of soup, roast beef with all the trimmings followed by a sensational chocolate mousse, the room was then prepared for the dance. Everyone began to mingle with one another, anxious to catch up with other family members, some of whom hadn't seen each other for some time.

One of the first guests Thomas sought out was his cousin Colin. Since that day that Colin had come to talk to him in his office, and confided in him his concerns about Leo, he had heard nothing more since. He quickly identified his Aunt Dorrie and Uncle John sitting with his other aunts and uncles, but of Colin and his family there was no sign. He quickly made his way over to them.

'Are you going home, Aunt Dorrie?' Thomas noticed his aunt and cousin had their handbags over their arm. 'Aren't you staying for the music?'

'No, Thomas, we're going home. I don't believe the music will be to our taste any more. Don't you agree, Rhoda?' Dorrie addressed her daughter.

'Yes, of course, Mum.' her daughter was quick to agree.

'Thomas, will you thank Tom and Ellen on our behalf, for a wonderful day. We'll just slip away without disrupting them. And, Thomas, it's really good to see you all.' John Finlay spoke so softly Thomas had to lean forward to hear him.

'I'll certainly do that, Uncle John. Are Colin and Margaret leaving now as well?' Dorrie and Rhoda had turned to say good-bye to Eve and Harry and the others, so it was John who remarked, 'I shouldn't think so, I see them seated across the room there,' and John nodded over briefly in the direction of another table where Colin, his wife Margaret and their sons were seated, and showing no signs of leaving.

'I must go over and say hallo to Colin.' Thomas addressed this to Dorrie, but she seemed to keep her head averted, and it was John who just nodded rather soberly in response. Thomas said his goodbyes before threading his way through the guests to speak to Colin. But he was deep in thought as he crossed the room. Something was amiss with Dorrie and John, but what it was, he had no idea. Perhaps it was just Dorrie's new found religion and beliefs which were reflected in her. But he would have thought such beliefs would have made his aunt a much warmer person, but to-day he had felt a coldness in her brief conversation with him.

Colin however, greeted him very warmly and pulled over another chair for him. He seemed most eager for Thomas to join them.

'Thomas, it's good to see you. We've had a wonderful day and it is good to see Ellen so happy. I, for one, will never forget her kindness to all us Finlays when we were evacuated to you during the war. Ellen deserves all the happiness she can get.'

Thomas nodded, remembering too that awful morning when he and his father had driven through a desolate destroyed Belfast to bring Aunt Dorrie and Uncle John and their family to safety.

'Mum and Tom are certainly very happy, I think Mum really needs him in her life.' Thomas hesitated only briefly, and then went on, 'I was wondering if Leo and you had managed to sort things out between you. Did you speak to your father? Was he able to help resolve things between you?'

At the mention of his father, Colin's eyes suddenly filled with tears and Margaret, who had been sitting quietly, listening to the conversation between the cousins, quickly grasped her husband's hand tightly, her eyes scanning his face.

'I'm sorry. Am I intruding on something, Colin? I didn't know. I'm sorry.'

'No, please, it's all right,' Colin made a conscious effort to pull himself together. 'I wanted to come and tell you everything but I was so upset I just did not wish to speak of it.' Colin smiled wanly at Thomas. 'But I do particularly want you to know that my parents have more or less disowned me.' His voice held such a weary, defeatist tone that Thomas's heart went out to him.

'Whatever do you mean Colin? Disowned you?'

'Well, when you start getting letters from your own mother saying you are evil, that the devil has entered your soul, that you are a compulsive liar. Then when she ignores you sitting over at the very next table at the wedding reception, and crosses to the other side of the room when she sees me approaching, what else am I to think?'

'Oh, God, I'm so sorry, Colin. And to think I was the one who suggested you speak to your father. But surely he doesn't believe any of this of you?'

'I daresay he probably doesn't, but for the sake of peace he has to be seen to be supporting his wife.'

'Surely he'll make your mother see sense?'

'I'm not so sure, Thomas. If you read those letters they would make your flesh creep, they are so vindictive towards me. But then I truly believe Leo had most of the say in their wording.'

'You are probably right, Colin. He has to justify himself I think. Is that why he isn't here today, do you suppose?'

'No, no. He was booked some time ago to go to South Africa to meet some evangelist. He has been in touch with this man for some time who has a church in Cape Town. He's due back next week. So that's where he is at the moment.'

'Oh, I see. I did wonder. Because knowing Leo he would be much more likely to brazen it out with you than to avoid you.' Thomas had always felt that Leo Finlay was quite glib and smooth, much more so than his elder brother.

'Look, enough about me.' Colin made a conscious effort to straighten himself up. 'Let's not spoil the remainder of this lovely day. Go and fetch Jean and the kids to join us and we'll watch the dancers and perhaps take to the floor ourselves.'

'Look, I'll go and bring them over, and I'll round up Charles and Sheila and the children as well. Colin, Thomas and you can gather up a few more chairs. We might as well all sit together to enjoy the remainder of the evening.' Margaret rose to her feet as she spoke and proceeded to weave her way across the floor to where Thomas's wife and family were.

'I understand Aunt Maggie and her family are moving into Lucie and Paul's annexe while Tom and Ellen are on honeymoon in Jersey. It seems an ideal housing solution for them. Don't you think?' Colin was anxious to keep the conversation away from him and his family problems.

'Yes, it certainly seems to be. Tom will have no further use for it and Eve and Harry have such limited room at their cottage, it must be a relief to them. Not that they would ever say. Lucie has very generously said that she doesn't want any rent from them, at least until Rachel gets work. So Maggie has been very appreciative of the offer.'

'Maggie seems to be fitting into the family circle very well indeed, Thomas. For someone who was so rarely in touch, and whom we knew so very little about, for all those years, here she is, almost as if she had never been away.'

Colin seemed determined to enjoy the family who were beginning to gather around pulling their chairs close to one another. Thomas was glad his cousin was diverted from his worries, even if only temporarily, by the goings-on at the dance. His mood seemed to have lifted considerably and they had a very enjoyable couple of hours just watching the dancers and all their relatives and friends interacting with one another. In fact, it seemed no time until everyone was rising to their feet to clap and cheer, as the bride and groom prepared to leave for their honeymoon. With the bride and groom's departure, the guests too, gradually began to disperse, and Thomas and Colin and Charles gathered their wives and children and their belongings together, said their goodbyes with promises to keep in touch.

CHAPTER 4

The day after her mother's wedding Lucie began, with the help of Rachel, to spring clean the annexe to enable Aunt Maggie to move in as soon as possible. Lucie did this so promptly mostly to ensure that Eve and Harry did not remain cramped for living space in their little cottage. Tom had already removed his most treasured, sentimental possessions to Ellen's house. These included his father's mahogany desk from his general practice room, his mother's favourite chair, a few ornaments, clocks and pictures. Lucie and Paul had insisted that Maggie and Rachel had the use of another room adjacent to the annexe, insisting that Maggie should have a room of her own.

'We can't thank Paul and you enough, Lucie, for all the kindnesses you have shown to us since we arrived here.' Rachel was busy in the kitchen, taking down curtains to put in the washing machine along with the bedroom ones she had already put there. 'Everyone has been very kind. We can hardly believe we are lucky enough to be allowed to live in this annexe, it is really wonderful. The whole place is truly beautiful.'

'Well, it was going to be lying empty with Tom's departure from it, so Paul and I are only too glad to see it being occupied and made use of.'

'As soon as I get some work I'll start paying you some rent, Lucie, and you really must take it.'

'Well, we'll see, Rachel.' Lucie and Paul had never even thought of rent money during the whole time Paul's father was there. He was a relative, and that was it as far as they were concerned. Lucie reckoned the same went for her aunt and cousin Rachel. She couldn't see herself taking anything from them.

'What sort of work have you thought of, Rachel?'

'I fancy looking for a small shop to rent and selling ladies underwear but it's really only a thought at the moment. I do have some savings. I have a bit of capital from my house which I sold before I came here.'

Lucie made no immediate reply and occupied herself washing out the larder, but she was quite taken aback at Rachel's ambition. Rachel mustn't realise that any shop in Belfast was at risk of being blown up, or at the least of being evacuated on a frequent basis due to yet another 'Bomb Scare'. Then Lucie chided herself, she was a doctor and a doctor's wife with no experience or foresight into running a business.

'That will entail some hard work, I would imagine, Rachel,' she eventually said rather lamely, then added quickly 'I know nothing about running a business, absolutely nothing, but that's what being at university does for you, and seeing sick people in a G, P. practice doesn't help in that field either.'

'Well, I certainly could never have done what you have done, Lucie, listening to people's complaints. I'd never have the patience for it for a start. But setting up a business isn't entirely new to me, I did have one in Canada selling similar items,' then Rachel hurried on, 'but that was some time ago and it fell through.'

There was something in Rachel's tone of voice that told Lucie not to ask many questions about her work in Canada, so the next hour was spent in companionable silence with the two women cleaning windows and cupboards and washing floors.

While she worked, Lucie's mind wandered to her mother's wedding day and Lucie was thankful it had been so successful. It had all gone off without a hitch. The only cloud to Lucie's enjoyment was Matthew's coolness towards her. He had been like that for the last four years and he was no different to her yesterday, avoiding her company yet without appearing rude. He had never understood how she could forgive Patrick Mullan, her ex-husband, for his involvement in their father's death. And although Lucie felt she had still done the right thing, she did often wonder had she known Matthew would have felt so bitter towards her, might she have had second thoughts. It wasn't that Matthew totally ignored her, certainly he always greeted her politely but in the last four years had never sought her company and had politely but firmly turned down any family invitation Paul and she had offered. It was so heartbreaking and Lucie knew her mother and Charles had both tried talking to him but according to them, Matthew's answer was always the same, he had no wish to discuss it.

Lucie's mother maintained that Matthew was, naturally, still traumatised over his father's death and she believed if they could find and charge the perpetrators who pulled the trigger that fateful day, Matthew would come round. He still loved Lucie, Ellen was sure of it. In the meantime, Lucie must live with this awful estrangement from her eldest brother, something she found extremely difficult to do.

Now, just a few days ago, Thomas had told her in confidence about the awful estrangement which had sprung up between Colin Finlay and his family, and although she was not close to any of her cousins she empathised with Colin and hoped it would be resolved very soon. It sounded so much worse than Matthew's ignoring of her, she could never, in her wildest dreams, envisage a time when her mother would disown her.

'This furniture is something else, it is truly beautiful. I really love the blue sofa in here.' Rachel and Lucie were standing in the living room of the annexe, both admiring their morning's work. 'The furniture here is so different, Lucie, from that in Canada. Everyone over there is into the modern, contemporary look. But this is so special, so superior.'

'Actually, most of this belonged to Tom's parents, Rachel, but he has no need of it at present. He did take a few pieces with him to Mum's house. Things he likes to look at and appreciate on a regular basis. He very kindly left this with us, so the least we can do is cherish it.' Lucie hastened to add, 'He will be delighted to know you are enjoying it, Rachel.'

'Well, I certainly will enjoy it, Lucie and I'll make sure that Mum and Lynn take good care of it for him while we're here,' and Rachel smiled openly at her cousin.

The very next day Maggie and her family moved into the annexe of Paul and Lucie's house on the Malone Road and the following week Rachel rented a rather run-down terraced house in one of the side streets in Belfast, with a view to converting the downstairs into a shop. She chose the site she said, because the rent was so cheap. Then a few days later, she said she had purchased a good stock of ladies underwear and intended to open the shop as soon as she had downstairs converted. When she showed Lucie a sample of some of the bras and knickers she had bought Lucie was quite shocked, it was all so provocative and daring.

CHAPTER 5

'I can't understand Rachel's interest in selling such racy underwear items here. I would never have imagined there was much of a market for that sort of thing in Belfast.' Lucie had been meaning to tell Paul about Rachel's choice of merchandise on several occasions, but with the latest terrorist attacks during the last week injuring and killing so many people, he had had several emergencies to deal with in theatre. Indeed, during the last couple of years Paul had become more and more involved in the trauma unit, as well as still being available for neurological operations. So to mention something as trivial as Rachel and whatever goods she had for sale, seemed so wrong in light of the major traumas Paul and his team had been trying to deal with. Besides, in the last week and indeed longer, he was at the hospital until well past midnight, trying to save the lives of those people caught up in the latest terrorist attack.

Now this evening he had arrived home early, Robert and Louise were in bed and Lucie and Paul were enjoying a quiet meal.

'Is her stock of goods really that different, my love? Perhaps we haven't been looking in the right places for it.'

Lucie could see Paul was smiling quite indulgently at her, he was not going to take her seriously, she could see that.

'I've no doubt she is working very hard. She is transforming upstairs and downstairs of that house. She is making what was the sitting room into the shop floor with a good solid wooden bench as a counter. She is also putting up two or three cubicles for potential customers to try on their purchases. She has worked hard and so too, has young Lynn; if anyone can sell that underwear she will be able to. She is such a gorgeous looking girl.'

'I must admit, Lucie I haven't seen much of either Rachel or Lynn, they seem to be working long hours, especially Rachel, according to Maggie. Maggie says Rachel leaves very early in the morning and gets home very late at night. Then again, my hours recently are such that I have seen very little of anyone, including you and the children, darling. But the police made a few arrests today, so we can only hope there will be a bit of a lull in all the shootings and bombings.'

'Paul I'm sorry, I shouldn't be bringing up such a subject as racy underwear. It must sound so petty in comparison to what you and your staff are dealing with in the trauma unit. I am sorry.'

'Well, don't be, Lucie. Anything that brings a bit of light relief to our conversations at the minute is welcome. And indeed anything that brings a bit of happiness to Belfast has to be all good.'

'I never thought of it like that and of course you're right, People do need something to give them a bit of a boost and if Rachel's bras and pants, and suspender belts can do that, she should do well. And isn't that what we want for Aunt Maggie and her family, that they prosper and do well in Northern Ireland? And that they all stay safe.'

Paul and Lucie both fell silent then, remembering that they had been unable to keep Lucie's father safe, that had been out of their control. As it was for so many people in Northern Ireland, who had lost loved ones.

Suddenly Paul suggested that he would take a walk round to the annexe to ask Maggie round for a drink and Rachel and Lynn too, of course, if they were home. Lucie was delighted to hear Paul making such a suggestion, taking it as a sign that her husband, who had been under such pressure and faced with such sadness from relatives who had lost loved ones, was more relaxed and was prepared to forget, even temporarily, the traumas he had faced in the past few weeks.

It transpired all three women were at home when Paul called and were delighted at the invitation. That first invitation set a precedent for many a pleasant evening spent in one another's company in Paul and Lucie's sitting room or in Maggie's. On the evenings that time was spent in the annexe Paul always brought the intercom system so he could hear the least movement or sound the children made.

One particular evening in late October when the nights were drawing in and the deep blue velvet curtains had been drawn, giving a warm cosy feeling to the living room of the annexe, Rachel broached the subject of Tom's antique furniture which occupied the room so beautifully, and gave such an air of elegance to the whole place.

'I am really keen to try to buy some of these beautiful pieces of furniture from Tom. We feel bad using it day and daily when it doesn't even belong to us. I know antique furniture to be very expensive, but the shop has been doing very well and I am in a position to offer Tom very good money for it. And it would be cash in hand.' Rachel looked over at Paul 'As his son, Paul, what do you think?'

Paul contemplated Rachel's question for a moment, and then assured her he would speak to his father. He did emphasise that the furniture was indeed very valuable and his father might not wish to part with it but pass it on to his grandchildren. Rachel stressed she would be willing to reimburse him so handsomely, that surely the money could be put in bonds for his grandchildren. Before parting for the evening, Paul promised he would speak to his father and Rachel was more than happy with that and was quite optimistic about the sale.

Paul was uneasy about the whole thing and said so to Lucie as they were preparing for bed. 'I'm not really into antiques, Lucie, but I imagine Dad's are worth a small fortune. Surely Rachel can't have that class of money, between paying the rent for that place in Belfast and buying the stock for her shop, she couldn't possibly be that well off. According to your Aunt Maggie, although she sold her house before coming here, by the time she paid off her mortgage she only had a few thousand left.' Paul paused for a moment 'I wouldn't want Dad to part with it all for a paltry sum because they are relatives.

It's not the money, darling, it's just I wouldn't want him to regret not keeping it for the grandchildren.'

'Paul, love, I don't think we need worry very much about it. Your dad is so sentimental I can't see him parting with it and he knows it is irreplaceable, he has said so many times. To be honest, I would worry more about Rachel and wanting to spend that type of money. She could leave herself in dire straits. I can't imagine the shop making a fortune or anything like it.'

'Well, she sounded very confident this evening, but knowing the trade here, it may not last. But then again maybe Rachel came home with far more money than her mother thinks, or else she's right, and the sale of ladies underwear is booming. Anyway, I'll speak to Dad as soon as I get the chance, but I don't intend to influence him, it has to be his decision.'

'I'm glad things are going well for her, Paul. They did take such a big risk coming here in the middle of all the troubles. I'm sure Aunt Maggie was worried if she was doing the right thing by coming back home. I do believe everything is working out well for them.'

A few days later Tom tactfully told Rachel that he couldn't possibly sell his furniture, it held such sentimental value for him, but they were welcome to enjoy it all while they lived in the annexe. When Rachel tried to pursue it and press money on him, Tom was staggered at the figure she mentioned, but stressed he simply did not want to sell. Rachel acquiesced and said she understood he would wish to keep it for his grandchildren.

'Mother, when are you going to allow me to see upstairs and what renovations you've done? What's the mystery about it all? You just keep telling me it's out of bounds until everything's finished. But I haven't seen any workmen about in the last two or three weeks. So I'm just becoming more and more intrigued, so much so that I think I'll sneak up any of these mornings.' Lynn was in the process of unpacking and sorting some exquisite underwear that had just been delivered to the shop that morning, and Rachel noticed how her daughter unfolded the bras and knickers so reverently and carefully.

'Lynn, I promise to show it all to you within the next day or so but there are a few things we need to discuss before that.' Rachel continued to study her daughter intently, 'You must decide very soon Lynn, if you wish to continue your education here in Northern Ireland or if you just want to work in the shop.' Rachel hurried on as Lynn made to answer, 'I don't want your answer now, darling. I want you to think seriously about it over the next few days. This is Wednesday, we'll talk about it next Monday morning and you'll also see the transformation I've made to this rather seedy, shabby house.'

'Fair enough, mum. And I know who I would like to talk to about the education system here. I'll talk to Jason, Matthew's son. He's at university here in Belfast. I had quite a chat with him at Ellen's wedding reception. I'll go and see him.'

'That sounds a good idea. He should be able to tell you what attainments you need to get into university and what degrees are available for study.'

CHAPTER 6

Even though Rachel worked in the shop until late in to the evening and arrived home as her mother and Lynn were preparing for bed, sleep evaded her that night. Lynn's eagerness and interest in seeing the bedrooms above the shop was a great source of worry to her. How was she going to keep her secret lifestyle and her real source of income from her daughter any longer? She had managed it very well in Toronto, even the humiliating time when the authorities had closed her premises down, stating she was running a brothel. A statement Rachel had thoroughly disagreed with, because as far as she was concerned she was running an escort agency. And although this time she did not intend to escort men any further than her bedrooms above the shop, she still viewed this new venture as similar in that it was only the more well-to-do men she was intent on entertaining.

But what was she to tell Lynn? Should she tell her the truth? Or another whole parcel of lies as she had told her in Toronto? In Toronto she had said she was simply providing some form of accommodation for homeless girls who occasionally brought their boyfriends home. At least this time there would be no one else only herself doing any entertainment. She was on her own in this operation and intended to keep it that way. But Lynn was older now, not the innocent, fourteen year old she had been then but a seventeen year old trying to pave a career for herself.

It was her mother who had insisted on coming to Northern Ireland. She wanted Rachel to make a clean break from her lifestyle. She should realise, Maggie told her, how lucky she had been to escape a prison sentence in Toronto, she might not be so lucky next time. But even in this beautiful country, beautiful, in spite of the violence that was all around them, Rachel was finding it impossible to change her ways. She reckoned the need to give a man some sexual satisfaction must be in her blood, in her genes. Or was it the thought of the money? She wasn't convinced it was, she could do all right selling underwear, in fact it was doing well enough. But in her heart she knew that the sight of those handsome, well-dressed men going up the stairs in her shop, gave her a tremendous glow of satisfaction and fulfilment that the lure of money never could.

'Mum, these rooms are stunning, so tastefully done and the scent and aroma of the perfumes is so, well, so comforting and relaxing.' Lynn was astonished at the grandeur of the bedrooms – her mother must have spent an inordinate amount of money on them to achieve this look. Not that there was a great deal of furniture in them, just a large bed, a comfortable easy chair and bedside tables with beautiful lamps on them. But everything was so opulent and grand that it took Lynn's breath away. The bathroom was so luxurious, it was obvious no expense had been spared, with marble tiles lining the walls from ceiling to floor and the aroma of expensive soaps and perfumes pervaded the atmosphere.

'Mum, it's just magnificent!' Lynn was lost for words. 'But what do you intend doing with it all? I can tell you it will be lost on students.'

'No, it isn't for students, Lynn.' Rachel answered. 'Let's go back downstairs, I'll make a cup of tea and explain to you what I hope to do with those rooms.'

Afterwards Rachel felt quite comfortable with what she had told her daughter. She did acknowledge truthfully to herself that she had lied a little by omission, but believed she had told Lynn enough for her to cope with. She had gone to great lengths to explain about the troubles and traumas in Northern Ireland, and how some men were finding it almost impossible to cope, both with their own fears and that of their wives and families. Rachel had come up with the idea that she should advertise discreetly that she was willing to listen to those men, and even give them a little physical comfort. Some of them, she told Lynn might be judges condemning someone to a prison sentence. Some might be policemen who had witnessed further terrorist attacks. Perhaps even a doctor might be glad to talk to someone after having to deal with the dead and injured following yet another terrorist attack. And when Lynn had come over and hugged her mother tightly exclaiming that she thought it a wonderful idea trying to help others, Rachel felt very guilty, but pushed her feelings to the back of her mind; this was enough for Lynn to cope with.

Maggie had never envisaged herself going to Dorrie to ask her to pray for Rachel and her granddaughter. She desperately needed help from someone, somewhere, and she had thought of her sister and how she had turned to religion. Surely if anyone could help her, Dorrie could. She had been unable to sleep or eat since her last visit to Rachel's lingerie shop. Certainly she was very impressed with the level of business her daughter was doing. It seemed to be thriving and Maggie knew that was good, but when Rachel was so evasive about upstairs and did not offer to show her mother around, Maggie knew, with an awful certainty what it all meant. Rachel must have resumed her old way of life, and since that stark reality had hit Maggie she had been totally preoccupied as to how she was going to help her daughter to change. She had basically run out of ideas. Bringing her and Lynn home to Northern Ireland had seemed the ideal solution. She had believed things would be different here, but apparently that wasn't the case. Now, as she usually did, she thought back to all those years ago in Poyntzpass and her own scandalous behaviour, and she was not proud of herself. Her only excuse was that she was desperate to escape the poverty trap she had found herself in. But after meeting her husband she had never strayed, not once. But the same could not be said for Rachel and her marriage. Her behaviour had led to her divorce. She had been in despair at the thought of her daughter once more engaging in ... well, in prostitution. How she hated the word, but that's what it was, prostitution. Then somehow, Dorrie and her eagerness to pray for people came into her mind. She believed Dorrie could help her, hadn't she looked after her and her siblings so well all those years ago, after their mother's death. And hadn't she told Maggie in her letters to her, that she prayed to God every day and he answered her prayers. So although initially, Maggie had had little time for her sister and her new found beliefs, now, although she might be clutching at straws, she hoped, no, she believed that Dorrie might help her daughter. And perhaps she, in turn, could help Dorrie mend the rift between her son and herself. It was Lucie who had told her all about some disagreement or other Colin and his mother had had. They were having a few drinks together at Paul and Lucie's, when Lucie asked her if she knew anything about the fallout. It seemed to be something no one wished to talk about. The only thing was, according to Thomas, it seemed to be something to do with money having gone missing from the church fund. The least Maggie felt she could do, was to offer some help to heal the rift.

Dorrie welcomed Maggie with open arms and enthused again, as she seemed to do each time they met how wonderful it was that she and her family had returned to Northern Ireland. While Dorrie made tea, insisting Maggie join her in the kitchen while she did so, they talked of Ellen's wedding, and Dorrie seemed so happy for her sister-in-law. She remarked that Tom Greenlees was an honest, upright man and he was just what Ellen needed. When they had carried the tea and cakes into the living room, and sat down to relax, Maggie told Dorrie the real reason for her visit and her need for prayers for Rachel. The transformation that took place in Dorrie then, at the mention of prayers, took Maggie by complete surprise. She became so animated, so inspired and so pious that Maggie was momentarily carried along with her sister's emotions and felt that surely those beautiful prayers would be answered.

When Dorrie had finished praying and had said her last amen, Maggie tentatively suggested trying to help bridge the gap between Colin and his family. Almost immediately

Dorrie's manner changed, and became an ugly, foreign thing which frightened Maggie and shook her to the core. Dorrie and John's son, Colin, according to Leo, was of the devil, Dorrie informed Maggie and she did not allow his name to be spoken in this house.

On her way home to Lucie and Paul's, Maggie pondered at length on her sister's awful bitterness towards her son. It upset her so much that her own troubles with Rachel seemed lessened, somehow. She was glad Dorrie had never known anything about her behaviour with men. She probably would have disowned her. But what awful deed had Colin done to warrant such a vicious reaction from his mother?

CHAPTER 7

'Please, Colin, I have to take this job, you know that. It's so good of Mr. McClure to create the vacancy in his office for me. It is such a wonderful Christian gesture on his part, so I would never let him down. He knows our situation and is extending a hand to help us.'

'I know he is, Margaret, and I'm so glad we made the decision to return to our old church without wasting any more time. Everyone has been so welcoming and understanding towards us. And although I do know you have to accept Stanley McClure's offer, I want you to know, my love, it is not what I want for you.' Colin was struggling with his emotions. 'I never dreamt you would have to go out to work. I had this dream, you see, where I would work and keep you in some kind of luxury.' He smiled wanly at his wife. 'And now we have both been offered a job on the selfsame day. Perhaps that bodes well for the future.'

'Oh Colin, mine's only a part-time job. It will fit in well with the children and getting them to and from school. But yours is wonderful, stepping into a top management job in freight. I'm so proud of you.' And Margaret smiled so happily at her husband, that he realised she did not mind in the least about going back to work. Suddenly, the dark cloud that had been hanging over him for weeks lifted, and he could sense that somehow or other, Margaret and he would weather the storm. Besides, they had no choice only to move on, for both their sakes and that of their children. But in all of this good news, he thought so much about his parents. Were his parents really lost to him? He hoped not, but in spite of his letters to his mother to try to explain what had happened, he just continued to receive hate mail from her, telling him the devil had entered his soul, and he must seek forgiveness from God for all his lies.

So now he must concentrate on bringing some happiness to his wife and family. He would guard this new job with his life and nurture the friendships of those who did believe in him. As for Leo, Leo did not matter to him anymore. He must have told their parents some awful lies to make them behave towards him as they were doing. He had confided in some of the elders in his Church that Leo was of no consequence to him. He knew some of them were quite shocked at how adamant Colin was and while they did say they understood how he felt, he must try his best to forgive his younger brother and pray for him. Something Colin knew that, at present, he was incapable of doing. What Leo had done to himself and his parents was so awful that Colin found it difficult to believe that anyone, never mind his own brother, could have been capable of such treachery.

In spite of this terrible rift with his family, he knew Margaret and he were capable of being very happy, just with each other and the children. Added to which they had a wide circle of friends, and now they also had the means to strive to get out of debt. All thanks to Mr McClure and Mr. Orr in the Church who had demonstrated so vividly their belief and trust in them by offering them such secure, worthy jobs.

It was a bitterly cold Sunday night in January and Leo was very pleased with the evening collections. He had never expected such a good attendance from his congregation this evening. It had been snowing most of the day and although it had eased off considerably, a lot of the country roads were almost impassable. The numbers who had made their way here this evening must be the most devout people, he reckoned or else, indeed he hoped, they came because they enjoyed and believed in everything he conveyed to them in his sermons. The very thought of him having such influence on people gave him the most wonderful feeling of elation and power. He knew though, that he would always have to strive to keep that influence and interest ignited. Now that he found himself alone, with no one to fill in for him at any time, he Leo, would always have to be available to his congregation.

However, when he had counted his collections from this evening's service, he knew it was worth all his sweat and agony. It was too bad Colin had discovered his bank accounts, that was a big slip-up on his part and he had agonised over that whole incident. But he had no regrets about how he had handled it all, he had to succeed, and if his parents and Colin had to suffer, so be it. Success was within his reach and he knew it. Why, people were actually cashing in their savings to support him, and others were selling some of their plots of land and donating the money from the sale. So if some of his family had to be isolated and humiliated, it was a small price to pay for success and achievement. He did have good support from a fair sized group of people, and the whole-hearted support of both his parents. Rhoda, his young sister made no secret of the fact that she just idolised him. A hero worship he could well do without. He only just tolerated his sister; he found her to be a dour, uninteresting being. But he would never want her or his mother to know how he really felt about her.

He knew his mother believed he could do no wrong and she fervently believed all his prayers to God were answered. A few weeks ago she had approached him about offering up some prayers for Rachel, his Canadian cousin. She had told him all about Maggie coming to visit, and confiding in her all about Rachel and what she was working at, and she felt that if only Leo would pray for her, all might turn out well.

He found Rachel in quite exuberant form the morning he visited her. He felt he needed to speak to her before remembering her in his prayers. She informed him shortly after he entered her shop that Lynn had been accepted by Queen's University to study English Literature. She would start in September, and as this was only March, she would work in the shop until then. She informed Leo that she had never envisaged her daughter getting into university so easily but her qualifications from high school in Canada were very acceptable to the university.

Over a very welcome cup of tea, Leo congratulated Rachel on her venture into business and then expressed his delight that Lynn was going to further her education. Then he told her the real reason for his visit, about her mother's worries for her, and how he had promised his own mother he would pray for her. He reassured her he would do so and in return he felt that God would keep her safe. Perhaps in return she might see her way to offering a donation towards his new church. He was rewarded with a warm embrace, a very happy smile and a very acceptable sum of money from her. He returned her embrace wholeheartedly and assured her every penny of the money would go towards his church fund. Before he left, Rachel expressed fears about other members of the family learning anything about her, and assured him he could rely on her financial, if not spiritual support, if he promised to be discreet about her. He, in turn, promised he would have no problem doing that, her secret was safe with him.

'John, Leo has been to see Rachel and has told her how wrong her lifestyle is. I believe he must have given her quite a sermon, because she has promised to do her best to take stock of her life and try to reform.' Dorrie was keen to keep John up to date about Leo's commitment in getting the gospel across to everyone, to save souls and commit them to the Lord. She felt this was vitally important at the moment because John seemed to have lost his enthusiasm for Leo and his ambition to build a new church. He had told her many times since the family rift that he would rather have his eldest son back in the warmth of the family circle than any new church Leo intended to build.

'I appreciate your concern for Rachel, Dorrie, but my main concern is for Colin and his family and how they must be feeling, separated from us all. The whole thing is wrong, I tell you, and we should be doing something about it. Not taking on Rachel and Maggie's problems.' John could hardly believe he had just had the courage to convey his feelings but he had gone beyond the stage of being sensitive to Dorrie's feelings and what she believed. He only knew he doubted that Colin would have said such things about Leo and the bank accounts if there hadn't been some truth in it all. He had always believed Colin to be honourable and truthful, but apparently Dorrie believed otherwise. She had insisted Leo could produce proof that the money was all for the church. It was just Leo's way of collecting it and saving it. But neither Dorrie nor he had seen any such proof, and John was beginning to suspect his younger son of dishonesty. He himself had, after all, been in business a long time and had seen men try to wriggle out of many a dilemma. If he thought Colin and his family were going to suffer because of untruths told by Leo, he knew he could not be accountable for the punishment he might consider justifiable in dealing with his son. He had never had any time for dissembling and lies, and in this instance it all seemed to be in the name of building a church, and preaching the word of the Lord.

By June of that same year, 1977, when Rachel was doing her book-keeping one evening, she looked back on her last four months of work and was very pleased with herself and what she had achieved. There was just one thing she could not understand about herself, and that was her all too ready agreement to donate money to Leo's church fund every month. It was so unlike her, she was always so astute and careful with her money, but somehow or other, she had been carried away with the thought of helping Leo and his church. She reckoned she must be turning into a right big softie, or she had had some kind of a "brainstorm" One thing she did know, if she could turn the clock back he would have got very little money from her, because, as far as she knew, the new church was hardly mentioned.

CHAPTER 8

October 1977

The hall that Leo Finlay rented for his evangelical services on Sunday morning and evening had once been the church hall belonging to the Presbyterian church on the Larne road. However, it was situated on the opposite side of the road from the church and at the end of quite a long lane. It was also in quite a state of disrepair. The members of the Church had decided, rather than spend money on renovations, to build a new hall on the stretch of land immediately beside the church and to have an up-to-date, thoroughly modern hall suitable for many functions. When the hall was built the church members declared themselves well pleased with it; it was well heated, had a very modern kitchen and was indeed considered a huge success.

When Leo and Colin first viewed the old hall, they were dismayed at the state of it and how it had been so neglected. It had a leaking roof, windows which refused to shut properly and a heating system that rattled and groaned, seeming to complain when it was switched on. Leo simply could not see how it would ever be fit for use again, but Colin thought that, with the right approach, it could be made habitable. He reassured Leo that he knew a good builder who could soon have the place put to rights. And true to his word, the man had the roof repaired, the windows replaced and a new boiler installed within a few weeks. Leo had never established how much it had all cost Colin, simply because he had never asked him. And the place was certainly serving him very well now. He had managed to buy a few extra seats at auction which supplemented the ones already there, so he was well able to accommodate his ever growing congregation. He had brought the desk from his parents' sitting room at home, to serve as his pulpit. It was all quite adequate, but nothing like the new church he aspired to, and which some of his congregation were beginning to ask questions about. These questions put him under immense pressure. Just tonight three of his elders, who had themselves donated very generously to the fund by selling some of their plots of land, had stayed behind to ask him how things were progressing. One of them, Gerald King, had even suggested he would go to the Planning Office in Downpatrick and explain the need for urgency for the building to proceed. So Leo reassured him, by promising to do exactly that himself the next day, but explaining that planning approval was notoriously a very lengthy procedure, and they must be patient.

It was some time after they left the hall that he felt disposed to count the evening collection, and as always, he was delighted with people's generosity. His coffers continued to swell and if only he could help Valerie decide if she wanted to go to New York or to Cape Town to get married and to live, they would soon be on their way. He knew it would not matter very much to him where they went, he knew now he had the power that was necessary to persuade people to give him money in order to preach the Word of the Lord. He knew that no matter which part of the world he travelled to people would listen to him. He had realised some time ago, that he held some strange power or fascination over them.

Leo had just finished putting the last of the collection into his briefcase, and was in the process of switching off the main lights in the room, the light in the front porch was enough to see to lock the outer door, when he thought he heard a sound from the outer porch. Perhaps someone had forgotten something; he looked round briefly as he made his way towards the porch, but the rays from the porch light were not enough after all, to illuminate the place. 'Is anyone there?' he raised his voice a little as he approached the doorway which led into the porch. There was only silence; the noise must be coming from those long straggly branches which overhung the hall. He must organise to have them cut back during this coming week.

As he opened the door and stepped into the porch he was aware of something or someone standing there, still and silent as a statue. 'Oh, hello, I wasn't expecting anyone, is everything all right with you?' as he strained to see who it was. And then he saw the flash of the knife and the face seemed illuminated by the glint of the metal, a face he knew so well. Then he felt the pain in his chest and knew that Valerie and he would not be going to New York or Cape Town, he would not be going anywhere.

'Rhoda, Leo did not come home last night, I've made his fry as usual for him but he's not in his room, I checked it.' Dorrie was annoyed with her son, she was a real stickler for routine, but here she was hanging around waiting to clear up her kitchen, but of Leo, there was no sign. He was always up and about from around seven o'clock any morning. He must have gone to Valerie's house after the service and decided to stay overnight. 'Have you Valerie's phone number by any chance?' This Valerie girl seemed to have taken Leo by storm. He was now thirty-four years of age but had never shown much interest in girls until now. He seemed quite besotted and that surprised Dorrie. Valerie was such a mouse of a girl, of average height, slightly built with light brown hair cut in a severe fringe across her forehead. She seemed to have so little to say for herself that, at times, Dorrie felt like shaking her. So unlike Leo, who was so forceful and had such magnetism. But still, they said opposites attract.

'Mum, I certainly don't have Valerie's number. I'm not very close to her.' Rhoda answered quite shortly, she had little time for Leo's girl-friend, she seemed such a bore. Still, she supposed her mum wouldn't rest until he was home. 'If you like, I'll take a walk to her house. I know where she lives, it's only a couple of drives away, and I'll tell him breakfast's ready.'

'No forget it Rhoda, he's bound to appear soon.' Dorrie had just finished speaking when the front door bell rang. It was

Rhoda who went to answer it, and Dorrie began to fill the kettle to make tea for whoever it was. When she turned round on hearing the footsteps resounding on her kitchen floor, initially she only saw Rhoda standing over from her, so white-faced and trembling. Then she saw the two uniformed policemen, and before they began to speak she was already screaming for John to come downstairs. She knew by their faces, and the whole atmosphere, that something truly terrible had happened to her youngest son.

CHAPTER 9

John lay, still and silent in the bed, listening to Dorrie's even breathing, reassured she was fast asleep and would more than likely remain that way for some time. The family doctor had been quite adamant that the sedative he had given Dorrie and her daughter, Rhoda, was a most effective one.

Both women had dissolved into uncontrollable hysteria when the police had informed them that Leo was dead. He had been found dead in the porch of the church hall and had died sometime during the previous evening. The two policemen who delivered the awful news had behaved with such professionalism and sensitivity that John knew he would always remember them. When Dorrie had screamed for him to come downstairs, they had said nothing until John was present. It was they who had suggested to John that he should get the family doctor for his wife and daughter, when they realised how truly hysterical the two women were becoming. Then they explained to him they needed someone to identify the body. Did John feel he was up to such an ordeal? He assured them he would do it, but first he must inform his sister-in-law Ellen and her husband Tom of Leo's death. He would want them to come and stay with his wife and daughter while he went with the police.

It was only while they were driving in the police car towards the church hall that the police told John they thought his son had been murdered, and that his body still lay in the porch of the hall. It could not be moved until Forensics were satisfied they had finished their search for clues which would help trap the murderer, and establish the kind of weapon that had been used to kill him.

Now as he lay beside his wife, John recalled the horror of the whole day, the moment when he saw the policemen in his kitchen, the drive to the hall, and then, the grotesque sight of his youngest child lying in a pool of blood in a Christian place of worship. The sight seemed to make the whole place so totally godless, and bereft of any divine or even decent presence. He did not need anyone to turn Leo's body over so that he could see his face in order to identify him. He knew without doubt it was Leo lying there, he knew the shape of his head so very well, he knew his hair-style, and even though some of it was now matted in congealed, dark blood, he recognised that mop of blond hair. Leo had always been proud of the fact he had stayed so blond since childhood.

Later, when the police told him he was free to go and they would see him safely home, he found he was longing to see Dorrie, to enfold her in his arms and make everything all right. Yet, perversely, he dreaded seeing her, having to witness her misery and grief at their son's death. He felt he would be unable to cope. He was in the very depths of despair himself, in some black pit he could never imagine climbing out of.

When he arrived back home it was Ellen and Tom who were there to help him into the sitting room. They offered him tea and insisted he eat something. They reassured him that both Dorrie and Rhoda were fast asleep, and would likely be like that until the next morning. Ellen had informed other members of the family, and some of the elders in the church, and also Leo's former minister, of Leo's death. John was grateful to his sister-in-law, he knew someone had to deal with practical issues, but for now he was not capable of doing so.

Now, as he waited for the dawn to come, indicating that this dreadful night was coming to an end, he remembered Colin and Margaret's visit earlier in the day and how they had both been a source of comfort to him. He had seemed bereft of feeling all day, but on seeing his son entering the sitting room with such concern on his face for his father, John's tears had flowed freely, and Colin, he knew, was finding it difficult to cope and to keep his own tears at bay.

'Who would do such a thing, dad? The police will soon find out whoever is responsible, I'm sure.'

John nodded mutely, too overcome with the tears running down his face, to make any coherent answer. He gripped his eldest son's arm as Colin went on 'How is Mum, Dad? I would give anything to hold her and cherish her, but Ellen tells me she is heavily sedated. Would she be any more accepting of me now, do you think?'

'I don't know, she is in no fit state for anything, and I believe she only sees Leo in front of her.'

Even though he was very distressed, Colin thought wryly that Leo was the only person his mother had seen in front of her for some time. But this was not the place for such thoughts. As John watched his eldest son leave the house with his wife, he felt a moment of panic that they might not call back for some time and momentarily considered how often they might call if Dorrie was kept sedated for a time. But as soon as that thought entered his head, John was appalled at the very idea. He was not thinking straight, this tragedy was affecting his thinking. Besides, now in the early hours of the morning as he looked at Dorrie, still lying sleeping deeply beside him, he realised she had had plenty of sedation to last for some hours. Moreover, Colin had promised before he left, that he intended to call regularly to see his father and mother.

The inquest into Leo Finlay's death was held on Friday 20th October, 1977 in the Courthouse in Belfast City Centre. The murder of such a young man, and him a wonderful evangelist with the prospect of a long and happy, God-fearing life ahead of him, had raised considerable interest among the people living in the area and more especially in his congregation, many of whom grieved deeply for the loss of their spiritual leader. So the courthouse was packed with young and old alike when the Coroner delivered his verdict that Leo Finlay had been murdered by person or persons unknown. The victim had died from a single stab wound to his chest which had penetrated his heart, causing massive bleeding from the aorta. The murder weapon had been a popular, kitchen type knife. Possibly one used for carving meat, and measured about eight centimetres in diameter. Death would have been almost instantaneous, due to shock and loss of blood.

Colin had attended the inquest alone, insisting Margaret might find it all too distressing and he knew she was relieved when he said he would go alone. His Aunt Ellen had informed him the previous evening that his mother and Rhoda would not be present either, so Colin was able to sit with his father, rendering what support he could, as they listened to the Coroner's words and the events which had ended Leo's life.

When the Coroner dismissed the court, Colin and his father were kindly escorted away through a side door, away from well meaning people jostling with one another in the hope of speaking to Mr. Finlay, and offering their sincere condolences. And of course, away from those who were there simply to pry, and might only have a ghoulish interest in the whole proceedings.

Five days later John and Dorrie's son's body was released for burial. It was a strictly private family burial, and he was laid to rest in the churchyard adjacent to the Presbyterian church he had attended since he was a little boy. John knew it was important that Dorrie was present, because he believed if she didn't go, she might regret it for the rest of her life. So with the help of her sisters and Ellen her sister-in-law, she was able to be there, and was respectable and alert during the service. Even later, when relatives returned to their niece Lucie's house for tea, she amazed John by insisting she wanted to come, and he took it as a sign that his wife was determined to try to cope with this tragedy.

CHAPTER 10

For the immediate family of Leo, and indeed for the extended family, the months following his inquest and subsequent burial were black pits of despair, and a time to simply struggle through on a daily, indeed on an hourly basis. Some of his family lived in a perpetual state of anguish and grief, unable to work or function properly; others did their best to bury the horror they felt at the brutality of his death and the loss they had suffered.

Colin and Margaret were among those in the family who did their best with the daily grind of their life without letting their feelings overshadow their children's welfare and happiness. They were just so grateful they both had their new jobs and must concentrate on doing their best there. They realised that their friends who had offered them the jobs in the first place, must feel justified in the decision they had made and so they had no intention of letting them down.

For John and Dorrie, their life seemed one long nightmare, with Dorrie's form fluctuating between bouts of uncontrolled and blood-curdling weeping, to ones of semi-comatosed sleep due to heavy sedation. John had tried everything he could think of to help his wife. He loved her so much and was finding it unbearable to see her like this. Even Rhoda seemed to have given up on her mother; she, who had been so understanding and tolerant immediately after her brother's death. She had been able to pick herself up very quickly, considering how she had worshipped her young brother. She was now back in her office job in the Civil Service, and seemed to be coping very well indeed. Many times during his long, lonely nights when John thought of the house so changed and of his daughter, he wondered if Rhoda had just simply wished to escape the agony of watching her mother, and the hopeless feeling it must give her. Certainly he could not blame Rhoda for returning to work in order to escape the horror of everything. He intended to support his daughter as best he could to help her cope with the destruction of their happy home life.

As for himself, he longed for comfort in his grief, for someone to listen to him, to put out a comforting arm to him and offer some solace. He knew he could not expect it from Dorrie, she was totally self-absorbed and selfish in her grief. She, who had always been so generous in her feelings and emotions towards him, now had ceased to think of him. How he wanted to shout aloud that he too, had lost a much loved son. Colin was kind enough and considerate to him, calling most evenings on his way home from work, when his mother would have gone to her bedroom. But even his kind words did not fill the aching void in his heart.

The advertisement occupied a small corner of the Belfast Telegraph, and on a sudden impulse John wrote the number in his diary. More than likely he would never ring it, but the words of the advertisement had intrigued him. The advertisement was simply in the form of a couple of questions. Are you unhappy? Are you in need of some emotional and physical comfort? These questions were followed by a phone number and John recognised it as a local one. He really felt that he could answer those questions with a resounding Yes, but he doubted if he had the courage to do anything about it.

He knew the street very well, he had had occasion to wander through it many times as a teenager on his way to Smithfield Market. Although not a very salubrious area it was still decent enough, with a mixture of terraced houses and shops lining it. The lady who answered the telephone explained that there was a back entrance off the wide alley which ran along the back of the street. She also explained that if he came to the back entrance, he could go directly upstairs and as the rooms were numbered very clearly, he could let himself into Room Two. He decided he must take the bus, as any car left unattended in Belfast, either day or night, might be the subject of a 'Controlled Explosion' by the Army, as every unattended car was suspected of containing a bomb.

After checking that Dorrie had had her sedation, and that Rhoda would be in all evening, John set forth on his rendezvous and was pleasantly surprised at how elated he felt at what he was about to do. He was quite amazed at his own courage, perhaps not so much courage but did his actions smack of desperation? Probably – but it was now January and he had bottled up his feelings over the last three months since Leo's death, and Christmas and the New Year had been non-events. Now, as he sat in the bus that would leave him in Smithfield Square, he felt he was getting some control over his life at last.

He found the terraced house eventually. It appeared to combine living accommodation with a shop, which was something many people did. He made his way along until he discovered the alley she had explained all about to him, and as all the houses were numbered at the back as well as the front, he soon found number ten, and went in through the back door as she had instructed him. He was quite surprised to find that the hall ran directly through from the front door to the back, with the stairs immediately to his right. He found Room Two with ease, as it was the room just facing the stairs as he stepped on to the landing. He entered a room which almost immediately gave him a sense of peace and ease, something he had not experienced in the last few weeks. The room was very simply furnished, but everything in it seemed to state elegance and refinement, and he was enveloped in the beautiful odours and atmosphere of the place.

He had just seated himself on the beautiful easy chair, the only one in the room, when the door opened and a woman in her forties appeared.

'Oh, my God, Rachel, I didn't know. Oh, God, this is terrible' John made to rise from the chair, but seemed incapable of any movement. 'I didn't know. Your advert, it didn't say anything about, you know, sex.' He was so ashamed of himself, how could he have been so naive, and him a business man all these years. 'I'm so sorry, I'll go, Rachel, I'll just go. I truthfully just wanted to talk to someone, that's all. You probably don't believe me, but it is true.'

In answer to all this agitation, Rachel quietly approached him where he sat, totally mortified. 'Please, John, you weren't to know. It is a different phone number I use for here and I also try to modulate my voice a little in case my Canadian accent puts people off.' Then she took his trembling hands in hers, in an attempt to ease his discomfort. As she held his hands he went on, 'I don't want sex. I only wanted what your advert says "comfort and someone to talk to". You must think me pathetic, really pathetic.'

'John, I don't think anything of the sort, look what you have been through. And, not everyone who comes here wants a sexual relationship. A few are content enough with a few cuddles, although not very many. I know you already know about me, John. I know my mother told Dorrie all about me. And she asked Leo to pray for me. Leo visited me fairly often, simply to let me know he was indeed praying for me, and for Lynn and my mother. I have to tell you, though, John, his prayers came at a price.' Rachel had made a conscious decision to talk about Leo, and to be as truthful about him as she could.

In that room on that evening Rachel reckoned that Uncle John did indeed need comfort. She had heard from other family members how poorly Aunt Dorrie was, and she wondered how John had coped with it all. He needed to talk to someone, and she felt if she handled the situation properly, he might open up to her. He must have been desperate to have answered her advertisement, because she knew or felt she knew, he was just a God-fearing and respectable member of the public and church. But hadn't she had three or four of Leo Finlay's elders from his church visiting her recently. They had been very clear and adamant about what they wanted, and were more than willing to pay her good money for it. Money, Rachel now knew, that must come from gullible members of the public who were similar to herself.

Afterwards, on the way home on the bus, John marvelled how well Rachel had coped with his presence in that bedroom. She had insisted on making tea for them both, and when she returned, had encouraged him to tell her everything about Dorrie and how he was coping with all the strain and stress both of the loss of his son and his wife's mental instability. He had initially been very reticent to talk about anything very much but when he looked over at Rachel, her gentle smile and firm nod encouraged him to talk to her, and when he began to talk, she pulled the chair over beside him and settled herself in it. She too, began to talk to him, just about her own family, about her time in Canada, about how she had become involved with the law over there. She told him about her mother's determination to return to Northern Ireland in the hope that Rachel would find a different occupation, but unfortunately she had found the lure of her original employment too strong. As the conversation flowed between them he found the situation a healing one and believed that he had done Rachel some good, too. When Rachel said it was time for home he could scarcely believe it, the whole evening had flown.

When he entered his own home it was with some renewed energy and spirit to deal with whatever lay ahead. One thing he did know, Dorrie and he must talk. Talk about anything, it didn't matter what it was just as long as they kept talking.

CHAPTER 11

It was the week before Christmas and although most of the schools and universities did not officially break up until a couple of days before Christmas Eve, they were already winding down and doing very little work in terms of true studying. Queen's University was one of those institutions which believed a good concert, an excellent Nativity play, and a resounding carol service were essential before the Christmas recess, and they also believed in recruiting the best of the talent from their huge numbers. So it was that Lynn Compton and Jason Hampton were attending the same carol practices together; then going with the crowd to their favourite pub, the Botanic Inn, afterwards for a pleasant drink.

They both found some solace and cheerfulness in one another's company. Being young and resilient, they longed to try and forget the horror which had invaded their whole family. They yearned for a more normal Christmas and the celebrations to go on as usual. But the family circle was having difficulty coping, there would be little celebration in anyone's home, the tragedy of Leo's death hung over everything like a thick, black cloud and pervaded the whole atmosphere. Most of the family felt that if the police could find poor Leo's killer they might be able to move on a little, but so far they did not seem to have any leads. They had told the family they had quickly dismissed any suggestion of a terrorist murder, as stabbing was not really a hallmark of I.R.A. activity. Bombing or shooting was their preferred method of assassination, besides, the IRA usually took great pride in announcing when they were responsible for yet another horrific murder. So no one believed Leo Finlay died at the hands of terrorists, but certainly someone had wanted him dead, but who and why? He had been an evangelist devoted to saving souls and to showing non-Christians a more Christian way of life. Who on earth would do such a thing? Everyone who knew him seemed under suspicion, according to the local gossip. Even his girlfriend Valerie, it seemed, had been taken in for questioning by the police. But it appeared her alibi for that evening had been watertight, she had been visiting a girlfriend's house, and that whole family could vouch she had been with them until very late in the evening. She had also been given a lift home by her girlfriend's father. There was endless speculation, but everyone agreed that the police needed to find the killer of Leo Finlay, and very soon.

Now as Lynn and Jason sat together over a quiet drink, commiserating with each other that this Christmas was not going to be one to look forward to; they confessed they felt a bit guilty about that, when it was obvious the other older members of the family were suffering agonies over Leo's death, and had no thought of Christmas.

'Lynn, would you like to come over some afternoon soon and see my new collie dog. It is the only thing that cheers me up, and it might do the same for you.' Jason's face lit up when he spoke of his new dog. 'I have just bought it, it cost me £300. I used some of my student loan I have to say, but I know you'll love him.'

'Lucky you, Jason, I love animals but because we live in Lucie's annexe I abandoned any notion I might have had of getting anything, not even a kitten. Aunt Lucie's good enough, but I would not want to impose.'

'Well, where we are, Lynn, it is semi-rural and I have plenty of scope to take him walking, plus we have a good sized back garden, well fenced in. I have no lectures either next Monday or Wednesday, what about you?'

Jason seemed so keen for Lynn's approval of his dog that she felt she must go, and a quick look at her diary confirmed she was free on the Monday. She told him she would cycle over to his house and hoped to see him around two o'clock. Jason was inordinately pleased that Lynn seemed eager to see

'Monty' because so far his parents had shown no interest, although his young sister Emily seemed to dote on him.

'That's terrific, Lynn. I have the car to-night, so I'll drop you off home and I'll see you Monday. And I do hope you like my collie as much as I do. I'm hoping to show him at a special collie show sometime in February. If I decide to do that, would you come with me? Will you think about it?'

'Certainly I'll go. Is it one of those shows that give prizes for appearance, behaviour and performance from the dog? I've never been to one, but I have seen them on television and I've read lots about them. Maybe my mum and grandma might come too, they love anything like that. That's if mum isn't working. She works nearly every night, but I'm sure she would take it off for something like that.'

'Mention it to them, it's only a thought at the moment, but maybe if my mum and dad knew you were going they might, just might, decide to come and support me. But I insist that anyone of our family who want to go to the show must come and get to know 'Monty' a little first. I want him to be on his best behaviour and behave impeccably and I have realised he just loves an audience.'

'Mum and Grandma have asked Lucie and her ones for Christmas dinner, a very quiet one, mind, so I'll mention it to Lucie then and see if she would like to come with us.'

When told about her nephew's new pet and his hopes for showing him sometime in the New Year, Lucie knew that, much as she wanted to support Jason, she did not think she could go to the house because of Matthew's animosity towards her, but she did tell Lynn that Paul and she would definitely go to the show and render a bit of moral support. Lucie felt that the interest in this pet of Jason's might just brighten their lives and help them to forget the horror of Leo. She firmly believed that pets could soothe people in times of sorrow and distress and it would be such a change to go and see a gathering of dogs, all looking their best, instead of watching her mother and Tom and Aunt Dorrie trying to cope with their grief. There would be little point in including them, especially Uncle John and Aunt Dorrie, as her aunt spent most of the day sleeping, or reading her Bible and praying. As for Uncle John, everyone wondered how he coped with it all, but he had confided in Lucie that he had started to go into town a couple of nights a week, just for a browse round, but really to get away from it all. He also visited Colin and Margaret on a regular basis.

CHAPTER 12

John found it extremely difficult to talk to Dorrie about anything. She seemed to have withdrawn from him into some private world of her own, and John despaired of her and of everything. He did blame the level of sedation their family doctor had approved for her use, and shortly after the first night he had talked to Rachel, he set about trying to remedy that.

The first week, when he decided to withdraw Dorrie's day-time sedation, was fraught with difficulties. Dorrie on one hand, weeping and begging him to give her her pill, then on the other, being so abusive to him, and using foul words he had never dreamt she was capable of saying. Many times during that week John was so tempted to give in and let both his wife and himself have some peace of mind. But he held out, and sometime during the second week of abstinence he noticed she was more accepting of the situation. Certainly she seemed much more alert, and they seemed to be able to hold a certain level of conversation together. She still took her night-time sedation and John was more than agreeable to this, she needed a good night's rest if she was to face the next day.

John soon established a routine for them both, he prepared lunch, which they ate in the kitchen, then they went to the sitting room with their cups of tea, and it was here John encouraged Dorrie to talk. During the first couple of weeks the only questions Dorrie asked were 'Who could have done such a terrible thing? And did John think Leo had suffered very much?' His replies were always the same 'the police would soon catch whoever was responsible' and 'No, Leo hadn't suffered, everyone had assured them Leo's death had been instantaneous.' He could not answer her first question with very much assurance in his voice. It was three months now since his son's death, and the police seemed no further on with their investigation.

One afternoon however, Dorrie surprised and delighted him by enquiring if Colin ever called to see them.

'Yes, love, Colin calls some evenings on his way home from work. You are usually in bed, and he was not sure if his presence might upset you more, he wanted to give you time to grieve.'

'John, I shall always grieve for Leo, as so too will you.' Dorrie was having difficulty speaking, choked by those tears which were never far from the surface. 'But I have another son, and Leo and he were very close once, so he must be grieving too. I would like to see him. I want to see him, that is, if he doesn't mention anything about the money or our break-up.'

'Dorrie, that is all so irrelevant now, both to us and to Colin.' John was anxious to heal the breach between his son and his wife as soon as possible. 'I'll ring him tonight and ask him to please call on his lunch hour tomorrow, because you would like to see him.' John was smiling for the first time in three months and he thought he saw the glimmer of one on his wife's face.

After ringing to confirm that she could see him, John visited Rachel that same evening and as he sat relaxing in the room which had been such a haven to him in the last few weeks, he told his niece all about Dorrie and her sudden desire to see Colin, and how pleased he was about it all. He believed, he told her, that Dorrie might just be turning the corner and was maybe learning to cope better with her grief.

'It's all down to you, Rachel, and I can never thank you enough for listening to me and helping me so much. If I had not come here I don't believe we would be saying anything to each other even yet. You have shown me the importance of trying to communicate, and reach out to one another. I fear what would have become of Dorrie and me. I love her so much, Rachel. I always have done. I might not have agreed with some of her actions recently, but my feelings for her have never changed.'

'I know that, John, just relax and think of her, and what you mean to each other.'

'You have helped me so much, Rachel, I wish I could be of more assistance to you.' John was hesitant about his concerns about putting any pressure on his niece regarding her life-style. 'I mean, I worry about you and the road you are going down since you came here. Is there anything else you might diverse into that might still bring you a reasonable income? These rooms, for example, you could let them out. There are business men who regularly come over here, always looking for accommodation. And you are right in the heart of Belfast, you would have no trouble letting them out, I should think.'

'Please, John you must not worry about me. I doubt very much if letting these three rooms out would bring me in the kind of money I can earn by offering my services to business men.' Rachel looked keenly at her uncle, 'I'm sorry. I know I sound very mercenary, but that's how it is. The only one I worry about in all this is Lynn. I don't know how she would feel if she knew what I really used these rooms for. I know I must tell her some time, but for now, I must keep it as quiet as possible.'

'I do believe that you are a good woman Rachel, otherwise you would not have been such support for me at this time in my life. But I am concerned for you, you know.'

Rachel laughed heartily at this. 'Me a good woman, John. I don't think there are many who would agree with that statement, But I shall hug it to me and in my darker moments I will always remember what you said.'

John had to be content with having managed to convey to his niece something of how he felt about what she was doing, without sounding too moralistic. He said good night and quit Rachel's premises, and made his way to the bus stop to catch the last bus home.

But a new horror awaited him when he arrived there; before he even put his key in the door Rhoda opened it, her eyes bloodshot with tears, and she seemed half crazed.

'Where have you been, dad? I've been ringing everyone looking for you. Margaret rang over an hour ago to say the police had been to their house and arrested Colin on suspicion of murder.' She looked at her father wildly. 'Please say it can't be so, Colin could not possibly have done this.'

'Shush, shush, Rhoda.' John felt numb, but he knew he must protect Dorrie from this latest horror. 'Let's go in the sitting room and you can tell me what has happened. But we must not waken your mother.'

It was some time before Rhoda seemed placated, and it was only when John said he was going to drive to the police station to see Colin and, he informed Rhoda, to make sure he had a good lawyer that she became more composed, even though her silences were still punctuated with sobs and hiccoughs. Then reminding his daughter to look after her mother, John fetched his car keys and in some sort of trance made his way to the police station.

'Oh, dad, I'm so glad to see you. To see anybody.' Colin looked quite demented looking and diminished, John observed, as he approached the cell where his son was. He seemed to have shrunk in stature since he had last seen him twenty-four hours ago.

'Colin, how has this happened? What have they done to you? How could anyone think you had anything to do with Leo's death?' John's voice tailed off, then making an effort to be strong for his son's sake. 'Have you thought of getting a solicitor? We have to get you out of here.'

'I was allowed one phone call when they brought me here and I rang Mr. Campbell, our family solicitor. He is coming first thing in the morning. Margaret had had the presence of mind to ring him, so she had already done that before I did. I knew she would contact you and I prayed you would call, dad. Please help me.'

Colin, his son, sounded so weak and vulnerable, this was not the strong, optimistic young man he knew and loved. In the space of a few hours he had become a wreck of a man. John could not make sense of anything that was happening, and obviously neither could Colin.

'We need to talk about the events leading up to you being here, Colin. I'm going to ask permission to be allowed in to the cell or that you are allowed out to me. There must be somewhere we can talk.'

The policeman on duty was a community one, simply used to dealing with routine misdemeanours, like shoplifting, drunkenness and the like. This case intrigued him so much, it was a murder one. And it was the man's brother who was accused of killing him. He had no problem letting his father into the cell to talk, but, he explained, he must sit guard outside, while his father was in there. Secretly, Constable Reid was eager to hear what might transpire between father and son. They had never had anything quite so exciting here before, even though they had had a terrible toll with terrorist bombings and shooting on all the security forces. Indeed they all lived in fear of that bomb being under their car, and that they might forget to check for any device before coming to work in the mornings.

But this was so different, a real scandal, a young evangelist who had his whole life ahead of him, murdered, and now they were saying his brother was responsible. And he, Constable Reid was right here at the forefront. He would have first-hand information on the whole thing. He could afford to be generous and let this man talk to the prisoner.

For the next hour John and Colin went over the events that had led to the arrest. It transpired that Colin had no alibi for the night in question, and on his way home would pass the church hall coming from his own church. Also the police had discovered the reason why Colin had left Leo to fend for himself and they were able to confirm that they knew the exact amount of money in each of Leo's accounts. For most of the time he was there, while concentrating on what Colin was saying, John was trying to decide what he would tell Dorrie, who just a few hours ago had told him she wanted to see Colin. What was he to tell her now? Could he and indeed should he, tell her of Colin's arrest? What then? Did that mean Dorrie would lapse back into the confused state she was only just starting to emerge from? He had no answers. He did not intend to rush home to tell her tonight, but would leave it in the meantime. Thank God he had sworn Rhoda to secrecy, before he had even left the house to come here.

CHAPTER 13

Rachel put a match to the scented candles in Room 1, as she normally did when she was expecting a client. Tonight it was for a Mr. Anderson who had phoned a short time before. Last week he had said he was Mr. Jones, the week before Mr. Smith, and before that Mr. Wilson. But Rachel was good with voices and she had come to recognise the same man calling each time. She knew, too, that he would be here a good fifteen minutes before his time, creep up the stairs and into the room without making a sound. And she would be there waiting for him. Invariably he did not talk much, but always eyed her lasciviously when he entered the room, then he was all hands, roughness and baseness.

But tonight when he arrived he seemed so different. He was spotlessly clean, something he was not always and instead of getting directly into the bed, he began to pace about the floor and to talk. And Rachel forced herself to listen, even though, for some strange reason, she was always anxious to be rid of the man. Every time he came he always reminded her he was an elder in a Church, and that his privacy must be sacrosanct. Rachel, in turn, had always to assure him that it would be, stressing that her privacy was equally important to her. He then surprised her by saying he would like to commiserate with her for her cousin's arrest. She had no idea how he knew Colin and she were even related, but she let it pass and simply thanked him. Mr. Anderson repeated again how sorry he was, and remarked he prayed for Colin Finlay's release every night. Surely no one could possibly believe he had anything to do with it.

'Well, the powers that be seem to believe they have some evidence, Mr. Anderson. He has no alibi from when he left the church until he returned home. They established that he passes Leo's church hall on his way home. The prosecution also know that Colin had left Leo because of money matters.' Rachel wondered about the wisdom of repeating any of this to someone out of Leo's Church but if Mr. Anderson was sincerely concerned about Colin and his welfare, she felt she had to be truthful with him and talk to him. Besides it suited her well, she felt she could not bear a sexual encounter with this man to-night. He seemed almost sterile in his cleanliness, no doubt because it was Sunday and he had come straight from church. She had actually preferred to see the man grubbier, more unkempt even. Then he seemed more human on those occasions.

'Money matters, what were they?' Mr. Anderson seemed very animated when he spoke. 'Leo controlled the money very well and very tightly, I do know that. So I don't see how they could have fallen out about that.'

Rachel remarked that none of the family seemed to have been told much about the estrangement between the two boys. The only thing that ever was said was that it was about 'money matters' but no one seemed to actually know much about it. As she spoke Rachel sensed that her client seemed disappointed in her answer, no doubt he had been hoping for a bit more gossip than was already going around. He lingered past his time that evening, and Rachel was inordinately relieved when he finally said he must go home. She was surprised and very appreciative when he actually handed her extra money for the evening, even though sex had not featured in their relationship at any time.

After he had gone Rachel pondered over the last couple of hours and what had actually transpired between Mr. Anderson and her, and she began to wonder if perhaps she was turning into some kind of agony aunt. As her mind ran on to their conversation, she began to compare it to John's and hers and how they had been. How she wished it had been him with her earlier, not a Church elder whom she found so very repulsive. She longed to know how John was, how was he coping with this new, awful trauma in his life. How she longed to talk to him, but he had not come back to 10, Waring Street since the night of Colin's arrest. So she only knew what other members of the family told her about him. According to them, John and Rhoda were both having a harrowing time with Dorrie. She could not be left alone, as they feared for her safety. According to Aunt Ellen, and contrary to what John thought best for his wife's mental health, their newly appointed evangelical leader in Leo's Church had decided Dorrie must be told the truth about Colin and his arrest. It seems that since then Dorrie had been prostrate, only eating scraps of food and was now back on her original sedation, and that had been ten days ago.

Rachel found she was quite heartbroken at this new horror for her Uncle John, and had found herself hoping and praying he would ring. Surely he would want to tell her how things were. They had shared so much, the trauma of Leo's murder, Dorrie's mental state and John's determination to cope. Now she felt they were so close – he was her friend, her advisor who only wanted to guide her and encourage her to leave the life she was currently leading. She thought a lot about what John had said about letting out the rooms. She knew he had her welfare at heart, and for her, he had, in many ways, replaced the father she had lost to cancer some years ago in Canada. She would like to think that John felt she was like a daughter to him and she believed that she was. The next time they met or he phoned she would let him know she was thinking a lot about his advice to her, but in the meantime Lynn needed financial support to get through university and into a good career. There was her mother too, who needed any financial help Rachel could give. And Rachel knew that, at present, she was most generous to both her mother and daughter. She could well afford to be, business was very good indeed. A business which she knew, in her heart, would be very difficult to give up.

'Mum, you'll never guess, there's going to be a dance after the dog show at the Belvedere Hotel. That's probably when the prizes will be distributed for the dog owners whose dogs were the best. Wouldn't it be fantastic if Jason won something? He really loves that dog. He has decided to enter him in the 'Most

Intelligent Dog' category. He was in two minds about entering him in anything, but as I said, sure it's only a bit of fun.' Lynn regarded her mother and grandmother sitting on either side of the fire in the annexe. It was a cold night in January 1978, and the fire had been so welcoming when she had returned home from university later than usual. She had gone to the library in Queen's to access information she needed and it had taken much longer than she had anticipated. But thankfully Jason had waited for her and driven her home in his car. It was on the way home he had told her about the dance in the Belvedere.

'I knew all about the show, but didn't know about any dance until yesterday. I suppose because I have officially entered a dog for the show, they have informed me of all the other entertainment. I hope you will come to the dance with me, I think it will be pretty good. I think Mum and Dad intend coming to the show, but may not stay for the dance, and probably your mum will feel the same. There's no doubt Colin's arrest has affected us all, the sooner his name is cleared the better. But in the meantime I intend to spend time around animals. They are a real source of comfort.'

By the time Jason pulled his car up outside the annexe, Lynn had promised to accompany him to the dance, even if no one else in the family wanted to go. She told him she would look forward to shopping for a new dress and getting ready for it all.

Now, sitting here with her mother and grandmother, Lynn realised how much she was beginning to love Northern Ireland. She loved the university. She loved where she lived and all her relatives, with no exception. They were all very dear to her. Even though there were frequent 'bomb scares', there were terrorist attacks in ever increasing numbers and gun battles between the differing terrorist groups, she still loved this place.

'Mum. We'll both need something to wear for this dance, I have nothing. Of course, I've never even been to a dinner dance before. But you too, need to treat yourself. That is if you are going.'

'With a dinner dance you really need a partner with you, Lynn. So I think I'll let Jason and you go on ahead. But as to-morrow's Saturday, we will go shopping and buy you a spectacular dress, because it is your first dance.'

Rachel felt she could do with going to do some shopping, it was something she could look forward to, especially for Lynn. There was nothing she liked better than buying presents for people. It was just what she needed. She had been feeling pretty low and had earlier to-day cancelled three bookings for this evening and rescheduled the men for another evening. She knew that, deep down, Uncle John's attitude to her and her work was dwelling on her mind. But at the same time, she would not let anyone's advice stand in her way of giving her mother and her daughter a comfortable life -style.

CHAPTER 14

In early January, 1978, when the courts had returned to work after Christmas and the New Year recess, the Director of Public Prosecutions, after spending considerable time perusing the evidence presented to him, determined that Colin Finlay had a case to answer regarding the murder of his young brother. The trial date was set for Monday 19th January, to be held in the High Court in Belfast. The jury would be notified and appointed according to the Rules of the Law.

Colin, who had been out on bail while waiting to know his fate, was promptly re-arrested and taken back to the courthouse, where he was formally charged with Leo's murder, and from there he was taken to Crumlin Road Gaol.

'Margaret, I have just been to see Colin and he does seem in reasonable spirits and remains optimistic about his future. He says his defence lawyer is working hard to prepare his case and prove his innocence.' John had called to see his daughter in law on the way home from the prison, 'I'll come and look after the children tomorrow, Margaret, while you go to visit him, He is so looking forward to your visit, He also said he wants your minister to call, so perhaps you could ring him.'

'I did that earlier, I knew he would probably want to see the Reverend Martin. He says he'll call tomorrow. But tell me what his defence think, there seems to be something about a kitchen knife, you know. The police were here about three weeks ago and ransacked the kitchen. They found my canteen of carving knives and because one of them is missing, they became very interested and took the canteen away. They quizzed Colin and I both about the missing knife, and I explained the knife had been missing for some time and could be anywhere. I know they didn't believe me, but surely a missing knife is not enough to condemn anyone, is it?' And now Margaret, who had been so stoical over the last few weeks, for her husband and family's sake, now sat down and sobbed bitterly. 'What have we ever done to deserve any of this? We have never harmed anyone, not ever. Colin did not even bear Leo very much resentment over the money, but decided to forget about it all and move on. Now they probably think he murdered Leo because of it. And they seem to think he might have done it with one of our kitchen knives.'

'That's the thing, Margaret, if you could just think what might have happened to the knife perhaps Colin would have no case to answer.'

'I've wracked my brains. Maybe I did take it over to Mum's house and left it there. Maybe we took it on a picnic, I just don't know.'

John was silent for a moment. It was obvious his daughter-in-law had no idea about the whereabouts of the knife and that was that. 'I was wondering, Margaret, if you would be agreeable to Matthew doing some 'off the record' detective work. I know he is anti-terrorist squad, but he is a great detective, and you never know, he might come up with something. He might be able to help us. I don't know. But I do know I have lost one son, and don't want to lose another to a prison cell. So is it worth a try?'

In answer Margaret immediately came across to her father-in-law, and hugging him tightly, said in a more positive voice, 'Of course, of course. I never once thought of Matthew, and as you say, he's very good at what he does.' Margaret's face brightened at the thought of some help and hope for her husband.

'I'll call over to his cottage now. It's a fairly short drive from here. I'll let you know tomorrow what he thinks. In the meantime, do try to eat something and get some sleep. Colin needs us to be well for him. And I think the only ones he really looks to are you and me, and his minister of course.'

'Tell me, John, did the police interview anyone else out of Leo's church? It might possibly have been someone who was actually at his service that night. Maybe Colin wasn't the only one Leo had duped regarding money.' Matthew regarded his uncle solemnly. John had appeared on his doorstep about an hour ago, and after Julie had made some tea and biscuits, Matthew, on hearing his uncle's request for his help, had suggested they go into the sitting room.

'This may sound strange to you Matthew, but I did not take much interest in the police investigation. I believe I was in total shock for some time, and then there was Dorrie. So I don't really know, but I think some people were questioned at a certain level. I don't believe they ever came up with anything even remotely like a motive for Leo's murder. So Colin is as good as they've got.' John's voice was heavy with sarcasm.

'Actually John, in my experience with a sudden death from foul play, many relatives have little interest initially with the police investigation. So you are not at all unusual here. But now there is an urgency to take heed as to what is going on, and if you hear anything in church, or from Dorrie's chief elders, no matter how trivial you might think it is, please let me know. I can't promise anything, but I will try and do a bit of undercover work for you, and you never know what I might come up with. I'm not really supposed to do anything like this. Investigate someone else's case, but I'll be very discreet.'

'Thanks, Matthew. I don't know why we didn't think of you before this, but I suppose we knew how gruelling working with the anti-terrorist squad must be, and how harrowing. But I'm going to hold onto the fact that you are out there, working on our behalf. But I won't mention anything to Colin. We don't want to raise any false hopes in the meantime.'

'I totally agree. I'll liaise with yourself and discuss anything I think might be significant with you. But we need to be careful, we don't want to jeopardise Colin's hopes of a fair trial.'

'I'm indebted to you Matthew,' and John gripped his nephew's hand in a firm handshake before bidding him good evening, and making his way to his car and to home.

'Rachel, Colin's trial begins on Monday, this is Thursday, that is only four days away, I am having difficulty coping, I'm ashamed to say.' On sheer impulse earlier that day John had decided to ring Rachel, he needed to talk to someone and Rachel immediately sprung to mind. 'Dorrie doesn't know yet that it all starts on Monday, I have become such a coward, Rachel. But I can't bear to tell her, I fear for her sanity.'

'But John, it must be awful for you. Your experience with Dorrie when the elder from the Church insisted she should know Colin had been arrested was so harrowing for you all. I think you must not tell her anything more at the moment.' When John had contacted her Rachel had encouraged him to call. 'If she's as fragile as everyone says, I don't believe it would do any good telling her this. Do you not agree, John?'

John nodded and continued 'This time I don't intend letting her minister in near her. I'll have to insist she is too unwell, as indeed, she really is.'

'Well, I hope you mean that, John, because I think it is what you really must do.' Rachel's voice was firm 'Remember, it is your house and you have the right to deny access to anyone.'

'Rachel, it is so good to talk to you, It is you who have helped me cope with so much, and especially with Dorrie, and that can only be a good thing.'

'I'm so glad to hear you say that, John.' Rachel still felt guilty that she had been unable to think seriously of John's idea to simply rent out the rooms upstairs, whereas he seemed so ready to accept her advice and try to talk to Dorrie. But now, she felt she had something of interest she could readily discuss with him.

'I need to talk to you too, John. As you know, I have a couple of elders from Leo's Church who come quite frequently, and they seem very keen to talk about Colin's arrest and trial. I have said a couple of things about his arrest and what led up to it. Not that I know very much, but I'm worried in case they might repeat something I have said and jeopardise Colin's trial. What do you think?'

'I can't see how it would. They are very unlikely to say anything, because people might wonder how they came by such information, and I do believe they would panic at the thought that people might suspect them of coming to see you.'

'I do believe that too, because when they do come here they stress time and time again, about keeping their confidentiality. And I always reassure them, so they are very unlikely to run the risk of exposing themselves.'

'In fact, Rachel, I was speaking to Matthew earlier, and he was wondering if there might be anyone else in the congregation who was unhappy about Leo's attitude to money. In other words, did he maybe take money from someone, and not put it towards the new church as he was supposed to, and did they find out about it? It's just a theory Matthew has. Perhaps you are in a position here to find out from some of them, if there was anything talked about, they may know someone in the Church who was disgruntled with him, apart from Colin. You would have to be very subtle, Rachel.'

'John, I never once thought of anything like that, and I've probably had lots of opportunities to find out something. Wouldn't it be wonderful if I could find out something for you, something which might, just might, raise doubts about Colin's guilt? I tell you, John, I intend to try,' and Rachel hugged her uncle closely, she felt so worthwhile suddenly and perhaps her house in Waring Street might prove useful yet. 'It's time for tea now and then we'll say goodnight.'

'Rachel, you must promise me you won't put yourself at risk from anybody.' The line of conversation they'd been having had made John realise how vulnerable Rachel was here at night, on her own. 'I don't mean the men from the Church. I mean any of the others who come.'

'I'm very careful John, and believe it or not, I have a panic button in each bedroom linked directly through to the police station. The police think it is in case of a robbery. If they did come and find me up here with a man I would have to say I was forced up. I'm sorry to tell you this John, but that's how it is. But then again,' and Rachel smiled brightly at him 'I might just confess all,' and she left the room to fetch the tea.

When she returned, John was quick to reassure her about his feelings. 'It may seem strange to you, Rachel. In fact, I find it a bit odd myself and I know I'm contradicting myself, when on one hand I want you to simply rent out the rooms to tenants and on the other your lifestyle makes no difference to how much I admire your spirit and wisdom.'

CHAPTER 15

Rachel seemed to have acquired renewed energy for her work in the evenings, so different from that Friday two weeks ago when she had cancelled some of her appointments, because she felt unable to face them. Initially, when she had awakened on the Saturday morning and remembered her promise to Lynn to go shopping with her, she was dismayed at how she felt. She had very little interest in going, but then when she entered the kitchen and saw Lynn's bright, happy face, her daughter's enthusiasm had rubbed off on her and she had had after all, a very enjoyable day. She had enthused so much about all the styles and the wide range of dresses in the shops they visited. She tried on several dresses in different shops, which were all thankfully situated close to each other and facing the city hall. So Rachel did not feel in the least tired, but was just happy to watch, as her daughter paraded and posed in different dresses, and then simply offered her opinion.

When Lynn appeared in a pale pink creation which flattered her slim figure and emphasized her dark hair and suntanned skin, she herself became very excited.

'Oh, Lynn, that's the one. You must have that. It's so beautiful. You are so beautiful.'

Lynn's eyes were bright with anticipation. 'I love it, Mum. But are you sure? Have you seen the price ticket? Because I have.'

In answer her mother just smiled lovingly, and remarked she would need the right sandals to complete the look. These too, proved to be quite expensive, but they flattered Lynn's slim feet and ankles so much that the deal was soon done. Rachel felt quite wanton at the amount of money she had just spent, but looking at her daughter's radiant face she knew it was all worth it.

So here she was opening her shop on a Monday morning, as she had done for the past eighteen months. But this Monday was very significant, because this Monday would see the opening of Colin Finlay's trial, and Rachel's thoughts were with him and his father. She was glad she had bookings for this evening. She knew it would keep her occupied, and hopefully her mind off John and how he was coping. She knew too, that Mr. Anderson, the elder from Leo's Church had booked with her for a session later on this evening. Although he had referred to himself as Mr. Jones on this occasion, Rachel had decided she would stick with the name Anderson when she thought of him. For a change, she was looking forward to his visit. She had, after all, promised John she would try and find out something about the congregation, no matter how small, from any of the elders who came to her. She had decided shortly after he had telephoned, that she would ask him directly if he knew anyone in the Church who might have had a grudge about money with Leo. After all, she had a good opening, she had told him about Colin and his resentment towards his brother. Initially she had been worried about having done that, but now she was very glad that she had divulged that information. She only had an hour with him – as she had explained to him over the phone, she had other bookings.

Now, she sincerely hoped one hour would be enough to find out anything. In the meantime she had put extra candles in Room 1 and extra pillows on the bed. She had sprayed herself more liberally than usual with Chanel No. 5. All these little touches were designed to seduce him mentally and Rachel had found in the past, they worked very well.

She had hoped he would be early, and she was not disappointed, he came about fifteen minutes before 7.30p.m. creeping up the stairs and into Room 1 as he always did. Rachel had made sure she was there when he entered the room and was at her most welcoming. She led him gently to the bed and indicated he should lie there. His mood however, was so totally different from that last evening when he had just wanted to pace about the room and talk. Tonight he just wanted to hug her and run his hands all over her body. Then he began to pull her down on to him, at the same time trying to remove some of her clothing.

'It will cost you a lot extra, Mr. Jones.' She was having difficulty extricating herself from him and trying to remember which name he had booked under this time. 'If you wish me nude, I mean.' Rachel spoke in her most persuasive manner. 'I don't do nudity.'

'Sorry, I just need good sex to-night.'

'And so you shall, Mr. Jones. I'll lie beside you for a moment or two,' and Rachel climbed up beside him. 'Now just relax and before we indulge in any sexual pleasure I need to ask you a few questions. Do you mind?' As she spoke Rachel was caressing his face and opening his shirt to caress his chest. Then her hand crept down to unzip his trousers, and then she began to stroke him, and as she stroked him and his body was responding urgently to her, she talked.

'I have wondered since the last evening you were here and I told you Colin and Leo had had their differences over money. Do you imagine anyone else in the Church might have had a disappointment with Leo over money? It would be interesting to know, wouldn't it?'

Mr. Jones lay silent for a moment, his breath coming in short, excited gasps and Rachel purposely stopped stroking him 'No, no, please, don't stop.'

'I'll continue shortly, Mr. Jones, I promise you, but first we need a brief break to talk.'

'As a matter of fact I do know somebody.' The words rushed from his mouth, he was frantic with desire, and Rachel felt very much in control and was elated. She simply caressed his thighs while she waited. 'I'd like to help Colin and I'm sure you would too, Mr. Jones.'

'There's a man in the Church, his wife has left him, about three months ago and, I believe, has taken the two children with her. She says it was because he gave most of his farm away to Leo Finlay, in an utter moment of madness, and of course, the evangelist took it. It seems to have left them with very little. A derelict farmhouse is all they have now and I believe he's living alone in it.' Mr Jones tried to drag Rachel down on to him again 'Leo, according to what this man believes, sold the land and banked the money in his own account. That would rankle with any God- fearing citizen, surely?'

Mr. Jones seemed very disturbed at the thought of such a thing happening, and during the next thirty minutes, between his bouts of gratification and ecstasy, declared that the man involved must have been really carried away to have given someone else their whole livelihood. When Rachel tried to establish who the man was, he was adamant that, because of Church etiquette and the confidentiality of any confession to him, he could never divulge that. It was all strictly confidential. In fact, as he was getting ready to leave Rachel, he remarked that he maybe had said too much and he had no desire to get anyone into trouble. Rachel consoled him and reminded him of her confidentiality agreement, but said rather strongly that he really ought to let the police know that there were others in the Church with grievances apart from Colin. She said he might find he would feel quite guilty if Colin were convicted, when some doubt might have been brought to bear on the case.

After Mr. Anderson had gone Rachel dismissed him and all that had transpired from her mind, until she had entertained her other two clients. It was when she was locking up for the evening and she was pondering on the information she had been told earlier, that she wondered if she should let anyone know something about it. It probably did not mean a thing, people did foolish things in their lives, and besides she had no idea who the culprit was. Then she remembered John urging her to take heed, and that no matter how trivial anything might seem to be, she should divulge it. As she put the key into the ignition she decided the only one she should tell was Matthew, he might find it of interest. She knew by going to her cousin she was running the risk of exposing her line of work and her means of income, but recently she had her suspicions that most of her family knew anyway. Something like that was hard to keep under wraps within a family circle, and indeed, within a community. Besides Colin Finlay, his family and their welfare must come first, before her pride and self- esteem.

Matthew and Julie greeted her very warmly, even though it was almost eleven o'clock at night. She explained urgently, when she arrived at their front door, that she had some information, some gossip about the congregation in Leo's church hall. She felt she had to explain why she was at their door at such a late hour. She stressed it might be of no significance, but she now knew that Colin had not been the only one who had suffered financially at Leo's hand.

'Please come in, Rachel.' Matthew opened the door wide and stood aside for her to pass. 'Julie and I are rather like night owls, so do feel welcome.'

Over tea and biscuits Rachel related to Matthew what she had learned, Julie having discreetly left them to it, explaining she never pried into any of Matthew's work, and he never encouraged it. It was only when he had success that she prided in it all she explained, as she left the room, with a loving glance at her husband.

Later as Rachel drove home to the Malone Road and the annexe, with all its comfort and security, she realised that not once had Matthew asked her how she came by the information. Where exactly she had met the man and where they were when she learned all this. This convinced Rachel Matthew knew all about her 'career'. But of course he would; he wasn't a member of the C.I.D. for nothing. She also realised with a jolt, that the first day of Colin's trial was over, and she knew nothing about it.

She was relieved when she entered the annexe that all was quiet, her mother and Lynn were fast asleep. That meant she had no explaining to do to either of them tonight. And when she entered the room she shared with Lynn she did not put on the bedside light, but undressed in the dark and crept into bed. Instead of lying awake as she usually did, she was soon fast asleep, all her worries and emotions cast aside for a time.

CHAPTER 16

Thomas reckoned there would be considerable interest in Colin's trial and expected quite a crowd to be present in the High Court. To this end he had organised those of the family circle who were attending, to set off early in order to get a car park, and also a good seat in the public gallery. He had agreed to do the driving and had arranged to collect Charles at his home in Dunmurry and then drive to Malone Road to pick up his stepfather, Tom. Uncle John Finlay had told Thomas he would much prefer to travel alone to his son's trial, even though Thomas had pointed out he was on Thomas's route to the court-house. Thomas respected his uncle's feelings, obviously the man wished to be alone with his thoughts, as no doubt many men who were awaiting such a harrowing experience would want. He would need time to think, to pray, and more importantly just to be alone. Uncle John had however, arranged to meet his nephews and brother-in-law outside the courthouse at 9 a.m. and then they would all enter together.

For Thomas, the whole sequence of events, since that day about eighteen months ago, when Colin had confided in him his concerns about Leo and the bank accounts; then Leo's murder, which had all culminated in Colin's arrest and trial, had become so surreal, so unreal. So that now as he drove to meet his brother, he seemed to be so numb and a sense of unreality surrounded him. After Colin had first told him about Leo and the money being put into Leo's private accounts, he and Colin had become close, meeting for coffee on a regular basis in the Trocadero Coffee Shop across from Thomas's furniture shop. Then, after Leo's murder, Charles and he had visited him at home, but somehow their regular coffee mornings waned off, and now as he drove into Beechpark Avenue to collect Charles, Thomas pondered a little on how that had happened. Had he been remiss in not maintaining contact or had Colin, grieving for his brother, decided to defer actual dates and meetings with friends? Whatever the reason, Thomas hoped he did not appear callous and uncaring in Colin's eyes, when, now that he had been arrested for murder, the opposite was the truth.

Charles greeted him sombrely as he climbed into the car. 'Here we are, brother, going to face what I would call a gruelling prospect to-day. I dread what the prosecution is going to come up with and how they'll talk to the jury. They are so very clever, you know.'

'I know that, Charles, but don't forget he has a good defence barrister.' Thomas nodded hopefully. 'We can only hope that the truth will prevail.' Then for one awful, treacherous moment Thomas wondered, 'What was the truth? And that old saying his father had. 'You never know anyone. You never know what anyone is truly capable of.' Those words, in his father's case, had turned out to be so true. His own son-in-law had been responsible for his murder. Then dismayed at such traitorous thoughts towards his cousin, he again reassured Charles, in a vague way that everything would be alright. They were quiet then until they reached the Gate Lodge at Malone Park, where they would collect Tom Greenlees, their step-father.

Tom was quite vocal on the last leg of their journey and was adamant the prosecution had a total lack of real evidence and he felt the case might be thrown out by the judge. He observed they had no forensic evidence whatsoever. It all seemed circumstantial.

Thomas was thankful, when they drove into the car park across the street from the High Court, to see a few remaining spaces. Even so, it was almost filled to capacity, which confirmed for him the high level of interest here this morning and how sensational it all was. But hadn't the victim been very young? And of course an enthusiastic evangelist with his whole life planned out to help others. And here, this morning, his brother was about to be accused of his murder. What a story the newspapers had to tell and what a story if, by some long shot, Colin Finlay were to be found guilty. Thomas had no doubt that people had a macabre interest in other people's tragedies, and no doubt that explained why this car park was so full.

As he entered the courtroom Thomas was suddenly transported back to that awful time five years ago when, in this same room and in the dock where Colin would shortly be brought to, his brother-in-law, Patrick Mullan, had stood accused of horrific offences which had culminated in Thomas's father's murder. He froze in the aisle leading towards the seats and then he felt Charles' hand on his shoulder. Their eyes met and Charles said very simply 'I know, old chap, I know. It is not easy ... memories.'

Thomas reached up to Charles' hand and clasped his own round it. As Charles continued, 'The truth will prevail here, Thomas, just as it did then. That man was guilty and got a just sentence. This man will be proved innocent, I'm sure of it.'

Then Charles began to follow Tom and John towards the few remaining seats, indicating that Thomas should follow, and just as they were deciding where best to hear everything clearly, everything seemed to happen at once. The jury were filing into their seats, suddenly there was Colin in the dock, and the judge had already seated himself and was surveying the whole courtroom in a disinterested fashion, over his glasses.

Charles had quickly realised the effect the courtroom had on his brother – in truth, he had been watching for it. He had known it would be traumatic for them both, he had lain awake most of the night, dreading entering this building again, with the memory of all the horror of the evidence unfolding against Patrick Mullan, and his part in their father's death. But unlike Thomas, he had steeled himself to enter the place and push those memories into the recesses of his mind, whereas he doubted if Thomas would have even thought about it. He would have been so concerned about Colin and concentrating on what he might be coming through, that he had not thought of anything else. Such was the sensitivity of Thomas. He thought back to that time in Kenya when he had been so wrongly accused of fraud. At least he had never been brought to trial for it. Charles had made sure of that, he had got him out of the country using a passport that had been doctored by him. Thomas, then had shown considerable courage and resilience by keeping cool and composed during his travels from Kenya to Northern Ireland and indeed during his dramatic escape out through the window of his home, when the police traced him there. Later, Charles had soon let his brother know when, in a small courtroom in Nairobi, Thomas was exonerated. So preoccupied was Charles with all his memories, that he almost missed the prosecution's opening address. Suddenly he was tense and alert as counsel began to describe, in a most dramatic fashion, Leo's murder and the discovery of his body. The effect of the man's words gave Charles an indescribable feeling of faintness and apprehension. The lawyer was speaking as if he was about to pass sentence on Colin Finlay, their cousin and Uncle John's son.

John Finlay's eyes never left his son's face as he, too, listened to the booming words of the counsel for the prosecution. By watching his son he was trying to instil some strength, some hope into that figure standing in the dock. Colin was a mere shadow of his former self, he had never been heavy, but now he had lost so much weight, he seemed shrunken and diminished, his eyes large and unfocused in his gaunt face. His hands gripping the front of the dock were skeletal and ghostly white. As John too, listened to the voice of prosecuting counsel describe the scene of his young son's murder, he was filled with foreboding and a real sense of dread. Without Dorrie by his side he felt so very alone even though he had other family right here in the form of his lovely caring nephews and brother-in-law. And wasn't Matthew Hampton out there trying to help, hadn't he promised to do his best for Colin? And Matthew Hampton was clever, no doubt about that. Now as he sat listening to the officious voice of the prosecution barrister, John was glad that Colin's wife, indeed none of their wives were present here to-day, it would be so traumatic for them.

Because a kitchen knife had been used to kill Leo, and the 'Shankill Butchers' a gang of Loyalists, were known to use knives to cut their victims' throats, the C.I.D. had considered the possibility that this man had been a victim of their violence. But this theory was soon discounted, the Shankill Butchers did not believe in a single stab wound to the heart. Certainly not, they believed in kidnapping perfectly innocent people, and then exposing them to prolonged, optimal torture, then invariably a taxi drive to the place of execution and the person's throat cut almost through to their spine. And almost, without exception, their victims were Catholics. Matthew Hampton, during his investigations into the atrocities carried out by the Shankill Butchers, firmly believed they had stooped to a whole new level of depravity and barbarism, unlike anything witnessed before in Northern Ireland. Matthew would give anything to be given a break in bringing to justice the perpetrators of such barbarism.

No, certainly Leo had not been tortured. He had suffered a one only, single stab wound; he was not only an upright Protestant but an Evangelist and he had been killed in his place of work, not driven anywhere to a place of execution.

Matthew, having access to the file for the murder investigation, had never thought it had been sectarian. He felt the answer to the crime lay somewhere in Leo's Church – a Church which Leo had dominated so efficiently, and that was the line of enquiry Matthew intended to follow. But if he were to help Colin, he knew he would have to work into the small hours because he had so much on his plate at the moment. It was he who had been charged with finding and arresting the feared Shankill Butchers. It was estimated that, to date, they were responsible for around twenty Catholic civilian deaths. That in itself was a mammoth task, never mind investigating several of the unsolved shootings of innocent Protestant civilians. No doubt it would be proven that the I.R.A. were responsible for those, but bringing someone to justice for any of them was extremely difficult. One of the enquiries of particular interest to him was the shooting dead of four Protestant civilians in a bar on the outskirts of Belfast. It had happened eighteen months ago, but so far no arrests had been made. But what raised Matthew's level of interest in this particular case was the fact that the gun used in the attack was of the same calibre as that used in the murder of his father five years ago. After his brother-in-law's conviction for his part in it all, Matthew had gone with another colleague to interview him in prison because Matthew did not trust himself to go alone. He knew he was capable of doing the man harm. During the interrogation when Patrick Mullan had been very anxious to help all he could, no doubt in an effort to salve his conscience, he had willingly given him the names of two I.R.A. volunteers whom he had met in Crossmaglen and given information to regarding registration numbers of police cars, their addresses and any other information he obtained. These volunteers duly passed this damning information on to their superiors in the I.R.A. Matthew began to try to track them down, but before they could be apprehended they had gone to ground, probably after Patrick Mullan's trial, and it was generally thought they had sought refuge in the south of Ireland. Was it likely they had come back up here? It could well be so – Matthew knew through his undercover work that if the I.R.A. wanted a job done and a particular volunteer to do it, it did not matter if they ran the risk of being apprehended, their superiors must be obeyed.

Now of course, Uncle John's request simply added to his onerous workload, but still he was happy enough to put out a few discreet enquiries. The information Rachel had given him a few days ago might just be worth pursuing, so he intended to visit a couple of elders during the course of the coming week if he could establish where they lived. Better still, he would ask Julie to accompany him to Church next Sunday evening, that way he could get the new leader of the Church to introduce him to some of the elders. They might be able to open up another line of enquiry which would prove useful to Colin's case.

Even though he was preoccupied with all these assignments, invariably his mind drifted back to Jason, and how little Matthew saw of him and how little interest he had in his son's hobbies, or had much time to participate with him in any of them. Now, it seemed, one of his son's dreams had always been to own a dog, something else Matthew was ashamed to admit to himself he never knew anything about. Indeed Jason had, about six months ago, gone and spent over three hundred pounds on a pedigree collie dog. He now spent most of his free time grooming it and forever teaching it obedience and a long line of fascinating tricks to perform. And more and more frequently Matthew had noticed that Lynn, Rachel's daughter was a frequent visitor to their home – she obviously shared his enthusiasm for animals. Matthew was delighted they had at least one another for company, even though young Emily worshipped the young dog, too. But her attention soon waned when Jason was trying to train the collie and Matthew had noticed that, when that happened Jason got exasperated with his young sister, and invariably Lynn and him were left alone to carry on. At least he and Julie would attend the dog show in a couple of weeks' time, which Jason had entered the collie in. He fully intended to show his support that day, and hopefully attend the dance that same evening.

CHAPTER 17

As Matthew made his way to his favourite coffee shop the following Tuesday morning to meet Mr. King, one of the elders in the Church, he was deep in thought and wondering how best to broach the subject of someone in Leo's Church actually having given almost all of his farm to Leo, by way of donation to his Church. It was the only lead he had in all this, this unknown farmer, who according to Rachel, had actually lost his wife and family as a result of his generosity. According to Rachel, the man in question had then found out the money had not gone into the Church funds, but seemed to have disappeared. But at least Mr. King had agreed to meet him, and that had raised Matthew's hopes – perhaps the man had remembered something important. Maybe, with a little persuasion, he might even overlook the confidentiality of the church and tell him who the man was.

On the Sunday evening after the service, Matthew had approached the preacher and introduced himself simply as Leo's cousin, and went on to say he would like to meet a couple of the elders who had been such good friends of Leo's. The minister, a Mr. Freeman, promptly took him over to where three or four well-dressed men were engaged in stacking up extra chairs which had obviously been used to accommodate the congregation. Mr. Freeman introduced Matthew to them and they greeted him very warmly. When he went on to say he was just following up some gossip he had heard about someone in the Church having a grudge against Leo and if that were so, it might improve Colin's chances of getting an acquittal – the men looked blankly at him and insisted they knew of no such gossip. Thanking them in his most polite manner, Matthew bade them good evening and then with what seemed to be an afterthought, he handed them a card each with his private address and phone number, and suggested if they did think of anything, no matter how small, to give him a ring. Later that very same evening Mr. King rang him, and told him he would like to talk to him and they duly arranged to meet here at Thompson's coffee shop on Botanic Avenue at ten-thirty this morning.

As he entered the cafe he recognised Mr. King as one of the four men he had spoken to on Sunday evening. He was seated at a small table in a far corner of the room, but he beckoned to Matthew immediately he spotted him. Approaching him, Matthew noticed he was dressed in a similar fashion to Sunday evening. His suit was obviously a very expensive one, well cut and pale grey in colour. His grey hair, smoothed back from his forehead, gave him a very distinguished look indeed. But the man, as Matthew pulled out the chair facing him, had a look of impatience and almost of anxiety about him.

'Mr. King, good to meet you again,' and Matthew stretched out his hand. 'Shall we order coffee while we talk?'

Mr. King shook his hand warmly 'I'll have Espresso, please'

The waitress was already hovering nearby and Matthew promptly gave her the order for two Espressos.

'I'm glad to meet you again, Mr. King. Obviously you have thought of something which might be important to Colin. The prosecution are still calling witnesses, I believe, to testify to Leo's utmost honesty in everything including money. I can see where it is all going, the prosecution are trying to convince the jury that it was Colin who was the dishonest one here, he wanted the money back out of the church funds because he was in debt. So let's hope the defence has ultimate proof that that was not always the case.' He paused and thanked the waitress as she placed the coffees on the table beside them. 'So no matter how unimportant you might think it, it may well prove to be otherwise.'

'Mr. Hampton, there is reportedly someone in our Church who parted with a considerable sum of money to Leo, money which just seemed to disappear. Certainly it never made its way to the church coffers, I believe.' Mr. King was stirring his coffee vigorously as he spoke 'Have you heard the same report, Mr. Hampton?'

In reply to Mr. King's question Matthew simply answered 'Yes.'

Then Mr. King went on, 'Where did you come by this rumour? I would have thought few people know about it. I don't believe many people in the Church know of it, never mind outsiders.'

'That's the thing, Mr. King, we think no one knows anything about a subject, and it is quite surprising how many people actually do know.'

'Did someone in the Church actually tell you this, Mr. Hampton? Or was it someone in the street?'

'I'm sorry I can't divulge my source of information. I'm not in a position to say. After all, it may not even be true.'

'That's very true, it may be rubbish. Did you hear it was actually the proceeds from the man's farm?' Mr. King was looking at Matthew very earnestly as he spoke.

'I really don't have much detail, but the main thing I think, is that the man concerned became very annoyed with himself indeed, for having been so gullible and parting with all his assets so readily. Justifiable feelings, I should think. Leo must have been a very convincing preacher indeed. I must admit I've never heard him. I never attended his church.'

'Indeed he was an excellent preacher of the gospel' Mr. King was enthusiastic 'He was remarkable; remarkable and gifted at saving souls. But,' and his voice tailed off 'Do you think he had a weakness for money?'

'The prosecution believe otherwise, so it is up to me to dig a little deeper and find out who the man is, if there is indeed such a person, and talk to him. Maybe he can help us.' Matthew beckoned to the waitress as he spoke, paid her and then rose from the table.

'Thank you so very much Mr. King. I feel more optimistic now, that you can corroborate what I've heard. There must be something in it. I feel compelled to follow it through and I hope we meet again soon.'

'Thank you for the coffee, Mr. Hampton.' and the elder made his way out of the cafe. He was so tall he had to stoop to avoid hitting his head on the lintel on his way out. As Matthew watched him leave he kept an image of him in his head. Something was telling him to describe this man's appearance and manner to Rachel, and he would do so as soon as possible. He preferred not to visit her premises, so a phone call from his home telephone would have to suffice- he felt he needed to be very discreet, not only for his sake, but for Rachel's and her age old profession.

Rachel was intrigued by Matthew's phone call. He rang her around six-thirty from home, he said he thought it might be more confidential than his office. Since then Rachel had thought of little else, only Matthew's description of the elder, Mr. King. She had little doubt he was indeed her Mr. Anderson, Mr. Smith or Mr. Jones, but really he was Mr. King, the chief elder in the new Elim church her cousin Leo had been so enthusiastic about. John too, had contacted her earlier to tell her how the day's events in the trial had gone, as he had promised he would. The prosecution, it seemed, were still calling witnesses to give evidence and it looked likely that it would be a long drawn-out affair. This evening she was glad she only had two clients. She was tired; the shop downstairs had been so busy all day. Now she felt she just wanted home, home to see her daughter and her mother and enjoy the rest of the evening with them.

The two men who had booked were quite undemanding and just wanted 'straight sex' and when they were leaving they had been more than generous as Rachel had thought they would be. After all, one was a bank manager, the other the proprietor of a local engineering firm. After they had gone, she was so tired she was tempted to leave the changing of the beds until the next day, something she never did. However, being such a creature of habit she began to strip them and put on fresh linen. The first thing she always did after her clients had gone was to go to each room and extinguish the candles, and to-night when in Room 3, there seemed to be a strong smell of something burning. She left the room with the intention of checking the other rooms and as she came out on to the landing, she was terror stricken by what she saw. The hall and bottom stairs were alight with flames. Her first thought was to get water to quench the flames, and she raced to the bathroom and filled a basin and returned to the burning stairway. Even as she doused the fire it seemed to make the smoke more dense and black. She began to feel faint and short of breath, and then suddenly remembering her fire drill she got down on the floor and began to crawl back into the nearest bedroom and close the door. She lay, her breath coming in short gasps and she felt herself becoming weaker. Then from somewhere in the back of her mind, she remembered the panic button and struggled to make her way over to it. She managed to press it feebly before blackness descended over her.

'Sir, I have just had an alert call from a local shop.' Constable Ferguson had been concentrating on preparing his reports of his day's work when he heard the faint buzz of the alarm. He was alert instantly and noted it was a shop in Waring Street. 'It only buzzed once, Sir, quite a short, feeble buzz and that was all. But there has been no further alarm since. What would you like me to do, Sir?'

'Do, Constable. Do?' the voice boomed at him. 'Follow it up, man. The place might be being attacked by the I.R.A. Get the emergency team round there and alert the fire service and ambulance at once, do you hear, Ferguson?' The sergeant glared contemptuously at the constable as he spoke.

Afterwards Constable Ferguson thanked God he had reported that one, single, feeble buzz when he had, and had alerted the emergency services, as his superior had instructed him. The small shop in Waring Street was well alight when they arrived, but the fire and ambulance services were both already there and someone was bringing a lifeless figure out through one of the upstairs windows. The constable watched dumbstruck as the ambulance crew went into action, covering the figure with blankets and delivering oxygen before placing the victim on a stretcher and into the ambulance, then sirens blaring, heading for the nearest hospital.

The local news at eleven o'clock that evening was awash with the night's activities by the I.R.A. They had petrol bombed several commercial premises in the city. However, there had only been one casualty, a forty-five year old woman who was in hospital suffering from severe smoke inhalation. She had still been on her premises, a ladies' lingerie shop in Waring Street, whereas all the other premises had been locked and vacated by the proprietors. The general public felt the I.R.A. were becoming more and more indiscriminate and their tactics even more base. Now they were bombing small private shops, not just the bigger superstores, but why on earth target a small lingerie shop? They had really stooped low this time, but then again there was no accounting for their actions, they were so unpredictable.

It was Lucie who took it on herself to let everyone know what had happened, as Maggie and Lynn had gone immediately to the hospital to sit with Rachel. So it was she who arrived at Matthew's door to tell him Rachel was very seriously ill in hospital. She decided to call personally with her brother rather than making a phone call to tell bad news. She told him immediately he opened the door to her that Rachel was in hospital, after having a petrol bomb thrown into her premises. She did not know how she was, she said, but was informing all the family, although Uncle John had already heard it on the news and knew it had to be Rachel. He had rung Lucie and asked what information Lynn had been given about her mother. Lucie had promised to find out and let him know.

'He seems very anxious that you should know immediately, so I told him I was coming straight here to tell you, Matthew.'

'Lucie, please come in,' and for the first time since his father's death Matthew hugged his sister, and as they entered his sitting room and took a seat, he seemed genuinely glad of her company. Had his resentment of her forgiveness for

Patrick Mullan and their father's death been forgotten about now they had a new trauma in their family at the hands of the I.R.A.?

'What a lovely fire, Matthew.' Lucie remarked as she entered the room. It was well past eleven o'clock at night and his desk was littered with papers.

'Lucie, when I'm working I'm ashamed to say I don't put on any news and I have been working here since six o'clock. I really appreciate you coming to tell me this at this time of night. Have we any idea how Rachel is?'

'I understand from the hospital she is very poorly indeed. She is suffering from severe smoke inhalation and is on continuous oxygen. Lynn and Maggie are going to stay with her. I know it is terrible, but I thought Uncle John's reaction was a bit extreme, but I suppose with Leo's murder, Colin's case and Aunt Dorrie's illness I think he is a little unhinged at present. He also muttered something about you absolutely confirming it was the I.R.A. and no other reason. What could he possibly have meant?'

Matthew reassured Lucie he did not know what line John's mind was going along, but he promised he would ring him and talk to him, calm him down. While he was speaking to his sister his mind was running ahead, why did the I.R.A. decide to bomb her shop? Was it just coincidence that she had suffered so soon after learning information from the elders in the Church and then his own meeting with Mr. King? But it must simply be coincidence because other places had been targeted that same evening. So he could reassure John when he rang him.

'Lucie, the C.I.D. will soon sort out who is responsible, all we have to do is think of Rachel and support Maggie and Lynn as best we can.'

'I agree totally, as long as I am assured you will ring John and calm him down. He is just coming through so much. I don't know how he is coping. In the meantime I'll hope and pray for Rachel's recovery.' Lucie rose reluctantly from her seat by the fire; she had been so inordinately pleased at Matthew's warm reception of her and she treasured how lovingly he had hugged her. She hated leaving him and this new sibling feeling of affection which surrounded them both, but it was really late and she had school books and uniforms to sort out for the children in the morning.

CHAPTER 18

The morning Lynn learned that her mother was going to be all right would be, she knew, engraved in her mind for all time. It was six days since that horrific evening when the fire had engulfed her mum's shop and almost destroyed it. Six long days and nights Lynn and her grandmother had spent in this hospital ward, only leaving to go for something to eat. Sometimes Aunt Lucie had sat too, just watching Rachel and talking to her, while she struggled for breath.

Then in the early hours of this Monday morning the 2nd February her breathing had eased, she was much calmer and began to speak to Lynn without any monumental struggle for breath. The evening before, Lynn had persuaded her grandmother to go home with Lucie. She seemed so exhausted that Lynn feared for her health, she was after all seventy-two. Lynn knew if Maggie became ill she would find it difficult to cope. Maggie had so readily agreed to go home and rest that Lynn knew she was on the point of making herself ill, and she was content to sit alone with her mother, just holding her and talking to her.

When the doctors came on their round and stood at the foot of Rachel's bed, they were amazed and pleased at how well she was. When they confirmed with Lynn that her mother had turned the corner and was going to be all right, adding a note of caution that she could be left with a 'weak chest', Lynn decided to ring Uncle John to tell him the good news. She had known he was very worried about Rachel. It seemed to Lynn as if he was almost as concerned about her as he was about Colin. Poor Colin, who was still standing in the docks of the High Court, listening to all sorts of accusations and suggestions about his way of life and habits. Now she understood the prosecution were doing their summing up, if that were so, then it was up to the defence to refute all those claims and so-called evidence, and get Colin acquitted as soon as possible.

John was anxious to visit Rachel in hospital. She was going to need help when she came out of hospital, if she intended to get her house in Waring Street up and running again. He had walked past it a couple of times in the past week, trying to assess the damage which had been done. But it was impossible to tell unless you were able to go inside because that, possibly, was where the true destruction lay. He hoped she had good insurance on the place. If so, and if she intended to renovate it anew, he knew just the man who could help her. He too, would do all he could to help her, because he still believed that she had been targeted that night in her house because of her questions to the elders of the church. And to think he had encouraged her to put herself at risk, for Colin's sake. Now he felt he had been totally selfish, but he had been so desperate to try to get some help for Colin. He had spoken to Matthew about it, who had assured him that it did seem to be the work of the IRA, but they were still investigating it all.

'John, it's good to see you.' Rachel was more composed than he was. 'Here I am, a bit damaged I believe, but they do reckon I'll be fine,' and she smiled at him, a radiant smile. 'The doctors think I may be able to go home in a couple of days. I hope so, I've so much to sort out – my shop, for example, and the insurance on it. And even more importantly I want Lynn to get to that dinner dance with Jason in a couple of weeks time. If I'm lying up here she won't entertain going anywhere.'

'Rachel, you really must think of yourself instead of thinking of other people. Could I remind you, you have been very ill.'

Rachel changed the subject, reluctant to accept any praise, only thinking of the worry she had caused her family. 'How is Colin? Trust me to add to everyone's woes by being petrol bombed and in the middle of such other trauma.' She paused as John looked taken aback. 'Yes, John, the police were here this afternoon to interview me and they reckon that it may have been the work of the I.R.A. and possibly a petrol bomb was used, but they are still working on it.' She paused, breathless for a moment. 'That's enough about me, how is the trial going? You must tell me.'

John nodded sombrely, his mind suddenly filled with thoughts of his son, now that he was somewhat reassured that it was the IRA who had been responsible for the fire in Rachel's premises, and nothing to do with any elders of Leo's Church or questions Rachel might have asked them.

'The prosecution have finished their summing up and the counsel for the defence started to give some convincing evidence of Leo's bank accounts, and Colin looked much happier as he listened, I have to say.'

'Well, thank God for that. And what about my precious shop? What's it like? Nobody wants to tell me. I am well insured you know. So I would prefer if someone would tell me the truth.'

And John could not deny her the truth and besides he knew she was anxious to know so that she could move forward. She would pick up the pieces and start again. 'I haven't seen inside the house Rachel, but according to the fire brigade the damage was mostly confined to downstairs and the hall and landing. The rooms above, though somewhat smoke damaged, did not suffer from the fire.'

'You're the first person I've been able to get anything out of, even Lynn and Mum, who were here earlier, simply patted my hand when I asked them the same question, and they told me not to worry.'

'I daresay they thought it was for the best, because no doubt you will be lying in bed there, concocting all sort of plans about the place. But I had to say, I could only ever be honest with you, you must know that, after how understanding you were to me the first evening I rang you and then came to see you. I tell you what, Rachel, if you let me have the name of your insurance company I could maybe get something moving for you. I also know a wonderful builder – my nephew – as it so happens, who always quotes a fair price and gets the work done in the time he usually says he will. If you agree, I'll get in touch with him after I speak to the insurance company. In the meantime, just concentrate on getting better and being discharged, so that Lynn and Jason may go to the ball leaving Rachel at home safe and well. Or perhaps Rachel might decide to go too.'

'Definitely not, John, I believe the dance is quite salubrious and not somewhere you may go without a partner, but I'll be delighted to see Lynn and Jason head off. Besides, they will have some company because Matthew and Julie intend going.'

'Well, my dear, please do take care, and I'll let you know how I get on with your insurance people, and I'll be back very, very soon,' and John leaned over and hugged her. In response Rachel squeezed his hand and whispered, 'Good night, Uncle John.'

The following morning John went to the High Court with a much lighter heart. Rachel would soon be discharged from hospital and the elders in the Church had had nothing to do with the petrol bomb placed in the hall in Waring Street. And to add to his brighter mood, Colin's defence team were very optimistic about their evidence and were delivering it all very efficiently. Rhoda too, was helping his frame of mind by taking a couple of hours off work to stay with Dorrie. Dorrie had seemed distressed yesterday evening, and was talking wildly about Leo, and although she had eventually settled down with her sedation, it had seemed to take much longer for the pills to have any effect. John was broken-hearted as he watched her and listened. She had idolised Leo, no doubt about that. He loved his wife, had always done, but he too was suffering the loss of his youngest son, but his grief had had to be shelved, while he tried to cope with Dorrie and her loss. Thankfully she was still in the dark about Colin and his trial. He had tried to make sure of that. He had arrived home each day at lunch-time and came straight home when court adjourned for the day to make sure Dorrie was all right. Was it the fact that he had gone out again last night to see Rachel which had distressed her? But he had been so sure she was settled for the night. It was only when he returned from the hospital he realised that was not the case. Rhoda told him she had only slept for the first half hour after he'd gone and then wakened up in a hysterical state. This morning though, she seemed fine and in much better form than she had been for some time.

The defence team had just finished exhibiting the numerous bank statements with substantial sums of money in them, all of which were in Leo Finlay's name and not under the Church fund account, as one would expect, Mr. Lawrence, counsel for the defence, was stressing emphatically to the judge and jury Then he went on to say they must consider where all this money had come from and why had it not been put to its proper use? Were some members of the congregation getting impatient that there was no sign of any church being built? Had someone in the congregation found out something about the money, probably money he had donated and he or she felt cheated? Mr. Lawrence went on to say his client, Colin Finlay, although in debt, as prosecution had pointed out, had managed to obtain an excellent job as had his wife, in an effort to pay off their debt. So it would seem certain his client had accepted that the money he had put into the church fund was lost to him. Also it was significant, Mr. Lawrence said, the firm who had appointed him as Head Manager of their freight company were holding the position open for him, so convinced were they of his innocence.

Just as the defence counsel finished exhibiting the bank accounts and was about to call a witness to vouch for Colin Finlay's character, there was a terrible commotion at the back of the court and every head was turned to try to establish the cause of the furore. A frantic looking, dishevelled woman was being restrained by two guards as she tried to make her way towards the dock where Colin had stood silent and stoical for the past three weeks. The woman was sobbing pitifully and shouting out through her cries, 'Leo, Colin, please come home. Colin, come down from there. I'm your mother. You must come home with me and help me look for Leo.'

And John, as he watched the security guards lead Dorrie away, and he left his seat to go to be with his wife, he felt as if both their lives were now finished, and this scene, in this courtroom, was the climax of it all. He would bring her back home, and from now on, he would be with her day and night, he would never leave her. He must depend on Tom Greenlees and his nephews, Charles and Thomas, to keep him truthfully informed about the trial.

As he left the courtroom, his arms around his wife's frail pathetic figure, he wondered how she had known to come here. Then he remembered that Rhoda had been keen to be brought up to date about everything last evening, and he had been more than happy to tell her about the good defence that had been launched for Colin. Although Dorrie had appeared downstairs at one point when he was talking, he hadn't thought very much about it. So this time he could not blame anyone for telling Dorrie about the trial; between Rhoda and himself they had managed to unhinge Dorrie themselves. Now he owed it to Dorrie to nurse her back to health and give her his undivided attention.

CHAPTER 19

Tom Greenlees and his nephews were deeply saddened, but also horrified at the scene they had witnessed in the courtroom, when Dorrie Finlay had tried to make her way to her son. They were saddened at the bare grief of the woman struggling with the security staff, and saddened too, to see the bowed figure of John leave them and go to his wife. But then weren't the sequence of events which had led to this close-knit family circle being here in this heart- rending situation, horrendous and unreal for everyone? How on earth had it all happened? How had it all come to this? And what was to be the outcome? Tom wondered about it all as he tried to bring his mind back to what the defence counsel were saying. He was surprised the judge had not adjourned the trial for the day after such a distressing disruption, but when John and Dorrie had left he had simply called 'Order, Order' and then instructed defence to continue with their evidence.

Tom personally wished the whole thing had been adjourned. He just wanted to get home, home to Ellen, to her calmness and her love. She would be so shocked to hear about Dorrie and what had happened here to-day. Ellen had always had a high regard for her sister-in-law. They had always been close and Ellen often talked about how supportive Dorrie had been to Rob during his childhood, and then later, so kind to Ellen after Rob's murder. To-day, as Tom watched his brother-in-law help his wife out of the room, his medical knowledge told him John was going to need a lot of help to cope and Dorrie too, if she were going to recover. Ellen would certainly be more than eager to help, and if Colin were soon to be acquitted, it might mean that Dorrie would be on the road to recovery. He trusted that it was not already too late for Dorrie.

Had she already gone into that dark abyss of mental instability where she was beyond help. How long, Tom wondered, had this been going on? In his experience as a general practitioner, mental health problems in patients were usually of a slow deteriorating nature, so he believed John and Rhoda must have been trying to cope on their own for some time, without seeking help. It was a desperate situation for them both. Rhoda was only a young woman who should not have to deal with such stress and trauma.

There was a short lull in the proceedings and the defence were just calling another witness. Tom made the most of the break.

'Charles, Thomas' he whispered, 'I'm going. I'm going home to Ellen. I think I can help John and Dorrie more by being with them, than being here. We aren't, in any way, going to influence the outcome of this trial by being present.' he looked at his nephews. 'What do you say, do you want to come? If not, I can make my own way home.'

'We'll come too, Tom. You're right, what use are we here to-day? It should have been adjourned, at least for Colin's sake, if for no other reason. Seeing his mother in such a distressed state I was afraid he might faint, but when he saw his father with her, he pulled himself together. So, let's go,' and Thomas began to make his way out of the courtroom. Once outside he turned to Charles and Tom. 'Perhaps someone ought to go to John and see what's happening and how they are.'

Tom nodded. 'If you leave me off at home, and then both of you call with him, I'll talk to Ellen and then we'll be round later, say, in an hour's time. Would that do?'

Charles had remained silent and thoughtful throughout. 'How long do you think Dorrie has been like this, Tom? I feel terrible that I didn't know. I mean, I knew she must be terribly grief-stricken, but to-day I saw a woman who has had a complete mental breakdown. I'm sorry to say that, but that's what I saw.' Charles became very distressed as he voiced his feelings, and tears were close to the surface.

Tom nodded soberly. 'Steady, Charles, this is very distressing for us all, but just think what it has been like for John and Rhoda and Dorrie, too of course. Dorrie, I'm sure is quite lucid at times, and is as distressed about her unstable behaviour as we are.' Tom tried to draw on his own experiences with patients in the past, as to how it might be for John. 'We do need to offer some help here, spend some time with them, if we are going to assist them in any way. We should be able to work something out between us. We'll try to have shifts between Dorrie's house and the courts, because I'm sure Colin needs to see a familiar face or two there, to give some support.'

'I really have to get back to work, Tom. I have already taken three weeks leave of absence and you know what the Civil Service is like, people have a habit of taking long term sick leave, but that's something I certainly don't believe in. But Sheila will be more than willing to help during the day, when the children are at school.' Charles was anxious about his employment.

'I think I would prefer to attend court as much as possible, simply because I was the one whom Colin came to with his problems initially. But as it is essential Jean is in the shop and office during my absence, I'm afraid we can't count on her.' Thomas felt compelled to be the one to attend court, even though he had come to dread it, dreaded hearing the booming voices of the barristers, dreaded watching the jury as they diligently took notes . But above all, he dreaded seeing Colin standing there, so silent and so accepting, as to what fate the jury would hand out to him. But in spite of all this he knew he could not bear to stay away.

The three men were relieved to get into Thomas's car and drive away from that building and head for Tom and Ellen's Gate Lodge, which as it came into view, had the effect of lifting their spirits somewhat. As they drove towards it, and Tom spied the pillars of Lucie and Paul's house, he remembered about Rachel and her imminent discharge from hospital.

'Let's hope Rachel is well when she comes home, but at least she has Lucie and Paul, both with medical knowledge and only a doorstep between them. She has her mother and Lynn, who, I'm sure are overjoyed to have her home so soon. I daresay Maggie will be distressed about Dorrie, but she must not get involved there, she has been through enough with Rachel. It will take her some time to get over the trauma, never mind the actual physical weariness of sitting in a hospital for days on end.'

As Thomas slowed his car to a halt outside his mother's house, he turned to Tom. 'I'll keep you informed about the trial, so please don't worry on that score and I'm sure Jean will be able to call and see Aunt Dorrie at some stage and see how she is.'

'Thanks, Thomas. Hopefully I'll see you soon and you too, Charles. Take care.' With that, Tom left them and went into the house to seek Ellen out.

'Oh, Tom, how could I not have known that Dorrie was so unwell; but I didn't, and I feel so awful about it. Anytime I called at the house she was usually resting upstairs, or sitting in their drawing room, but she seemed all right, if a bit dull and lethargic.'

'It is obvious Ellen, that John did not want any of us to know the extent of her illness. He probably believed it was very temporary and she would soon recover. So he was doing a cover-up job, and instead of getting better, Dorrie seems to have become much worse.' Tom hastened to reassure Ellen 'Look, Ellen, we had no way of knowing, love, how she really was, if John or Rhoda did not want us to know the extent of Dorrie's illness. But I have a feeling that he might be glad of some help, because I think it is no longer safe to leave Dorrie alone.' Tom rose from his seat beside the fire, where he had sat beside Ellen for the last hour. 'I'll make tea, then we'll drive over to the Shore Road and offer some help to John and Dorrie. After hopefully sorting something out with them, we'll call with Rachel on the way back and see how she is.'

John was deeply touched when he opened the door and saw Tom and Ellen. He could scarcely remember leaving the courtroom with Dorrie in his arms. He could vaguely remember the security man ordering a taxi for them, and him telling the man he usually came by bus, but how Dorrie had made it there, he had no idea. But he recalled vividly, and indeed knew he would never forget the security men's kindness to both Dorrie and himself as they stood waiting, and how that same kindness seemed to have almost a magical, calming effect on her.

When they returned home they found a very distressed Rhoda, who told them she had rung the police when her mother had disappeared, but had now just learned that she was safe. After John explained where her mother had been, Rhoda insisted she must go to bed with an electric blanket and she would give her hot fluids as she was concerned that Dorrie might be suffering from hypothermia. Rhoda said she would ring work, explain what had happened, and take the rest of the day off. She would of course stay with her to make sure she didn't wander off again. But in future the back door must be kept locked and the key well hidden. Rhoda insisted that her father too needed to rest, he had suffered such shock and trauma. They were suffering from acute embarrassment too, thought Rhoda, they had gone to such lengths to keep Dorrie's state of mind to themselves and now today it had been exposed. There would be no point in trying to cover it up any longer – to-day's scene in the courtroom had told so many people so much.

John was thinking how close his daughter and he had become in all this, and how, after her initial withdrawal from her mother and her illness, she had been a real source of strength to him. He did not know how he would do without her, when the front doorbell rang.

'Tom, Ellen,' and suddenly everything was too much for him. He simply put out his hands and clung desperately to his sister-in-law's arms and his eyes filled with tears. 'Oh, God, it's good to see you. You've no idea.' And Ellen, in spite of her brother-in-law's pitiful appearance, was glad to have such a warm welcome. She had dreaded the thought that John might continue to shut himself and Dorrie away from them all, as he must have been doing. To be so graciously received by him was a good sign.

During the next hour, as the three of them sat at the kitchen table, John had explained it was the safest place, it was quite soundproof, and Dorrie would not be able to hear them, as he told Ellen and Tom truthfully, how it had been since Leo's murder. He spared no detail as he talked to them, and Ellen marvelled at how this man had coped, with no one to confide in and share his burden.

'I know we are going to appreciate any help we can get, Ellen. We were basically all right because Dorrie never showed any signs of wanting to go anywhere, but that has now changed and she may well do it again. The simple truth is, she cannot be left, that is, until she is better. We are all right to-day, Rhoda is here, but if I need help to go out shopping for anything, I simply could not go. I intend to ring the doctor, of course, first thing in the morning.'

'If you're sure you don't need us today, I'll come around about ten-thirty in the morning and stay while you shop. Dorrie means a lot to us all, she and I shared some interesting and some very traumatic times together. So anything I can do now, I'll do it.'

'That would be good, in the morning, Ellen and thank you.' John said simply.

'On the way home we're going to call and see how Rachel is. And Maggie and Lynn too, of course. They have had a rotten time as well.'

'I know,' John's face was unreadable, 'but it's good to know Rachel is going to be all right'. He hesitated and then went on, 'Please give her my regards, Tom. Would you do that?' And there seemed to be an urgent tone, some sense of desperation in his voice as he spoke.

'Sure, we will, John.' Tom answered as he helped Ellen with her coat, 'and Ellen will be round in the morning, you can depend on it.' Tom longed to say more, to reassure John that Dorrie would be all right, but he found he was incapable of saying the words. Because the truth was, no one could say with certainty that Dorrie would become well again. She had suffered so much shock and grief no one could even hazard a guess as to what she had been through. Or John either. Tom firmly believed the man had had no chance to grieve for his son. He was so consumed by Dorrie's health and now Colin's welfare. And then to try to imagine how Colin must feel in that prison cell was just too awful to contemplate. Even to try to imagine what John was coming through was beyond him.

When Ellen and he called at Maggie's annexe to see how Rachel was, the next hour provided a little light relief – relief which Tom and Ellen were glad of, after being in John's home. Rachel seemed very well in spite of her ordeal, and when he passed on John's regards to her, she seemed very pleased in spite of all the trauma of court that morning. Rachel explained that Matthew had called earlier to explain about her shop, and it was he who had told her about Aunt Dorrie. Then when Tom went on to tell her that some of the family were going to rally round to give support, she seemed immeasurably relieved to hear that.

'I'm so glad, Uncle Tom. John really needs it and he will need to get out and about a bit, just for his own sanity. We do enjoy his company you know, in spite of the burden he is carrying. He is welcome to call here and see us anytime. Perhaps you would mention that to him. I would be able to make some tea, I do believe.' And Rachel smiled in a most attractive way as she spoke.

CHAPTER 20

Matthew slid the file back towards him once more; he had been to see Rachel earlier and had tried to encourage her to remember where the fire seemed to be coming from in her premises. But she said she could only recall the smoke and flames at the foot of the stairs, and nowhere else, and naturally she was very vague about it all. Now back in his office, he perused the file even more thoroughly than he had the first time. In the file lay the report of the I.R.A.'s bombing attacks on the shops in Belfast on the night Rachel was targeted. Something was very wrong here, Matthew instinctively felt it. Every shop or premises which had been targeted that evening had had incendiary devices placed there, except for Rachel's. She had had a crude petrol bomb placed it seemed, at the foot of the stairs. If the I.R.A. were responsible, why use a petrol bomb for her and incendiaries for all the others? And why the foot of the stairs and not through the letter box as they usually did? He needed time and inspiration to think about all this, both of which seemed in short supply with him at the moment. Perhaps if he spoke to some of the elders again, they might remember something about someone, no matter how trivial. But he felt he must go back to Rachel and tell her his suspicions, that perhaps the I.R.A. were not involved with the burning of her shop. He had promised to keep her informed, and he was obliged to do just that.

'Matthew, do you think someone might know you've been talking to Mr. King? Did they follow you, do you think? But then, that's stupid, to petrol bomb me, they would have had to know that Mr. King visited me, told me something, alerted me to something, and I passed it on to you. They may have followed Mr. King to my place and then followed him the morning he met you. They may think he suspects something. He too, would need to watch himself.' Rachel was very breathless as she spoke, but on hearing what Matthew thought about the crude device left in her hallway, she was beginning to think it was someone who knew she had talked. 'And Matthew, whoever it is may have even found out we are related.'

'I think, Rachel, I must discuss this with the C.I.D. team who are dealing with it directly. A possible road to go down is to have the media relay quite openly that your premises on that particular evening, was the only one to have a petrol bomb placed in it. We could see if the I.R.A. respond in any way to that, they take great pride in having the name of being organised, and this time it looks a bit irregular of them. But in the meantime, I want you to be very careful. Someone may think you know a lot more than you actually do. So please be very watchful.' Since Matthew's arrival at Rachel's home some three quarters of an hour ago, the whole talk had been about her shop. He had yet to ask her how she was, or how Maggie and Lynn were, he was concentrating so much on this case. A case which initially he had been resolved to just make a few enquiries about, but now was turning into something he had an obsession about.

'Rachel, I'm sorry. I haven't even asked about your health in all this. How are you really?'

'As you can see, Matthew, I'm well and the doctors are really pleased how quickly I have recovered. I know I'm very lucky indeed and I do intend to take care, believe me. It was a very frightening experience when I saw the smoke and flames at the foot of the stairs, and knew I had no means of escape. I just thank God I had panic buttons upstairs or I would not be here today talking to you.'

'That was good thinking on your part, especially in these times, to have those linked through to the police station. And now tell me, how is Aunt Maggie and Lynn?

'They seem to be delighted to get me home and are spoiling me rotten.'

'I'm glad to hear it, enjoy it while it's going, and I must say Jason seems to enjoy Lynn and her interest in his collie. He never stops talking about going to this dog show in the Belvedere Hotel in February and I am determined to be there, no matter what.' Matthew rose from his seat and made his way to the door. 'Keep an ear to the news, Rachel. You never know the C.I.D., may agree to the media broadcasting the unusual tactics of the I.R.A. the night you were petrol bombed. But be assured, I'll keep in touch.'

Rachel followed her cousin to the door. 'Matthew, you need to be careful too, you know. You keep warning me, and you are at risk all the time.'

Matthew nodded soberly on his way to the car. 'I know, Rachel, believe me, I know all about the risks.'

And then Rachel realised her mistake in speaking of his risk, he had just recalled his father's murder, when he had been the original target.

Six days later the I.R.A. announced they were not responsible for the petrol bomb attack in Waring Street, but were responsible for the incendiary devices in the other premises. And John Finlay, listening to the Northern Ireland ten o'clock news that same evening with Dorrie safely upstairs in bed, blamed himself for having put Rachel at risk in her premises. He was the one who had suggested to her and encouraged her, when they were discussing Colin's trial, to try to find out something from the elders in Leo's church which might prove to be of use to the defence team. What on earth had he been thinking of? Besides, the suggestions he had made and the information Rachel had obtained, had not got them very far with proving Colin's innocence. As far as he could gather Matthew had very little to go on, just some vague rumours of others having put substantial sums of money into the church fund. But Matthew had yet to come up with any concrete evidence, and Colin's defence team were doing their summing up tomorrow. Then the jury would be asked to consider their verdict, and on the face of it all, Colin seemed to be the only suspect they had. And because of John and Matthew's frantic search for evidence, Rachel had almost lost her life. If someone in the congregation were responsible, it seemed to John, proving anything would be very difficult. After all, the reason someone had placed a petrol bomb on Rachel's premises might simply be because they discovered she was a call girl and entertained men there. Some religious fanatic or other could well do it as a warning, no doubt about it. That is what many people would assume if they knew that Rachel kept those premises mainly to fulfil some men's needs. And even though John had tried to encourage Rachel to think seriously about giving up her line of work, perversely the last thing he wished to happen now was that she would be exposed as a call girl. He knew it was her main means of income.

The jury had retired to consider their verdict and the judge in his summing-up had stressed they could only find the prisoner guilty beyond reasonable doubt. He went on in his statement to say that Colin Finlay had had a motive, though some might consider it tenuous. He also had had easy access to the church hall where his brother was, it was on his route home, but then so it was for a lot of other people. Then there was of course, the question of the missing knife from Colin Finlay's pack, and which the defendant denied all knowledge of its whereabouts. Had that knife been the murder weapon? It seemed a similar one had been used in the attack, but the same knives were, after all, very common, very run of the mill.

'I don't know about all that, that the judge was talking about. I don't like it.' John had accompanied Thomas to court this morning and Ellen and Tom were also present. Charles' wife, Sheila, had offered to stay with Dorrie while they attended the hearing. They had left the courtroom and walked across the street to the small cafe to wait for the jury to deliberate on all the evidence which had been presented to them. After John had spoken, his companions were silent for a time – eventually Tom spoke. 'John, it is really only circumstantial evidence they are dealing with here. Surely no one could convict anyone on the strength of it, any number of people could have been passing the church hall and also possess packs of kitchen knives the same as Colin's. It's all so circumstantial.' Tom shook his head.

'Not everyone felt they had been robbed of their livelihood, as Colin had,' John replied. 'That to me is the most damning aspect of it all. I know there are rumours of others who have been fooled by Leo, but then we never got any real evidence.' John was beginning to feel more and more nauseated and weak as the day went on. He had been unable to eat any breakfast and still felt totally unable to look at food. He had such an ominous, anxious feeling in the pit of his stomach. Thomas, his nephew, he noticed, was simply a bundle of nerves. He had downed three large coffees within the last half-hour, and in between drinking them, had paced about the floor of the coffee shop, regardless of the impatient looks of other customers. Meantime, Ellen, the only woman who had attended the hearing at any time, sat quietly beside her husband, just being there, supportive to them all, in her own quiet way. But then Ellen had endured so much in the past, her first husband's murder and then her son-in-law's subsequent trial. Perhaps here to-day she might be more able to be accepting of the verdict than many others might be.

'Uncle John, I'll go back over, see if there's any sign of the jury coming back.' Thomas looked impatiently at his watch as he spoke. 'They've been out now for over three hours, it's almost five o'clock. I'll go and see what is happening,' and hurriedly Thomas left them and made his way back to the court.

He returned shortly after, and to John he seemed only to have been gone a few minutes.

'It seems the jury are coming back, we'd best get over there,' and Thomas turned immediately to lead the way back across the street. The others had no option but to leave their coffees sitting on the table and follow Thomas back into the courtroom.

As they entered the courtroom the jury had resumed their places, and the judge was asking if they had reached a verdict. The foreman of the jury rose from his seat and addressed the judge.

'We are sorry that we have been unable to reach a unanimous verdict. We need some more time.'

The judge then instructed them all to disperse for the night and to go to the hotel which had been designated for them. They must speak to no one about the case in the meantime. He would see them back here at nine-thirty in the morning.

'So the agony for my son is prolonged and relentless.' John muttered bitterly as they stood on the pavement outside the High Court.

No one had any heart to answer that. Any attempt at appeasing John at this moment in time would be so insincere, because he had stated a bald fact. The agony for Colin was prolonged. So quietly Thomas took his uncle's arm and led him to the car, and equally quietly said his good byes to Ellen and Tom who were adamant they would return in the morning. Rhoda intended taking another day off work and that meant her father and her aunt and uncle would be free to attend in the morning.

'John, it is good to see you. Please come on in,' and Rachel opened the door wide in greeting for John. 'Lynn's just gone over to see Jason, and Mum is getting ready for bed, so I'm on my own until Mum comes back into the lounge for supper. We know about the trial, Ellen came over earlier to tell us.'

'I had to see you Rachel. I've been desperate to talk to you.' John made his way into the living room of the annexe. Such a familiar room it was to him and all the familiarity of it seemed to bring him some comfort. He noticed some of the furniture was Tom's, no doubt he had left it here, as there would have been no room for it at Ellen's place. Some things never changed, he thought as he sat down on the old, familiar, blue sofa, and that could only be good.

'I asked Rhoda if she minded if I went out for a little while. I didn't say where I wanted to go and she didn't ask. I really was desperate to talk to someone for a little while, and I don't want to burden Rhoda any more than she already is.' He knew he was sounding quite pathetic and full of self-pity tonight, but he did not seem to be able to control it. As Rachel listened to him and watched him, her heart went out to him, but she seemed powerless to help.

'There, John, you are all right. Everything will work out in the end. Matthew is working away trying to find evidence to throw some light on it all. All is not lost, John, so let's try and keep one another's spirits up.' Rachel led her Uncle over to the blue sofa, aware how aged he seemed to be this evening. Just then her mother reappeared from the bedroom.

'John is very upset, Mum, as you can see.'

'And no wonder, John. I don't know how you have remained in control; it would have put a lesser man under. No doubt about that. Look, Rachel you stay where you are and I'll make supper for a change, for the three of us,' and Maggie disappeared into the kitchen. When she re-entered the lounge with the tea tray, she could see John was so much calmer and she could see clearly Rachel had, somehow or other, seemed to calm him down.

John did not stay very long with Maggie and Rachel, he was conscious that Rhoda had had a long day too looking after her mother and fretting and worrying about Colin at the same time. So after he drank the tea Maggie had made, he said a few thanks and good-byes before actually leaving. But the visit had brought a measure of contentment and comfort to him. The annexe and Rachel and Maggie's company and their cups of tea seemed to bring some normality back into his life, even if it was just for a brief time. On returning home to Dorrie and Rhoda he felt so much more refreshed, and more able to face anything which might come his way.

Rhoda had settled her mother, and when John went upstairs to his wife he was thankful she was sleeping peacefully, at least she was being spared the agonies and trauma the family were going through. Rhoda and he talked long into the night; he told her he was more upbeat about the trial because Matthew was determined to pursue a particular line of enquiry he had in mind. He believed he would uncover something about some of the Church members sooner or later.

'In the middle of all this, Rhoda, I'm getting concerned about your work. I know you have taken to-morrow off as well. Are your employers all right about this?'

'Dad, they do know, you know, about all we have been through and are still going through. It would be extremely callous of them if they objected. Don't you agree? Besides, I have insisted on taking it as holidays, which they think is very honourable of me.' Rhoda was anxious to reassure her father 'In fact Dad, I believe I have risen in their estimation, you know. So that is something a bit more cheery, in the midst of all this. My boss, or bosses I should say, have actually noticed me and are aware of the level of work I do, something they did not seem to have any idea about before all this. I was just there at a desk, plain, dowdy Rhoda Finlay. Now they seem to have realised I am a person, and actually one with brains.'

'Oh, Rhoda, that is good news and at a time when we have had very little. And Rhoda,' John added earnestly, 'you have never been plain to me. You have always been my beautiful, compassionate daughter.'

In response Rhoda hugged her father. 'How lovely of you to say so.' she wanted to add that Leo had always thought her plain and dowdy, he probably had thought her stupid too, but she had no wish to distress her father any more than he already was. 'Let's make a move to retire to bed; we just don't know what we might have to face to-morrow. By the way, dad, did you know Margaret intends to be present to-morrow? I believe her mother is coming down from Dungannon to look after the boys. She says she must be there for Colin. She has appreciated how often you have called on your way home from court, to bring her up to date on the days she was unable to attend. She is so confident of Colin's acquittal you know, she can't even consider the possibility of any other outcome. She is almost blasé about it all, whereas I'm the opposite, afraid to be too optimistic and then suffering further heartbreak.'

'That's exactly how I feel, love, but surely we won't be expected to deal with any more heartbreak; we have suffered enough.'

'Look, let's get to bed, dad. And do you know I believe Mum is lucky she knows so very little about it all. She is protected, at the moment at least.'

As father and daughter made their way to bed, they were both in agreement that Dorrie was safe and sound as she was.

CHAPTER 21

John tried his best to put the prospects of what the family might have to face the following day out of his mind, but he found he was reliving all the scenes of the trial, time and time again, and hearing the voice of the prosecuting counsel, accusing and compelling. Then the voice of the barrister for the defence counsel, defensive and equally assertive and always the image of Colin, standing there so very pale and so distanced from everyone and everything, awaiting his fate. His fate would soon be decided by the twelve good men and true of the jury. What if their verdict was one of 'guilty'? What then? What of Margaret and the boys? He had been so engrossed in Dorrie and her ill health that he had not thought too much about his daughter-in-law and grandchildren. And now he felt totally ashamed about that. But it was Dorrie who had filled his mind and thoughts these last few weeks. But now, in that darkened bedroom lying beside his heavily sedated wife, he felt he had neglected Margaret and his two grandsons. Sure, on the days she had not attended court, he had called with her, as he had promised to do, and tell her all about the day's proceedings. He always felt she was coping well and perhaps Rhoda was right, she was blasé about it, possibly because she could not contemplate any verdict other than 'not guilty'. Of course Margaret also had her parents, who supported her, and were devoted to her, her being an only child, and John knew them to be a compassionate, thoughtful couple. Somehow, with these more reassuring thoughts of his daughter-in-law, and his wife's contented deep breathing beside him, he was eventually lulled into a comparatively sound sleep.

As John entered the hall leading to the courtroom the next morning to wait for Tom and his nephews, he noticed Margaret, just ahead of him, about to enter the imposing courtroom. He was very relieved to see her father was with her and the vision of his daughter-in-law, leaning on her father's arm, eased his conscience considerably.

He was joined, shortly after Margaret and her father had entered the courtroom, by Tom, Charles and Thomas, and after a somewhat sombre good morning to one another, they too entered the courtroom and took their seats.

As usual John knew when the judge and jury were arriving because the clamour suddenly died down, and the atmosphere in that courtroom became one of the most reverent silence and expectation. Then the judge directed the jury to go to the rooms allocated and consider their verdict. At that the foreman of the jury rose from his seat, he too, seemed fraught with anxiety, 'My lord, what majority verdict would be acceptable to the court?'

The judge looked at the man for a moment, considering, 'I will accept a majority verdict of ten to two.'

The foreman of the jury looked somewhat less anxious as he led the way out of the courtroom, to once more consider the evidence before them.

Without consulting one another, John and his nephews rose from their seats, and with one thought in mind, left the courtroom and headed for the coffee shop, which had become their haven in the last thirty six-hours. They were so glad too, to see Margaret and her father come into the cafe shortly after and make their way over to them. It was so vital and also so comforting to be together as a family, in order to give support to one another. There was nothing any of them could do, only give hope to one another, while they waited.

And this time they did not have very long to wait. They had all just finished their coffee, with Thomas as usual on his second one, when Mr Leyton, their defence counsel, entered the coffee shop. 'The jury are preparing to return to the courtroom,' he addressed Margaret briefly and then turned and left the shop. John was left in no doubt that Colin's defence counsel was as anxious as they were about the verdict. They followed docilely out of the shop, across the road and back into that large imposing room, which they had occupied for endless hours and days over a period of weeks. But which was surely now coming to an end. And that alone, would be such a relief.

The judge now looked across at the jury, who had just filed back in, and taken their usual seats. The judge then addressed the foreman, 'Have you reached your verdict?'

The foreman of the jury rose from his seat, 'Yes my lord.'

'And how do you find the prisoner?'

'Guilty, my lord – by a verdict of ten to two men – my lord, guilty.'

There were loud, audible gasps and sobbing from the crowd in the court, but John was only conscious of his son. He stood swaying in the dock, shaking his head and seeming to mouth the words, 'No, no' then suddenly as the noise abated, he looked directly at the judge.

'I did not kill my only brother, my lord' as he held onto the dock in front of him.

The judge glanced at him for a long moment, and then in soft muted tones, instructed the prison officers to take the prisoner below, adding he would sentence him at a later date.

Suddenly there was a terrible disruption, and John realised Margaret was on her feet being supported by her elderly father. Her face was so deadly pale as to be almost death-like, but she addressed the judge in such a serene, implacable manner that every eye was turned towards her, and every ear was listening to her words. She spoke firmly and emphatically, 'My husband is totally innocent of this horrendous crime. The law is so wrong today – to find my Colin guilty on such feeble evidence, is a crime in itself. I and my family will stop at nothing to prove his innocence.' Margaret sat down, seemingly exhausted, and every eye was on her as they waited to hear if the judge would respond in any way. But he simply gathered up his files and proceeded out of the room, without looking either left or right.

John could only watch, stricken with grief, as Margaret spoke, and as the prison officers proceeded to take his only son down the steps, and back to his hell hole of a cell and utter desolation. And then John thanked God that his Dorrie, at least, was now beyond all this, all this suffering and misjudgement which he had witnessed today. Yes. He had finally accepted that Dorrie was beyond understanding as to what was happening. And he was beginning to believe that that was how it was going to be for his wife and their future.

Now as everyone filed out of court and he met up with Margaret and her father, he was amazed at her attitude and defiance. 'We'll show them John, I intend to fight this verdict and fight it until my Colin is released. I think it has all to do with that wretched missing knife, you know.' To John, Margaret now seemed almost hysterical, where before she had seemed so calm. 'If I could just remember what I did with it, where I last had it.'

John embraced her then, 'Matthew is working on all this, he is following a few leads, Margaret, so let us remain hopeful.'

Suddenly, in spite of all her force and courage, Margaret swayed, her eyes filled with tears and unable to speak, she just nodded dumbly at John as her father led her away towards his car.

Matthew was becoming increasingly frustrated with his lack of information regarding the cases he was currently working on. He had suspects regarding the Shankill Butchers, but he had precious little evidence to pursue very much. He had his team on the alert for any information regarding the IRA volunteers involved in the recent murder of Protestant civilians but so far they had reported nothing untoward. Now, added to all this, there was Colin, and he felt the pressure and the responsibility of proving his cousin's innocence. He had felt so close to uncovering something among the congregation of Leo's church, but here too, he had drawn a blank. He had gone back to three of the elders and although they were very pleasant, they said they could not help him. There was only Mr. King, who Matthew felt knew something about someone, but did not feel he could ever divulge it. Perhaps the man felt he himself was in danger. Matthew did not know, but knew he needed a break to help him solve some of these horrendous crimes. Perhaps he needed a diversion, and then he would be able to look at it all with renewed insight and a different attitude. He needed to get away from it all, the evidence, the lack of evidence, and his thoughts going round in circles until late in the evenings. And perhaps, the very thing he needed was the dog show, and the dinner dance to be held on Sat 15th of February. It wasn't usually his cup of tea, he preferred a good night at home by the fire with Julie by his side and a good strong glass of whiskey in his hand when he did get an hour or two off. But on this occasion he was determined to support his son and his so very faithful collie. To demonstrate his absolute support he had insisted on giving Jason money to buy himself a nice dinner suit, shirt and bow tie and of course a good quality collar for the dog. Matthew had insisted Jason must be well-dressed; he was convinced Lynn would look beautiful. Jason was overwhelmed at his father's generosity and admitted that up until now, when his father had pointed out the importance of his appearance, he had only thought of the dog's appearance, how he would look and behave.

Now the show was a mere two weeks away, and Jason and Lynn felt they had achieved so much with Monty; his coat was thick and glossy, his brown eyes shone, and as for his tricks, well, they both felt their collie friend had a fine repartee of tricks to show on the day of the show. Lynn also secretly felt and hoped that Jason would be delighted and very impressed when he saw her at the dinner dance. She hoped he would see a great transformation when she was dressed in her new pink gown and high heels. It would be such a change as to how he usually saw her, in jeans and her boots or wellingtons, and a sweat shirt which would have seen better days.

As for Matthew, he was becoming more and more frustrated by the day, there seemed to be no new clues regarding the Shankill Butchers, nothing at all on the four

Protestants shot dead. And all the time Colin was now languishing in the prison on the Crumlin Road, having been sentenced to fifteen years in prison for the murder of his brother. He must be feeling pretty desperate because he had taken to sending Matthew messages to help him prove his innocence. John brought these messages to Matthew in the evenings after visiting his son in prison, and the two men talked at length about finding the real killer of Leo. Although both men knew they were probably clutching at straws, they remained diligently optimistic and hopeful.

Meanwhile, Rachel was determined to keep herself occupied as much as possible. She had sorted out all the insurance on her house and had arranged to meet John's nephew, Gavin Finlay, this morning at 10, Waring Street. She wanted to get back to business just as soon as she possibly could, and hopefully her business would soon get back to normal, and would flourish again. Secretly, too, she fervently hoped that the elders of the Church, who had frequented her premises in the past, might return to her. Then perhaps she might be able to improve her methods of trying to get valuable information out of them. That was the only way she had any hope of helping John, and Colin too of course. She believed Mr. King knew something about somebody in the church, and perhaps next time he might confide even more in her. But then again, he might decide not to return at all. Probably the prospect of another fire would put a lot of men off, but still, Rachel knew from experience that when some men wanted a woman, they were usually quite prepared to take risks. So whoever she ended up employing to do the renovations to the house, she intended to pay them well to complete exactly in the time they specified. And while they worked she would continue to hope for Colin's release. She hadn't seen John since the evening before his son was found guilty, but Margaret had told her he called often with her to give her support and did see his grandsons from time to time. But most of his time, according to Margaret, was taken up with looking after Dorrie, having insisted Rhoda return to work, so he was left to deal with his wife and try to ensure she did not wander off. He depended on Ellen and Thomas, and Charles' wife to give him a bit of relief, which they were very willing to give, and then in the evening, he would not ask Rhoda to help after working all day. Margaret had stressed to everyone that they needed to understand if her father-in-law was no longer in the habit of visiting his relations it was because it was simply not possible for him.

'I can arrange for my men to start work here first thing on Monday, Rachel; that is, if you find my price acceptable to you. This is Wednesday, and I'll start now to measure up and do some calculations. I'll give you a ring by Friday at the latest with my estimate and if you are in agreement we can get started straight away.' Gavin Finlay smiled openly at Rachel as he spoke and she was immediately impressed by this man. He exuded confidence and professionalism and she felt that whatever his quote might be – if it wasn't too exorbitant – she would agree to his team starting work for her. As she watched him begin to measure up the place and check walls and floors some emotion flickered in Rachel's breast, an emotion she had thought long dead. It was some deep physical attraction that had been awakened in her, a feeling she had not had since the early days of her marriage to Roger Compton in Canada. Was it his rugged good looks, his vivid blue eyes, or his thick mop of greying hair which gave him such an attractive appearance? As she watched him check windows, roofs and doors she wondered if he was married, had he a family? She had never heard anything about him from any of the family, but then she had not been in Northern Ireland long enough to meet any of the extended family. As she watched Gavin pack his tools away, she made an effort to concentrate on the work which had to be done. Whatever this man's marital status might be he was outside her reach, no respectable man would want anything to do with her. That much she did know. Still she must remember her manners, and that he was one of the family.

'Gavin, you have my phone number and if you're not too expensive I would like you to start work on Monday. But now, would you like some coffee, or tea, perhaps, before you leave?' Rachel asked.

'Actually I would love some, Rachel. But let's go across the road to the coffee shop. The smell of smoke in here still lingers. Perhaps you don't notice because you have been here regularly. While we're having it you can fill me in about some of the changes you might want, now that you have the opportunity to make them.'

Rachel eagerly agreed. 'I'll just fetch my coat, check everything is OK before I lock up. Since the fire here I seem to have become obsessive about checking everything and have the compulsion to double-check everything before I leave.'

'I could well believe that. I'll go check upstairs for you while you see to down here before we go.'

Rachel appreciated that this nephew of John's did not make light of her compulsion to double- check everything. He seemed to understand how important it was for her to feel safe and secure.

Later that evening Rachel went over her first meeting with Gavin Finlay and how well they had seemed to hit it off together in that coffee shop. He seemed, she knew, to be quite impressed with her, but then of course he could have no idea what she used the bedrooms above her shop for. If he did, he would, she was sure, have a very different impression of her.

CHAPTER 22

'I don't like it, Bernard, it doesn't sound like our usual line of work that they want us to do.' Seamus considered his older brother across the room, 'besides, we are taking some risk going up north, when we know we are both on this 'wanted list' and have been for some time. I tell you, I don't like it.' and Seamus looked more and more miserable as he spoke.

'Seamus, we may not like any of it, the going back up north or the job they have lined up for us. The commander probably thinks because we have been off the scene for a time we are less likely to be caught. But I do believe that bloody CID team are watching the border and probably mum and dad's house on a regular basis too. No, I don't like it either, but what choice do we have? None, you know that, and I know that. We are dead men if we say no, indeed, if we even hesitate. So we have to go.'

Seamus was scared, he had been running scared for some time now, but indeed he was more terrified of his comrades, than he was of any CID. And to think he had started all this just by finding out a bit of information and passing it on, and now he lived in fear of his life. Now he just nodded in agreement and Bernard went on impatiently, 'I know, I know, how you feel, man. At least we have tomorrow and then a car will pick us up on Wednesday morning around 6.30, I believe. The thing is, Seamus, do we say to the foreman of the site, we won't be back, or do we just not turn up on Wednesday?'

'We daren't say, we've been instructed to say nothing and that's how it has to be.' Seamus shook his head sadly, 'I'll miss my job on that building site, the money was good, I liked my mates and never once did they ask us any questions as to what brought us down here. Yes they are great blokes, Bernie,

I wish I could stay.' And Seamus sounded stressed and anxious as he spoke.

'It'll be all right, Seamus, it's for the best and remember it's for the cause.' Bernard rose from his seat, and headed towards the kitchen of the apartment in North Dublin his brother and he had lived in for the last five years. They were happy to be there, and had remained there since they had first realised they were being hunted by the CID in Northern Ireland. Apart from that weekend in 1976, when they had fulfilled the mission the commander had demanded, they had not been back up north since.

'Let's have a beer each, Seamus, and raise our glasses to the cause.'

Seamus did not answer, he was anxious enough to have a beer, but he no longer thought much about fighting for the cause or even what it meant. He only knew he no longer wanted any part of it all, he wanted to stay here, here in Dublin where he was happy and could see his sweetheart, his beautiful girl, Josie, most evenings.

After Bernard poured the first two beers, it was so easy to consume another two and another two, and the two brothers finally made their way to bed very much later that evening, not even bothering to undress, but just to lie on their beds, they were so inebriated. But even considering the amount of alcohol they had both consumed the previous evening, the next day saw the two men dressed, ready and alert, when the car picked them up to bring them north the following morning. They knew very little about what their new job entailed, only that it was not information gathering, nor was it a shooting. They were assured by their car driver it was so easy, there was nothing to it. This reassured Bernard and Seamus Caughey a little. They would do their job and then return to their apartment in Dublin. The car driver had even hinted it might just be a matter of placing a few incendiary devices and then giving the appropriate warning to allow people time to escape. Seamus and Bernard were reassured that this time, the job did not involve a lot of energy or thinking, and they would be well away before anything untoward happened. And according to their driver, where it was all going to happen was quite out of the way. No one would suspect that they would be likely to be anywhere near the place or involved in any event which might happen there.

'Oh guess what, mum, Grandma Maggie, guess what?' Lynn burst into the living room in a high state of excitement. Her eyes were shining, her cheeks were flushed a delicate pink and her feet seemed to barely touch the ground as she sprung into the room. 'Monty won the obedience class, out of all those so beautiful, friendly dogs, he won. He also came second in the well-groomed collie appearance.' The words seemed to flow out of Lynn and then she stopped, smiled a little before going on, 'His tricks let him down a bit and Jason and I both know he was deliberately doing it to play to the audience, the wee rascal.' At the end of a very steady flow of words, Lynn sat down looking exhausted, but also very happy with her lot. Rachel, watching her daughter with that light heartedness of youth and its buoyancy, not weighed down with any traumas of life, was happy too, for her. Not that her daughter was callous and uncaring, far from it. There was no doubt the Finlay family's trouble had touched Lynn too, but it was not the all-consuming worry and trial it was for the older members of the family. And Rachel had no doubt that was how it was for Jason too. He too, felt for them all but he could still enjoy himself, be happy with Lynn and his beloved collie, Monty. Today, the dog show, with all its entertainment, had brought its rewards.

'Lynn, I think you should rest before you start to get ready for the dance, go and lie on your bed, I'll bring you up some tea.'

'Mum I couldn't rest, besides it's already five-thirty and Jason is collecting me at 7p.m. sharp and I have to bath and dress. Just think though, tonight we'll see Jason and Monty get their well-earned prize.'

Lynn went to her room and Rachel and Maggie did not see her until 6.50p.m., when she appeared in the lounge, dressed and ready to go with Jason. Maggie was the first to speak when her granddaughter entered the lounge. She had never been shown the dress Lynn had chosen that day in Belfast with her mother, and now Maggie thought Lynn could not have chosen better, it fitted her to perfection and complimented her dark complexion. She simply looked breathtakingly lovely.

'Oh Lynn, you look so gorgeous.' Maggie clasped her hands in delight at the sight of this, her granddaughter on what might be her debut into dinner dances.

Rachel was nodding in agreement, when the front doorbell rang and she went to it and announced the arrival of Jason, who looked so handsome and debonair in the outfit his father had bought him and as Rachel watched Matthew's son's reaction to Lynn' appearance and beauty and how he escorted her to his car, she was very thankful Lynn was her adopted daughter and that Jason and she were not blood related.

'Oh Jason, this looks wonderful, don't you agree?' Lynn was bubbling with enthusiasm now they were actually here, in this beautiful hotel and she was so looking forward to seeing Jason go up to that platform to receive the prizes he and Monty had won earlier. Then they would have dinner and afterwards they would spend the remainder of the evening dancing and enjoying the company of others.

'There's Amanda King, I knew she would be here.' Lynn tugged his arm, 'let's go and speak to her, she is in my year at Queen's, studying literature, same as I am. She has a flat in Belfast I believe. She doesn't live at home since her parents split up, so she told me.' As Lynn continued to guide Jason across the floor to introduce him to the tall, attractive brunette, she was doing her best to tell him exactly who the girl was. 'She is the daughter of one of the elders in what was Leo's church, I know that much.'

'Amanda, I'd like you to meet my cousin Jason.' Lynn smiled at Amanda King as she spoke.

'And I'd like you to meet Tony, my fiancé.' Amanda smiled broadly as she spoke. 'We have just got engaged this very evening. We decided we would do it tonight at this function which is so elaborate and being held in such a beautiful hotel. We did think Tony's dog might have a chance in the obedience class, but yours, Lynn, was miles ahead.'

'Congratulations to you both on becoming engaged. And Monty belongs to Jason, I'm afraid I have no claim on his success.'

'Look, ladies, let's head for the dining room and dinner. We're ahead in the queue and at least that way we'll all have seats together and have plenty of time to talk and gossip before the meal,' and at that Tony began to lead the way towards the dining room and the others meekly followed him.

'What about your mum and dad?' Lynn was looking at the couples already heading towards the dining hall. 'We should wait for them, Jason.'

'Sorry Lynn, I should have said, dad has met up with a former colleague, so the four of them are together.' Jason murmured. 'They've just gone in, so if we follow them we might be lucky enough to get a table near them.' When Jason and Lynn and their new found friends entered the ornate dining hall, with its glistening glassware and snowy white decor, they were pleased to see Jason's father had kept a table beside him, for Jason and his friends.

'Bernard, I think we've overshot the road to this place, the directions said the Strangford Road was on the left off this road. I think that was the second road we just passed.' Seamus was beginning to become anxious about this mission, it was such a dark night, the road to the hotel seemed far longer and more convoluted than he had imagined as navigator. Surely no one would open a hotel in such a rural place. If they had, he couldn't see how it could possibly be prospering.

'Seamus, that didn't seem to me to be a road, surely that was just a lane. I'll drive on. Keep your eyes peeled for the next road on the left.'

Seamus agreed, but all the time aware of the awful and dangerous packages in the back seat of the car, and the need to get them to their destination. 'I think we should turn, Bernard.' They had only travelled another couple of miles, but to Seamus it seemed like twenty, 'I tell you, that was a road back there. We've still to deliver the goods. Then we still have to find the phone booth we were told about and give the alarm.'

'O.K. O.K. brother, I'll turn and let's hope you're right.' and Bernard did a three point turn there and then on that unlit rural road.

'Ah Seamus, I think you were right, it is a road, not just a lane. Not much of a road, mind you, but still a road, just the same. You watch out for the hotel gates and signpost, and I imagine we'll soon be there.' Bernard seemed confident, they might be a bit late but still, they'd get there, do what they had to do, and clear off back to the south in no time at all.

Seamus breathed an audible sigh of relief as he spotted the sign and the gates. It was all really well illuminated and they were soon driving up the wide sweeping driveway.

They were soon working steadily and silently as they hung the bomb carefully on to a window. The bomb was now attached to four petrol cans each containing petrol and sugar designed to stick to whatever it lit. Once Bernard and Seamus had set everything in its proper place they headed towards their car in a much less stressed and anxious frame of mind than they had been on their outward journey. Everything was going as planned; true they had lost a few minutes by missing the road, but Bernard was confident he had made up the time by putting his foot on the accelerator. Now all they had to do was locate the phone booth they had been told about, and give the warning to the hotel that a bomb had been planted, and to say the premises should be vacated immediately. Seamus read out the directions to Bernard from the slip of paper he had kept folded in his diary. And soon they found the cross-roads indicated in his directions. Quickly he climbed out of the car and went into the booth, anxious to ring the phone number he had written in his new diary. This was the diary he was immensely proud of, his girl friend Josie had presented it to him on New Year's Day, and apart from the phone number of the hotel, only her phone number and her inscription to him, with all her love, was written within it.

It was Seamus, however, who discovered that the telephone within the booth was not working. And he knew, in that awful moment, that he and his brother were soon to be responsible for unspeakable carnage. And to Seamus' mind, as he ran back to the car, was the fact they would have to let their commander know and what then? They needed to try to find another phone booth very quickly, but what were the chances of such a thing being so convenient for them in this dark, unusual area.

The bomb would explode about thirty minutes after Bernard had driven out of that tree lined avenue leaving behind him what was soon to be unspeakable endless grief for so many innocent people.

When the meal was over, the tables in the centre of the dining room had to be moved to the outer edges of the room. This meant there was plenty of room in the centre of the floor for the dancing to begin and the band too, given plenty of room to set up their instruments. Matthew and Julie and their family and friends watched from their tables at the outer edge of the room, as the staff so efficiently prepared for the dancing and everyone relaxed, happy just listening to the music. Then suddenly the sound of the band's uplifting music was drowned by the large, unearthly roar of an explosion. Fleetingly, before he moved, and seconds before he saw the flames leap into the room, Matthew knew by the noise alone, that everyone here tonight was in grave danger. His first thoughts were for Julie, Jason and Lynn, and his mind could only focus on how he could possibly get the three of them to safety. He grasped Julie's hand and pulled her down on to the floor, shouting at her to keep crawling until she reached the door, and on no account to stand up. He turned towards the table beside theirs, where Jason and Lynn and their friends had been seated, but a swarm of people in sheer panic, now seemed to separate him from them. Where were they? He got down on the ground and began to follow the direction Julie had taken, all the time calling 'Jason' and looking for him and Lynn. It was as he caught up with Julie, and held tight to her, that he saw his son supporting and half carrying Lynn towards the exit. He shouted at the top of his voice.

'Get down Jason, right down onto the floor.' As he watched in horror, the fireball gradually seemed to fill the room. Whether Jason heard him, or some instinct told him to, Matthew didn't know, but Jason did get down on the floor, and edge towards the exit. Even though there was always the risk of being trampled by the terrified crowd bearing down on them, the floor was the safest place to be.

They could hardly believe it when they got safely outside and, although in a state of shock, they seemed uninjured. Then Jason spoke to his parents, 'I have to go back in there. Lynn's friend Amanda King and her fiancé are still in there, and I might be able to help. We should never have left them there; we should have all stuck together.'

'Oh please Jason, we got separated from them, but they will find their own way.' Lynn was scarcely able to utter the words, 'you can't go back in there.'

'No son, don't do it, it's too dangerous.' Matthew urged him. 'Besides, I hear the fire brigade. Leave it to them. I'm depending too, on my colleague and his wife getting safely out, knowing to keep low and to be safe.'

'No, I must go. I just left them to fend for themselves. You see I only thought of Lynn,' and before anyone could answer, Jason had re-entered the building, which now, to the naked eye seemed one huge fireball. As Matthew made to follow his son, he was stopped by one of the fire brigade officers.

'I'm sorry sir, we can't allow anyone in there.' He sounded sympathetic, but firm. 'Hopefully we'll soon have the fire under control, and we are well-equipped to rescue people.'

Matthew, Julie and Lynn could only stand, arms tightly entwined around one another and wait agonisingly for Jason to return to them. They watched in panic, as fire officers carried people out from that inferno, some screaming in pain and terror, others silent and listless. But of Jason there was no sign, and then suddenly Lynn sprang out of Julie's arms.

'There he is, I'm sure that is him in the hallway and he is helping someone. Oh thank God, thank God.' and Lynn raced away from her family and towards the entrance to the Hotel. Just as she did so there was a tremendous cracking sound from somewhere around the doorway of the building. Lynn could only watch in horror as a huge beam of wood crashed down towards Jason and the girl he was supporting. He was struck by the falling beam and collapsed in the hallway, the girl thrown out of his arms into the hall. Lynn began screaming and shouting for help and even as she did, two fire officers appeared and carried the two casualties out of the building and towards a waiting ambulance.

Afterwards Matthew could not recall how they coped with getting Jason and Amanda King to hospital but the ambulance seemed to be there in no time at all, and the two young people were placed on stretchers and driven at top speed to the Royal Victoria Hospital. Amanda was promptly admitted to the burns unit for treatment for her horrific burns. Jason was taken to the chest injuries unit because he was quickly diagnosed with a collapsed lung, due to fractured ribs caused by the beam's impact on his chest. Twelve people lost their lives that evening including Matthews's colleague and his wife who were unable to escape the inferno. Over thirty people were injured and this included Jason and Amanda King, Amanda had severe burns to her arms, upper torso and face and was to endure months of treatment and skin grafts. Sadly her fiancé lost his life in the explosion.

CHAPTER 23

'Oh Lucie, may I come in?' Matthew was standing anxiously at Lucie's door when she opened it in response to some impatient ringing of her doorbell. This anxious, flushed-looking man bore little resemblance to her brother Matthew, who always seemed so calm and composed.

' Matthew do please, come in.' It was eleven o'clock in the morning, and although Lucie had returned to her work part-time in her G.P practice, she had taken the morning off in order to try and help support Rachel and her mother and daughter after the horror of the previous evening.

'What's wrong Matthew? It's not Jason, Paul tells me all went well in theatre and his breathing is so much improved.'

'That's why I'm here, Lucie, to thank Paul for saving my son's life. He's a genius,' and Matthew reached for Lucie and held her closely to him. 'I love you, Lucie and I am sorry for my coldness towards you over these past years. You have such a big heart for forgiving Patrick Mullan for what he did. And it is only now I appreciate your capacity for forgiveness. Can you forgive me please?'

'Matthew, of course, I am just so glad we are reconciled.' Lucie indicated a seat at the kitchen table. 'Let's have some coffee and scones, just like we used to have.' and she checked the kettle for water and then switched it on, before retrieving scones from her bread bin and starting to butter them.

'I'll be glad to have some sustenance, Lucie, I haven't been to bed.' Matthew hesitated and then decided to go on, although he found it difficult, 'I lost a colleague last night and that too is soul destroying. He was at Julie's and my table, he should have got out but it seems he must have panicked and headed in the wrong direction.' His voice shook and Lucie could see her brother had had to endure unspeakable suffering during the last twelve hours. But before she could say anything he continued in a much brighter tone of voice, 'We already have an excellent lead into who is responsible for this latest, unspeakable atrocity, Lucie. The IRA rang to apologise and to say that there was human suffering and loss of life because they could not get a warning through, as the phone booth in the vicinity was out of order. In the middle of all Jason's trouble I could not go myself to find the phone booth, so I sent my constable and a forensics expert to check for finger-prints. They might not have found any fingerprints but guess what they did find? The diary belonging to whoever tried to make the telephone call.' Matthew sounded quite excited now, 'His name was on the diary, and now I have instructed all the roads leading into the south must be watched for him and his accomplice crossing the border.' Matthew could have told Lucie, there and then, the name of the owner of the diary, but he needed to keep that confidential. Besides, the name would probably mean nothing to her at present, but there would be, he hoped, another time when he could explain it to his sister. But the terrorists had still to be caught and apprehended as soon as possible.

Lucie and Matthew enjoyed their coffee and scones in a more relaxed air than they had done for some considerable time. Then Matthew, looking at his watch, realised he had been there for more than an hour. 'I'll go, Lucie, I said I would join Julie in hospital later this morning to sit with Jason. I take it Lynn is alright? I'm sure she is still suffering from the shock of the whole experience.'

'I have been in to the annexe a couple of times, Matthew,' Lucie answered. 'I gave her some sedation last night, and according to Rachel this morning, she was still asleep.'

'Best thing for her, Lucie, and when Jason is recovered, she is very welcome to come and visit him. In the meantime, assure her he is in good hands and is responding well. I think you can tell Lynn too, that we have a very positive lead as to who was responsible for such a barbaric act, and that I intend pursuing them until they are caught.'

As Matthew drove to the hospital to visit his son, he thought fleetingly of his Uncle John Finlay and his two sons, one dead and the other in prison serving a life sentence. But at this moment in time he had neither the time nor the energy to think of trying to resolve Leo's murder at present. Although he felt guilty about it, and the thought of Colin languishing there depressed him greatly, he was sure Uncle John would understand how it was for him. He must find and arrest these men who had almost ended his son's life and had successfully ended twelve others. He must find those responsible for such barbarity, before they escaped to one day create further grief for many more innocent people.

John Finlay was shocked and horrified when he heard the news on the radio the following morning of the destruction of the hotel, the horrendous loss of life and the numbers injured. As it was Sunday morning Rhoda was at home, and it was she who urged him to go to Rachel's to find out how the young people, and Jason's mother and father were. Rhoda and John had both known of Jason's interest in the collie show, as did most of the family, having been kept informed by Ellen and Tom, who both seemed very proud of their grandson.

Rachel in spite of her distress and the fact she had been up most of the night, hugged John closely when she opened her door to him, before bursting into tears,

'Oh Rachel this is awful, please tell me, how is everyone?'

Through her tears, and as John supported her into the sitting room, she was able to assure him the family was safe and although Jason was terribly injured, Paul was quietly confident he would be all right.

'Matthew and Julie are with him and I'm sure they intend to remain there. I understand Matthew is directing some orders from his son's bedside regarding last night, so John, I don't expect we'll see much of Matthew for some time. According to Lucie this morning, he intends to stick with this investigation until he has caught the killers and Lucie tells me he has a very positive lead on them.' and although Rachel did not elaborate, John knew she was letting him know that, at present, Matthew would not be able to help much with investigating Colin's case. They would have to be patient and wait a little while.

He shook his head sadly, 'I know how it is Rachel, Matthew's son and Lynn come first. Not to mention the relatives of those who lost their lives last night and all the other people seriously injured. I do know, I do understand, Matthew has to give this barbaric act priority.'

'John if you want to talk to me or Maggie at any time, don't hesitate to call with us,' Rachel hastened to assure him. 'That's if you don't mind other visitors who will possibly be coming to see Lynn and enquire about Jason.'

'Rachel, I would like nothing better than to come and sit a little while with Maggie and you but I'll have to leave it for a few days until we see how Jason really is.'

'I think that would be better. In all this I haven't even once enquired how Dorrie is. Is she any better?'

'I'm afraid not, Rachel, we still cannot leave her. In fact on several occasions she has wandered off, and has been brought back by neighbours and on one occasion, by the police. I think Dorrie's condition is well known now, especially since the incident in the high court. She is well known as Colin Finlay's mother.' John's voice was sad as he went on, 'I don't know what I would do without Rhoda and Ellen, they are devoted to her. But she is very difficult to watch twenty-four hours a day, and having to remember to lock the doors.' John sounded resigned now to Dorrie's behaviour, not once mentioning the hope she might improve. Then rising from his chair, 'I will go now, before you have any more callers, and I might give you a ring towards the end of next week.' As he made his way towards the front door he turned to Rachel, 'I almost forgot, what about your renovations? What did you think of my nephew? Were you impressed?'

'Gavin is starting work on Monday morning, John. He rang me two mornings after he had measured, with his estimate.' Rachel kept her voice non-committal. 'He seems very professional and I'm looking forward to the work commencing. I'm anxious to get my business up and running again. Maybe, just maybe, if some of the elders from Leo's church come back, they will decide to tell me something now that Colin has been sentenced.'

'Please, you must be careful, Rachel. I feel guilty enough that you might have put yourself at risk by questioning that Elder. I still wonder about all that, you know.'

'I don't intend to take any risks, John. Besides, we have to wait until the rooms are ready. Gavin hoped to have the bulk of the work done in a couple of weeks, so I would like to be back in business the week after that.'

John drove back home to Dorrie and Rhoda, quite clear headed in spite of the anguish he felt for all those innocent people who had lost loved ones last night, or had been injured in the bombing. He was indeed very saddened by it all, but he was also grateful that Rachel's daughter was safe, as were Matthew and his family. But as always, uppermost in his mind was the question. What was to become of Colin and his wife? What was their future likely to be like? If they could not prove Colin's innocence in the near future it would have a devastating effect on the whole family. He knew his mind was in deep turmoil because of so many things so that at times he feared for his own sanity. And was he being fair to Rhoda, to expect her to give up so much in order to help him? How did she really feel about everything? Certainly she never complained but he did wonder how she continued to go to her employment and come home in the evenings and help him with Dorrie. Sometimes he felt they truly could not go on much longer the way they were, and that something must change.

'Rhoda, I wasn't too long, I hope?' Those were John's first words to his daughter when he entered his home. Always on his mind was the sense of pressure not to be away from Dorrie or whoever was looking after her, for any length of time.

'Dad, you're fine, mum's fine. How is everyone?' and Rhoda took his arm and led him into the sitting room, and whilst she made coffee and brought in scones, she heard the latest news of her cousin Matthew and his family.

'Thank God they are safe, dad. We have had quite enough trauma and anguish, we could not face anymore, I think.' As she spoke John looked at his daughter, she had lost a lot of weight in the past couple of months, and now it struck him how weary she looked.

'Rhoda, do you want to go to church this morning, love? I'll look after things here.'

'No dad, I've no interest in going to church at the moment,' and Rhoda hesitated, looking slightly embarrassed, before continuing, 'Alan, a friend out of work, wishes to call with me for a time this afternoon. Actually I invited him to dinner dad, is that alright?'

'Oh Rhoda, of course, I'm delighted for you, bring anyone you wish to, at any time.' John was happy for Rhoda, 'you need friends, my dear, so I'll be most welcoming if he comes for dinner.' And John thought that it was just what this house needed, was a visit by a young man. They no longer had Leo and Colin's presence.

'Go now and have a rest, Rhoda. I'll take charge of mum and the dinner. You look a bit weary,' and John added, 'put on your very best dress, it's not often we have visitors coming, it will do us good, love, and maybe it'll do your mum some good too.'

Rhoda's friend from work turned out to be the manager of the office she worked in. As the evening wore on, and after dinner was over and Dorrie had been sitting with them quietly, and on her very best behaviour, John realised Alan Howard had quite an interest in Rhoda. Later when Rhoda had taken her mother upstairs to bed, he praised Rhoda enthusiastically for her resilience and fortitude during the ordeals they had had to face.

John was impressed with this young man, mostly because he had treated Dorrie with the utmost respect. Even when she had referred to him as Leo, he had just patted her hand and smiled at her. John also had witnessed the obvious concern and respect he had for Rhoda. He was beginning to think and to hope, that perhaps his daughter would, after all, have some happiness in her life. It was obvious too, that Alan Howard knew exactly how things were in Rhoda's and her parent's lives and it was good to see it was not deterring him from pursuing Rhoda. Somehow now the two young people sitting together and talking easily to one another, he thought longingly of the time he had met and married Dorrie, the wonderful years they had shared together, and he was deeply saddened by their present ordeal and trauma. Not for the first time too, did he consider that, because of Dorrie's state of mind, she was suffering much less than he was.

CHAPTER 24

'Colin, you must try to eat something we bring you. You need to keep your strength up while you are here. It is a hell hole, we know that, but Thomas and I are doing our best to get Matthew to focus again on your case now that Jason is almost ready for discharge.'

Margaret and Thomas mostly travelled together to visit Colin, who since his trial had lost almost twenty-eight pounds in weight and was a mere shadow of his former self.

'I know darling, I do try.' Colin's voice was strong and steady as he spoke, 'I have little appetite in here, that's my trouble, but,' and Colin brightened visibly, 'I still have my faith in God. I am allowed my Bible and I pray every day.' And his smile was bright and cheery as he regarded Thomas and Margaret. 'My time will soon come, my darling. Then we will be back together to lead a simple Christian life. How are my boys? Do they miss me?' and now his voice held a yearning note.

'They certainly do, always asking when you're coming home from your job in England.' Margaret and Colin had decided to lead their two sons to believe Colin had gone away to another job. This was something accepted very readily, as children do. Margaret did not tell her husband now, holed up in this prison, that her parents did their best to fill the empty space Colin had left and indeed they spoilt the boys rotten.

'And Jason, he is well then?' Margaret, from the very first day of Colin's imprisonment had believed in keeping her husband up to date with whatever was happening in the family. He had known about the fire in Rachel's premises and he had known all about the dog show and the barbaric act by the I.R.A that fateful evening. Margaret felt it kept Colin interested in the outside world and besides they never had had any secrets, so why now?

'Jason is up and about love. It's two weeks now since his admission to hospital, but you did know his right lung also collapsed – he was in a critical state – but fortunately Paul realised very quickly what was happening and got his other lung reinflated. I believe Amanda King remains critically ill. Mr. King spends most of his time there, whether she is aware her father is there or not, he doesn't know, but he is distraught. It can't be easy for him sitting watching her – all the time waiting for signs of improvement, day by day.'

Thomas had been sitting quietly listening to the conversation, and now he said, 'The police have announced they are following a definite line of inquiry and are watching all the roads at the border. So that's the good news. Matthew himself seems very optimistic about apprehending them, and it's really unlike him to say anything until it's all done and dusted. But please, Colin not a word.' Thomas felt he had just been indiscreet because here in this prison, even the walls have ears.

'I know Thomas, I know, I say very little to anyone.' Just then two prison officers came to announce visiting hours were over and Thomas and Margaret said their goodbyes one more time. They left that dreary, historic building and headed for Thomas's car.

'Colin is a remarkable man, Margaret. Initially he showed some impatience about proving his innocence. I know he sent Matthew some messages but he has realised Matthew has so much to contend with. So he has become very stoic and resilient. Another man would have cracked under the strain of it all.' Thomas was amazed at his cousin's strength of character in the position he was now in.

'Remember he has his faith, Thomas. I thought I would have to inspire him and keep him cheerful, but actually it is the other way around, he has been my rock through all this.' Margaret was smiling while she spoke. 'Mind you, I'd like to see him with a bit more meat on his bones, but it doesn't seem to bother him in the least.'

'I could see that,' Thomas agreed. 'Tell me about this girl King that you know. I don't know the family at all, but she seems very seriously ill.'

'We know the family through church, Thomas. It seems she and her fiancé were actually with Jason and Lynn that night when the bomb exploded. Her fiancé was killed and I understand she has horrific burns, it was Jason though that rescued her, or she too, would have been dead.'

'Matthew never mentioned any of that to me, Margaret, but I feel that he is totally engrossed in tracking down the perpetrators, so that's probably why.'

'Thomas if you hear anything that might help Matthew with Colin's case, anything at all please tell me, won't you?'

'Of course I will Margaret.' Thomas manoeuvred the car to a standstill outside Margaret's house. 'I won't come in for coffee today Margaret. I need to get back to the shop and relieve Jenny.'

And with a promise to ring the next time he was going to the prison, Thomas began his drive back along the Shore Road, towards Royal Avenue and his furniture shop. He had an evening's work ahead of him, his invoices and bills were beginning to pile up on the desk in his office.

Matthew and Julie collected Jason from hospital fifteen days after the explosion which had devastated so many lives – the lives of fathers, mothers, brothers, sisters, husbands, wives and an ever widening family circle. Before Jason left the hospital he insisted on visiting Amanda King in intensive care in the burns unit. When he entered the unit, a man whom Jason assumed to be her father, was sitting there holding her hand and talking to her. Jason explained who he was, and immediately the man was on his feet, hugging Jason and thanking him for bringing his daughter safely from the awful inferno, which had once been the hotel.

'She is in a drug induced coma and she is a very ill girl but I am so indebted to you.' Amanda's father hugged Jason again and Jason could see tears were very close to the surface.

'Sir, I only did what anyone would have done, but please tell me how she is?'

'They tell me she will need a lot of skin grafting, so she has a hard journey ahead, but the surgeon is a very long way off thinking about those grafts. He says she will need to be much improved before they can do anything about that.'

Jason went over to Amanda, touched her hand briefly, said who he was and said he would see her soon. Then, because he himself was still weak and vulnerable, and afraid of becoming emotional, he said a hasty goodbye to Mr. King and left the room.

Now that Matthew had his son safely home from hospital, he devoted most of his time to tracking down Seamus and Bernard Caughey, who he believed were laying low somewhere in the north. He had already established that their parents still lived just outside Crossmaglen and he had someone watching the house, on the off chance that one or other son would visit their parents. He had also gone back to Leo Finlay's elders in the church, in the hope that they might remember something, no matter how trivial, about someone Leo may have known, but he found they were of no help to him. He would really have liked to have coffee again with Mr. King, because he believed if anyone knew anything, he did. But it would be most insensitive he felt at present, if he were to try and arrange a meeting. The man's daughter was critically ill and he had also lost his future son-in-law, so Matthew decided that, for now, he had to abandon any thoughts of talking to Mr. King. The man had enough to contend with. But he did make a point of going to see John Finlay, to let him know that he had not had much luck in uncovering anything, and explain he could not possibly intrude in Mr. King's ordeal, to ask anything about anyone. He found John in good spirits, eager to tell him that Rhoda now had a boyfriend and together they took care of Dorrie a couple of evenings in the week, to allow him out. He told Matthew he spent some evenings with Maggie and Rachel, then some with Margaret and his grandsons. Matthew reckoned that Uncle John just getting away from Dorrie for a little while, just for a little diversion, was obviously doing him good. He looked better than he had done for some time.

'Two men have been arrested in Crossmaglen, on suspicion of carrying out the bombing of the Belvedere Hotel on the 18th February. They are also, it is understood, being questioned about the shooting of four Protestant civilians in 1976 and one in 1971.' As Mr. King listened to the news he had just switched on, on entering his home, he was overcome with such emotion he felt he would pass out. Could the police really have caught up with them so soon? But then they had confidently said from the beginning, they were following a definite line of enquiry, and no doubt tonight's news was the result of that. He sank down into a chair beside an electric fire, and automatically switched a bar on. He was glad his wife had come so promptly to relieve him tonight and had told him she intended sitting every night with Amanda. As the news droned on he felt close to despair. What use was it to him, if they had caught the terrorists if his daughter were to die, or indeed if she was to be so grotesquely disfigured? He got up suddenly, switched the TV off and reached for the telephone.

Rachel had just said goodnight to her first customer since she had opened up her premises the previous day. He had been quite undemanding and told her he had come from Fivemiletown to the city on business and was staying in a hotel in the centre of Belfast. It was obvious to Rachel he knew nothing about the fire in her premises and this was something she was glad about. She did not intend discussing it with any of her clients unless they specifically asked her about it. She was remaking the bed and was tidying the bedroom, and making sure her candles were all safely out when her phone rang. She recognised the voice immediately, and although she was weary and ready for home she knew the man on the other end of the phone was in some kind of awful despair.

She told him she would be waiting for him, and to come as soon as he could as it was getting rather late.

Matthew was very pleased how today had gone. He had gone to his office earlier than usual to contact his team, and make sure they were keeping keen watch on the border roads and the Caughey home in Crossmaglen. He was only at his desk about twenty minutes when his phone rang. It was one of his men from Crossmaglen.

'We have them both sir, we have got them both. One of them chanced visiting his parents earlier this morning and we nabbed him. It was easy enough getting him to take us to his brother.' The constable paused for breath. 'They are in cells in the police station here, sir.'

Matthew had already risen from his desk as he was listening to his colleague and was checking he had his car keys. Then he remembered the diary that had been found in the phone booth, and before leaving his office, he slipped it into his pocket.

When he arrived after over an hour's drive to Crossmaglen, the constables who were on duty were delighted with their couple of hours' work. The suspect had taken them to a derelict cottage only about half a mile from their parent's home, where they had both been living rough and here they found Bernard Caughey. There the constables also found a pistol the older brother had used as protection, and immediately Matthew issued instructions to have the firearm sent for analysis. Now this evening, as he went over the day's events, he was glad he had supervised the transfer of the two men to Crumlin Road Gaol, Crossmaglen police station was hardly a safe place to keep them. They could be targeted and set free by the I.R.A at any time.

He was preparing for bed when his phone rang, and he was surprised to hear Rachel on the other end of the line. Her voice was soft but unusually compelling, and she just told him it was urgent for him to come to Waring Street. Wearily he went in search of Julie, to let her know he had been called out, and didn't know when he would be back.

He arrived at Rachel's shop on Waring Street some fifteen minutes later and automatically noted that the place was beginning to take shape again, although there were still obvious signs of builders being around. A pile of sand and cement lay in the back alley and a wheelbarrow with bricks had been more or less abandoned for the evening. Obviously there was still work to be done outside by the look of things.

A light burned in the upper part of the house and when Matthew entered through the back door, he could see immediately the good renovation work that had been done. The cheap, teak staircase had been replaced by a much grander one. This one boasted a solid mahogany handrail, with ornate posts supporting it and served to give the whole area a more opulent feel. Matthew made his way upstairs, following the light, and opened the door to the room marked two.

When he entered the room he was immediately on high alert. His hand automatically went to the pistol at his waist. A man, whom he immediately recognised as Mr. King, sat in the chair by the window. On his knee was a towel with a knife on it.

'Don't make a move!' the words came out fast and rough, as Matthew scanned the room looking for signs of disturbance, but most of all looking for Rachel. He spotted her in another seat, over from Mr. King. To his surprise she looked quite calm and composed.

'It's alright Matthew.' As she spoke Rachel went over to him to lead him on into the room. 'Gerald has something to tell you. It is important. He has already told me, but I have stressed he needs to tell you all he knows.' Then Rachel went over to Gerald King where he sat, his head bowed – a picture of abject pity. And Matthew realised this man was no threat to anyone, even though he held a dangerous looking knife. And suddenly, before Gerald King spoke, Matthew knew exactly all there was to know about the knife and its significance. Quietly and gently he drew the chair, which Rachel had just vacated and indicated for him to use, over beside this broken man.

'I see you have a lot to tell me Gerald. I do need to caution you before you say anything. Do you understand?'

In a firm voice Gerald King said he understood very well. After Matthew had cautioned him he began to talk. It was as if he could no longer wait to say any of what he must say. He seemed to Matthew to be so impatient and just anxious to have everything over and done with. Matthew, reluctantly enough, could almost understand after months of saying nothing, it had suddenly become so important to speak and to tell all. As he listened and diligently took notes, the reason for Gerald King's confession soon became clear. The bombing of the Belvedere Hotel, his daughter's condition and the loss of his future son-in-law had made him realise he was being punished for not having confessed to the murder. Mr. King reiterated many times that evening, as he confessed to the murder of Leo Finlay, that his conscience no longer allowed him to keep such a dark and sinister secret.

'Tell me about the knife Gerald, is this the knife?'

'It was in my car you see. Margaret left it behind in the kitchen after a social evening. I brought it out with the intention of returning it to her or Colin, but I simply never got around to it.' Matthew had to wait some minutes while Gerald King pulled himself together and carried on. 'The knife happened to be there in the car that awful evening. I only wanted to threaten him, but I had come to know him and to know he loved money. And because he was doing it in the name of the Lord, he believed he was above the law.' And Gerald King's voice held a deep note of sarcasm.

'I lost everything, my land, my wife and now my daughter is seriously ill. If I lose her I will have nothing.' He paused, 'I am so sorry about Colin. I never imagined they would find him guilty. Then I realised they had believed him guilty because of the missing knife. It was all because of the missing knife. I retrieved it after I stabbed Leo. I had to take it away. There would have been finger-prints, you see. I brought it home and hid it in my wardrobe. It has been there ever since.' Gerald King looked over at Matthew.

'Leo Finlay may have been a relative of yours, but make no mistake about it, he was no man of God. I did the community a good turn. I know he took money from others in the church, but it was me who was the ultimate fool. I gave him everything and he took everything.'

Gently Matthew took the knife from Gerald King's knee, wrapped it in the towel and helped the elder to his feet. 'I think you know Gerald, we have to get someone to take you to the station. I will ring for someone.'

'Please Detective Hampton; I want you and you only to take me. It was your son who rescued my daughter and I assure you I have no thought of trying to escape from you.'

Before Matthew left the premises with Mr. King, Rachel asked Matthew's permission to ring John Finlay and let him know this latest development. Matthew readily consented, but stressed the importance of keeping it all very confidential, until Gerald King had been formally charged with Leo Finlay's murder. Because now that Colin had been proved to be so wrongly convicted, there may well be lengthy court sessions to ensure that this time the right culprit was found to be guilty beyond reasonable doubt.

CHAPTER 25

John came to see Rachel and Maggie at the annexe the next evening after she rang to tell him about Gerald King. By then the news of Gerald King's confession and imprisonment had been released to the media and although Colin was still in custody until the confession was authenticated, he too had been told of the latest developments. His initial response, when told of Gerald King's arrest, was simply, 'May God be with him.'

Rhoda and Alan were happy to stay with Dorrie to allow John to go out. Rhoda had tried to let her mother know, in the simplest terms, of Colin's imminent release from prison but her mother had just looked at her so blankly that Rhoda's tears came unchecked. It was her mother who sat patting Rhoda's hand, telling her everything would be all right. It was then that Rhoda knew Colin's release, and Gerald King's confession, had come too late for her warm kind-hearted mother.

'Rachel, I have you to thank for ultimately getting justice for Colin. I know if Gerald King had not come to you last evening, the verdict of guilty would still be hanging over my son.'

John was sitting on the blue sofa in the annexe, and Rachel sat facing him in the easy chair. Maggie, after making tea for the three of them, had retired to bed. John, watching his niece and her obvious modesty about what she had achieved for Colin, was in total awe of her.

'I believe Gerald King's wife left him some time ago because he gave his whole farm of land to Leo Finlay for the church and left himself with nothing. What on earth possessed him to do such a thing, Rachel?'

'He says he wanted more than anything to see the new church built, and of course Leo was always saying they needed more money. Then of course Mr. King discovered the church fund was almost depleted of money. So he began to believe Leo was simply a fraudster. By this time his wife had gone, Amanda had got herself a flat in Belfast and he was left living in an empty house.' Rachel continued, 'He was, as you can imagine, feeling very bitter and tormented. Remember this was a man who had had a strong faith in God, and then, because of one man, disillusionment came. He says he came back into the church hall that night with the knife, to threaten Leo. When he had watched him counting the collections from the church plates and putting the money into his briefcase he just snapped.' Rachel paused, 'The rest you know, John. I just want to say I never lose sight of the fact Leo was your son. It must be so hard for you.'

John nodded dumbly. 'He must have been very weak, a trait I was unaware of in him, I must admit. I can only hope and pray that God has forgiven him. Because he was my son, I wholeheartedly forgive him.' John was quiet for a minute then went on. 'One thing really puzzles me in all this. Do you think King was responsible for the petrol bomb? Did he think you suspected him for being responsible for the murder?'

'Indirectly, yes, he was responsible for the petrol bomb. He did admit it to me, but was most reluctant to talk about it. It seems every time he left here, because of his Christian beliefs, he felt plagued with guilt because he came here for sex. One night on impulse, he paid a young boy he knows well to put the petrol bomb in the hallway. It happened to coincide with the I.R.A's timing of their incendiary devices. He thought if he destroyed this place, I would have nowhere to continue trading and his guilt would be absolved.'

'But he almost had you killed, Rachel. How could he? There is no excuse for such barbarity.'

'John, he was not targeting me, just the building. He did tell the boy to make sure the place was empty, but because the other devices were going off in Royal Avenue, the boy just panicked, placed it in the hall and ran. I don't know who the lad was and I don't think I ever will now.' Rachel looked at John. 'And look at me, I am here. I am very well indeed. I am cured. I know I have so much to be thankful for. You are right. I could have been killed that awful evening. Thank God for my panic buttons in the bedroom and that young policeman who acted on hearing the sound of the alarm.'

'I know, I know.' John remembered how ill she had been and how these premises had looked the first time he saw them after the fire. His heart was full of praise for this woman, so resilient and caring. She had achieved so much in the last twenty-four hours. He could only hope that what she had achieved would perhaps, eventually be of some comfort to Dorrie. She might begin to understand Colin's innocence and it might even pave the way for her recovery.

'Colin's barrister believes Colin will be released the day after tomorrow. He says Mr. King will be formally charged tomorrow. We have so much to be thankful for, Colin out of that awful place and back into the heart of his family. He told me when I last visited him that when the time came for his release, and this was before Gerald King had confessed, one of his first visits would be to his mother. Since that day Dorrie came to the High Court, Colin has been desperately worried about her. He asks everyone who visits how she really is.' John went on, 'I hope Dorrie recognises him, but because of how her mind is at present, she may not, and then, of course, Colin has lost so much weight he doesn't look like our eldest son anymore.'

'I would love to go to see Dorrie too, John. I have not been in some time. I would be interested to see if she remembers me. You never know, she just might.' Rachel smiled as she spoke.

'Would you really come and visit? That would be lovely, Rachel. We will let Colin get his visit over first and then I will collect you some afternoon next week. Would that do?'

'Ideal, John. I can sort something out with Lynn regarding looking after the shop. She is back at university, but is fairly flexible with lectures at the minute. She will be happy to fill in behind the counter for me. She loves working in the lingerie shop and looks forward to working every Saturday. So I know she will be more than willing to help out.'

'Good. Now I must get back home and see how Dorrie is. Rhoda did think she would say something to her mother about Colin's release. In the meantime, let me know when Lynn can help out and I'll collect you. By the way, were you happy with Gavin's work and his quotation; you haven't told me anything about that, but I suppose with so much else going on that is hardly surprising.'

'His work has been excellent, and I have also asked him to call with me to-morrow to collect a cheque in payment for his work.' Then Rachel hurried on. 'He has asked me to dinner some evening, you know, John. He tells me he has been divorced for ten years, is that true?'

'Rachel, I'm delighted to hear you are going to dinner with Gavin. Yes, he had a rough deal with his wife I can tell you. She took up with an old flame of hers, and became pregnant by him. So needless to say, he has not bothered with any woman since. There is no one who would be more delighted than I would be, if Gavin and you hit it off.' John sounded very excited.

'Perhaps if he knew more about me, he would soon lose interest, John.'

'If you mean what you use your rooms for – he is already aware of that, Rachel. And if he has asked you to dinner, obviously it doesn't matter very much to him.'

With that John hugged Rachel before leaving. He seemed buoyed up, Rachel thought, as he walked down the drive. No doubt Colin's imminent release was the reason for his buoyancy.

Lynn was glad to get back to university and her studies. The work there she knew would keep her mind occupied. Her doctor had forbidden her to go back for at least a month, she had been so terror stricken and depressed. Since that awful night of the bombing of the Belvedere, her mind had been swamped with the images of people who had been brought out of that hell hole. Some already dead, others critically injured or horrendously burned. Then to see Jason re-enter that inferno was still something she dare not think about. He had almost lost his life, and only the skill of Paul Greenlees had saved him. She still had nightmares about his non-appearance out of that place, and how close those nightmares were to reality. The saving grace of it all was that Jason had managed to rescue Amanda King, and as a direct result of his act of recklessness, Amanda's father had admitted he had murdered Leo. The irony of the whole case was, now that Mr. King was locked up in prison, his daughter was making good progress in the hospital. And to think he had sat with her day and night and only saw his daughter in a coma, unaware her father was even there. Lynn hoped that now Amanda was recovering, someone would tell her how devoted her father had been. In spite of the terrible thing he had done to Leo, he was capable of love, love for his only daughter. Although Lynn herself had not been to visit Amanda, Jason had been there a few times and kept her informed of Amanda's progress. Perhaps the next time Jason was going to visit, she would accompany him.

She spied Jason on the Monday morning, the second week after her return to Queen's. He was sitting at their favourite table in the ground floor coffee bar, which looked out onto a busy thoroughfare. She had not seen him since his surgery, preferring to give him time with his family after his illness. She thought he looked remarkably well, despite all he had been through. As she approached his table, he looked up from the book he was studying and immediately stood up to meet her, almost overbalancing the lightweight table he was seated at.

'Oh Lynn,' and Jason put out both arms as she came towards him. He embraced her warmly. 'It is so good to see you, Lynn. Did you get my messages? I sent several, asking how you were.'

'Oh yes, Jason and I sent some to you. Everyone assured me you were doing well and I didn't want to intrude into your family life. Your mum and dad were so worried.'

'Your family told me you were really shocked and traumatised by the horror of it all.' Jason said. 'Thank goodness you had no physical injuries.'

'No, physically I was unscathed, unlike you, Amanda King and so many others.' Lynn hastened to add, 'I think I must be very weak, Jason. Everyone else seems so resilient, but me, I was just a shrivelling wreck.'

'Don't ever think such a thing Lynn. You are back now to resume your studies, isn't that everything? It tells me how resilient you are too.'

'I think the worst time Jason, was when you went back into the inferno. I had such nightmares about that. What if you hadn't come back out?'

'But I did come back, Lynn. Funny my parents would say the same; that was their worst moment.' Jason paused, 'I'll never know to this day why I did that, some instinct I think told me Amanda and her fiancé were in trouble. They had been directly behind us, so I realised something must have happened.'

Then they both fell silent – thinking of Amanda, her horrible injuries and the dreadful loss of her fiancé.

'Jason, I would like to visit Amanda, would that be possible? I know you have gone a couple of times.'

'That would be good, Lynn. I think, deep down, I go to see how she is progressing, because I did carry her out of that place. I have also deep pity for her because she lost her fiancé and what she is going to have to endure. I believe the operations, and the long stays in hospital she will have to come through will be horrendous. I would love it if you could come with me next time, it is not an easy visit, I have to tell you. At least one good thing has come out of all this, and that is Colin's release. Who would ever have suspected Amanda's father was involved in Leo's murder? I was totally stunned, Lynn, when dad told me.'

'It was mum who told me, Jason, even before Mr. King was charged. How she knew I have no idea, but she certainly has no intention of telling me how she came about such important information.'

'When we go to see Amanda, we'll not know whether she has learnt anything about her father or not. I haven't been for a fortnight, but I did ring and the staff told me she was now sitting up and watching television. Also her mother visits regularly, so she might well have told Amanda about it.'

'I feel very strongly that someone needs to tell Amanda, that in spite of this murder charge her father loves her and is dedicated to her.'

'I never thought of that, and I suppose it is important.' Jason said. 'Perhaps you and I could go, say Saturday afternoon. Would that suit you Lynn?'

'Yes, with my lectures so flexible at the moment, I'll cover some afternoon during the week in the shop and mum will be happy to do Saturday afternoon for me.'

'I'll pick you up around two and be prepared for, well, I don't really know what. On my previous visits Amanda has been under sedation, but she will be awake this time. Now that we have settled that, I am going to get you and me a cup of coffee.'

CHAPTER 26

'Is Jason collecting you on Saturday?' Rachel was waiting in the shop for John to collect her this Wednesday afternoon. She was going to see Dorrie as arranged, and Lynn had just arrived in from Queen's, with her haversack weighed down with books. She had told Rachel she was more than happy to look after the shop, and try to sell some of her expensive, provocative underwear. Lynn also said, if she wasn't too busy, she would make the most of her free time and try to get some studying done.

'Yes mum, Jason is collecting me about two. I must admit I have mixed feelings about going to see Amanda. That is selfish I know, but I don't know what to expect, you see. Is she scarred from the burns? How is she coping, now she knows her fiancé was killed?'

'It is really awful I know, Lynn, but just think of her and give her all the support you can.'

'I'll do my best mum, but no one seems to know if she knows about her father and his confession. It is all too awful.'

Lynn made a conscious effort to pull herself together. 'At least I have until Saturday to prepare myself. In the meantime you have to face Aunt Dorrie, which I think might be as equally harrowing for you, don't you think?'

'Probably Lynn, but I'll have to do my best to cope. After all, the good news in all this is Colin's release from prison. It is wonderful. I only hope Dorrie has some realisation of this, but according to John, when Colin visited his mother, on his release from prison, she was confused as to whether he was Leo or Colin. Not a good sign, I think. But we will see.' Just as she spoke Rachel recognised John's car drawing up by the kerb outside the shop. 'Bye darling, I'll see you in a couple of hours.'

Wednesday afternoons were usually quite quiet, because a lot of businesses closed on Wednesday afternoons for a half-day. But for the first hour after her mother left, Lynn was kept busy selling the beautiful lingerie her mother stocked. She loved the fine matching bras and pants, with their delicate lace and fine colours. She also adored the wide range of nightdresses and pyjamas, made of the finest silk or satin, and all neatly stacked and labelled to ensure easy sales. She marvelled her mother had been able to get her shop up and running again, all stock in place, as if nothing had ever happened, to either her or her business, and in such a short space of time. The petrol bomb had been planted early February, and this was almost the end of April. So to Lynn's mind, her mother had achieved a near miracle in less than twelve weeks. But then, of course, she had worked all day long and late into the evenings, once she had regained her health. So much so that Lynn wondered where her mother got her energy from and how she would ever cope with her mother's work ethos.

When there was a lull in people entering the shop, Lynn decided she would take a look upstairs. She hadn't seen any of the rooms since they had been redecorated after all the smoke damage. They were truly beautiful bedrooms, she thought as she walked from one to another. They even seemed more luxurious now than they had been originally. As she made her way back downstairs, she wondered how anyone who came to have a consultation with her mother could bear to tear themselves away.

'I never got opening a book, Mum. I have been rather busy.'

Rachel had returned, true to her word, about an hour and a half later.

'You'll see by the till roll my selling technique is quite good.' Lynn smiled and then suddenly remembered where her mother had been. 'How is Aunt Dorrie? Did she know you?

Sorry I should have asked about her first but I was rather proud of my sales.'

'That is fine, love. I am glad the time went quickly for you.' Rachel said. 'Dorrie did know me, believe it or not. Not at first I think, and then later she realised who I was. But,' Rachel hesitated, reluctant to believe how Dorrie really was, 'apart from that she is very unstable, but please do not say. John asked me on the way back what I thought of her and he insisted I would be truthful. I said I felt the Dorrie we knew was lost to us.'

'Oh no, mum, you mean,' Lynn was shocked ,'you think Aunt Dorrie is going to be more or less insane?'

'Lynn, I'm the last person to try and diagnose someone but please don't say the word insane. I detest it.' Rachel said. 'Mentally unstable she is but any more drastic description conjures up images of someone so out of control to be capable of vile deeds. That is not how Dorrie is. Certainly, if she got a chance she would be out of the house and away. Away where, John is not sure, but he thinks she is trying to find Leo. If that is the case, she has lost touch with reality, Lynn. Is that insanity? I don't know. I really don't. So far her own doctor has not referred her to a psychiatrist for a diagnosis. He still thinks she will make a partial recovery. I tentatively suggested to John he should get a psychiatrist to the house to assess her. I think the time has come for John to know the truth and then he will, given time, learn to accept it.'

'Mum you are a genius when it comes to helping people. No wonder they come to you here to talk. There must be so many needing to talk to someone after all the bombings, the shootings and the loss of life people have endured.'

Rachel was silent for a moment, 'Yes, love, people have suffered a lot and feel they need comfort in so many different ways.' Rachel felt the need to be deliberately vague with her daughter. She could never tell a lie to her and say the men only came to her for a chat. She knew when she had bought the premises at first, she had been evasive with Lynn, but perhaps the time was coming when she might have to be more truthful. She wondered if her daughter ever had any suspicions of what her mother actually did. But to her surprise now Lynn simply said, 'You are a born listener mum, and I am so proud of you.' As she gathered up her books she added, 'I think I'll call on Jason on the way home to make the final arrangements for Saturday.'

'Good Lynn, I'll see you later this evening.' Rachel hugged and kissed her daughter warmly before she departed. At the same time she heaved a sigh of relief, grateful she had been spared any more questions. After her daughter had gone Lynn felt the need to sit down and putting her head in her hands, wept tears for her daughter, for her innocence, and Rachel's profound guilt at misleading her most precious possession. And she vowed that afternoon, that at the next discussion she and Lynn had about her consultations, she would try to be more truthful with her. For now she intended to support John and his family as much as she could but at the same time she wanted to make a huge success of her business. No one knew when they needed money in the future and she felt she may well need it too. If that was going to be the case she was prepared to work hard and save hard for any unforeseen circumstances.

'Jason I'm so glad I went to see Amanda. It wasn't easy, she is so changed.' When Lynn and Jason had entered the ward where Amanda was, Lynn was shocked at the girl's appearance. She was almost bald and her arms, shoulders and chest were swathed in some type of light almost see-through bandages. Lynn's first thought for her friend was that her face seemed unscathed by burns. But as Jason and she approached her bedside, Lynn could see her eyebrows, which before had been delicate dark brown arches framing her beautiful blue eyes and oval face, were now two ugly, uneven scars dominating her appearance.

'I hope she didn't notice my initial shock, Jason. I did my best to hide it.'

'You were brilliant, Lynn, really good with her. I was glad you were with me. I don't really like going alone, you know.'

'Well, she certainly seems to welcome your visits and you have been so loyal.' Lynn added, 'I think she depends on you a lot. Probably because you were the one who rescued her.' Lynn smiled at Jason as she spoke. 'It's only natural for her to feel like that. I'm sure she sees you as her hero.'

Jason nodded and went on. 'It's good she's getting home this week. Good news for her and she's doing the right thing by going to stay with her mother in her apartment on the Antrim Road.'

'Yes, I said I would call and see her when she came home, do you want to come?'

Jason shook his head. 'Now that she's getting home, I'll skip the next visit but let me know how things are going.'

'O.K. Jason, I'll do that.' Lynn was reluctant to agree to going on her own, but Jason probably felt he had done enough and besides, Amanda's mother would probably be there. Jason might just feel a bit 'out of it' being the only man there.

'I'm not going for a couple of weeks. I said I would give her time to settle in. She has no appointments for any assessments regarding skin grafting. So I hope to go before all that starts. I have her phone number. I promised to ring before I'd call.'

'Thanks, Lynn. I feel strangely relieved that I'm to be spared the next visit, I'm ashamed to say. But that's how I feel.' and with that Jason gave her a giant hug before she got out of the car and with promises to watch out for one another in the coffee shop on Monday morning, Jason drove off as Lynn let herself in the door.

'Mum, I rang Amanda King today. I have arranged to call and see her at her mother's place. I intend going on Saturday afternoon, that is, if you don't need me in the shop.'

Rachel had arrived home from work about half an hour ago and Lynn was delighted to see her home early for a change. She did work so hard and Lynn always looked forward to spending time with her. Maggie and she had already spent a peaceful hour together reading the daily paper and doing the crossword. Now Maggie rose from her seat beside the fire and insisted she would make some tea and toast.

'How was trade in the shop to-day, Mum? Were you busy?'

'Yes, I was quite busy, Lynn. I could have worked a lot longer to-night, but to be truthful, I felt I needed a break. And don't worry about Saturday. I'll be fine serving on my own. Hopefully, you'll see an improvement in Amanda when you go.'

'I hope so, but I thought when I rang her earlier she was different – different towards me. She did say she would like me to come, but somehow I feel she's disappointed Jason isn't coming,' Lynn hesitated. 'I don't know – she was just different.'

'Lynn, probably everything is just beginning to hit her now since she went to stay with her mother. The loss of her fiancé, her disfigurement and now of course her knowledge of her father's confession and his arrest. It is all horrendous for her and I'm sure she'll be glad to see you on Saturday, even though Jason isn't with you.'

'How thoughtless of me, mum. She is coming through so much and I was so selfish. I thought she was beginning to cling to Jason.'

'You really like Jason, don't you Lynn?' Rachel was aware of her daughter's affection for her cousin.

'I really do, mum, we have a lot in common I think, especially regarding animals, but we are just good friends. Nothing more, you know.'

'I know that, but just the same, you never know what the future holds for you. Make sure Jason knows I adopted you, after your parents were killed. So there are no blood ties whatsoever.' Lynn smiled as she looked at her mother and then went to help Maggie with the tea and toast.

'Grandma, will you make sure Jason knows I am no blood relative of his?'

'What is this about?' Maggie looked puzzled as she handed Rachel her tea and toast.

'I merely suggested young Jason should be reminded that Lynn was adopted.'

Maggie nodded sagely, 'I'll certainly do that. And I'll be very subtle about it.'

'It's mum that wants you to do it, not me, Jason and me are fine as we are. This started because I felt Amanda was disappointed that Jason wasn't coming to visit her. Silly of me really, as mum pointed out, she has so much on her plate to contend with I'm sure whether Jason comes to visit her, or not, is on the bottom of her list. So don't worry, please, about Jason and me. I'll let you both know how Amanda and I get on when I get back on Saturday.'

CHAPTER 27

'Rachel, I think you should come home immediately. Lynn has arrived back from Amanda King's house a short time ago. She is totally distraught, and at this very moment she is packing a suitcase, and crying throughout it. She refuses to talk about anything. She is tight-lipped, except to keep saying it is nothing to do with me. She loves me dearly, she says, and will sorely miss me.' Maggie was having difficulty controlling the tears which were not too far away. 'What on earth could have happened, Rachel? Will you come home and speak to her? She says she has nothing to say to you. What can she possibly have heard?'

As Rachel listened to her mother tell her the state Lynn seemed to be in, Rachel's heart went to her boots. She realised the possibility of what had happened at Amanda King's house. Had someone told Amanda about her father coming to Waring Street? If that was the case, Amanda would feel totally justified in enlightening Lynn about what her mother actually did for a living, and how she managed to seem to be so comfortably off. Without another thought for her sales and the possibility of her customers coming in, Rachel checked her shop thoroughly, making sure all the lights were switched off, then putting her closed sign on the door, even though it was only 4 p.m. on a Saturday afternoon, she locked her doors. She then proceeded, with a very heavy heart, towards her car and home. While she drove she chastised herself for not telling Lynn the whole sorry truth. She might perhaps have been able to accept it, coming from her own mother. The human mind could react and accept sometimes in the most unexpected way, but now, if what she suspected was true, she feared her daughter was lost to her. Rachel knew her duplicity in such a situation was so much more unacceptable, than the stark truth was likely to be. Lynn herself never dissembled, certainly Rachel had never known her to. Indeed, sometimes she could get so brutally honest as to be quite hurtful. Now, as Rachel reached home, she feared that her daughter would have no respect for her now. She was panic stricken as she drove towards Paul and Lucie's house and saw a taxi sitting waiting, its engine running.

She parked her car out at the pavement and began to race up the drive to her front door and home. She had just entered the living room, when Lynn appeared out of the bedroom, her familiar blue suitcase in one hand, and a large canvas bag slung over her shoulder. Rachel stepped forward to speak to her, but Lynn, with such an expression of pure hatred on her face that Rachel knew she would never forget, put up her hand to fend off her mother and keep the distance between them.

'Don't come near me.' Lynn's eyes were blazing. 'Don't touch me.' She was screaming the words at her mother. 'To think I believed you, talking to men, helping them through some crisis or other. How naïve was I? I believed it all.' Lynn's voice broke now and she seemed to have become hoarse.

'I was going to tell you, really I was.'

'Don't give me that. You just hoped you would always get away with it.' Lynn moved towards the door, ignoring her mother's outstretched arms and agonising expression, as she whispered, 'Please, please don't go, Lynn. I'll do anything you ask.'

Lynn gave her mother a scathing, contemptible look by way of answer, as she opened the front door, then remembering something she closed it again and turned back into the room. Sidestepping her mother, she made her way to her grandmother's room and went in to Maggie. For a moment Rachel's spirits lifted, perhaps her mother could persuade Lynn to stay. But a few moments later her daughter reappeared, tears streaming down her face, and strode purposefully to the front door. As she stepped outside to go to the waiting taxi, her parting words to her mother were, 'And to think of Uncle John too, going to you. It's disgusting.'

Rachel shook her head wildly, 'No, no, Lynn, it wasn't like that. Not with John. You must believe me. Please, you must.'

Lynn made no reply but climbed into the taxi and as it sped off, she never once looked back towards the annexe or her mother, who was weeping heartbrokenly on the doorstep.

Amanda King thought a lot about her conversation with Lynn, after she had left her that Saturday afternoon. Perhaps by telling Lynn all she knew about her mother, and the men who visited her, it was a very ungrateful thing to do after all Lynn's cousin, Jason, had done for her. Amanda found it reassuring that Lynn and Jason were cousins. They were just good friends to one another. There was no romance between the two of them, nor should there be, if they were cousins. She herself had known a very happy romance with her fiancé Tony, but now he was dead. Gone from her forever, and he was never coming back. But she was young and nubile, and in spite of everything that had happened, she wanted to feel vibrant and alive again. She knew she was not pretty to look at at the moment, with her hair loss and the burns to her upper body. But she had noticed Jason did not seem to mind her disfigurement, and indeed she believed he hadn't even noticed them. He had been so faithful in visiting her in hospital and she always looked forward to his visits, but then Lynn had appeared on the last couple of occasions. When she actually arrived alone on Saturday with some lame excuse that Jason was studying, the knowledge she had been harbouring about Lynn's mother for a whole week, was relayed to Lynn that afternoon in the most forthright, brash manner Amanda could muster up.

When her mother had told her about her father's confession to Leo Finlay's murder and that he had also confessed to visiting Lynn's mother on a regular basis in order to have sex with her, paying handsomely for her services, Amanda had nursed this knowledge to herself since then. Now she was glad she had told Lynn how it really was. After all, why shouldn't she suffer too? As Amanda was doing. After all, Lynn had been lucky enough to escape unscathed after the explosion while she, Amanda, had been left maimed. Why shouldn't she see someone else being tortured? She had even contemplated ringing the police station anonymously to tell them about Rachel's house in Waring Street, but had decided it would be better just to tell Lynn. She knew the other girl had no idea what her mother actually did for a living. When Amanda thought back to the evening of the dance in the Belvedere, and how proud Lynn had been of the dress her mother had bought for her, out of her hard-earned cash, it was obvious to Amanda that the girl was foolishly naive. It was time someone enlightened her. Now, after all Amanda's revelations to her friend this afternoon, it was unlikely Lynn would be back to visit her any time soon, so she could look forward to Jason coming alone.

'John, I'm so sorry to ring you at home, but I didn't know what else to do, or who to turn to.' Rachel didn't add she had contemplated ringing his nephew, Gavin, but had resisted that temptation. They had had a lovely time together that evening last week, and had arranged to go out again on the following Wednesday. But she didn't feel she could call and tell him – at this early stage of their relationship – about Lynn and what had happened. Uncle John was the only one she could think of. Now her voice sounded weak, and so traumatized that John began to feel panic stricken.

'Oh, please, don't apologise, Rachel. Just tell me, what's the matter?'

'Can you come round, round to the annexe? Is Rhoda home? Is it safe to leave Dorrie?'

'I'll be straight round, Rachel. Rhoda and Alan are both here, so I'll be with you in about twenty minutes. So whatever's wrong, please, don't panic.'

John set the phone back on the receiver, and turning to Rhoda, said, 'I'm sorry, love. Rachel wants to talk to me. She sounds pretty desperate about something or other. But I'll be as quick as I can. I know we were looking forward to a quiet evening, after your mother was settled for the night. And I was looking forward to your company too, Alan.'

'That's all right, Mr. Finlay. Rhoda and I don't mind. We're more than happy here.' And Alan put his arm around Rhoda's shoulder and hugged her closely, not mindful in the least that her father saw the gesture. Grateful as ever for his daughter's understanding, John fetched his car keys and was soon heading into Belfast and along the Malone Road. All the time his mind was however, preoccupied with how Rachel, usually so calm and placid, sounded so panic-stricken and almost defeatist. Perhaps it was nothing untoward, but when he parked his car outside the annexe and she opened the door to him, he knew something terrible and heart-rending, had happened. And he wondered, as he stepped into the living room, and saw his sister-in-law, Maggie, white-faced and obviously distraught too, he wondered how much more trauma their family circle would be called on to endure.

'Rachel, Maggie,' he looked from one to another as Rachel closed the door behind him and silently indicated the seat on the other side of the fire from Maggie. He sat down and almost immediately Maggie burst into tears.'Please tell me what's wrong. Where's Lynn, has she been hurt?' And John's blood ran cold at the sound of his own words.

Rachel shook her head as she sat down on the sofa by the window, and John could see she was trying to compose herself to tell him what was wrong, so he waited patiently for her to regain her usual calmness.

'Lynn has gone, John, she has left me.' Rachel spoke so softly and her voice was shaking so much that in order to hear her distinctly, John moved to the seat beside her on the sofa.

'Did you say Lynn was gone? Is that what you said?'

She nodded in reply and then her voice, somewhat stronger, went on, 'She found out about me and my profession. What I actually do. I was actually going to tell her this week, I had made up my mind to do so. I felt I must, but someone else did it for me. She was visiting Amanda King earlier today and

I just wonder if she told her anything. But then again, what would she know?'

John was silent while he tried to digest what Rachel was saying. Lynn now knew her mother was a call girl. The strange thing was, he had never once considered Lynn in all this, whether she knew anything about the house on Waring Street or not. But if she was only learning about it now and especially from someone outside the family circle, it would have a dreadful impact on such a young, innocent girl like Lynn.

'You're sure that's the trouble. Did she tell you so?'

'She told me in no uncertain terms, as she made her way to the taxi.' Now Rachel had difficulty telling John the worst thing her daughter suspected. 'She believes you and I… You and I.' she could not bring herself to say anything more explicit.

John was shocked. 'I'll soon put that right, Rachel, I promise you. I'll clear our names regarding that.' Then, aware of Maggie sitting quietly by the fire, he turned to her. 'I want you to know, Maggie, I did visit Rachel on occasions, and those visits were invaluable to me, at a time in my life when I was desperate, but nothing untoward ever happened between Rachel and me. I hope you believe me.'

'John, I have known about Rachel since she first opened her premises on Waring Street and what her main means of income was. She knows how I feel about it and I am in no position to judge anyone. She did confide in me about your visits, but I believed her when she said nothing inappropriate happened between you. I do know you only wanted to share your troubles with someone and Rachel happened to be the one you initially confided in. So it never entered my head about anything going on between you.'

'Thanks, Maggie' and now John turned to Rachel, 'try to be strong, Rachel. And I promise you, I'll leave no stone unturned in an effort to find Lynn and try to encourage her to return home. Besides, I hope her common sense will prevail. Surely she will wish to finish her literature degree. That will bring her back.' John said. 'Has she access to money?

Obviously she must have cash if she ordered a taxi to take her to God knows where.'

'She has an account and I have been putting money into it each month for her. Whether she will continue to use it or not, well' Rachel shrugged. 'She may well think it's contaminated somehow now. Also, she will have access to money soon, money her parents left her when they were killed.'

'Let's hope we have Lynn back, and into Queen's again, before she even thinks of touching that money.' John smiled encouragingly at Rachel as he spoke.

'Well, John, you've given Mum and me some cheer this evening and I hope you're right. But she did tell mum she would make sure we would never find her. So your thoughts on this fresh trauma are encouraging.'

CHAPTER 28

'Where to, my lady?' the taxi driver slowed down at the bottom of the Malone Avenue and addressed Lynn over his shoulder. 'Do I turn left or right?' He realised this young lady was very unhappy about something, as was the woman who had begun to follow her from the front door of her home.

'I just want to find a good bed and breakfast place for the night, not in Belfast though. I want somewhere out of town.'

The taxi driver thought for a moment and then, 'I know just the place, a lovely bed and breakfast, clean, comfortable and safe. It has been approved for use by the army personnel, so I would strongly recommend it. I believe the prices are very reasonable too.'

Without any hesitation Lynn said, 'Take me there, please.'

'You won't regret it, miss,' and the taxi driver abruptly turned right across the Malone Road heading for Lisburn, a thriving garrison town situated a mere seven miles from Belfast.

As the taxi driver drove along the Lisburn road, Lynn had time to collect her thoughts and to realise the enormity of what had happened, and what she had done. She had just given up all she held dear, her mother, her darling grandmother, Lucie and Paul, Jason and his ever loving dog Monty, never mind all her loving aunts and uncles who had been so caring towards her for the past two years, since they had arrived in Northern Ireland. And she felt sheer, physical pain as she thought about it all. Then she thought of her mother, and how much she had deceived her, talking about helping men to cope with all their unhappiness, simply by listening to them, and Lynn's heart hardened, and she knew no matter how much she missed everyone, especially Jason, she must distance herself from her mother. The thing she found most tortuous to bear was the knowledge that Uncle John had been with her mother. How could they? And the two of them knowing Aunt Dorrie was so unwell.

Suddenly she was aware the taxi was turning into a driveway, and she saw a beautiful red-brick house, of interesting Dutch design, situated in beautiful gardens with lights flooding the front door and outer steps. 'Here we are, miss, leave this to me,' the taxi driver smiled as he opened the door, 'the proprietors know me well, you wait for a moment.'

Lynn nodded from her seat in the back and watched as the taximan rang the bell, and then have a brief conversation with a tall, fair middle-aged man. He returned to the car. 'Right miss, they have a room, last one as it happens. You go on over to the door there, I'll bring your case.'

The minute Lynn entered the warm inviting hall of the guest house, and the proprietor spoke to her, she felt immediately cheered and in somewhat better spirits. The bedroom too, that Mr. Frazier showed her, seemed to calm her spirits, whether it was the beautiful blue painted walls and the matching bed linen, or simply the warmth illuminating from the radiator by the window, she did not know. She thanked Mr. Frazier and paid him £ 40 for a night's accommodation, and after establishing the breakfast times, he left her, wishing her a good night's sleep, if he did not see her later, and he would see her in the morning. She did not bother to unpack anything; she would be leaving in the morning and although it was only seven o'clock in the evening, the bed was so inviting that Lynn, without bothering to undress, slipped under the duvet and nestled down into the warmth and comfort. She wakened with a start, and imagining it must be morning, switched on the bedside light to establish the time with her watch. She was very disappointed when she realised it was just eight-fifteen and she had only slept for three-quarters of an hour. Now the whole night stretched in front of her with all her agonising thoughts of home, of her mother, her grandmother and of course, Jason. Jason would wonder why on earth she wasn't in the coffee shop on Monday morning as arranged. Perhaps by then, some of the family would have told him that she had run away. He would feel so let down that she had not thought to contact him before she left. The truth was, she had considered ringing him, but was afraid he might have coaxed her into staying, and Lynn knew she must get away, away from her mother and all she stood for. She needed to get away from her mother's shop with its erotic lingerie and the memories of those luxurious bedrooms upstairs and what she now knew they stood for. Now she knew, understood so much, and could see everything so clearly. To have been so naive those couple of years, not to have seen the house on Waring Street for what it was. And the bitterness towards her mother filled her heart and mind as she climbed out of bed, uncertain of her future, but in no doubt about her feelings for her mother, and the knowledge that she never wished to see her again.

Now she brushed her hair, straightened her skirt and jumper and splashed some cold water over her face, before proceeding towards the guest lounge which Mr. Frazier had pointed out earlier. She didn't know why she was even contemplating going there – she was in no form for company. She only knew that further sleep was unlikely to come to her easily and some company would surely be better than just her own.

When she entered the lounge, the first thing she noticed was the television in the corner of the room and the rumble of voices from it. She was relieved to see it, it meant conversation would be limited, which was exactly what she wanted this evening. She spotted a vacant, easy chair in a corner and made her way over to it and without looking right of left at the occupants of the room, quietly sat down. Gradually, as she began to focus on aspects of the room, she realised there were only three others present, two who seemed to be eagerly following the TV programme. The other, a girl who seemed to be in her early twenties, was watching Lynn and now, as Lynn looked over, she nodded and gave a broad smile. Lynn gave a tentative smile in return, and then tried to show an interest in the TV programme.

'Do you fancy a quiet walk outside, by any chance? The grounds are lovely here. I'm a sales rep. and I stay here all the time. I wouldn't stay anywhere else.'

Lynn turned towards the girl who had whispered to her, she was obviously from Scotland because even though her voice was so low, the accent was unmistakeable. Lynn looked again towards the TV and the western film rolling on, and making a quick assessment of the girl got to her feet.

'That seems a good idea. I don't know anything about where I am, so the sooner I get my bearings the better,' and then she quietly followed the Scottish girl out into the hall, and through the front door. They went out into the garden, with its beautiful lawn, softly lit with authentic looking gas lamps which highlighted the dense shrubbery and ornate garden seats dotted round the entire grounds.

Her new acquaintance led the way to one of the seats at the far end of one of the lawns, and as they sat down side by side, she said to Lynn, 'What brings you here then? Are you another sales rep. like me?'

She sounded so sociable and so jolly, and her Scottish brogue was so attractive, that Lynn, in spite of her reservations about confiding anything to anybody, started to open her heart to this stranger. This girl, Lynn learned later during those couple of hours out in the garden, was from Glasgow, her name was Tracey Bell, and she was twenty-five years of age. She suggested, after Lynn had opened her heart to her, that- as she would be returning to Scotland and to Glasgow on the Monday morning, Lynn should come with her, as a passenger in her car.

'Lynn, it would be a good idea to come with me. You know, accompany me as a passenger in my car. After listening to your story I would really like to help you, but the decision must be yours. Your story is heart-rending and I would feel as you do, I'm afraid,' Tracey Bell went on eagerly, seeing such a simple solution to her friend's dilemma. 'I have a flat in Glasgow. You can stay with me until you sort yourself out. We can lie low here for the weekend and get a carry-out for a meal. I sometimes do stay the weekend here, simply to chill out and now I feel our meeting like this was meant to be. I'm really glad I decided to stay this weekend, otherwise I would not have met you at all.'

'But you don't know me Tracey – you know nothing about me.' Lynn was anxious to ensure Tracey knew what she was doing. She did not want this girl regretting anything she had said on the spur of the moment, out of pity for her.

'Well, I've been out and about now since I was eighteen, Lynn, about seven years and I'm a pretty shrewd judge of people. Regarding you, I really like what I see. But you sleep on what I have said tonight, and we'll have breakfast together in the morning. Breakfast's served between eight and nine, so let's say we'll meet in the dining room at half-eight.'

'Rachel, I'm very sorry, but so far Lynn seems to have vanished without a trace.' John had spent hours trying to trace Lynn's last movements. It was now Tuesday, the third day since Lynn had gone. And John had become more and more thwarted as he went from one taxi rank to another. He knew he felt committed to helping Rachel. After all, she had been brave enough to listen to Gerald King, even after the fire on her premises, and even when he appeared there with a knife. He did owe it to her now to help.

'If only I had thought to take the registration of the car, John.' It was almost as if Rachel could read his thoughts. It would have made things much simpler, but Rachel had been so distraught and intent on trying to persuade Lynn to stay that registration numbers had never entered her head. And who could blame her?

'I do intend to keep looking, I promise you, Rachel, but in the meantime we should let her bank know what has happened. They are the ones in a position to keep a check on her account, and to see where any money she withdraws is taken from.' John was reluctant at this stage, to bring anyone apart from family into this situation, but felt he had to make Rachel aware Lynn could be traced in that way.

'I don't think so John. If Lynn does not want anything more to do with me, what's the point in pursuing her?'

'I need to clarify our relationship with her, Rachel. And no matter how long it takes, I intend to do just that.' John was anxious that both his name and Rachel's would be cleared regarding their relationship sometime, some day.

'Would you like me to contact Gavin, just to let him know what has happened between you and Lynn. When is your dinner date with him?'

'I'm meeting him later this evening, John, and I need to make it perfectly clear to him why my daughter has left home. I'll know by his attitude if the knowledge I am a call girl has actually sunk in with him yet.'

'I'll be very surprised if it makes any difference to him, Rachel. Gavin has been through so much, you know. I believe he holds you in high regard, and that's another reason, Rachel, why I will continue to search for Lynn. No one in the family must think for one minute there was ever anything between us, only friendship. Even during our friendship I never thought too much about what you did for a living. You were a member of the family who has helped me so much, and now I would like to do all I can for you.'

'If only I could believe others in the family might feel as you do, but I am such a coward, I've told none of them, only Lucie. I've told her everything. That my erotic lingerie was just a cover for my real job.'

John was quite taken aback that Rachel had told anyone else in the family.

'I can see you're surprised, but I had to tell Lucie the real reason for Lynn going away. Besides, suddenly I am tired of deceiving people. Indeed I am suddenly tired of my whole lifestyle.' Rachel's voice shook as she spoke. 'Lucie has been wonderful, I must say. Not one word of condemnation from her, she did say she would have to confide in Paul, she could not keep the real reason for Lynn going away from him. I wouldn't blame him if he doesn't want me here in his annexe any longer.'

'Believe me Rachel, I know Paul Greenlees better than that. He is one of the most non-judgmental men I've ever met.

He would never put you out, and more especially because of Maggie.'

'I hope you're right John, I would not want to leave here, I love it and I know mum does too. Besides I would want to be here in case Lynn returns.'

John nodded, and then went on, 'Have you contacted Jason? I feel he is one person who needs to know why Lynn left, and so suddenly too.'

'I rang Matthew's house earlier and asked if Jason could call after his lectures today, I know he has a right to know. Perhaps he will be able to throw some light on how Lynn found out.'

'Well Rachel, I mean to go and visit Gerald King in prison. It won't be easy, he murdered my son and let my other son languish in a prison cell for a crime he did not commit. But my reason for going is to find out if he told Amanda about me visiting you, I suspect he did. And for whatever reason she has told Lynn. If she did, it sounds malicious to me, Rachel. Hopefully, Gerald King will enlighten me. In the meantime I will keep looking for Lynn, and you tell the extended family as, and when, you see fit. And just hold on to the knowledge that Gavin Finlay still wants to meet up with you, even though he knows a lot about you, Rachel. So that must count for something, surely?'

'It certainly does, John, and in spite of everything, I intend to dress up nicely to go and see him and enjoy his company.'

John was relieved to hear that Rachel still intended to go out. He rose from his seat, and hugging her tightly said his goodbyes, with promises to see her soon and let her know immediately the minute he heard any news.

CHAPTER 29

'Lynn, the ferry leaves for Stranraer at one-thirty to-morrow afternoon. I mean to pretend that you are my sister-in-law. I'm well known by the staff at the check-in desk, so it's unlikely they'll want any proof of that. But if they do, you have your passport with you, haven't you? Just show them it, the name will scarcely register with them, I'm sure. Besides I'll guarantee you won't even be asked.'

'Tracey, you have been so kind to me. I'm a stranger to you.' Lynn felt very humbled at her new-found friend's generosity and ingenuity. 'I promise I won't stay any longer in your apartment in Glasgow than is necessary.'

The two girls had just finished breakfast in the guest house Lynn had arrived at just two nights ago. Now, both were in the process of going to their rooms to pack their belongings and pay their bill. Tracey had insisted they both order Ulster fries for breakfast as it might be some time before they had an opportunity to eat again. She said she always tried to avoid eating on the ferry, it was so unappetising but also so expensive.

'Look, Lynn, the room in my apartment is lying there unused and to be honest, I'll be glad of the company. And please don't even think of paying me anything for it, at least not at present.' Tracey was adamant. 'Besides, you'll need to be careful where you draw your money from your account. That's a giveaway as to your whereabouts.' she hesitated. 'But sure you might just change your mind soon about everything and decide you want to go home. Homesickness is not a pleasant feeling, I can tell you. When I first left my home in York when I got this job in Glasgow, I nearly packed it all in. I was so homesick. So be prepared for that, Lynn.'

Lynn nodded dumbly as she rose from the table; she knew she was already beginning to feel the pangs of being away from those she loved. She would have loved to speak to her grandmother, to hear her quiet, gentle voice and try to get her to understand why she had to leave. But most of all she longed for Jason's company. Some day she hoped he, too, would understand why she had left everything so suddenly. How she could not bear to stay, not with the stigma and humiliation her mother had brought to them. Now, turning to Tracey, she said, 'I'll be fine, Tracey. This is something I must do. I'm glad I have enough cash to last for a few days because I never thought of my bank withdrawals, although I doubt if anyone in the family would actually check that out. And I intend to look for work as soon as we get to your apartment in Glasgow.'

"Well, believe it or not, there is plenty of work in Glasgow, if you just know where to look for it. I might have a few contacts, Lynn. But we'll talk about that later. Let's get back upstairs, and then I'll settle up with Mrs. Frazer and book my room for my next visit. I'll see you back here in thirty minutes time.'

Lynn and Tracey arrived at the docks around midday. They were in good time to get checked in and for Tracey to drive her Mini Minor into the hold of the ferry. Lynn was quite surprised, but also relieved that no one questioned her identity. She would have thought that, because of all the troubles in Northern Ireland, the security checks would have been very stringent. But Tracey had just casually remarked as she handed over the cash Lynn had given her for the fare, that this was her sister-in-law. The uniformed security man smiled openly at them both and wished them a good trip, assuring them it was to be a calm crossing this April morning.

It proved to be a quiet crossing indeed, as the security man had predicted, and because Tracey was engrossed in writing up her reports of her work, Lynn was left to deal with her thoughts and feelings as the distance between home and her new surroundings lengthened by the minute. As the ferry travelled on, leaving a trail of white surf, she began to feel an awful inevitability about everything that was happening to her. She knew she had, on impulse, given up so much. She had abandoned her home, her career, the love of her relatives, but most of all her friendship with Jason. But still, leaving Northern Ireland was something she must not consider regretting. She could not bear to continue to live with her mother, to expect nothing to have changed, in the face of what she now knew. It was impossible. This was something she had to do, she could do. She would soon find work, find other friends and study something else. And suddenly as she looked at Tracey, head bent low, scribbling notes in her diary, she was filled with a new resolve to succeed. This girl who had been befriended her was an inspiration to her. She had managed to strike out on her own, and now had a good job and a secure future. She needed to show her mother she could cope without her, and most of all, show Amanda King she could rise above the awful hurt she had inflicted on her.

'Tracey, I'm going to get you and me a coffee from the bar. How long is the trip on the ferry? I never even thought to ask you?'

'It's three and a half hours. We'll be there in less than forty-five minutes.'

'I'm beginning to look forward to seeing Scotland. You have impressed me with your reports of it. I intend to look for work immediately. I'm determined to find something, anything.' Lynn realised she was beginning to ramble. 'Sorry, you haven't finished your work yet, and here I am interrupting.'

'I was just about to finish off. So yes, coffee would be lovely, Lynn. And I'd love a scone and jam, please. I'm beginning to feel hungry and, out of all their food, their scones here are actually quite nice.'

'Right, be back shortly.' Lynn headed towards the bar and felt in a better frame of mind than she had since she left home. She now believed that meeting Tracey Bell and her friendship was meant to be, to help keep her sanity, and give her such a new start in life. She was indebted to this girl who was so laid-back about helping her and insisted she wanted no thanks for what she was doing. Lynn was determined that someday, when she was in a better position, she would return Tracey's kindness and understanding. She had helped Lynn at a time when she most needed it. With this girl as a friend she felt she would, in time, come to terms with the separation from other loved ones.

Rachel had not opened her shop since the Saturday evening when her mother had rang to advise her to come home. This was now Thursday, and because she had not been back she had not made any appointments with any of her clients. The truth was, she had no desire to open up, no desire to answer the phone to anyone, and certainly no desire to entertain clients. She scarcely had the desire to get out of bed in the morning and only for her mother she would have been starving. She made her light, delicate meals, chicken breasts with salad, her favourite lentil soup and lemon mousse, which Maggie knew Rachel had always loved. What she would have done without her mother Rachel hated to think. She had been such a calming presence in the house and had not uttered one word of condemnation about anything. Instead, she just listened quietly to her daughter when she wanted to talk, but always very persistent that she must eat. She also made sure Rachel had a hot whiskey at bedtime, stressing it was a good night-cap and might induce sleep. Rachel herself believed that it did seem to work, she did get a few hours most nights, which helped her face the next day.

Now this evening she was going to drive over to Matthew's house. She had decided to visit Jason at home rather than have him call and had rang earlier to establish he would be there, and when he himself had answered the phone he seemed delighted to hear from her. He assured her he would be home when she called and apologised he had been unable to call with her earlier. When Rachel replaced the telephone she knew Jason must wonder why she was coming and why she had been so anxious to talk to him. It was only to be expected that he would be curious. Lynn's non-appearance at university and not having called to see Monty, something she always did on a regular basis, and now Rachel ringing to make arrangements to see him. He was bound to wonder what was going on and Rachel was not looking forward to having to tell him. In many ways she hoped Matthew would be at home. Rachel felt his father might make things easier for her, simply because she felt Matthew already knew all about her house in Waring Street. After all, as a member of the C.I.D, it would be his business to know.

It was Matthew himself who answered the door when Rachel rang the bell. He greeted her warmly as he guided her into their cosy sitting room, where Julie and Jason were sitting with the Belfast Telegraph crossword spread out on the table in front of them.

After they had greeted one another, Rachel decided to be blatantly honest with her three relatives sitting in that room, who, she knew, were quietly wondering what the purpose of her visit could be. She did visit them from time to time and they did meet up frequently on family occasions. But they must know that the earlier telephone call to arrange a time indicated this was a formal, even serious visit.

'I needed to let you know, Jason,' Rachel had decided to address her words to Jason, to give him the respect he deserved. He had been a constant, loyal companion to Lynn since they had arrived here from Canada, and he deserved to be told the truth. 'Lynn has left home. Where she has gone, I have no idea. It is all because she found out I am a call girl, Jason. That is what I am.'

There was an audible gasp from Julie, and when Rachel looked over at her, she had her hands to her mouth and was obviously shocked by Rachel's statement.

'I know Rachel, I have known for some time.' Matthew stated quietly and then crossed the room to Julie. Sitting beside her he held his wife's hand and held it fast. As an awesome silence filled the room, Rachel got to her feet, desperately anxious to move somewhere, anywhere, the quiet was so stifling.

'I wanted to tell you Jason, the reason Lynn left so suddenly. You have a right to know the truth. You and she have been close friends. I have already told Uncle John about her departure, as I wanted him to help me find her.'

Suddenly Jason became aware Rachel was leaving and with a couple of strides he was beside her. Throwing his arms around her he kissed her on the cheek.

'I too, suspected what you were doing for a living. On one occasion when I called to see her in the shop Lynn showed me the opulent bedrooms. I did wonder about them, but I knew Lynn was very naive about it all, and I had no wish to plant any suspicions in her head. So I asked no questions about anything. But it makes no difference to me, Rachel. It is all your own business. I am more concerned about where Lynn has gone. I've been hoping every day to hear from her or see her and I couldn't understand it. And what do you think she will do about her degree? Do you think she has finished with that? I hope not, she was so keen at the beginning to succeed. Has she money with her? Will she have to go to the bank to withdraw some?' Jason turned to his father as the questions just spilled out of him, 'Dad, would it be appropriate for you to keep an eye on Lynn's bank account? And see where she draws her money from.'

'We will leave that for the moment, son. Let's wait and see if Lynn contacts one of us. Surely she will. She must know we would be very worried about her.'

Rachel made no reply, she knew how Lynn had been last Saturday evening, and she did not hold out much hope of hearing from her.

Julie, who seemed to have recovered somewhat from Rachel's statement, said she would make tea for the four of them. While she was in the kitchen, Rachel said she would take Matthew's advice and wait before rushing into looking at her daughter's finances. When Julie returned with the tea and some fruitcake, she seemed her usual self and said she would not be judging Rachel regarding her job, and she was welcome in their home anytime. Rachel thanked her and after she had drank some tea, having politely refused the cake, she wished them goodnight, with assurances to Jason that if she heard anything she would let him know.

Driving home Rachel reflected on how tolerant Matthew and his family had been. She knew it should have cheered her somewhat but all she really wanted was so see Lynn come through the door.

CHAPTER 30

'Constable Patton, will you set up the interview room for me this morning, I want to interrogate the Caughey boys and hopefully I'll start around ten a.m. I want to see them separately and I'm going to start with Seamus.'

Matthew had arrived at Crumlin Road prison at around 9a.m. He had received the official report about Bernard Caughey's pistol that morning to his office, and wanted to waste no time in getting to the bottom of the three IRA crimes he had been charged with solving. 'Are you free this morning, Constable, I would like you to be with me during the interviews with these men. It will be good experience for you David, just to watch if the suspects begin to crack under the strain. It is the cowards who usually do, you know,' Matthew paused, 'but I also want you with me because you take good, precise notes. I like that. What do you say?'

David Patton was delighted to be working with Superintendent Hampton again. He had only done so once before, but he had learned a lot from this man. His calm, patient approach to everything, and his astuteness and subtlety in leading the culprit into a trap intrigued him. There was no doubt the superintendent was talented at what he did, and he was highly thought of in his profession.

When Matthew entered the interview room at ten o'clock sharp, he was pleased to see the prisoner was already seated on a chair at the table where Matthew would be facing him. Constable Patton was seated adjacent to Matthew, three glasses of water had been placed on the table and Seamus Caughey was drinking one of them. He seemed nervous already, Matthew thought, and that had probably a lot to do with him giving instructions for the prisoner to be brought in at a quarter to ten, so he had had fifteen minutes to wait and wonder about his fate.

Matthew pulled up his seat and looked Seamus Caughey squarely in the eye, and for a second or two, he felt pity for him rise in his chest. How could such a personable young man, on the threshold of his life, become involved in terrorism and help deliver such violence and horror into the community. Surely this young person had been brain-washed. Then Matthew thought of his father gunned down with, he was sure, the pistol that was sitting on the table. He thought of the four Protestant civilians, their lives cut short by the same gun. But most of all he thought of the Belvedere Hotel, of the twelve innocent people killed, of his son's injuries, and then Amanda King and the trail of events that evolved as a result of her injuries. His heart hardened and he was once again the steely, determined inspector, resolved to get justice for those innocent people. Carefully and calmly he now withdrew the diary from his briefcase – the diary that had been found in the phone booth – all the time keeping a steady gaze on Seamus Caughey.

'Good morning Seamus,' in spite of his feelings Matthew's voice was affable and pleasant. The man facing him just nodded dumbly in response. 'Now Seamus, you know what you have been charged with don't you?'

Seamus Caughey just nodded again, and remained silent.

'Sorry, we need you to speak. My constable here must record an answer.'

'Yes, sir.' the answer now was low, almost a whisper.

'You are charged with planting a bomb which killed twelve innocent people and injured thirty -two others. You are now also charged with the shooting of four Protestants in a public house outside Belfast, and yet another man six years ago on the steps of a solicitor's office.'

Seamus Caughey was now deathly pale and seemed to be struggling for breath. Quietly Constable Patton refilled his glass from the jug and the prisoner gratefully drank from it.

'Now, I know you are responsible for three crimes, Seamus. I can only say if you confess everything to us here this morning, we will make sure you get a more lenient sentence.' Matthew paused to allow Constable Patton to take notes. Then fingering the diary, he said. 'This is yours isn't it Seamus?' There was no response. 'It is inscribed to you on the flyleaf, look,' and Matthew pointed to the inscription.

'Yes, it is mine.'

'Do you know where it was found?'

'Yes, I did try to ring from that phone, but it was broken you see. The line was dead,' and now Seamus Caughey was sobbing bitterly, 'we didn't mean to kill anybody, we didn't want anyone to die. The phone wouldn't work, that was the problem. That's what went wrong. We had to do it you see, since my brother made the mistake of shooting Mr Hampton all those years ago – instead of the policeman – we've had to do terrible things. Like the pub at Milltown and then the hotel. They said they would kill us, you see, if we didn't, and if we made any more mistakes. So we were trying to hide from them, you know, in that derelict place.'

It had been so easy in the end, Matthew thought, when they led Seamus Caughey away back to his cell where he would now await trial. Bernard Caughey was then ushered in. As he entered the interview room and looked at Matthew, he visibly paled and began to shake. And immediately Matthew knew this was, without a doubt, the man who had shot his father on the steps of that solicitor's office seven years before. Matthew knew Bernard Caughey recognised him straightaway. And how could he not? He had been shown photographs no doubt of Matthew, he had been informed of Matthew's movements. He had come armed that day to shoot him, but because of Matthew's father's bravery, Matthew was still alive, and now stood facing his father's murderer in this room.

Initially Bernard Caughey tried to bluff his way out of everything, but then Matthew showed him the diary and the pistol, with the analysis proving it had been involved in previous shootings. When he heard that his younger brother had already told them everything he too, pleaded guilty to the bombing of the Belvedere and to the shootings in the public house. He strongly denied having had anything to do with the shooting outside the solicitor's office seven years before. And Matthew knew this man meant to try to prolong Matthew's and his family's agony over their father's death.

Later that evening Matthew called with the remainder of his family to inform them that, even though the man was denying the charge, he had caught the man responsible for Rob's death. The first person he called with was his mother and Tom. He always thought of his mother's second husband just as Tom, he had never got used to thinking of him as his stepfather. It was Tom who opened the door to him.

'Hello, Matthew, good to see you.' Tom stepped back to allow his stepson to enter. 'I suppose you're just finished for the day, at half seven at night. It makes a long day for you.' Tom talked on as he led the way into their comfortable drawing room. A room which was still untouched since his father had decorated it. Matthew knew his mother liked it that way. Now he made his way over to her, where she sat reading the evening paper. He kissed her warmly and after enquiring how she was, he told them both he had important news for them. 'Today, I have finally charged two men with dad's murder, mum,' and suddenly Matthew's voice shook as he spoke. Making an effort to control himself, and hugging his mother fiercely, he went on. 'Bernard Caughey is denying the charge, mum. But I think we will be able to prove in court beyond reasonable doubt, that they were responsible. One drove the car to the car park outside the solicitor's office and the other one fired the shot.' Ellen and Tom were both silent as they tried to digest this news, and for Ellen, the whole horror of her husband's murder unfolded there in that room. She wept openly, something she had not done for some time. Quickly Tom was at her side hugging her and doing his best to console her.

'Why did they do it? And now, why do they want to deny it all, Matthew? Why?'

'I have no answers, they were given information by Patrick Mullan and when they supplied it to their supervisors they themselves were made to act on it.' Then Matthew proceeded to tell them about the other charges against them, the four

Protestants enjoying a quiet drink and the guests at the Belvedere Hotel rounding off a wonderful day after an innocent dog show.

'It seems they were made to do these other atrocities because of the mistakes they made over father.' As Matthew talked and Tom's words comforted her Ellen had managed to regain her composure. She looked at her son proudly.

'You have been wonderful in all this, Matthew. How you have survived it all and kept your head regarding your job, I'll never know. You deserve a medal.'

Matthew felt a warm glow encompass him at his mother's words and then he said, more light- heartedly, 'I think I will have a drink with you and Tom, mother. I'll leave my car here and get a taxi home. Then I'll collect it in the morning.'

'Good thinking Matthew, I'm delighted to hear it.' Tom was already on his way to the drinks cabinet. He could look forward to a drink with his stepson, it was something they so rarely indulged in, except at Christmas and perhaps at someone's birthday.

'I'll just ring Julie and let her know where I am, and why I'm here. I was meant to call with Lucie and Thomas and Charles but you could ring them later Tom. Tell them the bare bones of what has happened and then I will call with them all tomorrow and explain everything. I intend to take time off tomorrow.' Matthew suddenly remembered something. 'Also I need you to ring Aunt Maggie, Eva and Dorrie. They were dad's sisters and they need to know too. I'll also call in with them, not that Dorrie will understand. Sometimes I think she doesn't seem to remember what happened to dad. But maybe she is better not remembering.'

Tom reached Matthew his drink, then set Ellen's sherry on the small table beside her. Matthew noticed it was his favourite tipple, whiskey and soda, a taste he noticed he shared with Tom.

As he sat there that evening in May 1978, he thought it was most appropriate he should have this quiet celebration of his achievement with his mother and Tom. Yes, his mother was the most important person this evening, in his opinion.

CHAPTER 31

'John, I know everyone is doing their best, but if Lynn doesn't want us to find her it's going to be very difficult. So please, try not to fret on my behalf. To be honest, I have become much more accepting of Lynn's rejection of me. After all, what else could I expect? So yes, I am beginning to accept it.' Now Rachel changed the subject. 'It's good news about the arrests of the Caughey brothers. Each of us must hope there is, at last, going to be some justice for Uncle Rob. I know Patrick Mullan is still serving his sentence but the family felt that until they actually apprehended the person who pulled the trigger that day, they could not lay everything to rest.'

'I agree, Rachel. Even Dorrie showed some flicker of interest, of memory, that day I told her about the Caugheys. She kept repeating "Poor Rob. The IRA, you know, the IRA." Certainly she had some recollection.' John felt that his wife deserved to be treated the same as other members of the family, and had decided to tell her they had arrested the men responsible for Rob's murder. It was over a week now since their arrest and John understood from Matthew that the trial would begin in August. 'Do you see much of Lucie and Paul these days, Rachel? Living so close I always imagine you do, but I suppose with you all working it's not like that.'

'I've seen a fair bit of them recently and Lucie tells me she and Matthew are as close now as they were before their father's death. It seems Matthew understands why Lucie took pity on Patrick Mullan, her ex-husband. Matthew told her he felt pity for the younger brother Caughey. A young lad, with his whole life ahead of him, a life he should be enjoying. Now ruined because of how he had become drawn into a life of crime. Matthew realised his sister must have had similar feelings when she saw Patrick Mullan in that hospital bed, after his suicide bid. So, yes, Lucie sees a lot of her eldest brother and that is good.'

John realised that although Rachel was genuinely happy for Lucie and Matthew, she was thinking of her estrangement with her own daughter. John fervently hoped their separation would not last for six years.

'Actually, before I go, Rachel, my real reason for calling round to-day was to let you know I visited Gerald King in prison yesterday. It was not easy.' John was reluctant to relive anything of his visit yesterday, just remembering facing the man who had murdered his son, and who had also been prepared to let his other son take the punishment.

'John how awful for you,' somehow Rachel felt responsible for John having to visit Gerald King, knowing he had probably gone to find out if his daughter Amanda knew if he had visited Rachel in Waring Street. John's next words confirmed what Rachel had thought.

'He told me he had confessed everything to his wife; Leo's murder, his coming to you at night, and he also told me his wife had told Amanda everything. He was aware too, that, according to his wife, Amanda had taken great pleasure in telling Lynn all about you. I'm sorry, Rachel, but I had to tell you. Now we know the source.'

'It's no more than I suspected. Lynn left here immediately after coming from visiting Amanda. But I must not hold any spite against the girl; we don't really know how she has reacted to everything that has happened to her. I'm certainly in no position to judge anyone. And it all boils down to it being my fault. But I'm still glad you told me.'

'I notice Maggie hasn't appeared back into the lounge since I arrived. Does she purposely leave us together to have a chat, do you think?'

'Maybe so, I never thought much about it. But yes, she is usually in here at this time. It's eight o'clock and she usually makes tea around this time, and then goes to bed around nine-thirty.'

'Please ask her to join us, Rachel. I don't want her to feel I don't want her here.'

'I'll suggest she has tea with us before you go. I'll put the kettle on now.'

'After I have a word or two with Maggie and a cup of tea, I'll have to make my way home to relieve Rhoda and Alan. They want to go out for a drive later. It's Rhoda's birthday next week and Alan wants her to pick a good restaurant for her celebration. She will be nineteen, her last teenage year, so they want to celebrate. Alan says he'll bring some wine to the house so we can share a drink together before they set off.'

'Sounds pretty serious between them, don't you think?' Rachel was making the tea in the kitchen and spoke to John as she prepared the tray for the three of them.

John stayed for another half hour, not wanting to appear in a hurry when Maggie appeared for some tea. She talked at length about the men who had been arrested and how wonderful Matthew had been to find the evidence to arrest them.

As John made his way back home along the Shore Road, he thought a lot about Rachel and Maggie and how much they must miss Lynn. She had always been such a young, vibrant presence in the house and the place must be so quiet without her. Then his mind wandered on to Amanda King, and he wondered at the complexity of the human mind. What had driven her to tell Lynn anything about her mother? Was it the trauma she had come through and the ordeal of skin grafting still to come which had unbalanced her? Perhaps she wished to see others suffer as she was doing.

Amanda looked at the clock on the mantelpiece for about the sixth time. It was Saturday afternoon, and it was now a fortnight since Lynn had called to see her. She had fully expected Jason to call before this, even if it was just to tell her that Lynn had left home. Her mother had told her about it last week after returning from visiting Amanda's father in prison. It transpired that an uncle of Lynn's mother had called to see him at the prison and had told him about Lynn leaving home.

Amanda's mother seemed vague and ignorant as to the reason why Lynn had gone, but Amanda knew, without a shadow of a doubt, it was because of what she had told her about her mother.

She was disappointed at Jason's non-appearance, but she had made up her mind that if he did not come to visit her to-day, she would ring him next week and ask him along for tea. She could afford to be patient. She knew he cared about her. Why else would he have gone back into that blazing hotel to rescue her, and then to visit her so faithfully in hospital? The feelings he must have for her just had to be nurtured and she intended to do just that.

Jason had not considered going to visit Amanda in the near future, if at all – as far as he was concerned she was well on the road to recovery. Initially he had been very interested in her progress simply because he had rescued her, and had spared her the same fate as her fiancé. Besides, now he spent his spare time checking taxi drivers with descriptions of Lynn in an effort to jog some-one's memory. But he always drew a blank. Then he resorted to writing letters to Lynn, letting her know that whatever her mother did for a living did not matter to him, nor it seemed, to other members of the family. In those letters he always told her how much he loved her and missed her. Letters which, of course, accumulated in the desk in his bedroom. He had no address to send them to. His only consolation was Monty, his dear prize winning collie. He spent considerable time with him, brushing him, going for walks and teaching him new, innovative tricks. When he mentioned Lynn's name, the dog looked at him with such understanding in his limpid, brown eyes that Jason knew the dog missed Lynn almost as much as he did.

His parents had been very understanding about Lynn and the effect her absence had had on Jason. And when Jason pestered his father to look into Lynn's bank account in order to trace her, his father assured him he would give it some thought.

Lynn's cash was running low and the time was soon coming when she would have to go and draw money out of her bank account. She had mixed feelings about touching any of it. Even though some of it was hard-earned through her working to sell the lingerie in her mother's shop, she still felt it was money her mother had earned through her illicit dealings and had lodged it in Lynn's bank account for her. She had discussed it at some length with Tracey, after they had arrived at her friend's apartment in Glasgow. When Lynn saw the spacious flat situated on the ground floor of just six apartments, and when Tracey had shown her the spare bedroom, Lynn had been adamant that she must pay her some rent for such a lovely room.

'This is beautiful, Tracey. I couldn't just swan in here and expect such luxury for nothing.'

'Well, if it makes you feel better, Lynn, you can live here rent free for just two weeks, then I'll start charging you for your accommodation, say £15 per week. I expect you'll have a job by then. As I told you when I first met you, the news goes on about the unemployment in Glasgow, but believe me, there is work if you know the right people, so leave it to me.'

True to her word, Tracey, at the beginning of Lynn's third week with her, arranged an interview for Lynn with the owner of a restaurant and cafe whom Tracey was acquainted with. It was a cafe by day and then upstairs, there was a restaurant which opened in the evenings. It was quite a high-class concern and initially Lynn only worked in the cafe by day, but then the proprietor, a Mr. Simpson, told her he was quite impressed with her customer skills and offered her work in the restaurant in the evenings. Lynn readily accepted Mr. Simpson's offer; she reckoned going out to work in the evenings might ease her loneliness and sense of homesickness. Tracey had a boyfriend, who she saw from time to time in the evenings, but also Tracey's work was such that she worked long into the evenings, and often Lynn went to bed without having seen her friend that whole day. So Lynn had come to dread the evenings, it was then she longed to speak to Jason, to go to his home, to accompany Monty and him on their walks.

She longed too, to speak to her grandmother, and to chat over her usual cup of tea and slice of toast in the evenings. Indeed, if she were honest with herself, she missed her mother's companionship and easy chatter when her mother had come in from work. Many times she was tempted to ring Jason, but knew that if he were questioned about having heard anything from her, he would not be able to tell an untruth. It was not in his nature to dissemble. So she tried to keep herself occupied, she kept her room meticulously tidy and always arranged her clothes for the next day. So, even though she knew the work in the restaurant would be more challenging than the cafe was, Lynn was looking forward to it and was grateful to Mr. Simpson for giving her this opportunity. And another good thing about the move was that, of course, she would be earning more money. Mr. Simpson had assured her that the pay in the restaurant was so much better than that in the cafe, and he would discuss it with her further when she started. She had decided to open a bank account here in Glasgow, and forget about, in the meantime, the bank account her mother had opened for her. She intended to pay Tracey £20 per week for her room. It wasn't only the use of a bedroom she had, but the run of the whole apartment. There was no doubt Tracey had done everything she could to help Lynn cope with all she had discovered about her mother, and the changes to Lynn's life, as a result of such news.

Tracey seemed to Lynn to instinctively know when Lynn was feeling low and regretting not talking to some of the family before she had departed in such haste. Tracey, in those times, always managed to lift Lynn's spirits, assuring her she was young, Jason was young, and she was optimistic that they would get back together some day. They would renew their friendship when the time was right.

Most days, Jason came home from university after his lectures, on the pretext of writing up his notes for that day, but the truth was he waited eagerly for the phone to ring and rushed to answer it in the hall. After all, Lynn knew when his lectures were, how long each session lasted and he was convinced she must ring him soon. When he heard the girl's voice say, 'Is that you, Jason?' for a split second his heart lifted. Then he realised it wasn't Lynn after all. It was Amanda King, wondering why he had not called to see her. She was so looking forward to a visit from him and bringing him up to date about all her treatments. She sounded so eager to see him, that before he knew it, he had arranged to call with her the following Saturday afternoon.

CHAPTER 32

'Lynn, there's a programme on at eight o'clock tonight about the troubles in Northern Ireland and they specifically mention the Belvedere Hotel atrocity.' Tracey was scanning the daily paper to see what was on television, something she did every evening after work. 'Would you be interested in watching it? Or perhaps it might be too painful for you.'

'I think I'd like to see it, Tracey. Just to see how the programme is handled. I'm sure they'll tell us something about the latest atrocities that have happened.' It was October and Lynn had been in Glasgow for six months now, she worked three late evenings each week in Mr. Simpson's restaurant and three days in his cafe. She was glad she was kept so busy because it helped her stop thinking about home. She had, in a moment of weakness, a couple of weeks ago, dialled Jason's home number. When she heard his mother's voice on the other end of the phone, her courage deserted her and she replaced the receiver. Now she wondered if she had left it too late to contact him. He must resent her for her callous behaviour in leaving him without any explanation, and all because of her mother. If only she had sought him out before she left she could have explained everything to him. Now, when she reflected on her behaviour, she believed Jason would have understood and he would have kept her secret as to where she was. They could have kept in touch somehow. Now she was heartbroken about him and as the days went by she missed him more and more.

The first part of the programme talked about the latest atrocities. The commentator highlighted the killing of an RUC officer and the kidnap of another in June. The programme also showed the damage done to an RAF airfield when four planes were destroyed. Then he announced that they had two special guests this evening who had suffered in the Belvedere Hotel bombing some months before, a young lady who had been badly burned and the young man who had so bravely gone back into the inferno to rescue her. And Lynn could only watch, numb and mesmerised, as the announcer introduced Amanda King and the young man who was supporting her was Jason Hampton, her hero, who had risked his life to bring her to safety.

Tracey turned to look at her friend and was alarmed when she saw her white, stricken face. She immediately rose from her seat, turned the set off and turning towards Lynn put her arms round her and held her close.

'I'm so sorry, Lynn. I never dreamt such a thing would happen. How very stupid of me.'

Lynn shook her head. 'It's entirely my own fault, Tracey. You did ask me if I was sure I wanted to see it and I did say yes.'

Tracey stood quietly beside Lynn for a moment and then said. 'You and I are going to open the bottle of brandy I got last Christmas. It's been languishing in a cupboard in the kitchen ever since.' Tracey proceeded towards the kitchen. 'I know neither of us drink alcohol very much, but we're going to change all that tonight. We both need it, you especially, Lynn, and besides, you're off work in the morning.'

Lynn had never tasted brandy before in her life, she had had the odd lager or glass of sherry on occasion and that was all. But she found the brandy to be a delicious drink and Tracey and she had a few that evening. The programme about Northern Ireland was not brought on to the television screen again. The set remained silent, and Amanda King and Jason were not mentioned. And Lynn knew Tracey was giving her time to digest what she had seen and what it might all mean. Later, after they had locked up for the night and retired to their bedrooms, Lynn fully expected that sleep would elude her; that she would tumble and toss half the night. But she hadn't reckoned with the effects of the brandy and the amount she had actually consumed. As soon as she had undressed, put the bedside light off and slipped into bed, her eyes became heavy with sleep and she could feel herself drifting off.

'How do you feel this morning, Lynn? How did you sleep?'

Lynn opened her eyes at the sound of Tracey's voice and feeling guilty, quickly sat up in bed.

'My goodness, what time is it?'

'It's just gone nine o'clock. I've brought you some tea and toast, if you're up to having it.'

'I'd love some.' Lynn answered 'and in answer to your questions, I must have slept all night and I feel fine this morning. That brandy's some stuff, it must have knocked me out.'

'It's good, good in a crisis,' Tracey said 'but not on a regular basis, I think. It has achieved what I wanted it to achieve for you, and that was a good night's sleep. I think everything seems so much worse at night. In the cold light of day things don't seem as bad. At least, that's what I always feel.'

Lynn thought about what Tracey had said for a moment, but knew she still felt the same this morning as she had felt last night when she had seen Jason with Amanda. Jason was lost to her and that was the stark truth, and no doubt because of her own bad behaviour.

'I'm really grateful, Tracey. It was the right thing to do, and to be honest, I enjoyed sharing a few drinks with you. I don't think everything has hit me yet about Jason, but I will say this, I'm glad I'm working in the cafe later today. I need to keep myself occupied.' Lynn looked over at Tracey. 'I have to accept what's going on in Jason's life and his reasons for doing anything. I know I have only myself to blame for everything. But now, I think the time has come to close the door on all that and move forward, instead of looking back on what might have been. If I don't do that, and do it soon, my life will be empty and meaningless.'

'That's the spirit, Lynn. Do you want to slip on your dressing gown and have your tea in the sitting room? I have a cup sitting in there. I don't know about you, but I hate breakfast in bed, all those crumbs getting down your nightdress and into the bed. I brought the tea in expecting you to be under the weather, but that is not the case. Now, my first work appointment is for eleven o'clock this morning, so we have a little time to relax and pull ourselves together in the sitting room.'

Amanda was very pleased how the television interview had gone that evening. When her consultant, who was responsible for the suitable dates and sites for her skin grafting, had first asked her how she felt about taking part in a television programme about the Troubles, she had been very dubious about it. Her arms, upper body and forehead were badly scarred as a result of the burns, and because she had lost so much of her hair in the fire and new growth seemed so slow, she was currently wearing a wig. But when the consultant assured her she would be suitably dressed and well made up to minimise any scarring, she eventually agreed. She had given it all considerable thought, but maintained she would only appear if the young man who had rescued her was also asked to participate. She also insisted that the consultant must ask Jason personally to attend. Mr. Fleming assured her he was more than happy to do this, as he felt that Jason Hampton deserved to be there and his name made known to the public.

Jason was quite taken aback when Amanda's consultant rang him and asked him to participate. Because Jason felt he had only done what anyone else would have done, he told Mr. Fleming he did not relish such an interview. But when Mr. Fleming talked at length about that terrible night and the number of people who had been killed and injured, and how important it was for good news and good deeds to get the utmost prominence on television, Jason had agreed.

On the evening of the programme Jason found he was nervous about talking to people he could not actually see, and he was very self-conscious when the moment arrived for Amanda and him to enter the studio. He was taken aback too, when Amanda insisted she needed his arm to help her into the studio. She said she was feeling quite unwell, and made some reference to it probably being the tablet the consultant had given her to calm her nerves. But Jason had noticed Amanda had become more and more demanding towards him recently, ringing him a couple of times during the day and most evenings. After the show was over and they were on their way home, Jason resolved to be more forthright with the girl. He would have to make it clear to her that the only reason he had gone back into the Belvedere Hotel that fateful evening was simply because he had felt guilty that he had not guided her and her fiancé out with Lynn and him. He would make it clear he was concerned for her welfare because she had suffered so much both mentally and physically. He would tell her he admired her courage in how she was coping with her injuries, and also the devastating news she had had to bear regarding her father. But one thing he was intent on telling her, and that was the fact that there was no other girl for him but Lynn. He would let Amanda know that he had been trying to find Lynn and that he would never rest until he had found her.

'Well, Lynn I have to say, I am really surprised, you going out for dinner with Mr. Simpson,' Tracey had been rather shocked when Lynn had arrived in from work and informed her she was going out with her boss for dinner the following evening. 'I always thought Mr. Simpson was a married man. I don't know why I thought so, maybe just his age, I guess.'

'He's not that old, Tracey. In his late thirties, I think. And he was married, but he is now divorced, or separated, waiting for his divorce, I think.' Lynn talked on, anxious to reassure Tracey. 'Besides, I'm only going for dinner with him. Not embarking on a torrid love affair.' She knew her voice sounded sharp, but she needed to put matters straight with Tracey.

'I'm delighted Lynn that you are beginning to move forward and have a bit of a social life here in Glasgow. But I don't want to see you getting hurt again. That's for sure.'

It was a month now since they had watched the programme with Amanda and Jason in it and since then Lynn had only confided in Tracey on one occasion. Then she had made it clear she must forget about Jason and his relationship with Amanda. She did say she believed Amanda had told her about her mother simply because she was jealous of Jason and her relationship. She wondered too, she told Tracey, if he ever found out that his new girlfriend had told Lynn her mother was a call girl whom her father had visited frequently.

Lynn came home early from the cafe the following day. Mr. Simpson had told her to stop work at five o'clock instead of six as he would be picking her up around seven o'clock and she needed time to get ready. The restaurant her boss had chosen to take her to was situated in the suburbs of Glasgow and set in its own grounds. It was approached by a wide sweeping drive bordered by yew trees on either side. Lynn had to admit, as Mr. Simpson came round to her side to open her door and help her out of the car, she was very apprehensive about the evening ahead of her. The whole place looked so salubrious and so expensive that she felt out of place in her black crepe short-sleeved dress, the only decent dress she had thought to pack that awful Saturday afternoon when she had left Northern Ireland behind. But she need not have worried, Arnold Simpson proved to be the perfect gentleman, he praised her appearance, emphasising how appropriately she was dressed for the occasion. He introduced her to a delicious sparkling wine, which they had as accompaniment to their four course gourmet dinner. Later when he drove back to Tracey's apartment and left Lynn right to the front door she glowed with the memory of a lovely evening. She had never had an evening like it; Arnold Simpson had introduced her to a whole new world, and one which she knew she could enjoy very much, and one which she was also very much in awe of.

CHAPTER 33

'Oh, Lynn, I do hope you will be very happy, but I also hope you are sure you know what you are doing.'

Lynn had sprung the news of her engagement to Arnold Simpson just a few minutes ago. Tracey and she had just finished their tea, after having both come in from work about an hour before, when Lynn had fished in her handbag and produced a small jewellery box. Inside the box lay a magnificent solitaire ring which Lynn immediately put on her finger.

'Arnold and I have been together a few months now and you probably think that at twenty, I'm too young. But believe me Tracey, I've grown up considerably in the past year. The only thing that saddens me is leaving you, and leaving this apartment, which was such a source of comfort to me.'

'I'll miss you terribly, Lynn, but if you ever need me, you know where I am.' Tracey could have kicked herself the minute she said those words. Why had she said such a thing at such a time in Lynn's life? But she did think Lynn was far too young, and wondered if all this with Arnold Simpson was on the rebound from Jason Hampton. If that was the case, there was real cause for worry. Just the same, she hastened to cover up her mistake. 'I mean, coming up to your wedding Lynn, you're bound to need some help and you only have to ask me. Do you intend letting anyone in the family know about your wedding? It is over a year now, Lynn.'

'Arthur knows nothing about my mother and her trade. He knows nothing of Jason either nor my experience in the Belvedere Hotel.' Lynn was adamant. 'This is a new life for me, Tracey. I have to forget the old one. So please, Tracey, no more talk of that. And we both want a quiet wedding. When I broached the subject with Arnold he too, said that was what he wanted because he had been married before.'

'Lynn, as you know, I've always gone along with your wishes regarding your family and that is still the case.'

Lynn reached across to Tracey and hugged her tightly 'And I have always loved and appreciated your care and sensitivity and always will. In the meantime let's celebrate. I bought some brandy on the way home to have a toast to myself. I remembered how much I enjoyed your bottle those few months ago. And this I hope, is a much happier occasion than that was.' With that Lynn got up and went into the kitchen, returning with two glasses and the brandy she had purchased earlier. She wasn't altogether sure why she had felt compelled to buy the drink, but for some obscure reason Lynn had felt the need for it tonight.

On the first day of December in 1979 Lynn married Arnold Simpson in a registry office in Glasgow. They had both agreed that because of Arnold's previous marriage, a registry office wedding was most suitable. Tracey and her boyfriend Brian were the only witnesses and afterwards all four of them went back to the beautiful restaurant where Lynn had had her first date with Arnold. Later that evening the newlyweds flew to Greece for a week's honeymoon.

When Lynn and Arnold had first gone out together to the high-class restaurant and Arnold had been so very attentive and gentlemanly to her, Lynn had never foreseen that they would soon be talking about, and arranging their marriage. Now here she was living in a brand new detached cottage a few miles outside Glasgow, in a small village called Biggar. The first day after they had returned from their honeymoon and Arnold had taken her to see the property she was disappointed how inconvenient it would be for her to get to work from there. When she broached the subject with Arnold, he smiled knowingly at her. 'Lynn dear, you no longer need to worry about any work, I intend to provide for you. Besides, it would not do for my wife to be seen to be working for me.'

Now today, as she looked out at her garden, bright with daffodils and crocuses heralding the beginning of springtime at last, she thought how picturesque everything was and how she ought to appreciate it instead of dwelling on how lonely she was. But then the winter had seemed so long, with a heavy fall of snow in March which made going anywhere almost impossible. But it was now the second week in April and everywhere was at last beginning to feel warmer and Lynn was thankful to feel the spring sunshine on her arms, she had felt chilled through for some time now. She believed that where Arnold and she were now residing was even colder than Glasgow had ever been and certainly felt colder than Northern Ireland had ever felt. How she wished Arnold had allowed her to return to work, but he had been adamant that that was out of the question. He told her her job now was to take care of the cottage and the garden, and make sure his meals were ready for him on his arrival home in the evenings. During the last couple of weeks Lynn had been glad to get outside and had worked hard in the garden, but every time she looked out, it seemed more daunting than before. She was convinced the grass and weeds grew a hundred times faster than any of her daffodils and crocuses.

During the four months of her marriage Lynn had tried to meet up with Tracey on several occasions, but between the inclement weather and her trying to arrange a suitable time to obtain a lift with Arnold, nothing had materialised. So in the meantime, the two friends made do with long telephone conversations, taking alternative turns to ring one another.

Today she had tried to ring Tracey several times but there was no reply. She had rang her at lunch -time, as Tracey had always told her to do because if she was not too far afield with her job, she tried to get home for lunch. She so wanted to talk to her, to tell her that soon she would not be complaining about being idle, instead she would be saying she had too much to do. She had suspected for a couple of weeks now that she might be pregnant, but now, after missing her second period and being very sick this last couple of mornings, she realised it was a fact. And there was no one she wanted to share her news with more than Tracey.

She prayed she would be able to make contact with her before Arnold arrived home. She wasn't sure what time that would be as sometimes he was delayed in the office for a couple of hours, but he always rang to let her know if he was going to be late. This particular evening she hoped he would ring to tell her he was delayed, she so wanted to tell Tracey before anyone. She would not tell Arnold until she had her pregnancy confirmed, because she felt he might begin to fuss unnecessarily about her condition. In the meantime she would keep herself busy by preparing his evening meal of steak pie and roast potatoes. She had just finished peeling the potatoes for the two of them when the telephone rang. 'It must be Arnold,' she thought, as drying her hands, she went to answer it. She said her usual 'Hello,' and quoted her number, but the voice at the other end of the telephone line was a strange, female one.

'I would like to speak to Arnold Simpson, please.'

'I'm sorry he's not home from work yet,' Lynn replied, puzzled as to who it could be. She rarely got a phone call from anyone to home who wished to speak to her husband.

'Home, did you say his home?' the voice sounded much sharper now.

'Yes, this is his home.' Lynn was beginning to feel a little uneasy.

'And to whom am I speaking?'

'This is his wife, Lynn.'

And Lynn felt her blood run cold and she began to feel quite frightened when the voice at the other end let out a loud, raucous laugh which went on, it seemed to Lynn, for some time.

'His wife, did you say?'

'Yes, of course, I am his wife and this is his home.'

The voice at the other end of the telephone had stopped laughing and now stated firmly and coldly. 'You can't possibly be his wife, my dear. You see, I am. I am still Mrs Arnold Simpson. No doubt he convinced you he had obtained his divorce, which is of course, nonsense.' And she stressed each word and syllable as she spoke. 'Tell him I rang, my dear, and tell him you might never have known had I not rang directory enquiries and asked for a number for Arnold Simpson. There aren't too many with that name, my dear. Tell him all that, will you, please?' And suddenly there was silence and then the dialling tone came through.

After the call ended, Lynn sat on the telephone seat in the hall for some time, numb and disbelieving about what she had just heard. It must surely be some crank she thought, maybe someone who liked Arnold, and just wanting to stir up trouble. Then she remembered Tracey's advice, to make sure Arnold's divorce was finalised before she took those steps into the registry office with him. When she had mentioned it to Arnold, he had been very dismissive and was quite annoyed at her for even suspecting he would take such a step illegally.

She was desperate now to talk to Tracey. She would be able to advise her about what she ought to do. Without much hope of success, she rang her number with such disinterest and sense of hopelessness that she was surprised when her friend answered. Somehow, Lynn was able to talk calmly and coherently to her friend, she knew it was vital she told Tracey how it was. She told her of her pregnancy firstly, and there must have been something in her tone of voice which prevented Tracey from cheering. Then she told her about the phone call. There was such a long silence that Lynn began to panic. 'Are you still there Tracey?'

'Of course I am Lynn. I am thinking. I want you to say nothing to Arnold Simpson tonight about either your pregnancy or that telephone call. I intend to visit you tomorrow. I'll get a train, then a bus. It's Tuesday and Arnold will be at work. Please do not tell him I intend to come to see you.'

'Oh, that would be wonderful Tracey.' In spite of everything Lynn was delighted at the thought of seeing Tracey. It lifted her spirits so much. She had missed her friend's companionship during the last four months. Indeed she had been deprived of any company, only that of her husband in the evenings. And now Lynn began to wonder had it all been planned and quite deliberately done, keeping her here, isolated from the outside world, because the truth of the matter was he was still married. And worst of all, if it were true, the child she was carrying was illegitimate, and she was, in fact, just Arnold Simpson's mistress. How was she to face him this evening, knowing all this? Trying to act as a loving wife when the truth was, with that telephone call and the truth of her situation during the last four months dawning on her, any feelings she had had for this man had died, crushed by the realisation of what he had done to her and their baby. He had done it all to satisfy his own selfish needs. He had done it all because he had wanted a relationship with her. The repercussions had never entered his mind. He had given no thought to Lynn's future. He had wanted her, he had made that clear all along, but Lynn had been adamant she would never sleep with anyone before marriage. So, in order to satisfy his lust, Arnold Simpson had found a way around all that. He would go through with a bigamous marriage. That was the answer for him. And suddenly Lynn thought of her mother and she longed, in that moment, to talk to her. To tell her she had had no right to judge her, for now in the eyes of the world, her daughter was a slut and to make matters worse would be bringing an illegitimate child into the world. In that moment Lynn felt she needed her mother and grandmother more than she had ever done. She had, through sheer impulsiveness made a total mess of her life, and at only twenty years of age.

Later as she moved about the kitchen, putting the last minute touches to Arnold's meal she concentrated on Tracey and her advice. When she heard his key in the door, and then his step in the hall she was able, after all, to greet him as if nothing had happened to change everything in her life and her future.

'Tracey, I have some savings. Arnold has been most generous with the house keeping money each month. I haven't even spent the half of it since he started to give it to me when we came back from honeymoon.'

Tracey had arrived over an hour ago by taxi and had booked the driver to come back for her around three o'clock. That had given the two girls plenty of time to catch up, and then to try to decide Lynn's future, in as much as Arnold Simpson might allow. Lynn had already explained to Tracey that she needed to get away from him. But where would she go? If she came back to Tracey's apartment he would seek her out in no time.

'Go and do that pregnancy test now, I have brought the kit that you asked me for. Before you make any decision to go, you need to know you really are pregnant.'

'Right, Tracey, I'll go this minute. I have no doubt it will be positive.'

When Lynn returned from the bathroom she just nodded quietly to Tracey.

'Does that change your mind about leaving, Lynn?'

'It has made me more determined now than ever to get away from the biggest mistake of my life.'

'Well if you are sure, what are we waiting for? Let's get you packed and you can travel back to Glasgow with me. And don't forget your bank book or wherever you have the money you have saved.'

'It is all in a drawer in my bedroom. I never got a chance to go to a bank to open an account. So he did me a favour by not taking me anywhere.'

'You will need to book into a modest hotel for a couple of nights, Lynn, you can't come to me. It is too risky. Then we will sort something else out. But let's get started to pack up your belongings.'

An hour later Lynn's two suitcases sat side by side in the hall of the cottage, the battered blue one she had left Northern Ireland with, and the new one Arnold had bought her for their honeymoon. In her haversack she had stacked her money together with her passport. Also in the corner of the bag, now quite crumpled, was a snapshot of Jason and Monty she had taken the day of the dog show. She had lifted it just before she left her bedroom in the annexe that Saturday afternoon. Now she was leaving someone again, but whereas the last time she had been broken-hearted, today she had the utmost sense of relief. And just as she had made sure her mother wouldn't find her, she would make sure Arnold Simpson never did.

CHAPTER 34

'Mum, this is something I really want to do. Everyone's talking about the good investment property is, and I have far reaching plans for it all.' Seeing the anxious look on her mother's face Rachel hastened to reassure her. 'No, Mum, I'm not planning on opening a brothel. Actually I have very different plans altogether.'

'Well, Rachel, I wish you would just tell me what they are. Put me out of my misery.'

'Firstly, I plan to knock both premises into one. That is, if I am successful in buying the one beside my lingerie shop. I know it is a much bigger house than mine, in fact, the estate agent told me it was originally two terraced houses knocked into one some years ago. I know Gavin will do a wonderful job with the renovations. That is, if I do get it. Then I intend to apply for planning permission to turn my own property and the big house into one, and change its use to a home for the elderly with dementia.' Rachel looked over at her mother, anxious to gauge a response to this idea of hers.

Several expressions crossed her mother's face before she answered. Disbelief, then surprise, and then Rachel saw a wonderful expression of pride there, as her mother crossed the room and hugged her. 'Rachel, I think that's a marvellous thing to do. You must have given this enterprise some thought.'

'You could say that. In fact, I began to think about it after Lynn left home. I wondered how I could ever make recompense for how I've been and try to do something more worthy. While I don't expect it will change how Lynn feels, she may in the future, not be just so ashamed of me. It was after many sleepless nights and a lot of planning I can tell you that I eventually came up with this. I have had a year now to try and figure everything out, a year since I heard anything from my daughter. This project has helped me cope, keep my sanity, I must say. When the house next door went on the market I felt, in some strange way, that I was meant to have it. I'll know today if my offer has been accepted. Now, mum, I want you to keep it all to yourself. No one, only Gavin, knows anything about my plans. But when it is all completed I want to offer Dorrie and Uncle John accommodation. When Rhoda and Alan get married in a few months' time, John won't have as much support in looking after Dorrie. Dorrie is not getting any easier. She has escaped a few times and wandered off, which is so very distressing for all her family. If I can help I intend to, to the best of my ability. As I've said, mum, the only one I've discussed it with is Gavin over dinner on a few occasions in the last few weeks.'

'I'm sure Gavin would be delighted and relieved to know you were thinking of giving up your present occupation. Has he ever talked to you about how he feels about it all, Rachel?' Maggie had been intrigued for some time about Gavin Finlay, and wondered how he felt about her daughter. Certainly they seemed to get on well together but there was no indication that either of them was very serious about each other

'Mum, I did tell him about my experience with the law in Canada but since that time he has never referred to it. Perhaps he can't bear to talk about it, or perhaps he's not interested in me enough to care.'

'I think he's very interested in you, Rachel. Just give him time, according to John his wife let him down very badly. So he's probably very wary of women.'

'Well, I have only known him for about a year and that is only over dinner or at the movies, or his occasional visit here. So we are certainly taking it easy with one another, and that's fine by me, mum. I'm anxious to get this new project up and running, and perhaps someday I'll see my precious daughter. Everything else can wait.'

During the past year Rachel had waited and hoped to see her daughter return home as if nothing had happened. Then as hope faded that she might return of her own accord, she depended on John to find some trace of her somewhere, but he, distraught on many occasions, had drawn a blank. Lynn seemed to have vanished into thin air. Then Matthew suggested keeping an eye on her bank accounts to see where any money was withdrawn from. But her bank accounts remained untouched but Matthew said he was not concerned for her safety, but rather thought, with her looks and capability she would find work, no matter where she was. Matthew felt it more likely that she had been one step ahead of them all and had purposely left her accounts intact. Secretly Matthew was amazed how Lynn had so readily wiped her family out of her life, including his son Jason, whom he knew was still very hurt that she had not contacted him.

Jason had confided in him that it was Amanda King who had told Lynn about her mother. Indeed the evening Jason had talked at length to his father, he said he was anxious to tell him about Amanda King. It transpired that soon after their appearance on television, Jason had gone to Amanda in order to make it clear to her how he felt about her, and that he felt she had misunderstood his feelings for her. He told her he just thought he should help support her through her illness and the loss of her fiancé, but it was Lynn he loved and would always love. According to Jason, it seemed Amanda had become very aggressive, telling him Lynn was no good and her mother was a call girl, one whom her father had visited regularly for sex. Jason had walked out of her apartment then, and had never gone back. But he had heard through gossip at Queen's that she had recently become engaged to one of the doctors who was treating her.

Matthew felt proud of Jason, how he had handled Amanda, it could not have been easy for him, but he had absolutely done the right thing. Amanda had treated Lynn appallingly that Saturday afternoon, and Matthew often wondered had she led Lynn to believe that there was something between Jason and her. She certainly seemed to be the jealous type and it wouldn't surprise him if Lynn had not been in touch for that very reason. After all, she could so easily have contacted Jason from some telephone booth or other, but that had never happened.

Matthew felt guilty about Lynn, he probably hadn't devoted enough time to looking for her, but he always believed she would eventually make contact and he still thought that. She was, after all, only just over nineteen and with that impulsiveness of youth he believed she might well return as suddenly as she had gone. He had had of course, a very busy time in his work, and now the trial of Seamus and Bernard McCaughey was due to start in two weeks' time and he had had a lot of preparation to do for it. Also his cousin Colin was due to be awarded compensation for his wrongful arrest, and he was still trying to persuade the man that he was well entitled to it. Colin was reluctant enough to claim, he said. He was, he said, only too happy to be free and to take delight in his wife and sons. Also the people who had believed in him and had promised to keep his job for him had been true to their word, so what more could he ask for?

It was only after several visits to him and Margaret that Colin finally agreed to claim, and to believe he might be entitled to it. Certainly he felt Margaret and the two boys were entitled to something – they had suffered far more than he had. He personally, because he knew he was innocent, knew it would sooner or later be proven to be so.

When Matthew left their home that day he wasted no time in going to Colin's solicitor, in case Colin might change his mind, and told him on behalf of Colin to enter a claim. Getting involved in claims and compensation was outside Matthew's remit, but on this occasion he felt it necessary to advise his relation as best he could. Certainly Colin was a most deserving case.

Before going home that evening Matthew decided to call with Uncle John and see how Aunt Dorrie was. He could also give him the good news that Colin had agreed to put in a claim. Matthew knew that John felt very strongly that Colin, his only son, was well entitled to compensation.

When he arrived at John and Dorrie's house, he noticed Rhoda was just parking her car in the street, obviously just finished work for the day. It was a quarter past six and he hoped he would not be disrupting the family's dinner time, but he did not intend to stay very long. He would like to let them know about the McCaughey's trial in two weeks' time. He needed to prepare them for the fact that, apart from the Belvedere Hotel atrocity, they would be charged with his father's murder seven years before and also that of four Protestants in a pub outside Belfast in July 1976.

Matthew waited for Rhoda as she parked her car and they walked up the short path to the front door together. Before they went in the house Rhoda turned to Matthew. 'I never know how things are going to be when I come home. Dad does his best but you see, mum seems to have become very wily. She just waits for any opportunity that arises to get out the door. I don't know how dad copes.'

'Only with your help, I hear. Rhoda – You and Alan.'

'We do what we can, but believe me dad gets the brunt of it all.'

Matthew nodded as Rhoda opened the door and entered the narrow hall which led to the kitchen and living room. Rhoda led the way directly to the kitchen, obviously that was the first place she headed for each evening. John and Dorrie were seated at the kitchen table and it was obvious John was under some strain. He was trying to persuade Dorrie to eat the stew he had prepared. But now he stood up, smiling, his hand outstretched to his nephew. 'Matthew, it's good to see you. I know you're a busy man, especially in this country at present. Let's go in the living room. Rhoda, you take mum through and I'll make tea.'

'No Dad, you go with Matthew. I'll make the tea and then bring Mum in. She's fine with me.' And Rhoda checked the back door was locked as she spoke.

'It's good to see you, Matthew.' John reiterated as they entered the sitting room and indicated a seat by the window.

'I'm sorry I'm such a rare visitor but I have been rather busy, as I'm sure you appreciate, John. But at least Charles and Thomas keep me up to date about how Dorrie is. Not the best, I believe, John, is that right?'

John nodded his head sadly, obviously unable to put into words how Dorrie really was. 'Your two brothers and their wives have been wonderful. Calling at all times to relieve me so I can get to the shops, even if it is only for the morning paper and a jar of coffee.' Then doing his best to make light of the situation. 'This is Dorrie's home, she has everything she needs here yet she spends her time trying to escape from it.'

'It's awful for you, John. I wish I could offer some solution, but nothing springs to mind. But at least I have some good news for you. But we'll wait until Rhoda and Aunt Dorrie join us, we need to share it with them.'

Just as if on cue, Rhoda appeared with a tray with tea and biscuits, and her mother following quite docilely behind.

When Matthew related the news about Colin and his compensation, they all agreed it was the right thing. Even Dorrie, for a brief spell, seemed happy and kept repeating Colin's name several times. And when Matthew told them the date of the McCaughey's trial and the charges against them, Dorrie clapped her hands and kept repeating 'Good, good.'

Just as he was preparing to leave, Rhoda came over to him and proudly showed him the diamond ring on her finger. 'Alan and I hope to be married in about six months time. I do hope you and all the family circle will be able to be there. That's all we want, just family.'

'I wouldn't miss it for the world, Rhoda, and I hope Alan and you are as happy as Julie and I have been,' and Matthew kissed his cousin, but all the time wondering what John would do without his caring, loving daughter to help with Dorrie.

As Matthew drove home his mind was full of thoughts of the whole family. Whether it was Rhoda's statement about just having family at her wedding or the impending trial of the McCaugheys, responsible, he knew for his father's death, he didn't know. But because of the nature of his work, he knew he had very little time to be close to his brothers, and he would have to do something about that. At least he had made it up with Lucie and visited her frequently, but then he had ostracised his sister for far too long. And always, as he thought of Lucie and Paul, his mind raced on to Rachel and Maggie living in their annexe without Lynn's presence there. It must be very difficult for Rachel. Perhaps if Lynn watched the news, wherever she was, and realised it was the trial of those who had murdered her great- uncle, never mind the Belvedere bombing, it might encourage her to contact some one of the family.

CHAPTER 35

Lynn had read the news earlier in the day about Seamus McCaughey and his brother Bernard and the opening of their trial. She intended to watch the six o'clock news to hear about these men who had been responsible for killing twelve people and injuring many others. She knew it was something she would have great difficulty listening to, but she was totally compelled to do just that. Her new flat mate and land lady was Brian's sister who Tracey and Brian insisted would welcome Lynn to her apartment until her flatmate returned from a cruise in two months time. And Lynn, after three days and nights in an extremely dingy hotel in one of the side streets in Glasgow, felt it didn't matter much where she went. Just as long as she didn't have to see Arnold Simpson again. When Tracey told her that he had been around to her apartment the very next evening after they had left the cottage in Biggar, Lynn knew he was quite determined to find her. Tracey also said the man seemed angry to find that Lynn wasn't there, and she was glad Brian had been present. But, she reassured Lynn, she had done a good job of convincing him she knew nothing about Lynn's whereabouts, and he had left then, seemingly satisfied with that. Before he left though he informed her he knew Lynn was pregnant. Tracey was narrating all this information via the phone in Brian's house, just in case Arnold had second thoughts about Tracey not knowing where she was. Lynn was mystified how he could have suspected she was pregnant, she had scarcely been aware of it herself. Suddenly she remembered doing the pregnancy test in the bathroom of the cottage, and in her hurry to pack she had left all the evidence behind her. The used strip lying in the pedal bin, and the open package on the bathroom shelf. She had meant to go back into the bathroom and dispose of everything, but in her haste to get away it had slipped her mind.

The knowledge that Arnold knew she was carrying his child filled her with alarm. She believed he would stop at nothing to claim the child. He had talked at length, on many occasions, how he and his first wife had longed for a child, but it had never happened.

So when Brian and Tracey told her about Avril's place, although it was in Aberdeen, Lynn jumped at the chance to get away from Glasgow. She knew, in spite of everything, she wanted this child. She wanted some part of herself that she could love unconditionally, and hopefully, he or she would love her in return. After all, she had no one now who could possibly want anything to do with her, never mind love her. She was a failure.

At least she had enough money saved both in cash from Arnold's generous allowance and also her savings from Rachel and her own parents. If she had to use it, well that was how it must be, but she intended to pay Avril handsomely for the room in her apartment. She had been here five weeks now and she and Tracey had decided not to meet up for some time in case Arnold was having Tracey followed. Lynn knew he had the money at his disposal to do that and she wondered how long it would be until he caught up with her. But surely here in Aberdeen she would be safe for a time. What she would do when Avril's flatmate returned in three weeks time she did not know. Lynn knew that the reality now was that she had no alternative only to strike out and get a place of her own and be independent, because that was how it was going to be for her.

This evening Lynn had made shepherd's pie for Avril and herself, followed by a light apple crumble. At least here in Aberdeen she felt free to go and shop, even if it was only for groceries. In Biggar she had been isolated from any shop, and depended on Arnold to take her during his free time. After the two girls had ate and cleared up the kitchen they settled down in the living room to listen to the news at six o'clock. It was dominated by the ongoing troubles in Northern Ireland. A

P.I.R.A bomb had prematurely exploded on a passenger train on the outskirts of Belfast, killing three people and injuring five others. Two of the dead were thought to be the bombers. As Lynn listened to the voice of the commentator she realised the trial of the McCaughey brothers had opened that day. They were charged with planting the device at the Belvedere Hotel on the night of the 17th February 1978. They were also charged with the shooting in July 1976 of four Protestant civilians in a pub. A further charge of shooting a Mr. Rob Hampton in 1972 was also read out. On hearing her great- uncle's name stated so clearly, Lynn's heart missed a beat, and her hand went to her mouth to stifle a scream.

'That is my adopted great-uncle, Avril. They have arrested someone for him at last. I never knew Uncle Rob, but I have heard so much about him and how brave he was the day the I.R.A murdered him.' Lynn paused and looked at Avril, who seemed stricken by this piece of news.

'I am sorry Lynn, what can I say? Although I hear and read about all the atrocities, it never seemed real until now. Now I have actually met someone who has had someone belonging to them killed. It is really horrible when you realise the number of people who, like you, have lost one of their family.'

Lynn was silent for a time as the rest of the news droned on endlessly. She was lost in thought, thinking of Matthew and how much this arrest must mean to him. Had he been the detective who had brought them to justice? He had always said he would never rest until he saw whoever was responsible, in the dock. How she would love to talk to Jason to hear from him how everything was, and how everybody felt about this latest development. She would give anything to be with them all at this time in their lives, but it was all too late. She could never go back now. She was five months pregnant, and although she had felt her mother and her 'profession' brought shame to them all, it seemed to pale into insignificance beside her own shame and humiliation.

'Would you not consider phoning some of your family, Lynn? Now is an ideal time to do it. Even if it is just to inquire how everyone is. It must be hard for them all.'

'I know that, Avril. How I wish I could.' Lynn's voice broke, 'but you see I have left it far too late.'

'It is never too late, Lynn, you are young, and I believe your family would be absolutely delighted to hear from you. In fact I'm sure they would.'

'I don't think they would want anything to do with me. I have to go it alone. I brought it all on myself and I have to bear it myself. So no, I cannot contact anyone.'

Avril just nodded at Lynn's words, trying to understand how this girl must be feeling at the predicament she was in. How was she going to cope on her own? Avril knew she was intent on looking for somewhere of her own to live. What then? How on earth would she manage? And there and then she decided she would have a talk with Tracey to see what could be done to help this young and desperate girl.

The following evening before Avril left the office where she worked, she rang Tracey's number and was relieved when she answered the phone. She told her about her concerns for Lynn and how she believed if some of her family knew how things were, they would be on the next boat over.

'Can we encourage her to ring someone in the family, even just to talk to them?'

Tracey now was even more concerned about Lynn, she would have preferred to have her in her apartment where she could really see how she was. Indeed Tracey felt if she was sure Mr. Simpson had stopped searching for Lynn, she would bring her back to her flat. Even though Brian had told her about seeing Arnold Simpson with a woman who answered the description of his first wife, or indeed his only wife, she was still uneasy about him turning up at her door.

'Avril, apart from rummaging through Lynn's diary and looking for a contact number, I have no idea where to look for her relatives. I know they are from Belfast, and I know there has been publicity about her great-uncle recently, and maybe if I made a few enquiries the next time I am in Northern Ireland I could find out something. But it is all very secretive as to where Rob Hampton lived, but then, of course, it was his son they meant to kill because he was C.I.D. , so there is no way they are going to reveal addresses and everything. In the meantime tell Lynn I intend to come some afternoon soon to visit. I'll try to make sure I am not followed by our Mr. Simpson.'

Lynn brightened up considerably at the prospect of seeing Tracey again, and she knew she could rely on her to help her find somewhere suitable to live, at least until her baby was born.

It was the following week before Tracey found the time and resources to visit Lynn in Aberdeen. In order to ensure she was not followed at any point along the way, she took short cuts, she went via country roads instead of motorways, and was relieved and assured that no vehicle of any description was tailing her. Many times during her long drive she wondered if there was any need for any diversions and checking her mirrors. If Arnold Simpson had renewed contact with his wife, surely that was a good sign, and would only mean he was prepared to forget about Lynn. But Tracey still wasn't prepared to take the risk and put Lynn in jeopardy. Although what Arnold Simpson could actually do, if he did catch up with her was any-one's guess. As far as she knew he was not a violent man, and if Lynn did not want to associate with him, there was little he could do about it. But of course there was the child, and he did have a genuine claim to it. And he certainly was in a better financial position to rear it than Lynn would ever be, and probably in any court, because of his standing, he could maintain she had been a willing accomplice to his bigamy. And that she had been the one to want the ceremony to take place.

When Tracey arrived at Avril's apartment it had just gone one o'clock, and when Lynn opened the door to her, Tracey was glad to see her friend looked quite composed, almost as if she was resigned to her situation. She smiled delightedly, and hugged Tracey and then led the way into the living room.

'It's good to see you, Tracey. You've no idea how much I have missed you.' Then went on eagerly 'I've made lunch of chicken salad, so let's eat before we start talking. I'm always hungry at the moment, so I hope you are too.'

'Well, actually, after that long and rather convoluted drive to get here, I am a bit peckish. I'll follow you, if you just show me the kitchen,' and Tracey set her bag in a corner of the living room before she followed Lynn.

Over lunch Lynn told Tracey that she needed to start looking for a place of her own that she could rent from someone, or ideally, if someone was looking for a companion, some housekeeper who would not mind the fact that she was pregnant. Tracey said she had heard of such situations, and they seemed to work pretty well, but then again maybe it was just some romantic novel she had read it in. She thought Lynn should just concentrate on getting a small apartment as soon as possible.

'I have been buying the daily paper most mornings since I came here, but so far I have seen nothing. Neither anyone looking for a companion or indeed a suitable flat.'

'Something will turn up I'm sure, Lynn. Just keep looking.' Tracey thought that looking for an elderly person who needed someone would be ideal, and preferable to Lynn living alone in God knows where. With no one there with her, anything might go wrong. 'I'll keep my eyes open for you, Lynn. I know we need to be careful where you do go.'

Lynn nodded, Tracey was right. She needed to be careful where she ended up. She knew her baby's welfare depended on it. 'As usual, Tracey, you're prepared to help. And I tell you now, if I am ever in a position to help you out, I'll return all your kindness to me twentyfold.'

CHAPTER 36

'I made some fruit scones earlier today, Rachel. I'll make tea and we can have the scones with butter and jam. I thought they would make a change from my usual toast.' Maggie spoke to her daughter warmly, even before she had got her coat off and set her handbag down.

'Good idea, Mum. Any news of the trial, how it's going?'

'Yes, good news and bad, but I'll make the tea and then tell you what the six o'clock news said. But I'm sure we'll hear it again on the ten o'clock.'

'I know that, but it's hard to wait until then. I've been so busy clearing up after all the workmen had gone home that I'm late as usual.'

'Well, hold on a minute or so, then I'll bring you up to date, and you can tell me how your project's going.'

While her mother made the tea and hot, buttered scones for supper, Rachel hung up her coat and set out clean clothes for the next day. At the moment she was always getting covered in grit and dust and needed to shower vigorously and change her clothes every day. Besides she liked to spend some of the day discussing the renovations with Gavin, and she liked to look her best when he was there.

When she returned to the sitting room her mother was sitting in her favourite chair and the table beside her held the tea and scones.

As she reached Rachel her tea, Maggie said directly. 'The McCaugheys have pleaded guilty to the Belvedere Hotel bombing.' Maggie hesitated as she looked at her daughter; she was waiting expectantly, her face tense and white. 'I just thank God, mother. Thank God for that. I hope they suffer in prison as all the people suffered that awful night. But sure, they had to plead guilty, the shoe treads at the window matched theirs, and then of course the younger one's diary in the phone booth placed him right there.'

Maggie nodded and went on, 'They have, however, pleaded not guilty to the shootings in the pub and also not guilty to the shooting of my dear brother, Rob.' Maggie had been shocked to hear the men plead not guilty to these murders. Surely they must know they were damned here too. She thought of her nephew Matthew, and how much he needed to obtain a guilty verdict for his father's murder. She doubted if they would have been accused of these shootings without indisputable evidence. But now it seemed, they were all going to have an agonising wait while the trial continued.

'Mum, I would have every faith in Matthew and his team here. He would never have brought the case if he even considered failure. He knows so much depends on it, even his own peace of mind must be of vital importance to him.'

'We'll listen again at ten o'clock, but now tell me about your day, and how the work is going.' Maggie was keen on this new project of Rachel's and knew that if she only had it up and running, it would give her a lot of prestige and respectability.

'Well, the men took the counter and all the shelves away from the shop area today. I want to make that the reception area with an office and bedroom and kitchen area for staff. The whole of the downstairs next door will house the sitting room, dining room and kitchen for patients. I have told you just how much bigger this house is, haven't I Mum?'

'I think you have mentioned it.' In fact Rachel had told her mother so many times about the dimensions of the house next door, but considering that it had actually been two houses, it was not surprising that Rachel thought she had got a bargain. In fact she was delighted with what she had paid for it and was looking forward so much to the whole new enterprise.

'When it's all ready I'll have ten bedrooms – five single rooms and five double rooms.

So I hope to be able to accommodate fifteen elderly people. One of the double rooms will have a small sitting room, kitchen and bathroom. All the rooms will have their own bathrooms, of course. I have considered all the advice the health authorities gave me during the alterations. I can't afford to fail Mum, I have put so much money into it all.'

'I know that all right, Rachel, but I'm sure you won't. Such a home is badly needed and by the sound of yours, it is going to be quite exclusive.'

'That's the aim,' Rachel said, 'John called today and I have told him all my plans. But I haven't mentioned Dorrie yet. My idea is to have them both there in the self-contained flat in the place. But it may not be what he wants, you know. I really don't know. But now that Rhoda and Alan are getting married in November he'll have to get help with Dorrie.' Rachel said, adding, 'The good news is that Colin's case for compensation is to be heard on the 3rd of September. That's only three weeks away. So let's hope that goes well, for they really deserve it, after what they have gone through. The money he gets, Colin says, will help with his children's education.'

'Talking of education, did you know Maggie that Jason wants to become a barrister and intends to go to the bar? I'll say this for the young man, I still believe he loves Lynn, even though he has heard nothing now for nearly two years. According to Matthew, he says he shows no interest in any girl. But Matthew believes he's just wary after his experience with Amanda King. By the way,' Rachel went on 'Amanda King has married her doctor and according to someone in university, a wonderful job has been done with her scars. She too, deserves happiness after all she has gone through.' Rachel didn't elaborate on this statement but many times in the past two years she had wished Amanda had told her daughter nothing about her. She believed, had she had the chance to tell Lynn herself, she would still be here with her.

Rachel felt her one source of happiness now was during the times she met up with Gavin. They still continued to go out to dinner or to the movies and occasionally Rachel invited him to tea at the annexe. They enjoyed one another's company and could talk easily about a lot of subjects. Gavin had confided in her everything about his wife's betrayal and although initially Rachel had told him about her brush with the law she had never mentioned her divorce. But once Gavin opened up to her about his wife, she told him how her husband had felt the disgrace and stigma so deeply that he demanded a divorce, even though he had been aware of her occupation for years. Gavin always listened avidly to all Rachel told him but he never passed any comment about his feelings on the subject. Their relationship consisted simply of these evenings which ended with a hug and a kiss between them, before bidding each other good-night. Rachel felt she was content enough with his company and his affection for her. After all, what could she expect? She could never, in her wildest dreams, imagine anyone proposing to her again.

Gavin was delighted when Rachel successfully bought the house next door to number 10, Waring Street. He was looking forward to starting work on it to enable her to open up the small but select, nursing home. He had been quite surprised when Rachel first mentioned it to him and what her ambitions were. She went on to explain how she wanted to make some recompense to Lynn if she ever did come back home.

'It's so brave of you, Rachel, to take on a totally new enterprise, but I'll help you all I can to make a success of it.' Gavin looked at her searchingly. 'I hope you know that,' He had called round to the annexe to discuss when he and his team might start the work. It was late when he had arrived, and Maggie had gone to bed.

There was something in his tone of voice, a tenderness, which rendered Rachel incapable of speech. She just nodded soberly and reached for his hand.

Gavin squeezed her hand and held it tightly until she had recovered. How he would love to offer this woman much more than his skill as a builder and his company a few evenings a week. But the truth of the matter was he had a fear of a future with her. He had tried this last year not to mind too much that Rachel entertained men for money, but the truth of the matter was, he did mind. He minded very much, he was just simply, inordinately jealous. He needed her to himself; he did not want to share her with anyone. When he thought of her youthful, lithe body, her azure blue eyes and her thick, abundant brown hair falling to her shoulders, being enjoyed by any other man, he had always to try and block out the image and turn his thoughts to other things.

Now he held her hand and helped her to her feet. 'Let's go and have a look at this empire you've acquired and how we'll jointly transform it into a luxury home.'

Rachel, composed once more, followed him out of the door of the annexe, resolved to make the best of everything that came her way.

Lynn had had a rotten day and although it was still the middle of August, a cold wind had been blowing all day, bringing with it heavy persistent rain. She and Tracey had originally arranged to meet for lunch, but unexpectedly Tracey had rang Lynn earlier to say she had to cancel as something had turned up. Lynn thought her friend sounded very harassed, not at all like her usual calm self. But whatever was troubling Tracey, Lynn had no doubt she would hear all about it later. They were great confidantes and told one another everything, and Tracey had promised she would ring later. A telephone was the first thing Lynn had had installed in her new apartment when she moved in, the thought of going into labour and not being able to contact anyone struck abject fear in her. Her new home was drab and poky, but Lynn had been glad to jump at the chance of getting it, because she had been getting quite desperate. Now as she climbed the two flights of stairs to the flat, she wondered if Tracey might like to call round for some supper. She would be really glad to see her, as sometimes the loneliness and bleakness of the place was difficult to bear.

Now she entered the small living room and headed straight for the electric fire built into the wall. Although it wasn't much use at heating the entire room it was useful if you stood close to it to warm your body, and dry your wet clothes. After removing her raincoat and sodden shoes, she went to the phone and dialled Tracey's number. She answered almost immediately and when Lynn told her she had bought a chicken pie and some sausage rolls, Tracey jumped at the invitation to drive round and join her for supper.

While she waited for her, Lynn set out the small folding table in the living room and lit a single candle which she set in the centre. She turned on all three bars of the electric fire and then sat down to wait for the sound of Tracey's car and for the pie and sausage rolls to be warm enough to serve. But it was when she was in the tiny kitchen at the back of the flat, checking on the oven, that Tracey's car arrived. It was only when she rang the doorbell that Lynn realised she was here already. When she opened the door Lynn was shocked at Tracey's appearance. Her face was blotchy and swollen and her eyes red rimmed – she had obviously been crying, and by the look of her, for quite some time.

'Oh, Tracey.' Lynn in spite of her bulk, drew her friend into the room and closed the door firmly. 'What on earth's the matter?' She led Tracey to the chair nearest the electric fire. Then Lynn noticed her friend had a bottle of something with her, which she handed over to Lynn.

'I brought that for us to have a drink. I need one, I can tell you. And you're going to have one as well. The baby's over eight months now, fully formed. No harm can be done to him or her. So get a couple of glasses.'

Although Lynn had her reservations about consuming alcohol, she reckoned Tracey was right and the baby would be fine. Besides, she had never forgotten the evening she'd seen Jason and Amanda King on television and how a few drinks had helped her through. Now for the first time in their friendship, Tracey needed her, and she had no intention of letting her down. She took the bottle, realising it was brandy, probably not such a good idea she thought, but determinedly went to the kitchen and fetched the only two glasses that were there.

'Right Tracey, here you are.' She poured a generous drink for each of them and drew her chair over beside her friend.

As Tracey took the drink from Lynn she seemed to pull herself together. 'It's Brian. He's been arrested. Arrested for drug dealing, right here in Glasgow. It happened early this morning. He actually came to my apartment about nine o'clock and said he fancied having a coffee with me, which I naively believed. But he was just trying to evade the police, I know that now.'

Lynn was totally stunned to hear this from Tracey. Brian had always seemed to her to be above reproach. He had a wonderful job in a car sales showroom; surely he would not become involved in the drug underworld.

'I can see you're shocked Lynn, but it's true. Before the police left with him, I spoke to him alone, and he admitted it to me. In fact, he admitted everything. The new car he has, that wasn't supplied by the car firm, oh no, he bought it with the money from his dealings. The house he has talked about for months, that he hoped to buy for me and him, he had already bought it a year ago, only he has another girl in it, living with him, might I add. What do you make of all that, Lynn?'

'I'm so sorry Tracey. I think what you're telling me would put me off men for good. We don't seem to have made very good choices, do we?'

That statement seemed to brighten Tracey and lightened both their moods. Lynn refilled their glasses, but then insisted they must eat the food she had bought earlier, before they indulged in any more alcohol.

After they had both ate, Lynn decided it would be best if she didn't have any more, but Tracey continued with an abandon Lynn had never seen in her before. She knew her friend was suffering from the loss of someone she had firmly believed to be honourable, only to be so cruelly disillusioned.

As the evening wore on, Lynn realised Tracey was not going to be fit to go anywhere, so she organised the two easy chairs, end to end and then fetching a couple of spare blankets she found in the cupboard, made her as comfortable as she could. Then Lynn realised that she was delighted that Tracey had to stay. She had missed living with her friend and even another presence to share the long nights with her. Before retiring to her room she made sure Tracey was comfortable, and that the fire and lights were all switched off. She was thankful to crawl into bed. She was suddenly very tired and had a thumping headache. No doubt due to the brandy.

She wakened suddenly, surely it must be morning she was so alert. Then she realised that a pain in her abdomen and back had wakened her. Switching on her light, she saw by her bedside clock it was only 4a.m. She was still so tired and she must try to get a few more hours sleep. Now she regretted taking those three brandies, no doubt they were responsible for the pains in her stomach. But an hour later Lynn still had not slept, and she realised she was in labour and needed an ambulance to take her to hospital. Climbing once more out of bed, which she had been in and out of several times in the last hour trying to ease the pain, she pulled on her dressing gown and slippers and headed into the lounge. Unfortunately she would disturb Tracey, but she had no choice for that was where the phone was.

When she put the light on in the lounge, Tracey was immediately alert, much to Lynn's amazement. She had seemed more or less comatose with brandy when she had left her. Now, when she saw Lynn cross the room and lift the phone, she was on her feet at once.

'You're in pain Lynn, aren't you?'

Lynn just nodded as she dialled and in a steady voice said who she was, stated her address clearly and explained she was in labour, although her baby was not due for another four weeks. When she had finished the call and replaced the receiver, she noticed Tracey was straightening her clothes and patting her hair into place.

'Where's your bag, Lynn? I presume you've one packed for such an event as this.'

'Yes.' Lynn doubled over as another pain surged through her. 'It's in the wardrobe in the bedroom.'

'I'm going with you Lynn. We seem to only have each other at the moment, so we might as well stick together. How long will the ambulance men be before they get here?'

Tracey was beginning to feel anxious; the idea of trying to help Lynn deliver her baby filled her with terror. She would have no idea what to do. She should never have encouraged her to have those couple of drinks, probably that had been enough to trigger labour, that, and all the annoyance of their conversations about Brian and Arnold earlier in the evening. Tracey was relieved when she heard the ambulance pull up outside the flat and the noise of footsteps pounding up the steps. She already had the door open before they had appeared on the landing. After been shown into the room where Lynn was now pacing up and down, the two men quietly and efficiently set her in an ambulance chair, strapped her in, then carried her carefully down the steps, with Tracey, after locking the door, bringing up the rear.

CHAPTER 37

Lynn's baby boy arrived about four hours later, during which time Tracey had waited patiently outside the labour room doors, trying to sober up with the help of a couple of plastic cups of coffee from the vending machine in the hallway. Around 6a.m. Tracey heard a sharp, ear-piercing cry from the labour ward, and then one of the midwives appeared and informed her she could go in.

'Oh my, Lynn, such a beautiful boy!'

Tracey was entranced as she looked at the bundle wrapped so securely in her friend's arms. 'His hair, well it's so blonde it is almost white, and those blue eyes.'

The baby's eyes were wide open, and seemed to Tracey to be considering her in some depth, and as she reached her finger tentatively to his chubby finger, he held tight to her.

'Lynn, he's so beautiful, and he looks so intelligent too. I can't believe he's only just been born.' Tracey looked at Lynn, who was lying back on the pillows exhausted, but with a proud look on her face. She nodded and smiled in response.

'Have you thought about what you're going to call him, Lynn?'

'I'm going to call him after my dad, who was killed. Lewis, his name was, and also Rob after my great-uncle who was murdered. I'm calling him Lewis Rob.' Then suddenly as realisation hit her, Lynn began to weep.

'Lewis will have no dad, just as I haven't had for years. I know biologically he has, but I don't want Arnold Simpson to know anything about him or have anything to do with him.'

Tracey hugged her friend, who still clutched her son at her breast, until she seemed more composed. But Tracey wondered how they would keep Arnold Simpson, who was the baby's father, from him.

'Between us we will look after this wee mite. I intend to help all I can. I'm expecting to be godmother, you know. I know he'll help me cope with my troubles too, Lynn. And we will both pray your Mr. Simpson has given up looking for you. There's been no sight or sign of him since he came to my apartment. In fact, I think when you are discharged from hospital Lewis and you should come to me for a few days. You'll need someone, and it would help me cope with my troubles, having you there. Or if you're not entirely happy with that, I'll come to your place.'

Tracey paused as she looked at Lynn. 'It's up to you, but you mustn't consider going to an empty house.'

Lynn looked relieved, Tracey thought, to hear this. She must have had visions of having to cope entirely on her own.

'Would you mind coming to me, Tracey? I'll order a bed for you out of that furniture shop in Howard Street. There's plenty of room in the bedroom for it.'

'If you'd rather I came to you, I have a folding bed I can bring over in my hatchback. I have your front door key, so I'll try to fit it in tomorrow. I have a meeting in the manager's office in the morning at 11a.m. but after that I am free. Now you get some rest, I'll call later this evening.'

Just as Tracey was picking up her handbag, two nurses appeared to tell Lynn baby Lewis was going to the nursery, and Lynn was going out to the general ward.

In the main hall of the hospital Tracey approached the reception and asked if they could recommend a taxi service to take her home. The receptionist offered to ring for a cab for Tracey, remarking she looked tired and pale, and the receptionist would request it to be here as soon as possible. Tracey realised she must look quite a fright, between her tears last night, her over-consumption of alcohol, and then the wait at the labour ward door, were all telling a sorry tale. Suddenly Tracey felt so weary; she felt she could not face any manager's meeting. She would ring when she got back to her apartment and tell Mr Black she was unwell and unable to attend.

She was relieved to see the taxi driver come through the swing doors, and soon she was ensconced in the back seat and heading towards her apartment.

She was just settling the fare with the driver when she noticed a car pull up and park just beyond where her taxi was parked. The man who was climbing out of it looked vaguely familiar, and with horror she realised it was Arnold Simpson, and he was coming towards her, a determined look on his face. Hurriedly she thanked her driver and watched him drive away before turning to face the man who had caused Lynn such heartbreak.

'We meet again, my dear.' The man was smiling so knowingly at her – he had almost a leer on his face. How had Lynn been so taken in by him, she would never know.

'I see you are just getting a taxi back from Lynn's dingy flat. You are not able to drive this morning then. Had a few drinks perhaps? I won't detain you. Just tell Lynn, my wife Iris and I intend to fight for custody of this baby when it's born. The dingy flat Lynn is in is no place for a child. My wife and I have a beautiful home, we are back together now. Lynn, it seems, has nothing and nobody, only you. I'm the child's father and will be able to provide more, I think, than Lynn will ever be able to do.' He went on, 'Tell her after the child's born I'll see her in court.' He then turned on his heel and walked proudly back to his car.

And all Tracey could think as she retrieved her apartment keys from her bag and let herself into her flat, was that at least he didn't know the child had already been born. He hadn't hung about Lynn's flat until the early hours of the morning to witness what had really happened. So Lynn and the baby had a bit of breathing space at present, but it was only putting off the awful reality and the real prospect of losing her baby to this man with all his wealth and possessions.

And Tracey, as she showered and dressed, began to feel very sober and she made the decision to go to work after all. This meant she would have to ring for another taxi to retrieve her car from outside Lynn's flat, instead of spending the next hour having a bit of a sleep. Work was what she needed; it might help her decide what to do for Lynn for the best. She knew what she wanted to do, she longed to contact some of Lynn's own folks and tell them the whole situation. She had no doubt they would jump at the chance to help, no matter what. She was due to go on another visit to some of the supermarkets in Northern Ireland and she would so love to find some of Lynn's relatives and talk to them. But she had no idea where to start to look for any of them. They lived in Belfast, somewhere in Belfast, but Belfast was a pretty big place. She had on one occasion looked in the telephone directory but no one with Lynn's surname sprang out at her.

'John, it's nice to see you.' Rachel was standing in the middle of her new sitting room in 10 Waring Street, trying to decide exactly where to place the easy chairs which two employees of Thomas Hampton's furniture firm had just delivered. This time when Rachel was furnishing the home for those with dementia, she had decided to give Thomas free rein to furnish all the bedrooms, the large and airy sitting room and the spacious dining room. Whereas before, when she had first arrived here from Canada and bought the house on Waring Street, she had thought it best to furnish the bedrooms from strangers. That way no questions would be asked about the purpose of the bedrooms. Now she was done with this dissembling and Thomas was delighted to be given the opportunity to demonstrate his skill in making the best of any room. He had wanted to do the whole thing at cost price, but this infuriated Rachel. She pointed out, rather sternly, that the reason she was giving him the business was to help him make a reasonable living. When she told him this, she was rather surprised and embarrassed when he hugged and kissed her, and told her she was one in a million.

Now she looked at John as he entered the room, she knew he would help her decide about the chairs. 'Help me place these where you feel everyone would be comfortable, and have a good view of the goings-on out in the street.'

'Of course I will, Rachel, but firstly I called to let you know that Colin's case will be decided today, that is, the amount of money he is to receive. It has already been well and truly established he and his family deserve considerable recompense for what he went through.'

'John, I'm so glad for you all.' And Rachel sat down on one of her brand new chairs and regarded her uncle. 'I am really delighted for Colin. I know it took some persuasion to get him to pursue the claim. I'm sure he's glad he did it.'

'I knew you would be glad for him, Rachel.' And John promptly sat down beside his niece in the chair beside her and no further thought was given to how the chairs should be placed. 'Be sure to listen into the news this evening. Somehow I imagine it would be quite a headline and a change from the usual terrorist related headlines in Northern Ireland.'

Tracey visited Lynn on her way home from work that evening. It was only five o'clock but she persuaded Sister in maternity to allow her in. She had to visit her this evening, because she was scheduled to go to Northern Ireland on the first ferry out in the morning, and she knew she was going to have a couple of hectic days, targeting supermarkets with the body lotions and shampoos she was marketing. Lynn sounded wistful when Tracey told her she was going to her home town in the morning in the hope of restocking a few of the supermarket shelves.

'How I wish I was going with you,' Lynn remarked as she gazed at her baby son sleeping in the cot at the side of her bed. 'But of course that is out of the question.'

'Have you thought anything more about contacting some of your family?'

Lynn shook her head. 'It's become even more impossible to consider it, Tracey. Here I am with a newborn baby and I'm not even married. You go on the ferry in the morning and I'll be thinking of you and that time, a couple of years ago, when I arrived here with you. So much happened in such a short space of time, but my son is the most important thing to have happened to me. I intend to make him my priority now.'

Tracey could think of nothing to say in response to Lynn's passionate statement, so with promises to see her on her return in three days time, they kissed one another good-night. Tracey fretted all the way back to her apartment at Lynn's determination, not only to look after her son, but also not to contact any of her family. As she let herself into her apartment, Lynn wondered if she should have let Lynn know Arnold Simpson knew where she lived. But she still felt it was better Lynn didn't know until she was ready for discharge, and that would not be for a few days yet. Arnold Simpson didn't know of Lewis's birth, so Lynn was safe in the ward and free from any mental stress which even thinking about Arnold Simpson would be likely to bring on.

She went into the kitchen half-heartedly; she had little appetite for food since her encounter with Arnold Simpson that morning. She found a pack with two baked potatoes from Marks and Spencer which quite appealed to her. She put them in the microwave and set a tray for herself with a small bottle of wine, a glass and a knife and fork. When the microwave pinged she put her potatoes on the tray, carried it into the lounge, and before sitting down to eat she switched the television on. The six o'clock news was just being announced as she began to eat her potatoes, having opened her small bottle of wine and poured it into the glass.

She sat bolt upright, almost spilling her precious glass of wine, as she heard the name Colin Finlay announced and saw the figure of a tall, thin attractive man come down the steps of the High Court in Belfast, accompanied by another man. As she watched, a reporter made his way over to the two men and asked Colin if he had any comment to make on today's proceedings. Colin Finlay looked at the other man and nodded. The second man directed his attention to the reporter and introduced himself as Mr. Steel, Mr Finlay's solicitor.

'Mr Finlay just wants to say he is happy with today's outcome and will be putting the money to good use.'

At this stage the potatoes and wine on Tracey's tray were forgotten and she listened intently for further information. She was bitterly disappointed when the two men continued down the steps of the High Court and the cameras stopped following them. Then suddenly the reporter who had initially approached Colin and Mr. Steel turned to the camera and stated, obviously by way of a recap:

'Mr Colin Finlay of 16, Balmoral Avenue in Belfast was awarded an undisclosed sum of money for wrongful arrest and imprisonment for the murder of his brother, Leo.'

At hearing this, Tracey jumped to her feet and drained the glass of wine there and then, the baked potatoes forgotten about. This was a real godsend, no doubt about it. Balmoral Avenue, why she knew it well. At last she had an address, and on the very eve of her going over to Northern Ireland on one of her routine trips. Maybe she was a brazen hussy to even think of going to Colin Finlay's house. Perhaps Lynn had been right, and her family may not want to know anything about her after two years. But Tracey was not prone to self-doubt and she fervently believed any, and all of the family, would be delighted to know about Lynn, no matter what the circumstances.

CHAPTER 38

'It is a substantial sum of money Margaret, indeed it is. And it is very important we agree what we must do with it.' Colin was in the dining room of his home in Balmoral Avenue and had just received confirmation that he was to be awarded £200,000 for his ordeal, in relation to his brother's murder.

'It might be an awful lot of money Colin, but you did come through a horrible time.'

'I never doubted I would be released, although never in my wildest dreams did I think it would be through Mr. King and his confession.' Colin paused, and taking his wife's hand, went on. 'I would like to donate half of this money to Rachel and her new home for the elderly, if you are agreeable to this. That still leaves us £100,000 for the boys' future. I happen to know, because Rachel actually confided in me one day, she would like to take mum and dad in there. Not of course that dad needs to go, but just so he would always be with mum. She showed me the quarters she had designed especially for them, and wondered what I thought of them. I can tell you, Margaret, it is all really lovely, so safe, so comfortable and so homely. I think she was using me as a sounding board the day she showed me it all. She seemed unsure if it would be what dad would want, but she thought he might help her with the running of the place and she would pay him a salary.' Colin paused, while waiting for his wife's comments, then went on, 'I do know Rachel has borrowed money from the bank for this project. It would be good if she could start out with no debt.' Again Colin waited for his wife to speak. 'You seem hesitant, Margaret, uncertain.'

'Uncertain, Colin? Why I think it is just the answer to your dad's problems. He has no life, and our help and everyone else's is so limited. He is still left with all the responsibility of your mother. This way there will be other, more qualified staff, I believe to help with the decisions regarding your mum.'

'So Margaret you wouldn't mind if we donated a sum of our money to the home?'

'To be honest, I don't mind if you decided to give it all, Colin.' Margaret answered. 'You have a good job. I'm well paid for the few hours I work which fit in so well with the boys' school times and other activities. So we are quite secure.' Margaret leaned forward and kissed her husband passionately.

'I do think we need to keep some for a rainy day, Margaret. We ourselves have had a few, so we'll save some of the money, just to be sure. I also intend to tell dad what I've done. I think he'll feel better about Dorrie and him moving into the home.'

'I do know the £100,000 that we'll be left with ought to be more than adequate for any future rainy day. And let us hope there won't be any more rainy days like the ones we've just had.'.

Colin just nodded and smiled then said, 'Make us both a cup of coffee before I head into work. I have had a couple of days off after the court case, but I have a few important matters to deal with in work and I'm quite eager to get back to the grindstone.'

Margaret disappeared into the kitchen to make the coffee, and after suggesting they might have it in the sitting room and watch the passing traffic, Colin made his way there. Just as he was arranging the small coffee table between Margaret's and his favourite chairs, the front doorbell rang. Wondering who it could be, and dreading some persistent reporter who would want to interview him about the money, Colin made his way reluctantly to the door. A young girl of medium build, with bright golden hair stood there, an anxious expression on her face.

'Hello,' Colin said, waiting in anticipation for the reason for this strange girl's visit. Perhaps she was some journalist, keen to get the latest news on Colin's compensation and eager to write a story about his arrest and imprisonment. But in the brief seconds he had to assess her, he instinctively knew she was not from any newspaper. Her uncertain pose and hesitation in speaking to him told him this.

'Mr Finlay?' she asked in a quiet voice.

'Yes.'

'I would like to speak to you for a moment. It is actually about your cousin Rachel's daughter, Lynn.'

'Lynn?' and Colin's voice immediately held an excitement, an air of disbelief, as he sought to answer her.

'Please, do come in,' and Colin held the door wide as he spoke.

He called to Margaret then, as he indicated their modest sitting room to this young, strange girl, who had after two weary years brought them news of Lynn.

'Margaret, please come through to the sitting room. A lady here has some news for us of Lynn.'

Margaret joined her husband then, with the tray containing the coffee, and the young lady introduced herself as Tracey. She explained she and Lynn were both residing in Scotland at present. She told them she had travelled on the early morning ferry from Cairnryan and was here on business, but after learning of Colin's address on the news, she felt compelled to call to let Lynn's family know she was safe and well.

When Colin and Margaret heard Lynn was safe, their first reaction was to telephone Rachel and let her know.

'But I have so much more to tell you,' Tracey said. 'I think you must hear everything before you ring her mother and grandmother.'

'I'll make you some coffee, then. We were just about to have some, before you tell us anything more.' And Margaret was already on her way back to the kitchen.

Later as Tracey related the whole story of Lynn, how she had met her, their companionship, her bigamous marriage and her new-born baby boy, Colin and Margaret listened, not once interrupting this girl's sad story of Lynn.

'You can see why I felt I needed to contact her family. I'm worried about her welfare and that of her child. Arnold Simpson means business, I know he does. I have kept Lynn's confidence for two years, but I felt the time had come for her family to know how things really are for her.'

'You have absolutely done the right thing, Tracey and I think perhaps the first person I should ring is my father. He was the one who was involved in trying to find her at the onset of all this. Then Rachel felt he should stop, simply because she reckoned her daughter had no wish to be found. Now I know he would be delighted to meet someone who has obviously been such a firm friend to her, and helped her on so many occasions'.

Tracey glanced at her watch as Colin spoke. She had already been here for almost an hour. At this rate she would be working until nine o'clock tonight, and would be checking into the guest house much later than usual. She knew she only had to ring and Mrs Frazier would leave a key for her in its usual place.

'I would be delighted to meet Mr Finlay.' Lynn had told her all about John Finlay and her mother, and she had been intrigued by their relationship. Tracey thought it was unlikely that Lynn's mother and John Finlay had had a sexual relationship. There was quite an age difference and they were related.

'Have you time now to wait to meet him? He only lives about a twenty minute drive from here. So I can either take you to meet him at his house, or I can ring him and ask him to call here. But he may not be able to leave my mother if no one else is there, so I think we should go to him, if you are agreeable.'

'I think that would be best, I'll take my car and you can give me directions as we go. Then I'll leave you back home, before returning to my day's work.'

Soon Colin Finlay and Tracey were settled in the car and driving out of Balmoral Avenue.

Following Colin's simple directions Tracey realised they were heading for the Shore Road, an area she had been on many times in her travels as representative for Sally's shampoos and skin care. To think in the last two years she had been so near to Lynn's Uncle John's home, if only she had known she could have contacted him. But then again, when she thought of Lynn, she wondered if she really would have done anything sooner. Somehow she doubted if she would, whereas now she knew it was important that Lynn's family knew what was happening, both for Lynn and her baby's sake.

On Colin's instruction Tracey turned into a wide street and noted the name was St Judes Avenue. And then Colin was telling her to pull in and park outside a row of neat, gleaming terraced houses. Colin waited patiently on the footpath as she locked her car, then joined him, and silently followed him up a short pathway to a shining blue, front door marked Number 12.

They waited patiently for a response to Colin ringing the bell, and then Colin said in a low voice, 'Father must be busy with mum.' And even as he spoke they heard steps in the hall, and the door was opened by a tall, thin, grey haired man with an anxious look on his face, which was immediately replaced by a smile as he spoke to Colin.

'Colin, how wonderful. I did not expect you. Where's your front door key then?' Then he noticed the young girl standing quietly beside his son. He looked at the girl, then Colin, but suddenly remembering his manners, he opened the door wide.

'Please come in. I did not realise you had anyone with you. I'm sorry.'

'Dad.' Colin addressed his father as they entered the narrow hallway which led to the living quarters. 'This is Tracey; she has brought us good news of Lynn.'

For a few seconds John did not speak, as he led them directly into the living room where Dorrie was sitting quietly, a blank expression on her face and fully dressed for the day. He remained silent until Tracey and Colin were both seated, and then he turned to Tracey, his face alight with hope and anticipation.

'Is Lynn well, is she alright?' His voice sounded extremely anxious.

'She is very well, Mr Finlay. Very well indeed.' Then Tracey looked over at Colin, seeking his approval to continue, and to put Lynn's Uncle John in the picture. John listened intently until Tracey had finished.

'Well, we'll have to get her back home here. This is where she should be. With her mother and all her family circle as support. I can't see any judge taking her son from her if she was here with us. But we need to act fast and get everything into motion. You never know, you never know what a man like Arnold Simpson would be capable of, if he wants his son badly enough.' John began to pace across the floor, pausing now and then to pat his wife's hand or put an arm on her shoulder. She just smiled blankly back at him.

'I'll ring Sheila. See if she is free to sit with Dorrie. Then I shall go round to Rachel's place and tell her all the good news.' John was smiling broadly at the thought of being the bearer of such news, after all Rachel's heartbreak. 'I need to know when you are returning to Scotland, my dear. I intend to go with you, in my own car, of course. And I think I shall ask Matthew's son Jason, if he would like to come too.'

For a moment Tracey was unsure if it was a good idea that Jason be brought into all this at such an early stage. Then she thought to herself, why not? Their relationship would sort itself out one way or another. Lynn's welfare was the number one priority. Tracey explained that she had to get to work as soon as possible, because she normally only stayed one night in the guest house in Lisburn, catching the 12.30p.m.ferry the following afternoon. So they would travel to Scotland on the Wednesday, although Lynn and baby Lewis were not being discharged from hospital until the Friday.

Colin and Tracey waited until Sheila Hampton told John, when he rang her, that she would be over to stay with Dorrie within half an hour. As they travelled back to Balmoral Avenue, Tracey expressed her relief at having had the courage to call with Colin when she did.

'I haven't told you how I came by your address, Colin. I was so anxious to tell you about Lynn, it just slipped my mind. I heard it on the television news, and I could scarcely believe how fortuitous it was for me. Now, I have to admit a great weight has been lifted from me. I didn't realise just how concerned I was for Lynn until now.'

'My dear, it must all have been quite harrowing for you. But hopefully, Lynn and her son will soon be with her family. I must say I also look forward to their homecoming. It will be quite something.'

'John has the telephone number of the guest house, and he is going to ring me at 10p.m. tonight to make arrangements for the Wednesday ferry, and then hopefully, it will be plain sailing from there. I have arranged that John and, whoever travels with him, will stay in my apartment on Wednesday and Thursday evening. But, of course, before they go to see Lynn, I have to confess to her what I have done.'

Colin nodded, 'You have done so much for her. What we can ever do to repay you for your constancy and support I really do not know. If you ever need anything, please do not hesitate to ask any of us.' As they turned into Balmoral Avenue, and Tracey parked the car at the edge of the pavement, they said their goodbyes with Tracey promising to call on her next visit to Northern Ireland.

CHAPTER 39

When John had contacted Rachel after hearing all about Lynn from Tracey, he had simply told her without giving her any further information that he needed to come round to the annexe and to ask Maggie to be there. He stressed it was not bad news but he had so much to tell her he had to tell her personally. It was, he told her truthfully some news he had just learnt from Colin. But, he added, until he saw her he did not want to say anything more.

'News about Colin, what on earth would Colin have any news about? I just don't know. He has heard he'll get his compensation in about a week's time and John assures me it's not bad news. At least that's something. John, Dorrie and the family have been through enough.' Rachel knew she was rambling on a bit, then as she paused in her talking Maggie said she would put the kettle on for tea for her brother-in-law, commenting as she did so, that he always liked a cup of tea and a slice of cake any time he called. As she made her way to the kitchen Maggie added, 'You're only speculating what it might be, Rachel. Best to sit down and wait until he comes.'

Rachel nodded, knowing her mother was right and she was only speculating, and that in itself was very stressful. So taking her mother's advice she settled down to wait for John. She was thankful to hear his step on the path outside and had the front door open before he had pressed the bell. When she looked at her uncle, there was something in his expression which made her realise, there and then, that it was news of Lynn. She whispered brokenly 'Is it news of Lynn?' John just nodded and smiled. Before he even stepped over the threshold Rachel threw her arms around him and hugged him. They stood together for a few moments until Rachel became more composed and John said, 'Let's go in, I'll tell you all about it and Maggie can share in the wonderful news. But it's quite a story, so I'll need you not to interrupt, in case I forget something.'

Before John had finished telling the two women all he knew, they were both weeping silently for what Lynn must have been through since leaving home some two years before. When he had finished John said quietly, 'Lynn's troubles are over, we hope, and I shall bring her back to her family this week. And this girl Tracey is very confident that that is all Lynn wants now, to be back with her family. I intend to take the ferry over to Scotland on Wednesday when Tracey is returning – we'll travel together. And I'm also going to ask Jason to come along. In the meantime Rachel, you need to decide if you want to travel with us or stay and welcome Lynn home to her own house. If you do decide to stay, you might decide to have a party by way of home-coming. It would keep you and Maggie occupied. I've given you so much to think about, but it is your decision whether to come with us or not.'

Rachel shook her head 'I would rather stay here and welcome her back home with Mum here as well. If she wonders why I'm not with you, please explain that to her.'

'Now, John,' Maggie had risen from her seat, the tears over, and said, 'I boiled the kettle some time ago. But you really must have some tea before you go.' John said he would have a quick cup, and then he must get back home to relieve Sheila.

'Who is going to look after Dorrie while you're away? I can help out if I'm needed, John.'

'I'll ask Rhoda to take some leave. I think you would be better here getting ready for Lynn's return,' John answered.

'Well, tell Rhoda that if she needs me for anything to please ask.' Rachel didn't add that Dorrie could have come to Waring Street, as she had already employed two trained staff, one for day, the other for night, even though she only had two elderly ladies in the premises. She had yet to discuss the possibility of Dorrie and John coming to the home permanently. She had still to find the courage to broach the subject, but hopefully she would soon get around to it. In the meantime, the very next person she meant to inform about Lynn was Gavin and ask him to her daughter's welcome home party and to share a few drinks with them.

Tracey had arranged to meet John and Jason at the docks around 12.30p.m. When John had contacted her on the Monday evening to finalise the arrangements for travelling to Scotland, he told her that his daughter Rhoda had taken time off work to look after her mother. Then he also told her Jason was insistent on accompanying him. It was a long telephone call because Tracey confided in John she was uncertain as to whether to confess all to Lynn before her friend would see John and Jason. After a rather lengthy discussion, Tracey, who was usually very confident when it came to making decisions, left it to John to decide what to do for the best. He thought the shock of seeing the two men, without any forewarning, might prove to be too much for Lynn to cope with. In the end it was decided she would tell Lynn that John was here in Scotland, but in the meantime, they would keep Jason's presence a secret. When they met at the docks and had driven their cars into the hold and made their way up to the lounge, John immediately ordered a brandy for each of them. As they sat sipping their drinks, Tracey asked Jason how he felt about the arrangement.

'Tracey, I understand fully the need to be sensitive to Lynn's feelings here. She must surely be deeply troubled about how things have turned out for her, and I, for one have no desire to add to her anxiety and apprehension. I have waited two years to be reunited with her and I can certainly wait another couple of days. Whether she will be as glad to see me as I will be to see her remains to be seen.'

Tracey looked at this young man seated across the lounge table in front of her and was amazed at how anyone, who looked so young and naive, with his dark hair swept back from his forehead, and his blue eyes so full of expression, should have such insight into Lynn's situation. In that moment Jason Hampton gained Tracy's utmost respect and trust.

Now she felt that when she visited Lynn later this evening, and tell her how she had managed to contact Uncle John, she would do this with a much lighter heart, knowing her whole family would welcome her back without recrimination. Confident too, that Lynn's feelings for Jason must be as unchanged, as his quite obviously were for her.

Even though Tracey had talked herself through the scenario with Lynn, when she would bring Uncle John in to stand beside Lynn's bed, it was with some trepidation that Tracey and he left her flat later that evening, with Jason contentedly watching television, and drove to the hospital. Self-doubt assailed her as the car wound its way through the streets of Glasgow and John remained still and silent at her side. It was almost as if he understood what she was thinking, and was leaving her alone to sort it out for herself. What if she had been very wrong about Lynn and what she wanted? What if she really wanted to remain independent and fight her own battles? But as she parked her car in the hospital car park, with a resigned expression on her face, she turned to John,

'Well, this is it, John, let's go,' knowing it was too late now to turn back.

'Yes my dear, let's go in. I'll wait in the front hall until you speak to Lynn, then hopefully you'll come back to take me to her, with a huge smile on your face.' And John was smiling confidently at her. That smile immediately made Tracey feel better and with firm steps headed for the ward. She entered the ward, the grapes and the magazines she bought earlier, in a tight grip in the bag over her arm, and walked down towards Lynn. As she approached her she noticed the swollen eyes and the red cheeks, and knew she had been crying. As she neared the bed, Tracey looked at the cot beside Lynn and was relieved to see baby Lewis sleeping peacefully, his chubby finger against his mouth.

'Oh Lynn, what is it?' and Tracey threw her arms round her friend.

'I'm alright, Tracey now you are here. I thought you weren't coming.'

'I am a bit late, I know, Lynn but that's because I've brought you a visitor.' Tracey was rewarded immediately, when Lynn's spirits seemed to lift at those words. Throwing all her doubts to the wind, Tracey went on, 'It is your uncle, or rather your great uncle, I should say, John Finlay. He is waiting in the reception area, anxious to come and see you.'

The transformation in Lynn, on hearing those words, was remarkable. She flung her legs out the side of the bed, and grabbing her dressing gown where it lay over the back of the chair, said, 'Someone from home, Tracey, how did you do it? Someone from home, how lovely.' And instead of making any move away from the bed, overcome with obvious emotion, she sank back onto it, her eyes full of tears.

'I'm going to fetch him now, Lynn. So just you wait there.' And with a sigh of satisfaction and something akin to elation, Tracey made her way back to the reception desk and with a huge smile on her face, just as John had predicted. Too overcome with emotion to speak, she quietly signalled to him to follow her.

When she indicated the bed where Lynn was now sitting upright, her eyes fixed on the doorway, Tracey stood still in the ward, in order to let John greet his grand-niece as he saw fit. As she watched, she saw Lynn reach towards him, and as if he were her nearest and dearest, and not just the great-uncle she suspected of having an affair with her mother – she put out her arms and kissed him in a desperate and very welcoming way. Then Tracey knew she had done the absolutely right thing, and had brought Lynn back from the verge of a deep depression, to hope and happiness for her and her baby son.

It was John who told Lynn at the hospital bed, how Tracey, on hearing Colin's news on the television and getting his address, had decided to make contact with the family. It was John who told her her mother and grandmother could not wait to welcome her and her baby son back home, emphasising they were already organising a welcome party. And all the time he talked, Lynn sat up in bed, her eyes bright with tears, but smiling happily at both him and Tracey. Then John, looking over at Tracey with a questioning look, as if seeking confirmation from her, stated quietly that another member of the family had travelled to Scotland with them, but was uncertain about when he ought to come and see her.

'Is it Jason?' Lynn was alert immediately. Uncle John had said 'he', what other 'he' might it be? 'Do say it is Jason.' She looked at Tracey in some desperation, but with some hope in her beautiful eyes. 'Do say it's Jason.'

'Yes Lynn, it is Jason.' This was the first time Tracey had spoken since John had sat down beside Lynn's bed. 'It is Jason, so anxious to see you, but sensitive as to how you might feel about seeing him.'

Lynn looked at her friend in a puzzled way. 'How I might feel? No one knows how much I've missed him. But I thought he and Amanda King were an item. I saw the programme on television, you know.' Lynn's voice tailed off.

'Amanda King is married to the doctor who was looking after her. As I understand from Jason, he told her how it was. That it was you and only you he loved.' John said in quite a straight matter-of-fact voice, which carried more impact than any emotional tones might have done.

'Please, when can he come to see me? I need to see him.'

'I'll get a taxi tomorrow afternoon, Lynn, and bring him straight to you. Then we'll make arrangements for your discharge from here, book the ferry for Friday and take you and your son home to Northern Ireland.' John turned to Tracey, 'I'm sure you have your job to see to, Tracey. So leave it to me to make my own way here tomorrow.'

It was only then Tracey realised that Lynn would be leaving Glasgow and leaving her in the next couple of days, and suddenly she was consumed by an utter sense of loss and loneliness. She no longer had Brian, not that she had thought much about him in the last few days. His behaviour had killed outright any feelings she had had for him, but still, she missed his presence and his company. But now Lynn was going home, back to Northern Ireland and all that Lynn held dear, and

Tracey would still be here in Glasgow with a huge hole in her heart which her brave, resolute friend had occupied for the past two years. And Tracey felt, as she looked at John, Lynn and her beautiful baby, that she was the one who would now be bereft and lonely. And the days would stretch endlessly in front of her, with no one to confide in, to commiserate with or laugh with. There and then in that ward, Tracey decided that she desperately needed a change. A challenge, probably well away from Glasgow and Brian, her hopes of marriage, and setting up a home for him. That had all been pie in the sky. He had never had any intention of marrying her and making a home with her. But what could she do? She only knew about selling products that people really needed, that people were going to buy anyway, because they needed them. So how successful was she really?

The following evening Tracey visited Lynn in maternity at her usual time. It was a very different Lynn who sat at the side of the bed, telling her all about Jason having been to see her in the afternoon. He had hugged and kissed her, and seemed quite taken with baby Lewis, Lynn told her. He then went on to say that they would take the relationship very slowly, and see how it all went. Tracey listened with a full heart to all Lynn was telling her, and said she was absolutely delighted how things seemed at last, to be working out. Then she dropped her own bombshell when she told Lynn she had given a month's notice to her firm, and intended to come to Northern Ireland with the intention of setting up a small shop. This shop would be exclusive, specialising in good quality skin care and beauty products for women. She went on to tell Lynn she had a fair amount of savings, but would probably need to borrow some from a bank in order to get started.

'Tracey, you are actually coming to Northern Ireland. I seem to be going to have everything now, my family and you. It is all too much, it really is, you know.' And Lynn was smiling broadly at her friend, – 'so we certainly won't lose contact, you'll be in the same country as I'll be.' And Lynn's voice held an exciting note as she talked.

'I'll need you Lynn, when you get home to look out for suitable premises for me. I don't want you idling away your day with nothing to do. You can start to help me and the sooner the better.'

Lynn was about to protest that she would not get a minute, with looking after her son all day long. Then she realised Tracey was joking, and they both began to laugh, as neither of them had laughed for some time.

'I know someone who will just love looking for premises for you, Tracey. My mother would love to do it, and I'll ask her as soon as I've settled back at home.' Lynn looked at her friend. 'Just imagine Tracey, I'm going home.'

CHAPTER 40

On the Friday morning, the day Lynn was coming home with her baby boy, Rachel thought as she climbed out of bed, that things had a habit of not going according to plan. Throughout Wednesday evening and all day Thursday Maggie and she had worked hard to prepare the bedroom for Lynn and baby Lewis. She and Maggie had decided to share a bedroom, and that meant moving a single bed from Rachel's room into her mother's. She had then gone out on the Thursday morning, after enlisting Colin's wife Margaret's help, to purchase a cot and pram for her grandson. The cot fitted neatly enough into the boot of Rachel's car, but the pram would be delivered early on Friday morning.

Margaret and Rachel were in the process of erecting the cot, and making it up with new blue cot sheets and blankets they had also purchased, when the telephone rang. Rachel was surprised to hear Colin's voice on the other end of the phone telling her that Rhoda had had a slight accident in the house earlier that morning and had suffered a broken ankle. She needed a minor operation to put everything into place so that meant she would be kept in overnight. That obviously left the problem of their mother, and rather than ask anyone in the family to stay, Colin wondered if she could be admitted to Rachel's new home for the night. He knew she would be well looked after by the registered nurse who was in attendance, and if Rachel would agree, he would bring her there in a couple of hours' time. He was at his mother's house at the moment, and would get things organised for her. Rachel readily agreed to Dorrie coming to Waring Street and even as she talked to Colin, her mind was racing on. She would have her aunt admitted to the suite she had been secretly keeping for

John and her. Rachel herself would go there tonight, and sleep in the room with Dorrie. It was the least she could do, she decided. After all, John was in Scotland preparing to bring her daughter home.

After replacing the receiver, she went in search of Margaret and explained what had happened.

'Look we've a room ready for Lynn and the baby. I'll get mother to ring all the family, and tell them there's a party here tomorrow evening. If they could help out with a little food and wine, it would be appreciated. I'll also tell mum to explain what has happened, and why I am a bit behind in organising things. But I do think, Margaret, you should go to Dorrie's house now, and help your husband with packing a few things for his mother. I'll be at the home when you arrive.'

As Rachel dressed in the room where Dorrie was lying in a single bed close to the large picture window, she was relieved that both she and Dorrie had had a good night's undisturbed sleep. Dorrie was still sleeping soundly, even though the hands of the clock were creeping towards 9a.m. Rachel made her way downstairs into the small office she had organised early on in the renovations. Both the nurses were there, and when they saw Rachel, the night nurse explained she was just giving a report to Lorna, the day nurse. Rachel told both girls that Dorrie was fast asleep but would need to be up and dressed shortly. Then she said she really must go, but if she was needed, to ring her immediately. After checking that her two other patients, who occupied a twin bedded room were safe and comfortable, Rachel felt reassured as she left the home in Waring Street, that given time, she should make a success of the place. After all she had only opened her doors three weeks ago and already she had clients. Only two of course, and Dorrie, but even so, things were beginning to fall into place. Now she felt as if a great cloud had been lifted from her. Lynn was coming home, John had contacted her yesterday morning and he sounded so elated, that Rachel knew Lynn would soon be with her and her grandmother again. Hopefully when she heard about the home for the elderly, she would realise that Rachel had done her best to turn her life around and try to make some recompense for her past. They had a lot of ground to cover and bridges to build, she knew that, but they would take it easy with one another. She fervently hoped Lynn had forgiven her for her past 'profession' and that she would perhaps no longer feel so ashamed of her mother. Most importantly in the midst of all the activity going on and even though Rachel was most reluctant to admit it to herself, Gavin Finlay was still steadfast in his presence in her life, even if he had not expressed any deep feelings towards her.

Maggie was hard at work when Rachel entered the kitchen, she must have been up so very early. Two Victoria sponges stood cooling on the tray, and she was so engrossed in rolling out pastry, she did not hear Rachel come in.

'Mum, what time did you get up at? I don't want you overdoing it and then you won't be able to enjoy the evening.'

'I'm fine, Rachel, put the kettle on, and I'll just finish rolling out this pastry. I have the apples all ready and I'll soon have the tarts in the oven. Also, I made some porridge for us, it's on the cooker.' Maggie nodded towards the saucepan on the hob. 'I rang Ellen and Tom, Colin and Margaret, and Thomas and Charles' wives. They're sorting out different items between them to bring later. Lucie said Paul and she would supply the drinks. So we're well organised I think.' Maggie was rather proud of herself, how well she had managed everything and everybody during Rachel's absence. 'Oh, and Julie is going to bring the napkins and she said she would make some salads, then come early and help set everything up.'

'Maggie, you've done everything. You've left me nothing to do.'

'Well I didn't know what sort of a night you'd have with Dorrie. So yes, I got up early and got organised for my granddaughter coming back home.'

'Dorrie slept all night, after she settled down. She was restless until around midnight and then she became very calm and restful'.

'Well, after we get our porridge and tea, we'll go down to the room and have a rest before everyone starts to arrive with food and drink.'

'I hope we haven't forgotten anyone mum, but I think family will be more than enough for Lynn to cope with. Don't you?' Maggie wholeheartedly agreed, saying she was sure Lynn would be overwhelmed at such a welcome and homecoming.

Lynn could scarcely believe she was on her way home. Seeing her Uncle John coming into the ward, then to meet up with Jason the following day all seemed so unreal, and so far removed from how she had envisaged her discharge from hospital with her newborn son would be. She hadn't been looking forward to returning to her bleak flat and having to negotiate two flights of stairs on a regular basis with a baby. The only saving grace about that had been the fact that Tracey would have been there with her, if not during the day, at least at night.

Now, as Uncle John drove through the heavy traffic along the road to the docks, Lynn was sad she would not see Tracey for some time. Although she had given a month's notice to her firm, she would have to sort out the lease of the flat and the storage of her furniture until she acquired premises in Northern Ireland, and that might take some time. Lynn had promised Tracey she would have her mother shop hunting for her as soon as she arrived home.

She hadn't realised how much she had missed her mother during the last couple of years, until one of the midwives had asked her when her mother would be coming in to see her new grandson. Lynn had broken down then and told the midwife she had stormed out on her mother two years before but now she was going back home to her, and to Northern Ireland.

The midwife had hugged her and said, 'Aren't you the lucky girl then, going back to your mother? And your mother is a lucky woman you are returning home, some daughters just go off and never return. And your mother will be delighted with her new grandson, all women love grandchildren. Just you wait and see.'

And the midwife had been so cheery and confident that Lynn's reticence about meeting up with her mother had eased considerably.

After a three and a half hour trip on the ferry, and then almost another half hour in John's car, they eventually turned into Malone Avenue and were soon pulling up outside the annexe of Julie's house, where Lynn had spent such a happy time with her mother and grandmother. The trip had seemed endless, and Lewis had been fretful and irritable throughout, until Lynn had despaired and was now totally weary. But when the front door of the annexe opened and her mother's figure stood framed there, Lynn's weariness left her, and her heart bursting, and hugging Lewis close, she climbed out of the car and walked with firm steps towards her mother, who, arms outstretched, waited for her.

Gavin knew he really ought to make a move to go home but he was reluctant to leave the homely loving feeling which pervaded Rachel's annexe this evening. He had had a wonderful time with Rachel and her whole family, not to mention her beautiful daughter and grandson at last back home into the bosom of their family.

Somehow he saw everything this evening in a different light. It was so obvious to him that Rachel's family loved her unconditionally and without reservation, and Gavin had realised has he sat in their midst that he felt the same. He had simply let profound jealousy blind him as to how he truly felt about her. Now he appreciated how honourable she was trying to be, by giving up her lifestyle and the money it offered her, by venturing into new and uncertain work where she might face many hardships. And he knew she had done it all for her daughter's sake and no-one else's. She had never thought, he realised, of quitting her present job for his sake. And he wondered if she felt she had no future with him because of her lifestyle. Now as he sat beside Matthew and Julie Hampton, it saddened him to think that he might have, in any way, contributed to her sadness during the past year.

Now this evening, he was determined to tell her the depths of his feelings as soon as he could. They had wasted too much time already trying to remain friends while all the undercurrents of feelings and emotions flowed between them. Now he prayed she would feel as he did and reciprocate his feelings. As far as he was concerned the past was over and done with and they could look forward to a better future.

'The past doesn't matter, only you and I matter, and our future together, Rachel. I love you deeply and I want to marry you. Besides you have finished with that part of your life, and I have to admit I'm delighted about that. Perhaps if you had decided to continue with it I would have had difficulty coping. But it is simply jealousy on my part, Rachel. Nothing else only jealousy. I have no prejudices or moral stance of any kind about it. I hope you believe me.'

Gavin had contacted Rachel first thing the next morning after Lynn's homecoming and they had arranged to meet in their favourite coffee shop facing 10, Waring Street. Now when he looked at her he saw the tears were running down her cheeks, but still, she was smiling at him. A warm, loving smile and she was nodding her head vigorously. His heart lifted and reaching forward he tilted her chin up and kissed her in full view of the other customers and staff in the coffee shop.

CHAPTER 41

In the days following Lynn's arrival home, she looked back and marvelled at the wonderful family she had, and how each and every one of them had welcomed her back with open arms. Not a word of reproach was uttered by anyone and this in itself made Lynn feel guilty at how she had run away and made no contact whatsoever. Nor did there seem to be any sense of shame in any of the family that Lynn was now home, unmarried and with a baby son. The celebration of the homecoming was a huge success, with all the family being present. The tables were groaning with food and the drink was flowing. Everyone had been so generous, arriving laden with tempting eats and beers and wines and spirits. Those who had been told about baby Lewis had brought presents for him, which touched Lynn very much.

She had been home for four weeks now and thankfully Lewis was beginning to settle. She had had quite a few restless nights with him until her mother said she thought he was hungry. Lynn should think of supplementing her breast milk with a bottle feed. Rachel thought Lynn, who was still too thin and pale, was not producing enough milk for the baby's needs. Rachel and Maggie were of tremendous help during the day, insisting Lynn had a couple of hours rest. Jason called regularly to see her, and Maggie had insisted on a couple of occasions that they should go for a drive, and she or Rachel would give Lewis a bottle if needed.

Initially Lynn felt shy and reserved with Jason. She knew she had treated him badly, and had earnestly apologised to him. She did explain she was intent on contacting him, but when she had seen him with Amanda on television, she thought Jason and Amanda were now a couple. 'Oh Lynn, it was awful after you left. I didn't know what to think. Then when Amanda told me what she had told you about your mother, I understood a little of the shock it must have been for you. But what I couldn't understand was why you didn't contact me. But of course I never dreamt it had anything to do with the programme. Is that why you ended up in the registry office with Arnold Simpson?'

'I think it must have been, Jason. At the time it wasn't a conscious reason for doing it, but probably my subconscious was responsible. It was a disaster, I know, Jason, but all the same, I have Lewis and I love him deeply. No matter about anything else, I will love and cherish him.'

'I know that Lynn. Your son is adorable, and what you are saying is that whoever loves you, must love Lewis too. Well I think I already do.'

Lynn was so touched by Jason's words that, even though he was driving, she leaned forward and kissed him passionately.

'I'm so glad it wasn't true about you and Amanda.'

'And maybe this is the wrong thing to say Lynn, but I'm glad Arnold Simpson turned out to be a bigamist.'

As Jason continued to drive along the road to Helen's Bay, a place where all the family had such a soft spot for and wonderful memories of, Lynn knew that, deep down, she too was glad Arnold had turned out to be a bigamist. Even though there were those in society that would label her son illegitimate.

'It was when I discovered I was pregnant, and at the same time I discovered Arnold was still married, that all my bitterness towards my mother just dissipated into thin air. I knew then that I loved her no matter what, and I longed for home and you all. But I was convinced no one would want anything to do with me. And now I know how much everyone did care. You coming over to Scotland with Uncle John to bring me home, Jason, with not a second thought about it, pleased me so much. And then my mother opening a home for the elderly. Who would have thought she would do such a thing? And she tells me she did it to try and gain back my respect. To think she changed so many things just for me. And I blamed her in the wrong with Uncle John. He did tell me about going to talk to her after Leo's murder and Aunt Dorrie's illness. I felt ashamed of myself, Jason, jumping to conclusions. I should have known he is a really honourable man.'

'And hasn't everything worked out wonderfully well for him and Dorrie. Dorrie's staying on in the home after going there because of Rhoda's ankle fracture. She was just so settled and loved the attention the nurses gave her that John decided he would not move her,' Jason said.

'Mum can scarcely believe how calm Dorrie is now, and that is with little or no sedation. Once Uncle John saw how she was, sitting calmly at the low window watching the traffic in the street below, he was very agreeable to mum's idea that he lived there too.'

'I think it's a wonderful idea, and because it's a family owned home, everyone who visited Dorrie is relaxed and cheerful. Not tense and worried about her, as they were when she lived on the Shore Road.'

Jason had rarely visited his great-aunt in her previous home, he found the atmosphere so depressing and his Aunt always anxious and fidgety. But Lynn and he had been to Waring Street a few times and were amazed at the change in her.

'I think mum doesn't want to charge Uncle John anything. I know she told him she owed him so much for bringing me back safely. That was all she had ever wanted. But he maintains he will at least work there and help her all he can. He deals with all the supervision of the laundry, all the meals and the office work. Mum says she's beginning to think she will have nothing to do.' Lynn smiled as she spoke. 'I personally am only too glad to see her with a few free hours to herself, and I notice she can fill those very well in Gavin Finlay's company. I think he is a lovely man and I would be delighted if mum and he could make a go of it. Surely if you and I have managed to, so can they?'

'I hope so too, Lynn. In the meantime I imagine there is plenty to do in the home. She has eight elderly people in there now. So that takes some supervision, I should think.' As he spoke Jason glanced at his watch. 'We've been away for an hour and a half Lynn. Shall we make our way home?'

'I think we've driven far enough. Grandma's very good but she does get tired, and Lewis can be quite demanding at times.'

However when the two young people arrived back in Malone Avenue and entered Lynn's home, they found her son had slept since she had left and Maggie was sitting with her feet up, contentedly reading the daily paper.

Without preamble she spoke to Lynn, 'At long last the jury have returned to consider their verdict regarding the shooting of my dear brother and those Protestants in the pub.' Maggie couldn't believe how long this particular trial was going on, and that the McCaughey brothers, as they were always referred to, still pleaded not guilty. The trial had had to be adjourned half-way through, because the older brother had taken a slight stroke, according to the media. Maggie believed it was just a ploy to prolong everything, and would inevitably cost the government more money. But then she was very cynical about any terrorist who had been apprehended and brought before the courts.

'Oh Grandma, it is awful for you. Awful for everyone, especially Matthew who has worked so hard, and wanted so desperately to obtain justice for his dad.' Lynn hugged her grandmother tightly. 'But let's just hope, Grandma, that all his hard work will pay off.'

Jason, who had come in to the annexe to see Maggie and the baby, suddenly seemed tense and anxious at the mention of the trial. He nodded to Maggie, 'I hope so too. Dad has no doubt of their guilt. I won't ever forget that awful day and the months that followed. Mum and I feared for dad's sanity, you know.' He looked over at Lynn, 'I'll go home now Lynn, but

I'll be in touch.' He seemed very preoccupied now as he kissed Lynn goodbye and Lynn knew he must be thinking of his father and what he must be coming through.

Today Maggie, after having her rest, seemed in quite a talkative mood and obviously wanted Lynn to listen as she reminisced about when she lived here as a young girl. She told Lynn all about her mother dying at a young age and her father marrying again, only for him to die himself three or four years later. Then she turned to her granddaughter and in a questioning tone asked, 'Have you forgiven your mother yet, Lynn for the life she led up until now? I would like to know, love, because I have an important reason for asking.'

'Gran, I have forgiven my mother whole-heartedly. I had already done so even before I came home and saw what she had done to try to make amends. Does that answer your question?'

'Indeed it does Lynn, but I need to tell you that I too, offered my services to men for payment in Poyntzpass when I was a mere fifteen year old. And after I went to Canada I continued to do so until I met my husband.'

Maggie paused and saw a look of shock fleetingly cross her granddaughter's face, to be quickly replaced by a look of acceptance.

'Times were hard in those days, Lynn. I'm not making excuses for myself. I know I chose the easy way out to earn money. So whether your mother found out about how I managed to have a fair amount of money saved, or whether it is simply in our genes, who knows?'

'Gran that is all such a long time ago and I love you just the same, although I'm still glad you told me. I do appreciate it.' Then a thought occurred to Lynn, 'What about Great -Aunt Eve, what did she work at?'

'She got a wonderful job in an office in a huge department store shortly after we arrived in Canada. It was well paid, with good hours and a good pension with it, so no, Eve had no time for my behaviour, although she never judged me and we have always remained friends.'

'I was disappointed that Eve did not come to my homecoming, but I know Uncle Harry had had a heart attack. How is he now Gran, have you heard?'

'He's quite well. In fact I had a letter from Eve two days ago. Even though she has a telephone, she still prefers to write and always did. She says they will drive over here on Sunday to see you and Lewis.' Then looking over to Lewis's pram, Maggie went on, 'I think baby Lewis is getting hungry, he's getting restless.'

Lynn rose at once from her seat beside Maggie and went to the kitchen to prepare a bottle for Lewis, and some lunch for Maggie and herself and Rachel. Her mother had promised to be home for something to eat today. In the meantime her grandmother had given her quite a bit of information to think about. The fact that her gran had been a call girl too, as her mother had been did not upset Lynn now, as it might have done some time ago. Indeed, she was due to ring Tracey in a couple of days, to see how she was getting on with getting rid of her flat, and putting her furniture into storage, and she intended to confide in her what her grandmother had just told her. During her time in Scotland they had always confided in one another, and she knew her friend would be interested without being in the least judgemental.

CHAPTER 42

Tracey had expected to have reservations about giving up her job and her flat in Glasgow. She had loved her position, the independence of going out and selling and the freedom in travelling to different towns and cities had always appealed to her, so she was surprised to discover how much she was looking forward to her new venture and a new country. Since Lynn had rang her two days ago and told her Rachel had sourced a couple of empty premises in the heart of Belfast, which might be suitable for her, Tracey had wasted no time in booking her ferry, after paying for her furniture in storage for the next three months. Once more she was heading for the ferry which would take her to Northern Ireland to a whole new uncertain future. As she drove along she realised it was with the utmost relief she was leaving Glasgow and the soul destroying memories she had of Brian, and what he had done to her. His trial for drug trafficking was to be heard shortly, that much she did know, but she was just relieved she would not be in the same country as he was when his case was heard.

She had asked Lynn to find rented premises for her to live in until she had her project established but Lynn had been appalled at such a suggestion. She would be coming to her, it might be a bit cramped, but her grandma, her mother and Lynn insisted on it.

When Lynn had rang her, she had also told her to watch the six o'clock news to hear that the McCaughey brothers had been found guilty of her great-uncle's murder, and also of the four Protestants in the pub. Although Lynn had never talked much about that awful time for her family, she knew that Tracey, too, would be thankful to learn that justice had been done. The two brothers had been sentenced to twenty-five years each in prison, and Lynn said that her cousin Matthew was satisfied with how things had worked out. Then on a different note, Lynn also told her about her grandmother's past and how similar it had been to her mother's. Tracey was glad to learn that Lynn had been so accepting of what she had been told and knew her friend was well and truly over any resentment towards her mother, or any concern of any stigma which her mother's behaviour might have left on the family. Why Lynn's grandmother had told her about her past was a bit of a mystery to Tracey. Perhaps she had felt it might help to show Rachel in a better light, or perhaps it was just a matter of confession being good for the soul. Whatever the reason, Tracey thought it had obviously done Lynn good.

'Mum is going to sleep on the premises in Waring Street, Tracey. There is a small bedroom off the office there, and she insists she'll be fine. So I brought her bed out of grandma's room and I put it in with Lewis and me. It's a bit cramped, but I know you won't mind, Tracey.'

Tracey had arrived at Lynn's home about an hour ago and after tea and introductions to her mother and grandmother, Lynn was showing Tracey the modest bedroom she occupied with Lewis.

'Lynn it's grand for me. I hope you have room to attend to Lewis during the night. Does he wake up during the night?'

'Not at all, Tracey. He sleeps very well, so we've no worries on that score. But.' a sudden anxiety gripped Lynn, 'I need to know all there is to know about Arnold Simpson. You told me he was waiting for you one day when I was in hospital, and he said he would see me in court. And then you mentioned a letter, Tracey. Have you brought it with you?'

"Lynn, I was going to show it to you later, when we've had a meal and Lewis is settled for the night. And when you're mother and grandmother are with you.' Tracey said gently, 'There is nothing too immediate in it to worry about. Does that content you for a little while Lynn?'

Lynn hugged her friend tightly, 'I'm sorry. I haven't even said how happy I am to see you. How great it is to have you here. But you know that of course. It's just – I keep expecting to see him appear at the door. To find out where I am and even have Lewis abducted.'

'I don't think that's his style, Lynn. He'll do it the official way. He'll show everyone how important and successful he is. Mark my words, that's how I think he'll do it.'

Lynn relaxed on hearing Tracey and realized her friend was right; he was too officious to stoop to abduction and that sort of thing. He would much rather be seen to have won outright.

After dinner that evening, when Lewis was in his cot for the night and Rachel had returned from Waring Street, Tracey produced the official looking letter that she had kept in the side pocket of her handbag since receiving it three days before she had left Glasgow.

'Would you like me to read it, Lynn?'

'Yes please, Tracey.'

'It's from Arnold Simpson's solicitor and it's addressed to me.'

Dear Miss Bell

We are acting on behalf of Mr Arnold Simpson, who needs to trace Miss Lynn Compton, last known address being 2A Bridge Street Glasgow. She has vacated these premises recently, and as she is pregnant with Mr Simpson's child, he is anxious to see her. We understand you have been a constant companion to Miss Compton and would therefore have access to her current whereabouts.

We would be pleased if you could forward this lady's address to us as soon as possible.

'It is signed by Mr. Paul Rice on behalf of Mr. Simpson, Lynn, and that's it.'

'Did you reply to it, Tracey?' It was Rachel who spoke first.

'No, I'm afraid I didn't, Rachel. Perhaps that was wrong, but I had no intention of telling the truth, and as I knew I was coming here, I just ignored it.'

'Well that's a relief. I never dreamt for one moment he would involve you so directly, Tracey, and I'm so sorry about that. I knew of course you would never tell where I had gone.' Lynn felt she had been given some respite, but knew from the sound of the letter that Arnold was not going to give up easily.

'The good thing about the letter being from a solicitor, Lynn, means of course, that as Tracey says, he means to try to get custody legally. He has no thought of coming and lifting the baby.' Maggie had been listening intently.

'So Lewis and you are safe here, I feel. You'll just have to bide your time I think, and see what happens.'

'Of course Grandma, you're right. You're a gem for thinking so straight-forwardly. I'm afraid my thoughts are all over the place at the minute.' Lynn managed a smile over to Maggie, although tears were close to the surface. Her grandmother's words were a consolation to her. They really could do nothing, only wait and see if Arnold continued to pursue it.

'Well it looks like my dear Lynn's friend has vacated her apartment here. After I received the letter from my solicitor saying he had had no reply to the letter he sent two weeks ago, I went to Miss Bell's place and the apartment is empty. A sign outside says "To Let." Arnold Simpson addressed his wife of ten years across the dining room table.

'Well, what now dear?' Iris Simpson looked over at her husband expectantly. She had returned to their original marital home two months ago, and was glad to be back among her favourite things. She had thought she would never forgive Arnold for setting up house with that slip of a girl who had worked in his restaurant. But when Arnold had told her the girl was pregnant, was practically homeless, and he intended to get custody of the baby when it was born, she had been delighted. Delighted with the thought, that having lived with childlessness for ten years, suddenly there was hope for a baby for Arnold and herself. Surely he had a right to this child, and with them the child would have love, security and good prospects for the future. She would encourage him to fight for custody and surely they would win. They had to win.

'You must find out where that girl has gone.' Iris said. 'I think when you find her you'll find our Lynn and your baby.'

'I know, I know.' Arnold was preoccupied with trying to remember anything Lynn might have told him about where she lived in Ireland. He had not cared enough to listen, but was only interested in satisfying his lust for her. He was also trying to remember anything she might have told him about her friend Tracey. Even though he had known Tracey vaguely before he even met Lynn, he had not been remotely interested in what she did for a living. He only knew that now he really had to find out, but it could not be all that difficult to do. He intended to start tomorrow. There was no way he was going to let a twenty year old girl get the better of him. He had the money to fight her in court and to see it through. She, as far as he knew, had none.

'Colin, I could not possibly accept such an enormous sum of money from you. I don't mind paying off the loan I took out for this place. My reward has been to see your mother so calm and settled, and that's with very little sedation. She gets a light sleeping pill at night, but that is all. During the day she is quite happy to sit at the window and watch the throng of people going about their business. As for your dad, he works very hard and I know he too is very happy. When Dorrie is settled in the evening Gavin might call to see his Uncle John and we sit in their sitting room with tea or perhaps the occasional glass of wine. We are good company for one another, Colin. The arrangement is ideal and it suits us all, so please, don't feel you have to help.'

'Rachel, I need to do this, if not for you, for my parents.' Colin was very firm. 'If it makes you feel any better, put the property in my name as well as yours. But I won't be taking a penny out of it, and I'll sign with a solicitor to that effect.'

Rachel went over to him and threw her arms around him. 'That would make me feel better, Colin. I would be happy with that.'

'Right, the deal's done. Get the wheels in motion, Rachel and I'll get the money to the loan company and pay them off.'

'I just borrowed eighty thousand pounds, Colin. So you'll have twenty thousand out of it.'

'No, you will, Rachel. Bank it; you never know when you might need it.'

Gracefully Rachel said she would put it into a savings account in her and Colin's name, she might need it to help Lynn, even though when she was twenty-one, her daughter would inherit the money her parents left her in their will. She might need it all for the fight she might yet have, to keep custody of her son.

CHAPTER 43

1981

'Jason and I are going to do some Christmas shopping this afternoon, Grandma. We can take Lewis with us in his pram. We'll only be away a couple of hours and he's very good when I take him shopping.' Lynn was surveying the Christmas list she had made out earlier that morning, and she was daunted when she realised all the relatives she had included in her "presents to buy for" list.

'And we were hoping to call with Tracey to see how she's getting on in the new shop.' Tracey had chosen the smaller, cheaper premises which Rachel had sourced for her. The shop, which had potential for a good comfortable flat above it, was situated in Cromac Street, just round the corner from Waring Street.

'The bank was very supportive, you know Grandma, when Tracey approached them for a loan. She said the bank manager was charming and very thorough when it came down to learning about her experience in the skin-care range. And I think he was quite impressed with the savings she had.'

'Right, Lynn, you and Jason go ahead, do some shopping and call with Tracey. But Christmas is in a week's time, the shops will be so crowded, so please leave Lewis with me. I'll take him round the avenue for a walk. He'll be much happier looking at the houses and children out playing than he would be with jostling crowds. Don't worry,' Maggie added. 'I'll make sure he's warm and he's well strapped in. I'll also visit Ellen and Tom in the Gate Lodge. I've been meaning to do that for some time, they always seem to be the ones to call here. I know Tom still loves this annexe, and it brings back memories of when he lived here, so close to Lucie and Paul.'

'Are you sure Grandma?' Lynn hated imposing on Maggie, but she knew she genuinely loved looking after Lewis.

'Go on and get ready, Lynn. Don't have Jason waiting for you. His time is precious, I'm sure. His workload in trying to qualify as a solicitor early next year must be arduous and intense for him. He must be anxious to be finished with it all.'

'Well I'll tell you this Grandma, and then I'll go and get ready. Jason wants to go to the bar and become a barrister. So he certainly won't have finished studying for some time.' Lynn smiled and then went on, 'He says he wants security for both of us in the future.'

'Oh how wonderful, a barrister you tell me?' Maggie was impressed, even though she had really no idea whatsoever what being a barrister entailed. But still, it sounded good.

Jason parked his car in one of the car parks close to Royal Avenue and the City Hall. And Lynn thought as they walked along, admiring the Christmas decorations with their variety of Santa Clauses, snowmen and shining lights, that she could not be any happier. She was home and by some miracle, Jason still wanted and loved her. She knew he also loved her baby son and for that reason alone, Lynn knew she would always love him.

As they approached the giant Christmas tree at the City Hall, the carollers began to sing their Christmas songs and soon Jason and Lynn were in the City Hall grounds, entranced by the voices of the choir. During a lull in the singing, suddenly Jason pulled Lynn forward towards them all, then turning to her he got down on one knee and produced a small box from his pocket.

'Lynn I would like to marry you. Will you say yes?'

Lynn, shocked and embarrassed at the suddenness of Jason's proposal, was aware that the choir were waiting, looking at her expectantly.

She nodded eagerly, then pulling Jason to his feet, addressed the carol singers, 'Oh, yes, please Jason!' And she kissed him passionately as he struggled to place a beautiful antique ring on the third finger of her left hand. Then the choir encircled the two of them and began to sing "Away in a Manger."

It was three hours later when Jason and Lynn returned from Christmas shopping. Rachel was already home in the annexe, as was Tracey, waiting impatiently for the newly engaged couple. Jason and Lynn had called in, both at Tracey's shop and then at Rachel's Home and shown them the ring, and demonstrated their happiness in one another.

'Mum, look, isn't my ring beautiful!' Lynn held out her hand, 'It is Jason's grandmother's, you know. His grandfather Rob bought it for Ellen in an antique shop, not very long before he was murdered.' Lynn's voice shook, 'And to think she wanted Jason to have it to give to me.' Lynn was crying now, and it was her grandma who hugged her and held her tight. 'Just think Lynn, it would make my dear brother Rob so very happy to see Maggie's granddaughter with the ring he bought for Ellen.' Maggie held Lynn's ring hand tightly. 'Be happy, my love. It is what Rob would have wished for us all.'

'I'll tell you, Lynn, we'll have a party here on Christmas Eve night and ask all our friends and relatives to celebrate.' Rachel said.

'Good idea Rachel. And we'll tell everyone then that we hope to marry shortly after my graduation in May.' Jason responded.

Tracey was determined to renovate the rooms above her shop into a comfortable apartment for herself as soon as she could. At present it was just a large empty space, but she knew with a little ingenuity and some money she could convert it into a comfortable elegant home. She was very happy in Lynn's place, and very appreciative of her family's kindness in accommodating her in their family home so readily. But now Lynn and Jason were engaged, she was anxious to clear the way for them to make their home with Maggie, if that was what they wanted. Not that Tracey thought Lynn had even considered where Jason and Lynn and Lewis might live. She was just so happy about being engaged to the man she loved that she hadn't thought much beyond that.

Now Christmas and the New Year were over, and trade, although slow in many areas, as was to be expected after the money people had spent over the festive season, was busy enough for Tracey. Probably because women always felt it necessary to look after their skin and their bodies. Besides, in order to attract custom, and because it was in line with the other January sales, she had advertised special offers on her skin-care cream. And that seemed to have brought custom to her door. And tonight, she had a date, the first since she had left Scotland, and left Brian with all his disloyalty and his craving for material objects behind. She had heard from one of her ex-colleagues in the firm she had worked in, that Brian had received a two year prison sentence for drug trafficking. She was surprised at how little she had cared when she heard that. She was also ashamed of herself when she realised that it was primarily because he had deceived her with another woman that was the real reason for her callousness towards him, and not because of his drug trafficking. Now this evening she was going to dine out with the bank manager who had been so helpful to her in acquiring the loan for her business. She had to admit to herself, as she tried to decide what to wear to impress this young man who had had such an impact on her, that she hoped this evening might lead to something much more for them both. But then again, she had believed Brian and she would be together into old age, so for that reason, she must look on this as simply a dinner date. A thank you on both their parts for more business rendered. She intended to behave with the upmost decorum and dignity and leave it to Timothy to pursue their relationship, if that was what he wanted.

Finding out Lynn's friend Tracey, had left Glasgow to go to Northern Ireland had been very easy for Arnold Simpson. His detective had simply gone to the flat she had vacated and soon found the name of the landlord for that particular block. After some persuasion and some exchange of money, the landlord had then given him details of the firm she had worked for. They confirmed that Miss Bell had resigned some two months previously and had, they understood, decided to go to Northern Ireland in order to branch out on her own in the skincare industry.

So now he realised that of course, Lynn must have gone back to her relatives there. There could be little doubt about that, and her friend Tracey had obviously decided to go there too. Now it was up to his detective to find out exactly where they were. There could be no court case if no one could find his baby son in order to award him custody, and that, after all, was what this was all about. He needed to establish where the hearing for his case for custody of his son would be heard. Not that it mattered where it would be held, he still considered he had an excellent case, even though Lynn probably had gone back to her family. That was something he still had to establish, and although that might strengthen her case, he was still in a winning position, considering his status and his prosperity.

CHAPTER 44

1982

'Jason and I are thinking of a September wedding, Tracey. We haven't decided on the exact date, but I suppose that will depend on the hotel we want to book our reception in, and also the church we will get married in.'

Lynn and Tracey were seated in the sitting room of the annexe, Lewis was fast asleep in his cot in the bedroom and Maggie had also retired for the night. 'I need to go shopping for my dress and also one for Emily and you, Tracey. And I don't mind what colour you choose as bridesmaids, but I want the dresses to be very simple, just as I want the whole wedding to be. Getting a chance of happiness with Jason is all I want. Of course I want all my family, young and old alike, to be there. That would make me really happy.'

'Well, why don't you arrange a day soon, and bring your mum and Maggie with us, and have a really good day out? Now I have Elma employed part-time to help me, I can arrange some time out, and I know your mum can too. And if Julie requests it, Emily will be able to take a day off school. She definitely will need to be with us, for she's eleven and I'm twenty-seven, so it might be difficult enough to get the same dresses.'

'Well, I suppose we would need to be organised, this is the end of March, that leaves us six months, but even so, we don't want a mad rush at the last minute.'

'And I mean to show you how my flat is coming on, Lynn. I'm delighted with it, I must say. I hope you'll like it.'

'I'm delighted how your business is doing, Tracey, and I think your romance with Timothy is coming on too Am I right?'

'We do get on well together Lynn, but I'm taking it in easy stages. After Brian, I couldn't face any more heartbreak.'

'I can understand that Tracey, but Timothy seems genuine to me, he has no flash car or house. He is a very modest man.'

'I believe him to be decent, Lynn, but still, our relationship is in its very early stages.'

'I hope it goes well, Tracey, you deserve it. And thanks for pointing out to me that Jason and I should set up home here with Grandma. We never even considered doing that, we were intent on looking for a flat. And of course, Grandma and mum are delighted. I know mum was worried that, with her now living in her nursing home and Jason and I looking for an apartment, Grandma was going to be on her own. And although she is very sprightly, the years are there, I suppose. So Jason and I moving in seems the ideal solution.'

Rachel was relieved that she had been adamant that Gavin and she should wait a little while before mentioning their intention to get married to any of their family. She and Gavin had discussed it and Rachel felt she needed time to get her business up and running and to get to know her staff. Gavin willingly agreed to do this and said he would in the meantime put his apartment in Banbridge on the market and look for somewhere suitable for them to buy, with a view to renovating it. They both agreed that they needed to look for somewhere within reasonable distance from Rachel's Home. Now she felt that Gavin and she could take a back seat and let her daughter and Jason fully enjoy their day and all the celebrations around it.

Arnold Simpson was in good spirits as he sat at the breakfast table with Iris. It was only 8 a.m. and the ferry to Belfast did not leave until two o'clock in the afternoon, so Iris and he could afford to have a leisurely breakfast of bacon and eggs before leaving. Their overnight bag was packed and sat in the hall where Iris, after checking that they had all they needed, had placed it.

'I know, at least I'm fairly sure, I know where to find my son. The detective has been most thorough in his investigations; he soon found out where Lynn's family lived. Why, he even was able to tell me all about Tracey. Mind you, I did pay him handsomely for all his time and effort spent on this case, but you have to admit, my dear, it has all been worthwhile.'

'Arnold, I am delighted how everything seems to be falling into place for us both. You do know where the solicitor's office is where you have booked your appointment in the morning?'

'I know exactly, my dear, and I'll even have time before that appointment at 2 p.m. to have a look in Malone Park where my son is currently living. I think I need to know that, to give me a better idea what I might be up against in court.'

'I'm sure, Arnold, there will be no comparison between what we can offer your son and what you ex-girlfriend can offer him.'

"I know dear, but I still need to be forewarned. We'll drive after dinner this evening to Malone Park and try to discover the house my son is living in and perhaps we might even catch a glimpse of him.'

'We need to start out, Iris. I know it's a good couple of hours drive, but I did want to take my car, that way I feel I'm more independent. Besides, as you know, I'm not too keen on flying, especially short flights such as this one would be, between Glasgow and Belfast. All that noise going up, and then the racket coming down again. I detest it all.'

April the 20th was a particularly fresh, sunny morning and Lynn had finally managed to get everyone who intended to go shopping with her, rounded up. They had arranged to meet in White's coffee bar at 11 a.m. It was the earliest Rachel and Tracey could manage to get away from their business commitments, and Lynn accepted that. She knew it was so much easier for her to make arrangements for a day out shopping. She only had to organise her grandmother and her son, then pick up Emily at Matthew and Julie's house and drive the short distance into Belfast.

It was quite some time later, simply because, after meeting in the coffee bar, they had relaxed and enjoyed their coffee and scones in a most leisurely fashion, that they all finally decided that if they were going to do any shopping, they would need to move. As they began to troop up Royal Avenue, Lynn was amazed to see the clocks hands were at ten minutes past one. They had spent two hours together over coffee, simply chatting about this and that. It was time they began to concentrate on doing some serious shopping. They were all just in the process of admiring the brides and bridesmaids dresses in Jean Millar's bridal shop, and young Lewis was contentedly draining his cup of juice, when a loud-speaker announced there was a suspect device in the shopping area. Everyone must vacate all the premises in the area immediately.

Silently and calmly the women replaced the dresses and left the premises, and then stepped out onto Royal Avenue where the police where shepherding people away from where the device was thought to be, to the top end of Royal Avenue.

Arnold Simpson had seen Lynn with his son in his pushchair, accompanied by three or four other women entering the bridal shop. He had found this intriguing, and wondered who could possibly be getting married. Not that it mattered much; he had found his son, that's what mattered. Iris and he had sat outside the house in Malone Avenue earlier that morning, watching and waiting and were rewarded when Lynn and his son – accompanied by a much older lady appeared. They had watched while they climbed into a car and then they followed discreetly, parking not very far from them in the large car park on the Dublin Road. Iris and he had followed them on foot, at a safe distance away, and saw them join Tracey and another lady in a coffee shop. Iris and he waited patiently in a man's outfitting shop across the way, while they seemed to spend an eternity over their coffee and scones.

Now the police were beginning to guide people to the upper end of Royal Avenue, all because of a 'bomb scare'. He had never known what it might be like to be part of all this inconvenience and upheaval which he had read that the people in Northern Ireland tolerated day after day. He had watched it all unfolding on the news, but had no idea how disruptive it actually was. Taking Iris's arm, he approached a police-man and explained he had an appointment in a solicitor's office in that part of the avenue they had just cordoned off.

'I'm so sorry, sir. That area is totally out of bounds. All the offices have been vacated. Believe me, the solicitor in question will understand only too well why you are not able to keep your appointment.' The constable nodded in sympathy. 'I really must move you on now sir. It is dangerous to remain here.'

Lynn was standing in a shop doorway with Lewis securely strapped in his buggy. Her mother, grandmother, Tracey and Emily huddled closely around her, when suddenly her eyes fell on a familiar figure in his black blazer and white shirt, as immaculate as ever. It was Arnold and her breath froze in her chest, even as her heart seemed to hurtle on.

As their eyes met across the crowd of people jostling on the pavement, Arnold Simpson gave her a knowing look which struck fear in Lynn. Her immediate reaction was to shield her son with her entire body, where he sat in his buggy, so innocent and unaware of any threat to his security and happiness.

Then suddenly, even as Lynn bent over her son the ominous silence which had surrounded the people waiting so patiently for the device to be declared a hoax, was broken by the sound of an awful explosion, and everything seemed to shift and change for Lynn in that instant. She was conscious of being lifted further towards her son, and both of them being carried by some awful force further into the shop doorway. Then the sound of breaking glass and people screaming and crying dominated the whole area. But still Lynn was only conscious of the need to hold onto the buggy and shield Lewis, who was now crying hysterically. And all the while she remembered that other time, and that other sound, of another explosion and a fire, and she wondered, as she was thrust forward by the blast, how anyone could possibly be in the wrong place on two different occasions and still hope they had any chance of survival.

CHAPTER 45

'Please sir, my son – I must see my son. Where is he? Lynn was aware she was lying on the pavement, a rough blanket over her, and a man in uniform bending over her.

'Your son is safe, my dear, you'll be pleased to hear. Not a scratch on him, even though a shop window cascaded on you both. You shielded him very well, and a lady by the name of Rachel, your mother I believe, is with him.' The police constable moved closer to her, 'Do you think you would be able to stand, my dear? You have some superficial cuts to your face and hands, but that seems to be all. We believe shock made you faint. We need to clear the area as soon as possible, so if you feel able to move you will be escorted to where your mother and child are.'

Lynn assured the kind constable she was fine and managed to struggle to her feet. But all the time she was frantic to ask him more questions. What of Grandma? Of Tracey and Emily? Where were they? But fear made her speechless in that place of destruction and death and injury. Meekly she allowed the constable to escort her to safety, which was an office building of stout brick walls which seemed totally unaffected by the blast.

As they entered the building, it seemed, to Lynn's eyes, to be filled with people all shocked and horrified at what had happened to their innocent day's shopping. When her eyes became accustomed to the semi-darkness of the ground floor of the building, she began to make out the familiar figure of her mother holding Lewis tightly in her arms. She rushed towards them both, weeping with relief and gratitude that they were both safe, but anguished as to where the others might be.

Shaking violently, she embraced and kissed her mother and son before speaking in a low, fearful voice.

'Where's Grandma, Tracey and Emily?'

'Take it easy, Lynn. Tracey and Emily are over in that room off this one. They've minor cuts from falling glass and are having them cleaned up.' Rachel hesitated for a moment, and then added, 'Grandma has gone to hospital, she has sustained a leg injury, I'm afraid. She tried to reach Lewis and you when the explosion occurred. But a plank of wood from a shop window caught her right leg.'

'Oh mum, is she alright?'

'She was wonderful, Lynn, chirpy as ever when she was getting into the ambulance. So please don't worry. The police rang Gavin and he will be along soon for us all. And once we're home I'll ring the Royal and see what's happening to mum.'

Maggie's X-rays showed she had sustained a fractured pelvis and hip as a result of the impact with the plank, and she needed surgery to pin her fractured hip. But bed rest was the desired treatment for her fractured pelvis, and that imposed rest would probably need to be somewhere in the region of four to six weeks. Rachel knew exactly where she intended to bring her mother once she was discharged from hospital and only needed to rest; she would bring her to her home for the elderly. It was not ideal for Maggie, who was so alert and anxious to remain involved in all family matters. But Waring Street was where Rachel had now made her own home and she needed her mother with her at all times, in order to concentrate on getting her back to her former good health.

On the same day the provisional IRA exploded the bomb in Belfast, they also exploded one in several other towns. Four people were injured in Belfast, in the other towns eight people were injured and two young men killed in Magherafelt.

Arnold Simpson was dimly aware of a light shining in his eyes and the sound of low whispering voices somewhere, invading his consciousness. He tried to move, but found he was unable to, without horrendous pains gripping his legs, his arms and then his entire body. He tried to shout out, to make the owners of those low voices aware of his suffering, but no sound came from his throat.

What was wrong? Something terrible must have happened. But what? As he wrestled with his memory, trying to make sense of where he was and what was wrong with him, some fleeting gruesome images began to swamp his thinking and then suddenly, with an awful flash of remembrance of the explosion, and people being hurled around the street, he let out a shrill agonising cry. Almost immediately a tender hand was placed on his brow and a soft, reassuring voice spoke to him.

'Mr. Simpson, there, there, everything's alright. Are you in pain?'

Arnold could only nod dumbly, but now could make out the figure of a young girl in a white uniform. 'Please, where am I?' He eventually managed to say.

'You are in hospital. I'm your nurse-in-charge. You have been injured in an explosion and have not been very well, but you are coming on fine now. The doctor will be round tomorrow to talk to you about your injuries.' The young voice was reassuring, 'I'll get you something for your pain now, Mr. Simpson. It will make you feel so much better.'

'Don't leave me nurse, please don't leave me.'

'I'll only be a few moments, just to draw up some medication and then I'll be back to stay with you.'

He heard the sound of her footsteps on the floor receding from him, and panic rose in his throat and he wanted to cry out, but his whole body lacked the energy to do anything. Then he heard the noise of her steps as she came back to his bedside, he felt her soft hands on him and was aware of her working at something in his arm. Then almost instantaneously he felt relief from his pain and worry, and he was being transported into bliss. Then suddenly his memory, for a brief moment, jogged him wide awake and he thought of Iris. Where was she? Why was she not here, here with him? Then his mind drifted off and he thought no more about anything as the morphine began to take effect.

Iris Simpson's injuries from the explosion were serious. She had suffered a fractured skull, which in the long term would lead to memory loss and some confusion. But physically she should recover fairly speedily. Her husband Arnold however, had lost an arm and a leg in the blast, and rehabilitation would prove to be a long and arduous battle to regain mobility and independence.

It was at least three weeks after the explosion, when Lynn was assured that her grandmother would survive her injuries, before she told her mother about seeing Arnold on the footpath opposite her, just before the bomb went off.

'Mum, I'm so worried about Lewis. What was Arnold doing in Belfast that day? He must have meant business with me, I know by how he looked at me, and then at Lewis in his pram. How do I go about finding out what he's going to do? Have you any ideas?' Lynn had bottled up so much during the last weeks that now she sounded quite frantic, fear of what might happen to her son had dominated her thoughts, while at the same time worrying about her grandmother.

'Lynn, I wish you had told me this sooner, love. I never thought of him coming here to look for you. I suppose that was stupid of us all.' Rachel was worried too, but was anxious Lynn did not realise that. 'I wonder if Matthew could find out anything for us. I think it is worth mentioning to him. But I would imagine Arnold has gone home again after that bomb, plus all the other bombs which he must have heard about on that day. That surely would be enough to scare him off and to think twice about ever coming back.'

'Oh mum, I never thought of Matthew. That would be great, even if he could just find out if he went home. It would give us a little more time. Could you try to get in touch with him now, mum?'

'No reason why not, Lynn.' And Rachel made her way over to the telephone to ring her cousin and ask for his help.

Three days later Matthew was able to establish that Mr. and Mrs. Simpson had not returned to Scotland, but both lay in the Royal Hospital with serious injuries. Mr. Simpson had lost an arm and a leg in the explosion, and Mrs. Simpson had suffered a very serious head injury. After discovering the Simpsons had not returned home, Matthew consulted the list of those injured in the blast on the off chance they might be among them. He could scarcely believe it when he saw the two names, Mr. and Mrs. Simpson from Glasgow, leap out from the list he had requested from head office.

'I would just love to visit this man on Lynn's behalf, and tell him in no uncertain manner that he has no hope now of winning any custody case for his son. He and his wife would never be able to look after him. They will, by the sound of things, need looking after themselves for some time.'

'Matthew, it's not like you to be impulsive, but I do understand. But we just need to tell Lynn what you have found out. Let her decide what is for the best.'

Matthew had arrived at the annexe earlier that afternoon in order to give Lynn the news first hand. But on hearing she had gone round to visit her grandma in Waring Street, he had decided to tell Rachel what he had discovered.

'I leave it with you and Lynn, Rachel. Of course the decision must be Lynn's. She might prefer to let things drift, but I think she would be better to know exactly where she stands. Give me a ring if she wants any further help from me.'

'Thank you again for everything, Matthew. At least Lynn will now know where Arnold Simpson is, and how he is.' Rachel said. 'After that, the decision is hers.'

Impulsively, Rachel went forward and hugged her cousin as he made his way to the door. 'Throughout this whole business, Lynn's disappearance, Colin's compensation, you've been wonderful and thank you again.'

CHAPTER 46

'Oh mum, please try to understand, this is something I really must do.' Lynn had been told by her mother the evening before what had happened to Arnold and his wife, and she was horrified when she heard. 'Arnold is Lewis's father after all, nothing can ever change that. Now that I believe he may not pursue custody of Lewis, I, selfishly – perhaps, am beginning to see things more clearly, and in a different light. I would like Arnold to see his son, I feel it is the least I can do, especially in the circumstances. He may not welcome me, but surely he will be delighted to see Lewis. And we'll take it from there.'

'I think it is a lovely gesture, Lynn. No, more than that, I think it is a most generous gesture, considering how Arnold Simpson intended to try to take your son from you through the courts. I am worried for you, you know. Would you like me to come with you?'

'Mum, now please, don't be silly, there really is no need. The way Arnold is, from what Matthew has told us, he is not capable of doing either Lewis or me any harm.' But Lynn added, 'I would like a lift to the Royal, and as I don't expect to stay long, perhaps you would wait for me?'

'Of course Lynn, I'll do that. I'll go and get my coat this instant.' Since Maggie had been moved into Waring Street Home, Rachel had changed her mind and had returned to the annexe. She knew Maggie was well looked after and she was anxious that Lynn, after escaping a second IRA bomb explosion with only minor injuries, should have company and support until such time as Jason and she were married. And now today, considering what her daughter intended doing, she needed support more than ever.

As Lynn walked along the long corridor in the Royal Hospital, with Lewis safely strapped in his chair, her mind was swamped with thoughts of all that had happened since she had left home, so unceremoniously three years ago. Her chance meeting with Tracey, now her closest friend, her relationship with Arnold, her pregnancy and her darling son.

But most of all she thought about how she had survived two IRA explosions almost unscathed. Yet Arnold and his wife, here on such a short visit, had sustained such horrific injuries. She believed some guardian angel must have been looking out for her, and her heart melted at the thought of what Arnold and his wife must have suffered, and she vowed, as she walked towards the ward where reception had told her Arnold was, she would do all she could to help him and make things easier and hopefully, happier for him. There was no way she could hold a grudge against him now, when she thought of what had happened to him. And the uncertain future he had ahead of him.

The corridors in the hospital seemed endless to Lynn, and she began to doubt the wisdom of actually coming to visit Arnold. After all, she could simply have written to him and sent a photograph of Lewis, but that, to Lynn's mind, would have been the coward's way to do it. Besides, he had every right to see his son in the flesh, to touch him and to speak to him.

She realised suddenly she was almost at ward 15, and that she had already passed wards 17 and 16. She had been so engrossed in her thoughts she had almost forgotten to look out for the ward the girl at reception had told her Arnold was in.

On entering the ward she approached a nurse, whom she assumed was quite senior, as she had three stripes on her left arm and wore a white fall, as opposed to the small cap student nurses wore.

Briefly she asked if she might see Mr. Simpson for a few minutes, and when the nurse asked her if she was a relative, she explained, pointing to Lewis in his buggy, that this was his son. And she thought it might help Arnold if he could see him.

The nurse looked mystified and intrigued for a moment, but then, she assumed her professional manner and smiled at Lynn.

'I think that would be just lovely. He is over here in a private ward, off the main ward. If you just follow me.'

The nurse made her way across the main ward and then indicated a door which was open, no doubt to enable the nurses to observe the occupant of it. Tremulously Lynn asked her if she would tell Mr. Simpson he had a visitor, so he would be somewhat prepared.

The nurse entered the room with Lynn and Lewis at her heels, and as she approached the bed she said, in a soft voice, 'Mr. Simpson, you have a visitor.'

The man in the bed turned over and looked at the nurse, and then at Lynn, who was still holding tight to the buggy. The man who looked at her now, obviously shocked at seeing her there, was a stranger to her and wore no resemblance to the man she had thought she had married in that registry office in Glasgow.

Arnold had been a dapper, confident, handsome man, but this person, who was looking with such delight at her and the small boy in the pram, bore no resemblance to Arnold.

It was a frail, weak old man who was reaching out his right hand in greeting to her. It was only when he spoke that Lynn took some hope in his recovery. His voice seemed undimmed by the trauma he had suffered; it still held the same assured, modulated tones she always remembered.

Spontaneously she grasped his hand and indicating Lewis, who was attempting to undo his straps and climb out of his buggy, she simply said, 'This is your son, Arnold. I have brought him to see you.'

At those words a huge smile transformed his gaunt, bony face and he attempted to sit up higher in the bed. In doing so, his left arm was stripped of the blanket and Lynn could see his arm had been amputated above the elbow.

'Oh Arnold, I am so sorry for your plight.' And Lynn's eyes filled with tears as she spoke.

'It is so good of you to come to see me, Lynn, after how I treated you. I too, am so sorry. I have had plenty of time to think about everything since the bomb in Royal Avenue. As I'm sure you are aware, Lynn, I will not be pursuing custody of my son. Not anymore, and I wish you every happiness with him.'

Lynn had bent over the buggy to release Lewis, and now lifted him onto the side of the bed beside Arnold. Initially however, Lewis just seemed interested in the ward and all the machinery which was attached to the wall above Arnold's bed. Then gradually his eyes rested on Arnold and his outstretched arm, and then, his own small chubby hand reached forward and touched Arnold's hand. As Lynn watched father and son, she saw the tears begin to run down Arnold's cheeks unchecked. She went over to his locker and extracted some tissues from a box that had been placed there.

'Arnold I want you to know you can see Lewis – that is our son's name – anytime you like. If you want to be involved in his welfare and education that too, will be fine by me.' Lynn hesitated, and then went on, 'But I just want him to live with me.'

Arnold, Lynn could see was too overcome to speak, but eventually he nodded and smiled at her.

'And Mrs. Simpson too, can be involved in his life. But you are his father, and it is because she is your wife, naturally, she will be part of everything. And that too, is fine by me.'

Again, Arnold just nodded and smiled, and was now attempting to hug his son as Lewis sat happily enough at the side of the bed.

'How is Mrs. Simpson?' Lynn asked.

Arnold made a conscious effort to pull himself together, 'She is improving and the nurses bring her to see me very regularly. She is the one who is mobile, whereas I'm not. But I still have my memory for everything, whereas Iris's short term memory is giving her a lot of problems.'

Lynn said sincerely she was sorry about that, but she wanted Arnold to make a recovery and get back on his feet. That way he would be able to play a part in Lewis's upbringing.

'Now I must go Arnold, as you can see, Lewis is getting restless. The novelty of coming here is beginning to wear off.' While she spoke, Lynn was trying to distract Lewis, who had climbed down from the bed and was now rifling through Arnold's locker. A locker, she noticed, which contained little else other than his pyjamas and soap bag.

'The next day I come I'll bring something to tempt your appetite, Arnold. I never thought of that today, I just wanted to bring Lewis.'

'Lynn, you could not have brought me anything that would have made me any happier.' And Arnold seemed delighted and transformed as he spoke.

Before strapping Lewis in his pram and preparing herself for that endless corridor walk, Lynn held Lewis while Arnold gave him a light hug with his right arm. With promises to be back soon, she strapped Lewis in and said goodbye to the man who had initially caused her so much anxiety, but now held no fear for her whatsoever.

CHAPTER 47

29th May 1982

'Emily, you look beautiful, but remember you are supposed to be doing your best to make me look beautiful too.' Lynn smiled indulgently at Jason's sister as she spoke. Emily did look exquisite in her full-length silk dress of pale pink, encrusted with silver sequins around the neck, sleeves and hemline. Emily was only fourteen, but had a slim curvaceous figure like an eighteen year old and the pale pink of the dress seemed to enhance her colouring and her hair, and gave her an air of forthcoming adulthood. This mature look surprised and delighted those who were watching her as she admired herself in the mirror in Lynn's bedroom.

It was Lynn and Jason's wedding day. A whole year had passed since they had first thought to set a date. But Lynn was adamant her grandma must be mobile, and able to attend and enjoy her wedding, the most important day in Lynn's life. And although she had not voiced her thoughts about Arnold and his wife Iris to anyone, only Jason, she was anxious that both of them would be at her service, to see her legally wed to her childhood sweetheart.

During the last year Lynn and Jason had kept constant contact with Arnold and his wife. They visited them frequently in hospital, and Jason had praised Lynn to all the members of her family after her initial visit to Arnold. It was Jason who had stated so categorically how sensitive and caring Lynn had been by visiting Arnold, and taking his son along to visit him. He maintained it was Lynn's visit to Arnold, and bringing Lewis with her, that had given Arnold incentive to master the prosthesis on his left leg and learn to walk again. Jason firmly believed that having his son in his life had given Arnold inspiration to overcome the awful trauma inflicted on him that fateful day in Belfast.

After Lynn had left the ward that first day, Arnold's thoughts were in disarray. How a young girl like Lynn could have even bothered to come near him, after how he had treated her. Why, he had even threatened her with court and gaining custody of their son. But she had obviously forgiven him and somehow her actions that day, and her words to him had shown her in such a wonderful light, that Arnold's biggest regret had been that he had not stayed with her, obtained a divorce and married her. But on her subsequent visit, when she brought her fiancé along, he realised he was being utterly selfish in his thinking. The two young people where obviously in love, and he could only wish them happiness in the future. After Jason and Lynn had left the ward, on Lynn's second visit to him, he resolved, there and then to fight the disability that had been inflicted on him.

He would get back on his feet, he would be mobile again. He could make his son proud of him yet. And above all, he would, as Lynn had said he should, play an active role in his son's upbringing. And who knows, it might even help Iris to regain some of her mental stability.

That same day, Arnold thanked God he had been so astute with money – he was wealthy and that meant a lot to him now. He would be able to retire and move to anywhere that appealed to Iris and him. And in spite of all that had happened, and the daily reports of bombs, and bomb scares in Northern Ireland, he thought that after his discharge from hospital and later, the rehabilitation centre, he might settle with Iris in Northern Ireland. After all, a nice house with mature gardens in a select rural area should be comparatively safe and free from any terrorist attack.

It was a full six months before Arnold mastered the prosthesis on his leg. The fact that he had also lost the lower limb of his left arm complicated his ability to walk and support himself. But still, with no other thought in his head only that of the vision of his two year old son, with his smiling face, fair hair and brilliant blue eyes before him, he persevered until the sweat ran down his brow and forehead and he thought he must pass out with all the effort.

Today, on this, Lynn's wedding day, Tracey, who was chief bridesmaid and should be thinking of getting dressed, was still in her dressing gown. She had spent the last thirty minutes sewing on buttons on Lynn's wedding dress, which had had to be taken in at the last minute. How Lynn kept so slim, yet seemed to have such an enormous appetite, had always mystified Tracey. Lynn insisted that had Tracey had a two year old to run after all day long, she would be thin too.

'Right Lynn, put this on this instant, or we are all going to be late for your big day.' Tracey secured the final button before handing the dress to Lynn who stood waiting, in the finest underwear that her mother had provided, to put her dress on.

Some thirty minutes later, all three young ladies emerged from Lynn's bedroom and to John, who had been given the honour of giving the bride away, the image of the three of them was unforgettable. The bridesmaids glowed with the natural beauty of youth, and the pale pink of their dresses seemed to bring colour to their cheeks, and was in unison with the delightful spring morning they were about to step out into.

As for Lynn, her dress, made of the finest oyster pink silk, clung to every fine line and shape of her slim body. John marvelled at the shining beauty of this young daughter of Rachel's, and how privileged he felt to be given the opportunity to give her away to the young man who obviously, through all his trauma, maintained a steadfast love for her.

'Let's go, my dear.' John addressed Lynn as she stood in the middle of the living room, obviously waiting for his approval. 'You look beautiful, Lynn, and Jason will be spell-bound when he sees you.' John extended his arm for Lynn to take, 'Now we really must get going, we are five minutes late already.' But John smiled as he spoke and then Lynn, her arm looped through his, walked serenely with her uncle out of the house, towards the waiting car.

When Lynn and John entered the porch of the church where Emily and Tracey were waiting for her, Lynn found now that her initial nervousness had gone, and that she was really looking forward to this day. Then, as the organ struck up the familiar Bridal March she began the walk up the aisle, now in tears, as she saw the familiar faces all look towards her and then young Lewis's voice cry 'Momma, Momma.'

As Lynn and John proceeded up towards the front of the church to join Jason where he stood with Alan, Rhoda's husband and Timothy, now Tracey's fiancé, her young son began to clap, his face alight as he saw his mother.

Suddenly, all the guests were joining in the clapping and Lynn knew it was going to be a wonderful day, the best day of her life. As she looked at everyone's face directed towards her, wishing her well, she saw Arnold clapping with his good hand against his wife's. She noticed too, he was standing firm and straight with only a stick for support. She saw and registered the presence of all her cousins, aunts and uncles. In particular she was delighted to see Aunt Dorrie there, dressed in a beautiful cream suit, being supported by Lynn's mother. She marvelled at her mother's determination that she would try to bring Dorrie to the church service. Dorrie might not understand much of what was happening, but Rachel had been resolute in believing she should be there. As John and she passed the pew where Dorrie and her mum were sitting, John nudged Lynn ever so discreetly, and they smiled at one another as they saw Dorrie clapping too.

September 1983

It was Lewis's first day at preschool and it was a poignant day in Lynn and Jason's life. They had been up since 6.30 a.m. that morning, organising his uniform, packing his brand new schoolbag with all the essentials the school had requested he would need to bring. He would be going to the preparatory school in Methodist College, the fees which would be paid for by Arnold. It was Arnold who had visited several schools in the area and had been given a tour and, on some occasions, endured prolonged discussions on the advantages of a particular school. After several discussions with Lynn and Jason, Methodist College was decided on. It was after all, situated close to where Lynn and Jason lived, it appeared to have democratic views and a multicultural outlook. But above all, as Arnold pointed out, its success rate in examinations and indeed in a wide range of sports was exemplary. And he held high hopes of his son excelling in the future. Arnold and Iris had bought a small Victorian style cottage at Helen's Bay over two years ago; this they had done in order to be involved in young Lewis's life.

So much had happened since Lynn and Jason's marriage a year ago. The happiest occasion since then had been the birth of their daughter Eva two months ago. They had decided to call her after Lynn's great-aunt, whose life story and romance had always interested them both. They also thought it would give Eve an interest in life again, because sadly her darling husband Harry had succumbed to a second heart attack over a year ago. That had been a huge blow to the entire family. Eve and Harry had seemed to be such an enduring twosome, who would go on forever, and Eve had been bereft at his death, but her step-daughter and husband had arrived back from England to take up residence with her and to take over the running of the farm.

It was just two weeks later that John wakened early one bright morning towards the end of September. He went over to the bed by the window where Dorrie slept. He called her name softly, and then realising there was some awful stillness about her, he wrapped his arms around her and turned her towards him. It was then he realised she was dead. He lay down beside his wife of over forty-five years, tightened his arms around her and covered them both with the duvet. And that was how Rachel found them some thirty minutes later.

Because John had always shared the bedroom with Dorrie, Rachel dealt with all the other patients in her Home first, before disturbing them. John worked so hard for her that Rachel was always anxious not to disturb him too early, and Dorrie rarely wakened before 8.30 a.m. every morning. When Rachel entered the room that fateful morning, she realised immediately something was terribly wrong. As she approached the bed she saw John's face, the agony on it, and the tears flowing down his cheeks, and she needed no other indication to tell her her beloved aunt was dead.

And her first thought was that Dorrie was now with her darling Leo, who she had yearned and pined for for so long after his death. And whose loss had made such a terrible impact on her health. It was only in the last couple of years, since coming to Waring Street that she had recovered a calmness and dignity which had been missing from her character for so long. And Rachel thanked God that her aunt had had a couple of years of peace, with no indication of that awful agitation and despair which had dominated her behaviour for so long.

After Dorrie's death, Maggie, who had remained at Waring Street after being injured in the bomb explosion, felt she would love nothing more than to see her sister, Eve, come to the Home too. Maggie felt, because there was only the two of them left, they ought to spend their last years together. After all, they had spent their whole childhood and teenage years together, and had even travelled to Canada together all those years ago. Many times Maggie had reflected on the daring of the two of them, making their way across the oceans to a whole, strange new country. Here they had had to try to find work, accommodation and some happiness.

She discussed the possibility of Eve coming on many occasions with Rachel and John, insisting Eve would be better here, in the middle of things, rather than in a remote farmhouse badly in need of repair, with only her memories. Maggie believed Eve's stepdaughter and husband would be happy to take over the farm. They were young and could make a success of it.

It was John who went with Maggie to visit Eve in Poyntzpass on several occasions and eventually Eve agreed to come and stay in Waring Street for a holiday. During this time she shared a room with Maggie and had her constant companionship. She saw a lot of her relatives, John and Rachel and lots of other members of the family. Ellen, who treasured such fond memories of Eve in Drumin all those years ago, was a constant visitor, as was Tom, her husband.

Eve's initial fortnight's holiday was extended on several occasions, then finally she told Rachel she wished to stay with Maggie, and could they discuss what the fees would be for a permanent residence.

Rachel stood in her bedroom in 10, Waring Street and looked with something like disbelief at the pale blue crepe dress which hung on the hanger outside her wardrobe door. Was she really getting married to-day? She could scarcely believe it but the dress and the pale blue matching shoes on the floor reassured her that she was. Was it true that Gavin Finlay had said he could wait no longer to make her his wife, even though the house he had bought on the Malone Road was still not ready for anyone to take up residence? He had wanted it perfect for Rachel, he had told her, but because it was a listed building it had taken longer than he had initially thought to obtain any planning permission. So now they were going ahead with their wedding at twelve o'clock in the registry office in Belfast and they were returning to the Home where they had decided to have a small reception to celebrate their union. Gavin had arranged a few days honeymoon in Paris and then they would return to 10, Waring Street to live until their new home was ready.

Later, after the service in the registry office, Rachel and Gavin made their way back to the Home to wait for their guests. As the place began to fill up with their precious friends and relatives Rachel looked round the room at all her loved ones, and her heart swelled with emotion when she thought of what they had all been through. She had particularly wanted to have her reception here; here was where she had first realised what her Uncle John and Aunt Dorrie were going through as a result of Leo's death and Colin's miscarriage of justice. It was here she had learned about Gerald King and his confession. It was here she had realised she must try to make some recompense to her daughter and give up her occupation in the sex trade. But most of all, it was here she had met Gavin and fell in love again, and wonder of wonders, he had fallen in love with her. She thanked God for her and Gavin's happiness and most of all thanked God that 10, Waring Street was now a warm, loving home, highly respected by the whole community.